THE
FALL-DOWN
ARTIST

THE FALL-DOWN ARTIST

Thomas Lipinski

St. Martin's Press
New York

Design by Judith A. Stagnitto

Library of Congress Catalogin-in-Publication Data

Lipinski, Thomas.

   The fall-down artist / Thomas Lipinski.

    p. cm.

   "A Thomas Dunne Book."

   ISBN 0-312-10461-8 : $20.95

    1. Private investigators—Pennsylvania—Pittsburgh—Fiction.

  2. Steel industry and trade—Pennsylvania—Pittsburgh—Fiction.

  3. Pittsburgh (Pa.)—Fiction. I. Title.

PS3562.I574F3 1994   93-45280

813'.54—dc20   CIP

First Edition

10 9 8 7 6 5 4 3 2 1

THE
FALL-DOWN
ARTIST

CHAPTER 1

As he expected, by the middle of the third page, the fingers of his right hand began to ache. The arthritis, a result of three greenstick fractures, was a variant that caused pain but only minor restriction of movement. Yeah, Dorsey thought as he worked at his fingers, shaking and loosening them, just enough restriction to reduce a classic hook-shot artist to a brawling rebounder.

Carroll Dorsey was pleased with what he had typed thus far; the final report, he felt, was going well. And why not? You're still describing the beginning of the case, he reminded himself, when things were going so nicely. Before the bottom fell out. Before you took the witness stand. "Should've known," he said aloud. "Damned lawyer; they should've known. They took Stockman too lightly. Never take that son of a bitch light."

From the far corner of the desktop, Dorsey took a can of beer in his right hand, holding it gently by the thumb and first finger, keeping the cold from the other aching knuckles. He leaned back in the swivel chair and turned toward a four-tiered bookshelf crammed with paperbacks and a small stereo tape player, from which the Basie band was now playing "Back to the Apple." On the top shelf were three photos of the same tall, heavy-shouldered boy in three different basketball uniforms. The first two were black-and-white shots, one of the boy with a crew cut in his Sacred Heart grade school uniform, the other of the boy with a bit more hair wearing a jersey with CENTRAL CATHOLIC printed across it. The third photo was a publicity glossy from Duquesne University.

"B.F." Dorsey saluted the photos with his beer. "Before fractures." He turned back to the Olivetti portable and drew himself to the desk.

Benito DeMarco was forty-seven years old, built like a brick shithouse, a pipe fitter, and a fraud. It had been over a year since his pickup had been struck from behind as he waited at a stop sign, and still, he claimed, the phantom pains rendered him totally disabled. The report's first three pages covered Dorsey's investigation. It documented the times and routes of DeMarco's numerous trips to hardware stores and building supply centers, Dorsey following close behind in a borrowed van. Attached to the report were copies of receipts Dorsey had obtained from sales clerks, proving that DeMarco had lines of credit and was buying supplies in contractor's quantities. Also accompanying the report was a tape shot from the van's rear window as DeMarco tore into a cement sidewalk with a pickax.

The good stuff, Dorsey thought, gazing at the typewriter keys, the stuff that speaks for itself. Now for the rest, which isn't such good stuff. Put it on paper and run. Just document your time for the bill.

Without further deliberation, he began a new paragraph, the pain in his fingers increasing, and documented that on October 26, 1984, he had appeared in the Court of Common Pleas of Allegheny County, at Pittsburgh, to provide expert testimony in the case of *DeMarco* v. *Fidelity Casualty*. After which his involvement in the case ended. And that, Dorsey reminded himself, coincided with the end of Fidelity Casualty's defense.

Dorsey sipped at his beer. Fidelity Casualty's attorney: so young, the product of a large law firm, so well dressed and groomed he seemed to Dorsey the result of reading *Esquire* too thoroughly. The guy was overconfident, figuring he had DeMarco's lawyer, Stockman, by the ass. As if Jack "Personal Injury" Stockman ever stood still long enough to be taken hold of.

"You'll be a surprise witness," the defense attorney had said at their first meeting. "I'm—the law firm, I mean—we're the ones who will hire you, not the insurance company. That way you're protected from discovery in pretrial, as part of attorney's privilege. You'll be called and sworn in, and we'll watch Stockman's face drop when you show the tape. Oh, Stockman will object when you're called, but he'll be overruled. And you'll put on your show. And we'll have kicked his ass."

But Stockman, he hadn't objected very hard.

Dorsey rose from the swivel and crossed the office to seat himself on the edge of a black leather chaise beneath the two front windows. The office was the converted living room of Dorsey's row house; outside was working-class Wharton Street, the late-afternoon foot traffic increasing as the workday ended. Dorsey leaned his heavy frame toward the window, resting his elbows on the sill. For a few moments he watched a woodpecker, lost in the city, pecking away at a telephone pole it had mistaken for a tree. As he watched, Dorsey rehashed his day in court.

The jury box had been empty. It was the first thing Dorsey had noticed on entering the courtroom, and he immediately asked the defense attorney what had happened. "Funny thing," the defense attorney said. "Soon as we got started, Stockman tells the judge his client wishes to waive his right to a jury trial. Wants to plead the whole thing before the judge." When Dorsey went on to ask the defense attorney for his thoughts on the matter, he was told to take a seat and wait to be called.

The judge entered and took his seat at the bench and the young attorney stood, patting his hair into place at his temple and self-consciously flattening the lapels of his suit jacket. He announced, a bit too quickly, that he had a surprise witness, and Dorsey came to the witness stand. Stockman, seated at the plaintiff's table next to his client, remained silent.

Led by the defense attorney's questions, Dorsey recounted his surveillance of DeMarco's activities. The sales slips were entered into evidence and examined by the judge. At that point, the defense attorney asked Dorsey if he would bring in the videotape player and monitor being attended to by a sheriff's deputy in the corridor.

Stockman objected. Not vigorously, with none of the pseudo-outrage Dorsey had come to view as standard courtroom procedure; he merely announced his objection, but for a moment further he continued to scan a file folder that lay open on the plaintiff's table. Then Stockman, a man in his mid-fifties, tall and gray-haired, rose and walked halfway to the bench, assuming center stage. Once there, he informed the judge that pretrial discovery procedures had failed to disclose this investigation.

"The discovery period," Stockman had said, turning to the defense attorney. "During which, I had assumed, I was provided with all the material and information the defense would present."

"Mr. Dorsey is a surprise witness, as I said." The defense attorney's words still spilled out too quickly. "More important, his services were retained by my firm. As a result, his work is confidential and protected from discovery as attorney's work product."

"Your employee?" Stockman asked. "Not that of your client, Fidelity Casualty? You are sure of this?"

"Mr. Dorsey is definitely in my firm's services."

Showing surprising agility, Stockman twirled, more than turned, moved to the plaintiff's table, and picked up the file folder he had been reading. He took it to the bench, still open, and presented it to the judge. While doing so he informed the judge that the folder contained a photocopy of Fidelity Casualty's claim file on Benito DeMarco, something he was sure the defense would be willing to stipulate to. Pointing with his finger, Stockman directed the judge's attention to a handwritten entry dated September 4 of that same year.

"The entry," Stockman said, "is signed by Raymond Corso, who is—and again I am sure the defense will stipulate to this—the local claims manager for Fidelity Casualty. The September fourth records show that Mr. Corso received a call from Mr. Dorsey requesting permission to continue. It does not say what it is he wishes to continue, but as Mr. Dorsey is a private investigator by profession it is only logical that Mr. Dorsey was referring to the investigation of my client. It is also logical to assume that since he was contacting Mr. Corso he was under Mr. Corso's supervision. As a result, Mr. Dorsey was working for Fidelity Casualty and not a law firm. As such, his investigation was discoverable and his present testimony is inadmissible."

Dorsey immediately remembered the call and had felt himself reeling backward in his chair. One call, he had thought, one fucking call! Made to Corso because you were in a hurry and this tenderfoot of an attorney couldn't be reached. One simple clarification for a fee invoice, that's all you needed. How did Stockman find it? What brought his attention to that entry? What difference did it make? Stockman always knew.

The judge ruled swiftly and Dorsey was dismissed. Walking past the defense attorney and out of the room, Dorsey worked out Stockman's scheme. Somehow Stockman had known Dorsey would be testifying about his investigation, and that's why he got rid of the jury. Stockman could object to Dorsey's testimony and the judge could throw it out afterward, but the testimony itself could never be erased from the jurors' minds. Even if the testimony was thrown out before it was given, the jury would have known an investigation had been conducted, and nobody bothers to testify about an investigation that had no results. So Stockman chooses to skip the jury and deal with the judge, who will consider only points of law. A judge who is just a little bit pissed off at the defense for springing a bogus surprise witness on him.

Wiping the memories away as best he could, Dorsey returned to the desk, took the last page from the typewriter carriage, and signed his name. Attaching the invoice, he slipped the report and the videotape into a manila envelope. The letterhead at the upper left corner of the envelope read DORSEY INFORMATION SERVICES, CARROLL DORSEY, MANAGER. Well, he thought, licking the envelope's adhesive strip, at least Junior—the attorney—had someone to blame for how things turned out.

CHAPTER 2

After showering, Dorsey went through two towels drying his six-foot-four-inch frame. He put on a pair of fatigue pants speckled with paint, the waistband of which matched his age, thirty-eight. After struggling into a gray sweatshirt with matching paint speckles, he shoved his feet into a pair of worn jogging shoes and sat at the edge of his bed, listening for the front doorbell. From his bedroom window, through the growing darkness of the October evening, Dorsey could see the back of another row house across the alley from his own backyard. Beyond that was the Monogahela River, reflecting the soft glow of the mercury lamps strung along the Tenth Street bridge. Sitting there, Dorsey again ran through his court appearance, memories he had hoped to rinse away in the shower. Maybe, he thought, a shower of beer would do the trick. Jack "Personal Injury" Stockman. P.I. Stockman. The guy is hot shit.

The low electric buzz of the doorbell pulled Dorsey away from the courtroom and downstairs to the front door. Through the door's glass, partially blocked by a cardboard sign jammed into its left corner, he saw two men standing on the stoop. One was short and heavy, in his mid-sixties, carrying two brown grocery sacks. The second one was much younger and of medium height, wearing a necktie and a trench coat. Dorsey opened the door. The second man in, the younger of the two, stopped in the doorway and tapped a finger on the cardboard sign. Printed in green on white, it read CARROLL DORSEY, INFORMATIONAL SERVICES TO THE INSURANCE INDUSTRY AND THE LEGAL COMMUNITY.

"Forget yesterday," the younger man said. "You'll have a day all your own. Goes around and comes around. Al and I still like you."

"Thank you, Bernie," Dorsey said, a grin betraying his formal response. "And fuck you, I guess."

Dorsey followed his visitors into the hall. To the right were double sliding doors, and the older man worked a hand free and stabbed at a handle with his knuckles, sending one of the doors flying back on its overhead track. Dorsey reached ahead and flicked on the overhead light, and the three men entered his office. The man with the grocery bags went directly to the desk and dumped the bags on the blotter.

"Well," Dorsey said, "I see you both made it. More important, I see that the cargo made the trip safely too."

"It traveled well." Al Rosek took off his lined zipper jacket, draped it across the back of the armchair next to the desk, and dropped into the seat, shifting his weight from one buttock to the other until he was settled.

Dorsey sat behind the desk. "But Al, the desk is no place for this stuff. It should've gone there." He indicated a small office refrigerator behind the desk at the side of the bookcase.

"Bullshit. Me, I'm like the Teamsters. We haul the stuff, take it anywhere you want it to go, but we don't unload. Sorry, Dorsey, the shop steward says no crossin' of craft lines. It's a serious violation."

"That's how it's got to be, okay. Unions, backbone of the country." Dorsey swiveled toward the bags and tore at them greedily, pulling out five six-packs of beer and a large bag of Pennsylvania Dutch pretzels. "And the shipment, I believe, is correct."

"Got it straight, always do," Al said. "Thirty-one years—owned and worked the bar for thirty-one years now, and never botched an order. Two Irons, two Rolling Rocks for you, and a sixer of Michelob for this guy." With a tilt of his head, Al indicated Bernie.

"This guy?" Dorsey repeated, his voice heavy with concern, his outstretched hands pleading. "This guy, as you have the balls to call him, is Bernie. Bernie the attorney. Wisest of adjudicators, rival and close second to Solomon. This guy, Al, is the famous Bernard S. Perlac, attorney-at-something-or-other. Hell, Bern, what is that stuff you're an attorney at?"

"Lemme see," Bernie said, supine on the chaise. He wore a white oxford shirt buttoned to the throat, and his red silk necktie flowed gracefully across his breastbone to the top of his navy chalk-striped pants. "It was a school. I seem to remember attending a school of some sort. Lemme see, what did they call it? Thought you could help on this one, Dorsey. As I recall, you went there for a while. But I think I went there a little longer, after you blew out."

"I'd be wrong to help you; it'd be cheatin'."

"Never mind, I've got it!" Bernie sprang into a seated position. "Law. They called the fucking thing a law school. And so I sit here, at least until I lie back down, a law school graduate, an A-one lawyer. Bernard S. Perlac—yes, Dorsey, it's true—attorney-at-law. Get to you a little?"

"I get misty-eyed all over again," Dorsey said, cramming beer cans into the midget refrigerator.

"Comic geniuses." Al cracked open an Iron City. "Ever get some real jobs, put in some regular hours, there wouldn't be any time for clowning. Especially you, Dorsey, lucky enough to have a young thing like Gretchen to spend your time with. Girl like her, with a wreck like you? I can't figure it."

"Young girls find me exotic," Dorsey said, settling back into his seat, a Rolling Rock in his hand.

"The movie," Al said. "C'mon, Dorsey, we came to see this movie of yours. The new one."

"Showing your age, Al, really are," Dorsey said. "Not movies nowadays, Grandpop. These are videos. No white screen to unroll.

No film to crop every time it's shown. Videotape: shove in the cassette you're in business."

"Just show it, please?"

"Yeah," Bernie repeated. "Just show it, please?"

Dorsey took a tape cassette, a copy of the one he had mailed that afternoon to Fidelity Casualty, from a desk drawer and slapped it into the VCR atop his twenty-inch television.

"So what's on the program tonight?" Bernie asked.

"Something of a New Wave feature," Dorsey said, returning to his seat. "It's called *Cement Man,* a real tearjerker. How many hankies you equipped with?"

The TV screen went from black to gray, and then a row house much like Dorsey's appeared. The camera angle was on a diagonal from the left and pointing down from about shoulder height. From the covered walkway between two houses came a man in his late forties, wearing a stained navy sweatshirt. In his left hand he held a four-foot wrecking bar, which he began to use against the cement sidewalk. He worked the curved business end into an existing crack and put his back into it. Cement chunks split off into the air. After going at it for a few more minutes, he dropped the bar, lowered himself into a crouch, and began gathering the debris.

"This is it," Dorsey said. "Here it comes now, the part you're gonna love."

The videotape's subject carried a load of debris through the walkway and returned for another. As he bent down, his face was to the camera; his expression turned to a scowl of suspicion.

"Busted." Al left his chair for another beer. "Looks like this guy caught on."

"Just watch," Dorsey said calmly. No, he thought, DeMarco never caught on. Too busy working. P.I. Stockman, he's the one who caught on. Somehow.

Suspicion left the man's face and he went blank. Cautiously, he turned to left profile and reached a hand back to the seat of his pants. Now his face showed disgust as he fanned at his ass.

"Goddamn!" Bernie shouted. "The guy cut the cheese. Dorsey, you must've pissed yourself."

"Job like this, I take along a pair of plastic underwear."

"So what's his story?" Al asked. As they spoke, the man on screen went back to work on the sidewalk.

"Auto, personal injury. And, as you can see, a solid fake." Dorsey took another Rolling Rock from the refrigerator. "He's the one who got away. I thought Bernie might've filled you in on the way over."

"So this is the one," Al said. "Bernie told me you had a bad break, but he thinks you'll be all right."

"Really, Dorsey," Bernie said. He finished his beer and gestured for Dorsey to toss him another. "You haven't lost face around here. That young shit they assigned to the case should've settled and never taken on Stockman. Should've settled up and called it a victory."

"Settle. You lawyers like that, huh?" Al asked Bernie.

"Looking at me here flat on my back, Al, you may find it hard to believe I'm a good lawyer. Want to know why?" Bernie did not wait for an answer. "Because I very rarely go to court. Settle 'em ahead of time, that's the moneymaker. Hearings and trials, they're too much like work. Take time, too, time I can put to better use elsewhere. Like bringing in new business for the firm. Or maybe sitting at my desk billing more time for more clients. Better believe I like to settle."

The tape continued for another ten minutes of manual labor, until both Bernie and Al decided they'd had enough. Dorsey rewound the tape and returned it to the desk drawer. Al remarked he had been asking around about Dorsey; he hadn't seen him much lately. "My Rolling Rock seems to last a lot longer when you're not around," Al told him.

"My time's been filled with a little of this and that." Dorsey grinned with satisfaction. "Chased down some witnesses for a civil suit. Even had a job for Bernie's firm and did it pretty well. I was their hero."

"Unlike this DeMarco trial, which is no big deal," Bernie said. "You certainly were our hero, but only for a day; then we got over it and settled down to business. But, regardless, it was a good piece of work, which led to a brilliant settlement."

"Yeah," Dorsey said. "I did that. But mostly it's been insurance jobs lately."

"Checkin' out more deadbeats?" Al asked.

"Pretty much," Dorsey said. "Not with the camera, mostly just asking around about guys. Workers' comp, a little auto. Last few weeks, the stuff has been pouring in. I've put some thought into buying a bigger mailbox."

"Sounds funny," Bernie said. "How come you're getting so much? Stuff you're talking about, surveillance and even just checking on a guy, that usually goes to the big outfits because of the price. And some of the local carriers have in-house guys. Somebody must like you, want to make you rich."

"Like me? Somebody out there loves me—the claims manager at Fidelity Casualty. You know him, Ray Corso? Well, things may change after this DeMarco deal, but up to now I've been getting tons of work from him. Back in early summer, around the first of July, Corso calls and asks if I can come to his office for a talk, which of course I do. Well, Corso starts right in about how the company wants to get tough and run a lot of cases to ground. Really sew up some bad ones. Get aggressive, he keeps on saying. I don't think this guy could get aggressive in a whorehouse. But he comes right across with eight cases and says expense is no concern."

"Can't be; it doesn't work that way," Bernie said. "Corso's like all the rest, he's got a money ceiling on his authority. Tell you what: you send in big bills, really milk this thing, there's going to be invoices coming back in the mail with PISSED OFF stamped across 'em."

"Who's the investigator here?" Dorsey asked. "I talked to Corso, and I'm telling you the money is there. Already finished some of the jobs, and the bills were paid in full. Big bills like you wouldn't believe."

Bernie sipped his beer and shook his head. "Still doesn't sound right, that much work going to just one guy. Don't get pissed off and take it the wrong way, but you think your old man might have a little something to do with this?"

Dorsey stopped his beer three inches from his mouth and cut his eyes at Bernie. "No, I'm not taking it wrong, I'm taking it right, and I *am* pissed off. The old man, his day is done. Shot his wad a long time back. He doesn't have a thing to do with this."

"Okay, just guessing is all," Bernie said. "So, anyways, where's all this work at?"

"Not much here in the city." Dorsey sipped his beer, glad to be off the subject of his father. "Been hauling my ass all over western P. A. for months. Mill towns, mostly. Allenport, Monessen, Aliquippa, those sorts of places. Next week's work is all in Westmoreland County; then I go to Johnstown. Working on an hourly rate so the mileage is money. Doing in-depth shit like the man asks for."

"Guy could get rich," Al said, resting his beer on the curve of his stomach, "if he was smart enough to go to them places in a short-haul truck with a load of whatever. A guy could double his take, maybe triple it."

"Yeah, Al, sure," Dorsey said. "I've done a lot of surveillance from the back of a big orange sixteen-foot U-Haul. Who would notice me?"

CHAPTER 3

In western Pennsylvania, U.S. 22 is a road that requires concentration. There are three lanes; eastbound, westbound, and an alternating passing lane that can change midway through an S-bend or tight curve. The terrain is mountainous in part and always treacherous. But despite the danger, Dorsey drove his old Buick with only a fraction of his attention on the road. He kept drifting back to Bernie's question: Could the old man be pulling strings?

The old man, Dorsey thought, as he passed a truck just beyond the turnoff for Torrance State Hospital, the site of a number of involuntary commitment hearings he had attended, representing the District Attorney. The old man has a lot of pull, but not with insurance companies. He can still put in the fix for a guy to get a job with the county or city, but this is out of his league. He was always the working man's candidate, the man for the common people: Old Irish, common as Paddy's pig. The only way for him to get into the boardroom was to pour the coffee and serve lunch to the whitebreads. The old man can make a lot of things happen, but not in this ballpark, Dorsey assured himself. At Route 56, he pulled off 22 and headed south for Johnstown.

With the luxury of unlimited expenses, Dorsey chose to make an overnight stay out of what should have been a two-day commuting job. The first day he spent interviewing Carl Radovic's neighbors in the lower regions of Otterman Avenue. Slow and tedious work and, as Dorsey well knew, most likely futile. Though many investigations begin with a tip from a jilted lover or an angry neighbor who has seen the disabled guy next door fixing his roof when he left for the three-to-eleven shift, little or nothing comes from cold calls on the neighbors. But just such a canvassing was expected as an integral part of a disability investigation. Adjusting companies and investigators grew fat on such work every day, and Dorsey was willing to play along and get on the gravy train.

Otterman Avenue, unlike most of Johnstown, was on flat bottom ground in the basin that formed the business district. Dorsey thought of the area as the floor of a natural cistern, surrounded by hills, that filled itself with muddy brown water every forty years or so. The part of Otterman Avenue that Dorsey worked, far east of the shops and hospitals, was blue-collar residential. At 362 Otterman, Dorsey spoke briefly to an elderly woman who didn't know Carl Radovic; she was just the mother-in-law in for a visit. At 364, only a fourteen-year-old girl was home. Dorsey backed off quickly when she flashed him a twenty-year-old smile and invitation. At 370, directly across from Radovic's house, he met three unemployed brothers, all in their early twenties.

"Yeah, sure, fuckin' Carlie," said the oldest brother, who had nominated himself spokesman. Like the others, he was dressed in a faded T-shirt and raggedy Levi's; his hair was long and unkempt. The living room in which they sat held one easy chair and sofa. The air had a musty smell that told Dorsey the boys weren't helping Mother with the housework.

"Carl Radovic," Dorsey said. "Around five-five but wide through the shoulders, they tell me. Lives across the street?"

"Tryin' to tell ya we know him," the oldest said from his spot on the sofa. "Fuckin' guy's been around forever. Used to have his mother over there with him. She died couple years ago. Forget how many."

"No family? Married?"

"Him? That ugly bastard?" The oldest brother lit a cigarette and kicked out a cloud of smoke for punctuation. "He spends all his time nursin' beers down the corner, the Hotel Bar. So you're an insurance guy, huh? Checkin' on his back, on how he got hurt? Ain't supposed to be worth a shit. Used to be a hard-working sumbitch, but ain't worth a shit now. What's he gettin', work comp?"

"They don't tell me the numbers or what they're paying out for," Dorsey lied. Radovic had a hefty weekly check coming in. "So what's the guy doing with all his time? Can't spend it all in a bar. Who does the house repairs? Who keeps up the property?"

"Repairs?" the oldest brother said. "Gimme a break. Nothin' new on the outside and the drapes are drawn shut. Maybe he makes chicken movies." The two younger brothers, sitting at the far end of the sofa, elbowed each other and laughed.

Dorsey ignored the suggestion. "How about his comings and goings? Does he go out and come back about the same time every day?"

"Just to the Hotel Bar. We don't keep tabs on him." The oldest brother looked over at his siblings, waiting for his laugh. He got it.

"No sign of him working? How about when he goes out in the morning, does he carry a lunch pail? How about his car, is he driving something new?"

"He ain't drivin' 'cause he ain't got a car. Far as lunch is concerned, he don't leave the house till afternoon."

Finishing his interview with the brothers, Dorsey tried a few more homes on Otterman with even weaker results. He checked out the Hotel Bar, which he found with the help of a crossing guard, but only the bartender was in and he was busy loading the coolers and in a bad mood because of it.

Dorsey returned to his motel, the Sheraton on Bedford, and broke for lunch. With a Diet Coke from the machine in the hall, he tore into three chunks of a ham loaf that Gretchen had taught him to prepare. The ham loaf had been packed in a small Igloo cooler. Dorsey replaced the food with ice from the lobby machine, then topped the ice with six cans of Rolling Rock to chill for the end of the day's work. This completed, he slipped on a tie, flicked some lint from the lapel of his herringbone jacket, and set off to interview Dr. Tang, Carl Radovic's treating physician.

Sitting in an uncomfortable chair in Dr. Tang's empty waiting room, Dorsey pondered the fact that backwoods America is knee-deep in foreign-born doctors. Every small-town hospital seems staffed almost exclusively with them. Grinning, he recalled a neurologist he had interviewed in Greene County, an Asian whose receptionist had sat in on the conversation to assist the doctor over the rougher spots of the English language. The doctor was straightforward and honest, as Dorsey remembered, but somebody else was writing the great reports he signed.

"Things look kind of slow," Dorsey said to Dr. Tang's receptionist, the room's only other occupant, who sat behind a counter with a sliding glass partition. She was young, but Dorsey knew that even at her age she could have the keeper-of-the-gate syndrome suffered by so many medical receptionists. The higher calling to protect the doctor from answering questions. Nobody sees the wizard.

"It's a slow town," she said, shuffling some papers to the side, seemingly glad for the diversion. "Nobody works anymore, so nobody's got health insurance, like Blue Cross or Blue Shield. Most can't afford a visit to the family doc for a cold, let alone fork out an orthopedist's fee. Even the work comp patients are gettin' scarce. Fewer jobs for people to get hurt on. Yeah, slow it is."

"One guy got hurt at work. Otherwise I wouldn't be here."

"Who's that?"

"Guy named Carl Radovic. He's a comp case."

"Oh, him," the receptionist said. "Just pulled his chart this morning. You're next, by the way, soon as Dr. Tang finishes rounds at Conemaugh."

"Any chance of getting a peek at that chart?" Dorsey used his most ingratiating smile, chancing it. C'mon, he thought, let's have a look. There's a resident at Mercy Hospital who's showing me the way around a patient's folder.

"Sorry, it's already in the doctor's office, locked in a drawer."

"You familiar with Radovic?"

"A little. He's in every two weeks," the receptionist said. "And the way things are, I've got plenty of time to shoot the breeze, find out what people are all about. Like a good detective. You're a detective, right? What do you think?"

"Work on it," Dorsey said. "The field is bursting with opportunity."

"One thing I know for sure," the receptionist said, apparently pleased with her insider's knowledge. "He's a lucky son of a bum."

"How's that, lucky?"

"Really lucky, in a way," the girl said. "You don't mind gettin' a little bit hurt. Carl, now, he don't look bad, really."

"Let's get back to lucky."

The receptionist looked surprised at Dorsey's apparent failure to understand. "Guy twisted his back, right? Picked up something or other at the mill. Get this. The accident takes place two days before a layoff! Carl would've been gone, laid off. He stays healthy, he'd have gone on unemployment. Temporary benefits, even if some people think it's never gonna run out. But he's on comp, permanent. Stuff runs for life, unless you guys come up with a way to get him off."

Dorsey slipped into a well-practiced disinterest. "Radovic tell you this?"

"Some," the receptionist said. "He ain't got much, but he likes to brag like the rest. Most of it I got from a girlfriend; she's in personnel at the mill. Used to be, anyways. She's laid off now, too. From Carlisle Steel."

Before they could continue, the intercom buzzed, indicating that Dr. Tang had arrived in his office through a private entrance. Dorsey was shooed in by the receptionist, who reluctantly gave up her audience.

An Asian gentleman, wearing an ill-fitting suit that would

have disguised his profession in a larger city, rose from behind his desk and introduced himself as Dr. Tang. His hair was cropped short and his eyes were hidden behind thick lenses.

"Mista Dorsey," Dr. Tang said blandly, nodding to a chair in front of the desk. "You here to discuss Mista Ravic?"

"Radovic." Dorsey took his seat. "Carl Radovic. You're his treating physician, correct? You're treating him for a back ailment?"

"Yes, over the last few months. I see him on referral from Dr. Hurst, the plant doctor at Carlisle." As he spoke, Dr. Tang opened a manila folder and reviewed its contents. "The man has a problem."

"What's the diagnosis, doctor?" Dorsey took a sheet of paper from a manila folder of his own and handed it to the doctor. It was Radovic's signed release for medical information, photocopied from Fidelity Casualty's claim file.

"To me, looks like a disc," Dr. Tang said, eyes on the paper Dorsey had handed to him. "Herniated at L5-S1. Lots of pain; patient says he have pain running down his leg. Disc is out, striking a nerve. Possibly sciatic."

"Herniated disc," Dorsey mumbled, again looking through the folder on his lap, faking a search. "What do the tests say? CT scan, myelogram?"

"I examine him," the doctor said. His eyes abruptly left the paper and settled on Dorsey. "All the signs, he have all the signs. Straight leg is positive. Tender over the sciatic notch. Can't bend, and range of motion is narrow."

"Doctor," Dorsey said, "I'm not here to start an argument, but isn't it standard for some type of pictures, other than X rays, to be taken? What you just mentioned are clinical observations. Any test results in his chart?"

"CT scan." Dr. Tang's glare sharpened as he handed out the test report to Dorsey. Looking over the results, Dorsey concluded that Radovic suffered only the signs of advancing age for a laborer: spurring on several vertebrae and a bulging disc at L5-S1.

"There's a recommendation for a myelogram." Dorsey indicated the report, passing it back to Dr. Tang. "Has one been scheduled, doctor?"

"Not by me. Patient will not consent."

"But isn't a myelogram the way to go to decide whether or not surgery is indicated?"

"What can I say?" Dr. Tang grinned, as if in triumph. "Mista Radovic refuse even to consider surgery. Said this on first exam. He didn't care what I say: no myelogram and no surgery."

"Without your ever raising the question, he refused a myelogram and surgery?" Dorsey was intrigued that a steelworker would be familiar with a myelogram. Familiarity gotten from a good coach, he concluded.

"Correct."

"No myelogram, but you're sure it's a herniation?" Dorsey thought he'd take a chance, tempted by the opportunity to show off. "No myelogram, inconclusive CT. So really, doctor, you're basing your diagnosis and finding of disability on believing the patient's subjective complaints?" It was a short-lived and Pyrrhic victory, and Dorsey saw his error even as he committed it. Never alienate your subject, he reminded himself. Be a friend and get the information you came for.

First Dr. Tang stumbled, then he exploded. "Of course I believe. He come here and say he have pain, I got to believe. I'm not crazy! You know how serious that is, ignoring, disbelieving the patient? He say he hurts, I try to figure out why he hurts."

"What happens if you can't figure it out?"

"Then I send him somewhere else, let somebody else try. Not perfect, you know."

Yeah, Dorsey thought, somebody else will try. Somebody on the Pittsburgh Express, maybe. The patient goes right on the cycle, the treatment cycle. Dorsey had never seen proof, but he had been hearing about the Pittsburgh Express for years. Just rumors, rumors that small-town locals like Dr. Tang only treated patients until it was time for surgery. Then the patient was farmed out to one of a select number of neurosurgeons or orthopedists in Pittsburgh. After surgery, it was home again to the local doctor for a long convalescence and regularly scheduled examinations.

On his way out through the reception area, Dorsey picked up a copy of the CT scan. He also got the name of the girl at Carlisle Steel: Claudia Maynard.

"Think you'll find her at home?" The receptionist leaned through the open partition. "Not likely. That girl has been on the go ever since the layoff. Signed up for unemployment, and when it came time to get her mail-in claims she took off for Myrtle Beach. Might still be there."

That evening in his room, the Olivetti portable on the chair seat, Dorsey sat at the edge of the bed, pecking away with two fingers, composing his report of the day's activity. His attention was divided among writing the report, watching the Bulls and Knicks play an exhibition game on the room's TV set, and listening to Roy Eldridge strain his trumpet on the tape player, packed along for the trip. At the foot of the bed was the Igloo cooler with a fresh layer of ice over the Rolling Rock.

Threading a clean sheet of paper into the typewriter carriage, Dorsey once again realized that his ability to prepare a well-written report was his bread and butter. He often spoke like a leftover from the old films and recordings he loved, but knowing his way around a typewriter kept him in business. For years he had wondered who to thank, the nuns at Sacred Heart grade school or the instructors in his one year of law school.

Pulling on a beer, Dorsey worked his way through the morning hours, describing his interview of the three Grub brothers, as he had come to call them. Although they had not meant to, the three boys had provided useful information. Radovic was a loner, a lifelong bachelor whose only interest was the beer at the Hotel Bar. It didn't impact directly on the claim, Dorsey typed, but knowing this about Radovic was helpful in planning a surveillance. Anywhere that Radovic might go, other than the Hotel Bar or a grocery store, might be significant. He could be up to something. Maybe working on the side.

Dorsey next described his meeting with Dr. Tang, wincing as he forced himself to relive the botched job. But even here he found material to build on. He concentrated on the physician's defensive posture and the clear pleasure he had displayed when he told Dorsey that no myelogram or surgery would be done, thinking this ended the investigation.

A final section was reserved for the gift Dorsey had received from Dr. Tang's receptionist. "Low-key interrogation" was his label for the method he had used to obtain this information. There is a distinct possibility, Dorsey wrote, that Mr. Radovic had prior knowledge of a planned reduction of manpower at Carlisle Steel that allowed him to schedule his accident. Also, the most likely source of information, a personnel secretary, had been able to finance a prolonged stay at a popular East Coast resort. Dorsey went on to state his firm resolve, if possible, to interview the woman. Finishing the report and knowing he could never properly realign the paper once it was out of the carriage, he did his proofreading while the page was still in the typewriter. Then he put the Olivetti in its case, opened a fresh beer, and stretched out on the bed, watching the Knicks cross the center court stripe and listening to the last notes drip from Roy Eldridge's horn.

Bernie, Dorsey thought. That guy can be a pain in the ass. This work from Corso is a windfall, nothing else, part of the cycle. Some insurance exec tells his people to get tough on claims and hire investigators; it'll save us a bundle. Six months down the road a new exec may be in charge and come up with another idea: these investigations are a waste. Cancel them; we'll save a bundle.

Bernie don't know shit. There's nothing funny going on, and the old man doesn't have the pull to be part of it. It is what it is.

He missed Gretchen. He thought of putting through a call but she would never take it, not during her shift. Her work was too important, the future of her career even more so.

The following morning Dorsey rose and dressed himself in a matching gray sweatsuit and worn-down Brooks running shoes. By seven o'clock he was off on his daily forty-five-minute exercise session, walking at a brisk pace around the Johnstown basin, arms pumping in unison with his legs. It was a regime he had begun two years ago following the surgical repair of a ligament in his left knee. The injury had occurred in a football game on Thanksgiving morning. Bernie had invited Dorsey out to Mellon Park to play in a game between the younger members of his law firm and the staff of a local legal aid service. "A struggle between the haves and have-nots," Bernie had dubbed it. An hour into the game Dorsey had stepped forward to tag a ball carrier when a skinny paralegal on the other team dove into Dorsey's left leg, clipping him. In his hospital room after surgery, casted from toe to hip, Dorsey received a visit from Bernie.

"Nice guys," Dorsey said, brushing the Demerol webs from his thoughts. "Great buncha fellas. Professionals, straight-up and honest. Guys you can turn your back on and feel good about it."

"What's the bitch?" Bernie had said. "Lucky the guy was only a paralegal. Imagine the outcome if a lawyer, maybe a full partner, had caught you looking the other way."

After his walk Dorsey took a long hot shower and then dressed in a checked flannel shirt and blue jeans without a designer label. From the closet he took his army field jacket and draped it across the back of a chair. Watching daytime TV, sticking with the talk shows and avoiding the games, he thought again of calling Gretchen and again thought better of it. After an on-call shift she needed ten to twelve hours of recovery sleep. Instead, he went to the motel coffee shop and read the Pittsburgh morning paper over eggs and hash browns. At ten-thirty he packed his bags, checked out with an itemized bill for Corso, and put his things in the trunk of the Buick. Wearing his field jacket, he left on foot to begin his surveillance of Radovic.

Standing across the street and halfway up the block from Radovic's house, Dorsey checked his watch and wrote in his pocket notebook that he was in place and beginning the surveillance at eleven-fifteen. Relying on his own experience and the information gotten from the three Grub brothers, Dorsey figured an unemployed bachelor was never out of bed before eleven o'clock. Even then, Dorsey thought, he should be fighting a hangover.

It wasn't until five minutes after one that Radovic emerged

from the house and came down the porch steps, shaking the loose handrail and apparently deciding that repairs could wait. With the exception of a blue windbreaker, his clothes matched Dorsey's. Moving down Otterman he fought a stiff wind that played at the few strands of hair stretched across his crown. His gait was brisk and with his shoulders huddled against the wind he gave Dorsey the image of a neckless man whose fleshy head flowed directly into an overweight torso.

Two hours of crisscrossing the street pretending to look for a forgotten address had played on Dorsey's nerves and he started off after Radovic much too quickly, leaving him only a half-block lead. Easy, Dorsey coached himself. Remember the rules. Give 'em rope. You're in a small city, a tight-knit one. They'll pick up on you. There's only so much time. Make it count.

When Radovic passed the Hotel Bar without stopping, Dorsey cursed, having promised himself a cold Rock as a reward for his self-control. Block after block went by. Dorsey marveled at the fat man's stamina, giving him more and more credit for ducking the myelogram. Radovic took an abrupt left at the next intersection and Dorsey fell back even farther, fearing he had been spotted.

After a ten-count, Dorsey rounded the corner and found the sidewalks empty. Couldn't have gone far, he reasoned. Disabled or not, fat guys only move so fast. Unlike the sidewalk on which he stood, which was lined with worn-down private homes, the far side of the street held storefronts. Most were empty but some were secondhand clothing and furniture shops, the old owners' names obliterated with whitewash and the names of the newcomers announced on hand-printed cardboard signs. Dorsey chose to check the shops. He could be in one of those houses, he told himself, but if he is, you've lost him.

The first two shops were open but had no customers; the next three were closed. He passed a secondhand furniture store; from what he saw through the shop window Dorsey decided the owner had balls putting up a sign that said ANTIQUES. At the corner storefront Dorsey peeked through the dirt-streaked window and saw Radovic seated behind a folding table that served as a desk, diligently working the phone and returning Dorsey's stare.

"I'm made," Dorsey muttered, knowing he would have to go in and play the scene through. Entering the small shop, he noted that the table and matching folding chairs were the total of the room's furnishings. The drab walls were covered with reprinted Wobblies posters, photos of striking railroad workers in Altoona, and front-page newspaper stories recounting the famous steelworkers' strike of the 1890s. Dorsey's eyes went from poster to poster, following plaster cracks that served as a timeline, tracing the history of the American labor movement. The centerpiece of the wall to Radovic's back was a sheet of white butcher paper that announced, in black ink, that this was the Johnstown headquarters of Movement Together.

"Gotta get off. Gotta go," Radovic mumbled into the receiver. "Guy just came in." He hung up the phone and scratched his stomach through his windbreaker. Dorsey could feel the fat man's eyes roam over his unfamiliar face.

"Kinda on the cold side in here, don't think?" Dorsey asked, avoiding introductions. "Somebody must've forgot to hit the thermostat."

"Ain't no corporate fuckin' penthouse," Radovic said, his gut straining his jacket and pressing at the table's metal edge. "Poor town, fella. No bucks for heat. Little guys, that's what we got here."

"C'mon, no bucks, Movement Together?" Dorsey knew his best move would be to ease himself back out the door, but his more playful side was taking charge. Even as he spoke, an inner voice reminded him what an asshole he could be. "No money? I see the priest, your leader, on TV. At least I think he's still a priest. He's on TV, and not just on the news when you guys are getting back at the Japanese by busting up Toyotas with sledgehammers. He does his own commercials, and they cost. You have the shitty end of the stick. Put your office in for a bigger budget next year."

Radovic rose slowly from his chair and crossed toward Dorsey. "Who the fuck are you, tellin' me about gettin' the fuckin' shaft? You got nothin' new to teach me about that. We been gettin' it from the money boys all along. This place ain't about no shaft. This is gettin' even, kickin' 'em right in the balls."

"Hey, slow down." With a hard-case radical on his hands, Dorsey saw he'd better back off some. In just two days, he thought, in the course of one investigation, you have pissed off two people and thereby pissed in your own hat. Corso's easy money is getting to you.

"Asked you who the fuck you was."

Dorsey knew the laws on misrepresentations, although he did break them from time to time. But this was different. He had an angry man on his hands who knew him for a stranger in a town that had so few. Being only from the insurance company and not the evil agent of Corporate America could get him outside without a fight. Dorsey identified himself and the company he represented.

The tension lessened in Radovic's eyes but only a degree. Dorsey figured it to be a downgrading from murder to maiming. "Get the fuck out," Radovic said. "Got nothing to say, prick. Get a lawyer, he can talk to my lawyer."

"The company has plenty of lawyers. I trip over a couple everytime I visit the office. We can call them if that's how it's got to be."

"Said for you to get the fuck out." Radovic stepped around Dorsey and opened the door.

"Carl," Dorsey said, gambling, hoping to salvage something out of his blown surveillance. "I'm going to be straight with you. I've been behind you for a while and you move pretty good for a disabled guy. I'm winded just trying to keep up. Scooted right along, you did. No limps, aches, pains, nothing. You've got a little something going here, from what I can see of it. So c'mon, Carl, give me a little of your time."

"Time." Radovic gazed out at the street, tapping his toe. "I'll give you time, I'll give you a hard time. Gonna put in a call, get some of the boys over here. Same guys you saw on TV, with the Toyota that ain't worth a shit now. Remember what that car looked like when they got bored and gave up? No resale value, that's what we said about it. No resale value. I'm dialin'. What you gonna do?"

Hiking back to the Sheraton, Dorsey came to the grim conclusion that through his own temporary (he hoped) ineptitude, the investigation was a bust. He had a few facts that others might convincingly call opinions and nothing on which Ray Corso could act. Radovic had taken a long walk and used a telephone. Oh, Dorsey thought, how the workers' compensation board will be impressed by that! And that man is not being paid to be in that office, he's dedicated and ruthless, the kind that mans the ship even when the water is over his head. Still, maybe this mess can be saved.

Dorsey pulled the Buick out of the motel lot and for the first time on this trip he left the flat bottom of the crater that held Johnstown and climbed up Route 271, headed north. Passing the Flood Museum, Dorsey amused himself by thinking of the whole town as an extension of that institution. With hard times, flood memorabilia had become the town's primary industry. Street signs marked a walking tour; bars and restaurants were decorated with flood scenes where photos of boxers and baseball players once hung. Water retention had replaced steelmaking and coal mining.

Dorsey found Mundys Corner just south of where 271 links up with U.S. 22, several miles past the point of level ground. Though it was only a small village, it took Dorsey thirty minutes to find the correct house, glad it was thirty minutes that could be billed to Ray Corso. The house, set back from the road with only a dirt drive cutting through some pines, was like many found in the highlands, constructed of stone, with wood stoves and high chimneys.

Dorsey introduced himself through a locked screen door while a suspicious Mrs. Maynard examined him closely. Short and wide, her eyes squinted against the outdoor light as she looked up.

"You from the unemployment? My Claudia, she got the mail-in cards, she don't have to go to the office each week—to register, I mean. They give her a lot of cards; they do it to hold down the lines. You been gettin' her cards? She said onna phone she was sending 'em in regular."

Patiently, Dorsey explained again that he was not from the state unemployment office and that he wanted to speak to Claudia concerning an accident at the mill. "Private insurance matter," he told her.

Mrs. Maynard explained that her daughter was on an extended vacation; she wouldn't be home for two more weeks. It took some doing, but Dorsey persuaded Mrs. Maynard that her daughter might have said something to either her or Mr. Maynard about the accident. He was shown to an easy chair in a cramped living room, and Mrs. Maynard went for her husband.

"She liked it there, Claudia did," Mr. Maynard said from the sofa opposite Dorsey. Built similarly to his wife, he was dressed in matching green work clothes. "Told me she always got along real well with everybody at the mill, even the fancy office types. Even when she got axed in the layoff she didn't have no hard feelings personally. Didn't tell anybody off. The big shots stay and she goes, but she don't make a fuss."

"Sounds like she just sort of tolerated management types, the ones she worked for." Dorsey hoped to learn as much as he could through small talk before getting down to a line of questioning. "Sounds like she wanted to get along."

"Claudia grew up right. And she's loyal to her people."

"Mr. Maynard," Dorsey said, working on a casual expression, "this business I'm here on is pretty routine stuff. It's about an accident down at Carlisle Steel. Just a few questions to set the record straight."

"Sure, we can talk, if that's all it is," Mr. Maynard said. Dorsey caught the trace of reluctance in his voice.

"Claudia, she was in the personnel office, right?"

"Secretary, general clerk stuff." Mr. Maynard ran his hand through his sparse gray hair. "Kept track of overtime and pay rates, looked after the time sheets. Typed a lot, mostly for the personnel director. She said he liked her, liked her work. But when the time came she got the ax with all the rest. How come, if her work is so good? Anyways, each layoff broke her heart. She had to get the time cards together for the guys who were goin'. Nasty job."

"How about this last one?" Dorsey asked. "Must've been specially tough; she must've known she was being let go. Did she know very long ahead of time?"

"At least a week, as I remember. You're right, it was tough. But let's get back to what you came for. Some guy got hurt down at Carlisle? Maybe I know him. I'm retired from there, ya know."

"The guy's name is Radovic, Carl's his first name. Lives in town down on Otterman. Sound familiar?"

"Carl? Yeah, I know the guy," Mr. Maynard said. "Supposed to be in bad shape. Haven't seen him since I left the plant. Still, I hear things."

"How about Claudia, she know him?"

"Could be, but it's unlikely. Old bachelor like him wouldn't run with the same crowd as Claudia. Could've met him at the plant. Maybe he came into the office, about a mistake in his pay or somethin'."

"Just thought I'd ask." Dorsey thought this conversation might look good once it was reduced to paper, but it was going nowhere. "I saw Carl today," Dorsey said. "He's working for Movement Together, those union people."

"Union people? Gimme a break." Mr. Maynard used his hands in a gesture of dismissal. "That's some outfit they got there. Oh, there's *some* union guys, guys like Carl, but not many. Carl's a hothead, so his throwin' in with those people isn't surprising. Of course he was always just an errand boy, and I'll bet he still is. Not like my Claudia. She don't go in for marches or throwin' stink bombs in churches and department stores, but she knows the wheels, the big shots. Her bein' involved on that level I can live with, her workin' sometimes with the leaders. She even knows the priest, Father Jancek. Andy, that's what the young ones call him."

"She should stay away from him!" Unseen, Mrs. Maynard shouted from the hallway. "Priests should leave young girls alone!"

Mr. Maynard grinned. "She makes a lot out of nothin'. The priest's okay, when it comes to that. Claudia's seen him lots and nothing's come of it."

"Father Jancek: he's the guy on TV leading the marches?" Dorsey asked. "Saw him saying mass at the mill gates. Is he still a priest?"

"Can't say. One bishop says he ain't, the other says he is. Better ask the Pope. But you wanna talk about Carl."

"Claudia, she wouldn't've known Carl even through the priest?"

"No way," Mr. Maynard said. "Carl is strictly rank-and-file. Claudia knows the bosses."

Maybe, maybe not, Dorsey thought. But now at least he had something to put in his report.

CHAPTER 4

Three years earlier, approximately four months after his mutually unmourned departure from the Allegheny County District Attorney's office, Dorsey had purchased an electronic telephone answering machine. The unit came off the back of a truck parked in the Strip district, and Dorsey suspected it originated in the back of another truck. Proud of his bargaining powers, he was sure the tape would soon be crammed with messages from prospective clients. Sadly, this was not the case, and the aggravation caused by the silent tape led Dorsey to disconnect the entire unit. But now, with the newfound affluence brought by Ray Corso, the machine was back on the job. It had taken Dorsey and Bernie two hours and three beers each to get the unit up and running.

Dorsey pulled his mail from the black metal mailbox anchored in the brick by his door and searched through the envelopes for checks from Fidelity Casualty. Disappointed, he unlocked the front door and went through the hallway into the office. He dropped into the swivel chair and slipped a cassette into the tape player. While the Ellington orchestra softly played "Prelude to a Kiss," Dorsey played the answering machine tape, hoping for better results than he had gotten from the mail.

"I get through tonight at eleven," a young female voice said. "It's been a bad one today, so I know I'll want out fast. Please: at eleven, not twenty after. See ya."

"I'll be there," Dorsey muttered. "I'm always there. Most times." The next voice was also female, older and much more self-assured.

"Carroll, your father asked me to call." It was Irene Boyle, his father's personal secretary: Ironbox Boyle, the only woman Dorsey ever remembered working for his father. Hard and cold, as Dorsey remembered from his youth; that box has to be iron. Dorsey hit the stop button, hoping to kill the woman, but only silenced the voice temporarily. ". . . this evening. He would like you to come by this evening. Dinner's out. I'm sorry, but it's just not possible. He's got this affair, a gathering for a judge or a candidate for judge, I forget which. Be here around eight-thirty. He'd really like to see you."

He had planned a quiet evening of typing reports and listening to Ellington, with a little comforting companionship later on, but this message was a well-worded summons. Dorsey had not said no to Mrs. Boyle in all his thirty-eight years, not since she had partially filled the void when his mother died when he was twelve. Strong on discipline but without maternal love, she gave directions and never made requests. Dorsey smiled at the smooth manner in which Mrs. Boyle had avoided the possibility of dinner. Dorsey had not eaten at his father's table since the day in 1970 he'd dropped out of Duquesne Law School, the day before he enlisted in the army.

His mother had died when he was in the sixth grade, his first year of organized basketball, the type of milestone an old jock uses to mark the passage of time. At times Dorsey had thought that if she had to die it was best she had done it then, when he was tall and awkwardly uncoordinated, an embarrassment on the court. Dorsey had figured his performances to be humiliations; after all, his father never came to watch. His father's failure to attend his games became more of an issue than his mother's passing. Two more reasons to hate the old man.

Dorsey's prowess on the court increased in spurts. By eighth grade he had an unreliable jump shot, but his strong rebounding kept him off the bench. It was his junior year at Central Catholic when it all came together, when the hook shot was perfected, not only from a low post setup but also on the run, sweeping through the key, arching the ball over the defender's reach to end in a sweet glide through the net. After a forty-two-point effort against Bishop Serra, he came to the attention of Columnist Phil Musick, who referred to Dorsey as the best possible combination of Bill Sharman and Dave DeBusschere.

With fame came his father's interest. Throughout his senior year Dorsey watched his father, just before the game, shaking hands with innumerable priests as he strolled through the gym. When the team fell two victories short of the state finals, the local papers carried a photo of Martin Dorsey with his arm around his son's bare shoulders, whispering words of condolence in his ear.

At Duquesne—his father and the clergy at Central Catholic had insisted he attend a Catholic university—Dorsey continued to gather press clippings. Twice he led the team into the NCAA tournament and once to the NIT. For two years straight he beat crosstown rival Pitt with soft hook shots at the buzzer. And his father's interest continued to grow. Martin Dorsey attended all the home games, normally seated with several priests two rows behind the bench. On several occasions he took the coaches and players to dinner afterward. And when the team couldn't go he treated the local sportswriters, ensuring that his son's name would be mentioned in their columns.

Early in his senior year, Dorsey was introduced by his father to Dorothy Madigan, whose family had been political in Pittsburgh ever since there had been a city and county to run. They dated occasionally, but Dorsey never saw a future for them. Also at that time Dorsey began to receive repeated lectures from his father about the benefits of a law school education.

"Basketball is fleeting," Martin Dorsey had told his son, seated in the study of his Point Breeze home. "The NBA is an outside possibility but not a very realistic one. You're no guard, and you're too short to last at forward. Even if you should squeak by, it'd only be for a year or two. Law school will give you a profession. For life." At age twenty-two and looking toward his last collegiate season, Dorsey had let his father's words blow past him.

Early in that last season, on a snowy night in Morgantown, Dorsey's life changed. Three minutes into the second half against West Virginia, Dorsey moved up from his forward's position to double-team the WVU guard. The guard had his back to the Duquesne defender, dribbling the ball with his arm dangerously extended far away from his side. Dorsey moved for it, sure of a breakaway basket.

Whether the WVU guard had spotted him in the corner of his eye or had just coincidentally chosen to change direction Dorsey would never know, but as he closed in on the ball it began to move away, the guard twirling to his right. Dorsey dove for the ball, his right hand and fingers extended, and missed. As his hand was driven into the court's wooden floor, the three fractures sounded like one ugly snap.

At the university hospital, while being prepped for surgery, it finally occurred to Dorsey that attending law school might be the thing to do. He finished his undergraduate work and prepared for the LSAT examination, and in between he continued to date Dorothy Madigan, along with a handful of other women. Several times during the summer that followed he went with Dorothy to her family's summer place in the mountains near Ligonier. Dorsey found Dorothy sensual, with her raven-black hair and dark eyes, and sex with her was like comingling with the gods, but he could not commit to her. And each time he let his father know this, he suffered the hard disapproval of his father's steely look.

On Friday, May 29, 1970, Dorsey completed his first year at Duquesne Law School. He was living in a small apartment in the Squirrel Hill section of the city, and his father had asked him to dinner. With the after-dinner coffee, his father had his say.

"I think a wedding in June, next year, would be best." Martin Dorsey set his cup on its saucer and stared at his son.

Dorsey knew what he meant but tried to play off it. "You've

met someone new?" he laughed. "Hadn't heard about it. I hope you'll be happy together."

"No joking, please." Martin Dorsey was all business. "I won't have you laughing about your future, not after so many plans have been made."

"Plans? I've got some vague ones," Dorsey said slowly, his eyes digging at his father. "Sounds as though you've gone ahead and finished them for me. Let's hear how my life is to unfold."

Martin maintained his composure, appearing to consider his son's request. "This is as good a time as any. Your contribution will be to finish law school and pass the bar. And marry Dorothy, of course. That's the key. Arrangements will be made for you to join one of the midsized law firms in town. You'll spend a few years making a lot of friends and doing very little work; then you run for office: city council or one of the county row offices, whichever. Then you start the climb. End as governor, maybe senator."

"All laid out for me, right?"

"Yes," Martin Dorsey said. "All laid out for you. Despite yourself."

Dorsey's first instinct was to run, and that's the one he followed: he ran to an army recruiting station and enlisted the following morning. He knew a simple no wouldn't cut it with his father so he asked for immediate induction.

Basic training was a merciless grind of pushups, obstacle courses, and firing ranges, but for all its confinements, Dorsey was enraptured by the sense of being where his father couldn't touch him. After basic he was accepted into Ranger school; he washed out just three days short of graduation. Even though the completion of training would have earmarked him for Vietnam, Dorsey was discouraged by the dismissal, which he found surprising and unexplained. Dumped into a Military Police unit, he spent the remainder of his hitch chasing drunken soldiers at Fort Dix, New Jersey.

Following his separation from the army in 1973, feeling his oats and wanting to send a little spittle into his father's face, Dorsey joined the county DA's office as an investigator. He did so by relying on his MP experience and his father's name. He had used his father's influence, but not as his father planned. The old man, Dorsey thought, wanted to put you in a row office, but you used his pull to get a job far down the ladder. Turned the tables on him.

The end of the DA job and the end of Dorsey's satisfaction came with the election of two reform candidates to the three-member board of commissioners of Allegheny County. This latest demand to throw the bums out resulted in drastic cuts in manpower and spending. The DA's staff was sliced in half, but Dorsey stayed on, while men with more seniority went looking elsewhere. One assistant DA assured him he'd been kept on because of his ability. But at a going-away party for one of the departing investigators, a second assistant DA, falling-down drunk, asked Dorsey to give him a fuckin' break, "You're here because the DA owes his job to your old man, and the old man owns his future too." Three days later, after two days of unexplained absence from work, Dorsey called in his resignation and applied for his investigator's license.

His father's home was much smaller than many of the lavish homes near it along Wilkins Avenue in Point Breeze, but the pointed brick of the wall surrounding the front garden lent it an elegant touch. As Dorsey drove the Buick through the wrought-iron gate, he admired this expensive enclave in the midst of the city's decaying east end. He wondered just how badly the blacks who lived a few blocks away on the wrong side of Thomas Boulevard ached to get their hands on this old mick and his fellow landholders. Parking the car in the short circular drive, Dorsey took the garden path to the front door.

"Ah, very good; you came," Mrs. Boyle said as she answered the door.

"Called me, didn't you? Gave me my orders?"

"But you didn't call to confirm." Mrs. Boyle had just a trace of reprimand in her voice. Perfect, Dorsey thought, grinning. Perfect old hard-ass. Battleship-gray hair and matching skin wrapped in a plaid wool suit.

Leading him as if he were a stranger to the house, just another favor seeker here for his interview, Mrs. Boyle walked through a living room filled with antique furniture and adorned with Belleek china to a pair of cherrywood double doors. Gently and without knocking, she held one door slightly ajar but did not look in.

"Carroll's here. He just arrived."

"Please, Mrs. Boyle," the voice on the far side of the door said, "have him come in now. No need to have him mill about the house."

Avoiding her eyes, Dorsey passed Mrs. Boyle and looked upon a cherry desk with his father sitting behind it; when he was a boy he was never sure where the desk ended and his father began. Martin Dermott Dorsey, bald with only wisps of hair behind each ear, reminded his son of history-book pictures of William Jennings Bryan, staunch and purposeful, protecting the country from a threatening cross of gold. Wearing a navy wool suit and red bow tie, the older Dorsey smiled and gestured for his son to take one of the two wing chairs facing his desk. Behind his head and broad shoulders, mounted on the wall, were clusters of photos of then Commissioner Dorsey with every notable or celebrity who had passed through the area during his terms in office. The other walls were lined in bookshelves, and from a corner a console stereo gave out the soft tones of "Moonlight Serenade."

"Glenn Miller. You still like him, Carroll?"

"My preference is for Ellington and Basie, but I like Miller." Dorsey settled into the chair. "Some things stay with you."

"Thank you for coming, especially on such short notice," Martin Dorsey said. "A drink? How about it? You're home, you know."

"Beer, please," Dorsey said, watching his father rise from his seat and cross the room to the liquor cabinet concealed in one of the wall units. "Beer's okay."

"Beer I have," his father said, taking a can from an ice bucket that Dorsey knew had been filled in preparation for his visit. "I knew the answer, Carroll. I haven't seen a real drink in your hand in ten years, at least."

"Didn't see me in Georgia, those first couple of months in the service." Dorsey took the green can from his father. "Had all the moonshine I could hold down, which ain't much. Puked blood for two days after the stuff burned the lining of my stomach. Almost got a medical discharge, as you may recall."

"You must have truly been a mess," his father said, retaking his seat.

"Mrs. Boyle's call," Dorsey said, after a long pull on his beer. "She said something about you having a social gathering tonight."

The older Dorsey contemplated the glass of whisky he had poured himself and spoke as if reading his words from the gold-plated rim. "Little get-together for Danny Weitz; he's the fellow running for district magistrate over your way in South Side. Final stretch, you know; elections are only a few weeks away. Danny gets the shakes, like someone is going to find a Republican in South Side to challenge him and make it interesting. It's crap, but Danny always came through for me. So even if I don't like him, which I don't, I show my face over there a couple of times per year. Still, this magistrate's job, it could've been yours. Not a bad deal, really."

"What, sitting in some storefront on Carson Street dressed like the asshole on 'People's Court'?" Dorsey shook his head. "Listening to cops from the boroughs call drunk drivers and flashers 'the perpetrator'? Please, give me a break. Besides, nobody would listen to a district attorney dropout. I'm not popular in law-enforcement circles."

"Your true talent may lie in being unpopular," Martin Dorsey said. "But arrangements and compromises and understandings are reached every day by reasonable men. You want in, you're in. Tomorrow, if you like. You like?"

"No," Dorsey said. "I'm just not ready to wage the war against crime and solicit campaign contributions at the same time. Don't have the energy level for it. Besides, as Mrs. Boyle no doubt told you, I'm busy enough these days to have a machine taking my calls."

"Business is good, huh?" Martin Dorsey rested his glass on the desk blotter and then removed it, inspecting the wet ring it left behind. "Glad to hear it. Maybe it makes the reason I asked you to stop by null and void."

"Suppose you reveal your reasons, allow my input, and we'll see." Dorsey grinned. "Picked that one up in a meeting between two lawyers. They were hoping to settle a domestic dispute by using my input—videotapes."

"Carroll, please." His father had his hands out in supplication. "No more cute shit for a few minutes?"

"Fine, let's get to it."

"You and I," Martin Dorsey began, "father and son, but with nothing but a name in common. A lot of crap has taken place over the years, but I can't change that and you don't want to, so that's that. But you did toss away a lot of chances, chances to be much more than you are."

"I'll drink your beer," Dorsey said, "but the lecture you can pack up your ass."

Martin Dorsey smiled thinly. "I don't give lectures, I make speeches. I'm a politician, remember? Regardless, I have to start out this way. Making things your fault makes me feel better. Makes what I'm about to say sound much more caring. Makes me feel I'm giving the prodigal son his room back."

"Now that you have yourself completely fooled"—Dorsey saluted his father with his beer can—"please continue. Tingling. I'm simply tingling."

From the desk's deep center drawer, Martin Dorsey produced what appeared to be a leather-bound photo album. On the red cover, in raised gold script, it read *Steel Center Restoration Project, Phase One*. Martin Dorsey pushed the album toward his son and began his presentation.

"I assume you realize that I have not been sitting on my hands since leaving office. I'm a politician, like I said. And a politician is a deal-maker; it's his job to make the best deal all ways around. It's always been my favorite part of public life. I know how to make deals, and there are lots of people with money who know I know how. People with money who are looking to make a move."

"Keep going," Dorsey said, crossing the room for another beer. His father waited for him to return to his seat before continuing.

"I've been very busy," his father said, "making money by closing deals. Making sure the government-backed loans come through, discussing the possibility of a tax break for a company looking to move into the area. I know the people to talk to and I know how to talk."

"Who's disagreeing?"

"This time," Martin Dorsey said, tapping his finger on the album cover, "the deal is huge. I'm in with a business group, real top-drawer men with enough vision to see that the old way of making money is dead. Steel, foundry equipment, tractors: that's all out the window."

"Lots of people disagree," Dorsey said.

"You one of them?" Martin Dorsey opened the album and nudged it to the edge of the desk, flipping the pages before his son. The first pages held photos of idle and decaying steel mills and equipment plants. In the foreground of these pictures were railroad lines overgrown with vegetation. A few pages later came blueprints and diagrams for new commercial construction. Near the end began a series of artist-conceptualized drawings of sleek metallic-looking industrial buildings, long low barns with additions for office space and newly paved parking lots.

"Your people behind the new industrial push?" Dorsey asked. "All that high-tech stuff? These are the folks trying to buy up old mill sites, am I right?"

"Right you are," his father said. "High tech is a piece of it, but any interested firm is welcome to come take a look. We're going to pave the way for them, literally. The mills and plants, we'll buy them up and knock them down. Hell, with the shape they're in, a good stiff wind will do the job for us. Then rebuild and attract the new companies, the new employers, the new blood. This place, Steel Center, is up in the Mon Valley. The deal for that place, my deal, is cinched. But it's just the first of many. Look around; every river valley in the area is on its last legs. We'll rebuild them all."

"It could happen," Dorsey allowed. "The papers have stories about Carnegie Mellon and Pitt research projects that the high-tech people should eat up. But this stuff is all in its infancy. Be careful with your dough."

"Again, all types of companies will be enticed," Martin Dorsey said. "But you seem concerned about our ability to attract high tech. Well, don't be. Listen, son, they're here. There's a company, up off Route Twenty-eight along the Allegheny, that's already putting out all types of electronic equipment. Defibrillators, the electric paddles they use to whack a person after a heart attack? They're making experimental ones that are implanted into a patient's chest like a pacemaker. They can't fill the orders, there's that much demand."

"Sorry, Pop," Dorsey said. "I'm in no position to make an investment, if that's what this is about. Business is good but not that good."

"Carroll, I do wish you would stop looking at the world through a green beer bottle," Martin Dorsey said, shaking his head. "You think I started this speech with a near apology for our lives just to hit you up for a donation? You're right, you don't have what it takes for a deal like this. But I do. Not in money, in services; that's where my value is, and I stand to make a mint. I asked you here to let you know I intend to cut you in on my take. What you'll get is a fraction of a fraction, but it will pay the mortgage on your Polack town house and keep People's Natural Gas from removing you some winter from the preferred customers list."

"Save it," Dorsey said. "I'd just have to hire an accountant who would steal it in the end. Besides, why so generous in your old age?"

"Who's generous? What am I giving away?" Martin Dorsey asked. "I'm seventy-one years old, and money doesn't mean what it used to. I can get all I want just by reminding a few guys here and there about some old debt from years ago. It's the deals that matter, making things happen when maybe they're not supposed to. Convincing people to see things my way against what they think is their better judgment. Keeps me going like I was thirty again. But you, you're young and you're not ambitious by anyone's standard. You need money to get along. And this I can provide right now."

"Don't need it," Dorsey said. "Thanks, but I get along okay."

"Yes, you do need it; think it over. And don't thank me because thanks are not in order. I'm old and I want to feel good about myself. This will help to do it. Makes me feel that everything between us has turned out okay. It's my illusion, my present to myself."

"Don't need it," Dorsey repeated, shaking an empty can and thinking he had closed the discussion.

"Think about it," Martin Dorsey hissed, his eyes suddenly cold. The effect was not lost on Dorsey.

"I'll toss it around."

"Good," Martin Dorsey said. "Now get out. I'll give you a call."

Chapter 5

Although it might have its rivals, Dorsey was sure the emergency room at Mercy Hospital was the city's most hectic. Located in Uptown, the hospital sat in the middle of a crumbling neighborhood in which a number of federal renovation projects had fallen miserably short. Patients, mostly violent trauma victims, were abundant, and the most popular insurance was the Department of Public Welfare card. At times the emergency room resembled a battlefield aid station, echoing with the screams of the injured and filled with a rush of interns and residents in blood-smeared white smocks. And yet Dorsey knew Gretchen embraced it as the finest classroom she had ever entered.

In a misting rain Dorsey drove through the hospital's parking lot and saw Gretchen at the ER door, examining her reflection in the glass. She was dressed in her customary working clothes: the Reebok shoes that allowed her to stay on her feet for hours, corduroy slacks, button-down oxford shirt, and white smock with nameplate. Dorsey could see that a twenty-four-hour on-call shift had done little to disturb her professional appearance. Tall, just a fraction under six feet, with slim legs and hips and just a hint of breasts, she looked striking and dignified.

Dorsey pulled up and tooted the horn. A short black man in a security guard's uniform joined Gretchen at the door with an umbrella and led her out to the car, opening the passenger door.

"You late again," the security guard said. "You always late. Take care with this woman. She'll leave your ass behind."

"Thank you, Henry." Gretchen slipped into the car and brushed a drop of rainwater from her hair, which was short and tightly curled. "Let's hope he learns in time. Have a nice evening."

" 'Night, Dr. Keller." Henry returned to his station inside the ER door.

"Sorry, I really am." Dorsey put the car in drive and started back through the lot. "My father called and wanted to see me." From the car's tape deck, Sinatra sang "A New Kind of Love."

"And the Celtics and Atlanta went into overtime." Gretchen smiled and jabbed a finger in his shoulder. "The residents' lounge has cable TV. We do get an occasional break." She gave him another jab, then settled into her seat. "But you said your father called. That's something different."

"Well, actually he didn't call. Ironbox Boyle did the calling. She said that although he refuses to feed me he was willing and even interested in speaking with me."

"What was on his mind?" Gretchen looked off at the water as the car started across the Tenth Street bridge, heading for the flats of South Side.

"Says he wants to make me rich."

"That would be a decided improvement." Gretchen leaned her head against the window and closed her eyes. A grin worked its way across her face. "After he puts you in the chips, you can send a limo to pick me up twenty minutes late."

"The shift was a bad one, huh?" Dorsey asked. "You said so in your message."

"A madhouse," she said, letting the other matter drop. "Oh, the first six or seven hours were smooth enough. I even got a few hours' sleep in the lounge. But then things started downhill. About ten this morning we got an eight-year-old boy with a broken left arm. The fracture was about midshaft in the ulna, and it was a clean one. No shattering and no splintering. We didn't even bother with the orthopedic resident; I did the setting myself. Plastered myself, too. Well, halfway through the casting the cops come in with this guy for detox and he's in the absolute depths of the DTs. The whole deal, seeing snakes and slapping at the bugs he says are swarming on his pants. Next thing you know, and I'm not sure how it happened, he breaks loose from the cops—one of which was a female, you'll be pleased to hear."

"There's nothing wrong with female police officers." Dorsey turned onto Wharton Street. "It's just that most of them look more like female impersonators than female police officers."

"Thank you for your tolerance."

Dorsey pulled the Buick to the curb in front of his row house and Gretchen opened the passenger door and rushed up the front steps in the rain. Dorsey hurried behind her to unlock the door. Inside, she tossed her wet smock over the staircase handrail and continued down the hallway to the kitchen. Dorsey followed behind.

"So, the boozer breaks loose and he's a wild man, smacking the walls and stomping on snakes. And, of course, the only thing between him and my eight-year-old patient, who is frightened half to death, is me, having just sent the nurse to the phone to answer a page on my beeper."

"Things got a little rough, sounds like." Dorsey bent down to search for a frying pan in a cabinet below the sink. "Bet he took the first round, but you came back and cleaned his clock in the second."

"You can be sure neither of us went the distance," Gretchen said, seating herself at the kitchen's Formica-topped table. "I stood straight and tall, hid my trembling knees, squared my shoulders, and yelled for the guy to back off. He in reply smashes right into me. We both go down, and I slipped away and rolled into a ball. At that point the kid was on his own, I'm afraid, but the cops must have caught their breath. They took hold of the boozer and dragged him out."

Dorsey set down the frying pan. "You okay? Sure there's no damage?"

"Fine. Slight bruise on the right hip, but it's okay. The kid was a wreck, though. I gave some thought to slipping him a Valium, but the nurse came back and was able to calm him. She's got kids." Gretchen took a deep breath that came out as a long sigh, signaling that the story was over and the incident forgotten. "I'm hungry. What's to eat?"

"Bacon and eggs," Dorsey said, peering into the refrigerator. "You like the way I make them."

"Not always." Gretchen laughed. "But tonight they sound good. I'm going to grab a shower while you cook."

"Your robe's in the bedroom closet," Dorsey said. "Hey, before you go up, take a look at the medical in that file." Using the frying pan, Dorsey indicated the manila folder on the tabletop. "You take your shower, I'll never get you to do it. It'll take five minutes, no more."

Gretchen opened the file and studied the contents for a few silent moments. "Can't anybody in this part of the state drive without getting hit? It's all I ever see you handle, that and some really hokey comp cases. And something else: must everything I look at be from these cock-and-bull chiropractors? It's insulting, equating me with them."

"C'mon, I don't do that." Dorsey forked bacon into the pan. "Besides, there's some X rays and a CT scan report in there."

"And both of them say nothing." Gretchen closed the file and rose from the table. "No pathology; no disc problems, herniated or bulging. A whiplash case is what you have." Gretchen pushed the folder away. "Let the bacon fry crisp. I'm going to take a long shower and try to loosen my hip."

Dorsey lowered the flame under the bacon and went to the office for his tape player. When he returned he plugged it in above the kitchen counter and put in a cassette of Benny Goodman's 1938 Carnegie Hall concert.

He had first met Gretchen in the waiting room of a large law firm in the Oliver building. The firm did a lot of insurance defense work, and Dorsey was there to be deposed on a personal injury case. Gretchen had accompanied a fellow ER physician who was being questioned about a negligence suit filed against the hospital. Seated on the waiting room's brown herringbone sofa, Gretchen spoke first, curious as to what Dorsey was doing there. She had been in Pittsburgh for only two weeks, he gathered, was a little on the lonely side, and talked to anyone she rubbed up against. In doing so, she went on to explain that she had just finished her intern training at Hershey Medical Center near her native Lancaster.

Dorsey was irritated by her at first. The case he was to be deposed on had some serious holes in it, double- and triple-checking that should have been done but proved impossible. But Gretchen was a notch away from being soft-spoken and in an odd, endearing way could not be put off. When Dorsey explained his business she became intrigued, and as Dorsey was being called off to a corner office Gretchen asked if he would like to meet later for a drink. Yes, I would, Dorsey had answered.

Dorsey fell hard for her. She was young but not so terribly that he found himself explaining himself and his favorite TV shows from boyhood. She was strong and she was tranquil and, though they argued, her even manner usually won out. Everything I've never had, Dorsey would tell himself, everything I've never had. He knew the beer and jazz was a kick for her; beyond that he didn't know why she loved him in return. After six months she kept half her wardrobe at Wharton Street.

"Please turn that off—please?" Gretchen entered the kitchen, pulling tight her terry-cloth robe. Dorsey hit the stop button, and the tape fell silent. "Over the last twenty-four hours, with the exception of the basketball game from Atlanta, I've been cut off from the world. Let's catch the cable news."

At the end of the counter sat a portable TV with the cable lead running under the windowsill, courtesy of Al's electrical prowess. Dorsey flicked on the set, then went about dividing the food onto two plates before sitting down across from Gretchen. Gretchen chewed each forkful slowly and patiently watched the TV screen.

He wondered if the food was registering in her mouth and admired her powers of concentration.

"Hey." Gretchen indicated the TV with her fork. "Isn't that the priest you told me about?"

Dorsey twisted in his seat and watched as a short, slight priest, bald but with a full salt-and-pepper beard, was led away in handcuffs by sheriff's deputies. As the videotape played, a monotone commentator explained that Father Andrew Jancek and thirty members of Movement Together had been arrested when they attempted to block the main gate of a steel mill in McKeesport. The mill was scheduled for demolition, and Movement Together had vowed to impede the work. Following their arrest, the commentator went on, the priest and his followers had been released when bail had been posted by the organization's attorney, Jack Stockman.

"What is this shit?" Dorsey muttered. Not enough money coming in from the insurance companies, P.I.? Or is this just branching out, tired of kicking my sorry ass? New worlds to conquer, or just dabbling in labor? For money, of course.

"What did you say?"

"Nothing," Dorsey said. "Eat your eggs."

After making love, they rested in bed and Dorsey gave Gretchen a full report on the meeting with his father. "He says my little piece can grow into a big slice. I said no, he got persuasive, and I said I'd think about it. Which I will do. But for now, what do you think?"

"I'm not crazy about his motives, but money is nice to have around."

"I wholeheartedly agree about the money," Dorsey said. "But tell me what you really think."

Gretchen propped herself on one elbow, her nipple grazing the hair on Dorsey's chest. She smiled playfully. "What I think is this. It's a wonderful world we live in when a jerk like you can make a living like you do, have someone offer to make you rich, and, best of all, get laid by a classy broad like me."

CHAPTER 6

Hell's wrong with him?" Al Rosek stood behind his oak bar cleaning beer mugs and rinsing them in clear water. He wiped his hands on his stained white linen apron. "Somebody stick a little Iron City where his Rolling Rock oughta be?"

Al's Bar consisted of a long room with the countertop running along the right, beginning at the entrance from South Seventeenth Street. To the left were three Formica-topped tables, each with four chairs. At the far end was a step-down entrance into a large back room, which held a tiled one-time dance floor and a jukebox. Dorsey and Bernie stood at the center of the bar, a few steps from the beer taps.

"My friend must have your indulgence," Bernie said, filling his glass from a Michelob bottle, careful not to splash his newest dark suit. "Have you never before seen the pensive look of the gifted investigator? The man has a theory, a case. He is not merely sneaking pictures or conducting interviews—and, let's face it, only Johnny and Merv make the big dough holding interviews. But

Dorsey here finds a pattern is developing. Now he must unmask the conspirators!"

"Liked it better when you were taking pictures of people in bed," Al said, leaning across the bar on his elbows. "That way, you showed the films and we all shared in your triumphs."

"Up yours," Dorsey said through a mouthful of beer, twisting the green long-necked bottle, illustrating the technique Al was to use.

"Buddy, I'm sorry," Al said. "Ain't seen ya in a while, missed givin' you a hard time." He waddled to the end of the bar to fill a customer's glass.

"Must be very important, this case," Bernie said. "Up yours? Really, that's not up to standard. It's a disappointment to those of us who have come to rely on your wit for a reason to live." Bernie sipped his beer. "So, anyways, last week you were in Johnstown."

"Last week in Johnstown," Dorsey said, "was where it finally came up and bit me in the ass. Well, actually, it was *this* week, when I was in Greensburg and Somerset. Another one of Tang's patients—the girl in Somerset, I mean. And while I'm going over it there were some locals in Pitcairn and Homestead that need a closer look. If I can get Corso to let me retrace my steps, pay me for it, I could make something out of it. Maybe build your goddamned pattern for you."

Bernie tapped his empty bottle on the bar top, signaling for a refill. "This Radovic in Johnstown, I know a little about him. Our firm does the defense work for Fidelity Casualty, just locally. They send cases over, every now and then, for us to look at in the early stages, and me being the lowest man on the totem pole, they all come to me. Radovic was in the last batch. Conjecture is all you have. Maybe the Maynard girl tipped him to the layoff, maybe not. But there's still the medical from Dr. Tang. You may not like the guy, but you haven't come up with a way to get around his medical opinion, either."

"There's some fresh reports you haven't seen," Dorsey said. Al returned with two beers, collected money from Bernie's change pile, and leaned forward into the conversation. "The woman out in Somerset," Dorsey said, "the one who's Tang's patient; I filed my report on her. Anyway, she has a history of knee problems; some cartilage had to come out when she was a kid. She worked at this plant where they did specialty steel, and two weeks before the plant is to close she's in this fender-bender. Neither car has more than two hundred dollars' worth of damage, but she runs to Dr. Tang, and now she has lateral compartment syndrome. Can't get around and sure can't work. She gets a disability check from another carrier, but Fidelity Casualty is on the hook for the auto liability. Lost wages, present and future, services lost to her parents she lives with, maybe she'll claim loss of consortium with her boyfriend. Depending on their favorite position."

"Wait. Hold up." Bernie gestured with his right hand to silence Dorsey. "How much is fact and how much is dreamed up?"

"Next-door neighbor was pissed and had a lot to say about her." Dorsey sipped at his beer. "I knocked on his door and caught him on his way to the evening shift. The guy, he's laid off from the same plant and he's got a night gig at a gas station on U.S. Thirty, feeds the kids with it. Believe me, he's less than crazy about the young chick living next door with her retired parents getting eight hundred a month for shit. He told me the story was all over the shop, before the layoff, that she was going for disability. She bragged about it, said she had a friend who could show her the ropes. This friend supposedly told her it was now or never."

"Not so special," Bernie said. "There's been plenty of this before. A place is supposed to close down on Friday at five? Guess how many employees fall and hurt themselves at four-thirty. It's common, real, everyday stuff."

Dorsey followed Al's eyes as they drifted away from the conversation. Stepping out of the back room was a short squat man in his late fifties. Dressed in work pants and well-worn brown sweater, he wiped his bald pate and close-cropped side hair with a cloth handkerchief. His chest had the solid look that comes not with exercise but from a lifetime's hard labor.

"The cases stacked?" Al asked him as he stepped behind the bar and drew a glass of water.

"By the far wall, like you said." The short man drained the

water and drew another from the faucet. "Kegs, too. But they're right next to the tap hookup."

"How's it been, Russie?" Dorsey asked. "Haven't had much time to talk."

"Good, good," Russie said. "How 'bout you and your dad, Mr. Dorsey? He's still good, right? You see him much? Good fella, always a good fella."

"Just the other day, I was over his place." Dorsey's words sounded slow even to himself after Russie's rapid fire. "He's good, asks about you."

"Good fella, real good fella." Russie stepped back around the bar, making for the door. "You got any work for me, any of you guys, gimme a call here at the bar."

When Russie had gone, Bernie asked Dorsey why he gave the old bum the time of day. Dorsey told him it was none of his fucking business.

"Anyway," Dorsey said, "getting back to what we were saying, the plant closing was a complete surprise. The guy I talked to, he had sixteen years in, two terms as shop steward. He had no idea of what was coming. But he says he thinks maybe the girl did."

"Good," Bernie said, shaking his head. "So now you have two."

"There's more," Dorsey told him. "I've had a lot of work these last couple of months, you guys both know that. Mostly from Corso. A lot of it is work comp and auto. Now the majority—not all of them, but a majority—are these blue-collar singles. Some old and some young, but all are on some type of disability and negotiating on the auto settlement. And from what I pick up, they all were a nut hair from being laid off. There's an epidemic of chintzy bullshit going on."

"Bernie's right," Al said, back in the conversation, ignoring a customer at the bar's far end. "Guys have been doin' that since I was a pup. Seen it myself down the street at J and L before I got this place. Young single guys like you said, they love that shit. They get plenty on disability, more than enough, and they take their time gettin' better. Layoff time comes and the older guys with responsibilities, they get in on the act too."

"Maybe so." Dorsey drank beer directly from the bottle, shunning the glass Al had set before him. "Seems funny to me, that's all I'm saying. All these people were the same: radical types. Acted like I carried a disease and tossed me out of the house like I was the cat who pissed on the living room carpet. Everyone the same."

"Anything else?" Bernie asked. "Besides Radovic and the girl. Anybody else treating with Tang?"

"One more with Tang," Dorsey said. "Another knee case. The rest are back problems treating with a group of chiropractors in Latrobe. Those bastards will say anything."

"Bad times," Al said, shaking his head sorrowfully. "Chalk it up to bad times. Guys, they go nuts. Way of life is changin' and nobody knows how to change with it. Things used to be: a steady check from the mill, now and again a short stay on unemployment, then back to the mill. Guys were content. Most have never seen anythin' like what we have now. All they want is somethin' steady comin' in. Reliable. Drives 'em crazy."

"Ain't blaming anyone, Al," Dorsey said. "Just trying to be a success in my chosen profession."

CHAPTER 7

The town of Washington was too short a drive, twenty-six miles, for an overnight stay, so Dorsey was forced to commute along Interstate 79 for the two-day job on Kenny Borek. He spent the first day on an uneventful surveillance of Borek, who left his apartment only once, for an afternoon newspaper. Although Borek's Beau Street neighborhood was busy with shoppers and other pedestrians, forcing Dorsey to reposition himself several times, he was sure enough of Borek's movements to file his first day's report.

The morning of the second day was equally dull, so much so that Dorsey intended to knock off at noon and move on to the next job. With most of his concentration split between his father's offer of riches and daydreams of Gretchen, he interviewed a half dozen of Borek's neighbors and decided the man qualified as a hermit. Most of them didn't recognize Borek's name, and only one elderly woman was willing to venture a guess that he might be the young man who rented the second floor of the house next door. To wrap up the assignment, Dorsey spoke to the owner of the corner grocery, where Borek had purchased his newspaper the day before.

"Young guy, rents Ethel Stimic's upstairs." The owner, a small elderly man, stood behind a low counter loaded with bread. Wearing a cardigan sweater over a checked flannel shirt, he stuffed newspapers with advertising supplements as he spoke. "Comes in for cigarettes and the paper, smokes Winstons. Heard he was in a crack-up."

"He's the one." Dorsey watched a sly grin work its way over the shopkeeper's face. "He's off work because of it. You don't see him much, huh?"

"Cigarettes and the paper, that's all he comes in for." The old man held on to his smile, annoying Dorsey. What a lunatic, Dorsey thought.

"Haven't heard about him working anywhere, have you?" Dorsey asked. "Something under the table, bring in a little extra dough?"

"All I know is he smokes. And if he can't read, he's wasting a quarter every afternoon."

The old man's grinning got the best of Dorsey, and he decided to close out the conversation and head for Midland, the site of the next job. He gave the shopkeeper a business card and asked him to call if anything occurred to him about Borek.

"Some kinda detective, huh?" The old man settled onto a stool behind the counter. "Supposed to be interesting work. You look bored, like I'm keepin' you from something."

"We get our slow days too." Dorsey turned for the door.

"Maybe I can pick this one up for you." The old man pulled the sweater closer to his chest.

"What have you got?"

"You sure can't be their ace, I can tell," the old man said. "Why waste your time going door-to-door? This Borek got hurt in a bad car crack-up, hurt so bad he can't work. Tell ya something. I've been on this corner for thirty-seven years. Know 'em all, every house, every car and its parking spot. And none are missing. Borek, he got hurt driving a car, but he sure don't own one."

In the front seat of the Buick, Dorsey reviewed portions of Borek's claim file, spreading the statements and forms across the unholstery. On the day of his accident, Kenneth Edward Borek, age thirty-one, was operating a 1972 Electra, license plate 618-KE3. There was no indication that a full check on the ownership had been run.

Dorsey drove to the Washington barracks of the state police, where for twenty minutes he sat in a chair of plastic-covered cushions waiting for Corporal Dennison. During that time Dorsey again decided to refuse his father's offer. And then again the thought of being able to keep up with Gretchen financially, as the years went by, crept into his head. Money's the biggest problem you two could have, Dorsey told himself. She'll be making plenty and you'll bring in shit by comparison. Lots of tension from that. It could be avoided.

"This is what you do for a living?" Corporal Calvin Dennison watched the lines of information forming on the CRT at his desk. Tall and black, with short-cropped trooper's hair, he laughed and gave Dorsey a playful slap on the shoulder. "Figured you for sheriff by now. You were hot shit, DA office detective. Good to see you got humble, good for the soul."

"You've done pretty well yourself." Dorsey sat in a chair opposite the CRT. "Let's see, you were a rookie at the Monroeville barracks eight or nine years ago. And now, after eight or nine years, you make corporal. That's one hell of a leap."

"It's the skin." Dennison slipped a palm across his ebony chin. "Upper echelon still got it in for us. Figure if we're too slow to go on the take with the rest, we just don't have the stuff for the job. Me, I have every intention of taking a payoff and breaking the color line. Not for myself, you understand. I'll be acting as a pioneer, in the service of my brethren."

"What about the car?" Dorsey asked.

"Not really supposed to do this," Dennison said, craning his neck around the CRT to smile at Dorsey. "But you were a fellow soldier in the war against crime."

"Some people might figure me for a deserter."

"An amnesty is granted," Dennison said. "Ford did it for the pussies who ducked out to Canada; I can exercise my official powers as well." Dennison looked closer at the CRT. "Okay, here it comes. Electra, same plate. Registered to Carmen's Rentals, Main Street in Brownsville. Hate the place."

"Carmen? Why do you hate his place?"

"It's Brownsville I hate, not Carmen." Dennison cut the power to the CRT. "Nasty place, cramped little hole near the river. Carmen, he rents old secondhand bombs for cheap."

Back in his car, Dorsey concluded that Dennison could be right; Brownsville might be hell, but the road to hell was paved in rose petals. U.S. 40, the National Road, was the route to Brownsville through wooded countryside and farmland at the roadside. Touching on little hamlets named Scenery Hill and Richeyville, it was Dorsey's favorite stretch of road, especially when autumn turned the woodlands into smears of reds and browns and yellows intermixed. For twenty miles or so, U.S. 40 could pull him away from depositions and court appearances and remembering to give the subject of his surveillance a block-and-a-half lead. And as he pulled into Brownsville, crossing the bridge and turning left at the Russian Orthodox Church to get to the business district, the beauty of the countryside held on to Dorsey long enough for him to conclude that factory towns were aberrations. Just sooty pockets of life dropped into valleys that were green in summer and surrounded by even greener hills.

The show lot at Carmen's Rentals, dominated at the center by an office trailer, was located near Water Street and was clogged with junkers. Dorsey figured them to be second- and third-hand models picked up cheap at the wholesale auction near Harrisburg. When he pulled into the lot and stepped away from the Buick, he found a comical pride in having the best-looking machine in sight. Once inside the office he identified himself to a receptionist and asked to see the owner. Leaving her desk and opening an inner door, she told an unseen someone that the guy from the insurance company was here.

"How's that, insurance company?" a voice from the office said. "Here about the accidents?"

Dorsey shouted past the receptionist that he had come to

discuss several of them. The receptionist quickly ushered him in and closed the door as she left.

A fat young man dressed in jeans and a terry-cloth sportshirt rose from his seat and offered his hand across a metal desk, the kind Dorsey remembered from community recreation centers. He introduced himself as Carmen Avolio and poured them each a cup of coffee from the Mr. Coffee sitting on a corner filing cabinet. Dorsey took the plastic cup in his fingertips to save his palms from burning.

"So, what's it gonna be?" Avolio strained his recliner chair to its limit. "How much higher can my rates go?"

"The accidents." Dorsey hoped to string Avolio along. "Face it, there's been more than one."

"Too many in too short a time," Avolio said. "The guy on the phone, the agent, that's what he said. Still, look what's on the lot. Crap on wheels. Shit, I get another rate hike, they should just come and shut me down."

"It's the medical." Dorsey sipped carefully at the coffee. "Crap, sure, but they've got people inside them when they get smacked. Borek, for instance."

"Fuckin' shit, man." Avolio pulled his weight forward and rested his elbows on the desktop. "Listen, I rent cars, fuckin' cars. Fast and cheap. A guy comes here because he can't come up with the daily rate at Hertz or Avis. Only way this place stays open. I start demanding customers take a defensive driving course, I better turn the place into a Seven-Eleven."

"Business is good? High volume?"

"Real good," Avolio said. "Rural place like this, where people are hard pressed for enough cash for even a used car? Sure, business is good. Young kids, they like to have a car for the weekend even if it's only a rental. I have 'em coming from all over, hitchhiking to get here. And that's where these accident-prone assholes come from. From all over."

"All over where?" Dorsey asked. The fat man began counting on his fingers.

"There was Borek from Washington, then a guy from

Greensburg, another from Homestead, and a guy from Union-town. Last was the little blond chick from Somerset, fucked up her knee in a crash on One-nineteen."

"Karen Stroesser?" Dorsey asked. Stroesser was Dr. Tang's lateral compartment patient.

"She's the one," Avolio said. "Couldn't make up her mind which car she wanted. She'd look at one, then ask how heavy it was, kept banging her foot on the bumpers, testing them. Finally she takes out this Chrysler, one of the big ones. And one of the best cars on the lot. Had hopes of having it around for a while. It'll be okay, the dents and all are pounded out, but people get leery when a car's been in an accident. They think the frame's bent no matter what you tell 'em."

Dorsey asked for copies of the rental agreements and four out of five names were familiar: Borek and Stroesser, Klazak from Homestead, and Stark from Greensburg. Only the Uniontown man was a stranger. All four had been the subjects of investigations done for Fidelity Casualty. Before leaving the office, Dorsey placed a call to Ray Corso. Carmen collected two dollars for the copies and three for the toll call.

Dorsey gave Corso a quick rundown on what he had found, hoping his voice conveyed what he thought was the gravity of the situation, an organized rip-off. He also suggested that they meet as soon as possible to map out a strategy.

"It's certainly something to think about." Corso sounded preoccupied. "Write up the report and enclose the rental agree-ments. When they get here I'll have the legal people look it all over. Then maybe we'll get together and review a few things."

"Ray, please listen." Dorsey was fighting Corso's famed iner-tia. "Four, maybe five guys, here alone are putting shit over on you. All have lost wages to figure in on a final liability settlement. We have to talk."

"Send in the report," Corso said, ending the conversation.

Dorsey knew Corso's history and knew he was a jumper. Claims work is filled with nomads moving from company to com-pany, and Ray Corso was a true bedouin. One step ahead of the ax, Corso moved to another job, pushing a hoax as a successful claims manager, just as his former employer learned to appreciate the magnitude of his shortsighted laziness. The Inert One. Dorsey thought the nickname was well earned. Slow-boat, pipe-smoking asshole was another.

Next day, enjoying the scenery and a tape of Count Basie backing up Sinatra, Dorsey headed for Beaver County and Midland. As he drove, he ran through the pertinent facts of his next case. Edward Damjani, twenty-six years of age, resided in Midland. Employed by Kensington Steel as a crane man, he was receiving $335 per week in workers' compensation benefits. Diagnosed as suffering a low back strain, he treated primarily with a chiropractor and occasionally with a local orthopedic who was known to Dorsey as a claims whore. The medical reports showed Damjani to be a big man, six feet seven inches and 240 pounds. As Dorsey pondered the last of these facts, Basie and Sinatra closed out, the tape ended, and the radio came on.

"Friends in Jesus, this is Father Andrew Jancek. The past few years have seen disastrous changes in our lives, the types of changes that serve to illustrate how tenuous are our security and faith in our fellowman. Institutions on which we have learned to rely, institutions to which we gave our labor and loyalty, have purposely betrayed our faith in them. Our labor's fruit has been stripped from us and used to enrich others, who now turn their backs to us.

"To the workers of this area, a job is more than a weekly paycheck. The work we do shapes our lives: how we deal with others, how we raise our families, how we practice our faith and pass on our values. The theft of our jobs is truly the theft of our souls. Please join my friends and me in our efforts to recover our jobs and our dignity. Any contribution, large or small, in time or money, will aid in our crusade to halt the plans of our so-called industrial leaders to desert the working person. Thank you."

An announcer provided an address for contributions, which was followed by a weather update. "Christ," Dorsey said, "the guy does radio spots too." Makes sense, he thought, more sense than those late-night TV spots.

Crossing the Ohio River at Shippingport, under the shadows of the nuclear plant's twin cooling towers, Dorsey recalled that Midland was laid out like most river-valley mill towns. Kensington Steel occupied all the riverfront within the city limits, conveniently situated to receive bargeloads of coal and to expel refuse into the already murky water. Next, on the valley flats, were a few streets of small row houses followed by a main street dominated by merchants. From there the land went quickly upward, terraced with the homes of the sons of immigrants and those of displaced cotton sharecroppers. Wooden frame or brick, these homes appeared to have fingernails dug into the hillside, bracing for the next violent storm, natural or economic.

Ohio Street ran up the hillside, Damjani's home sat one and a half blocks up from the valley floor, one of several soot-stained brick houses lining the left sidewalk. Dorsey drove past Damjani's, made a wide U-turn at the next intersection, and slid the Buick to a stop at the curb across the street. His plans to conduct a series of neighborhood interviews changed immediately when he saw what must have been Ed Damjani walk down the steps of number 211's front stoop.

Goddamn, Dorsey thought, this has to be the biggest mill hand on record. He had expected a large man, but one who was running to sloppy fat at the waist. Damjani's figure ran like a V from shoulder to hips, and the rolled sleeves of his flannel shirt strained at the seams. With surprising vigor for an injured man, he strode down the street, away from Dorsey. Hoping to pass himself off as a shopkeeper, Dorsey stripped off his tie and sport coat, allowed Damjani a one-and-a-half block lead, and began his surveillance.

Lagging behind, Dorsey watched Damjani turn right onto Merchant Street, Midland's business district. When he followed around the corner and Damjani was nowhere to be seen, Dorsey felt a hard chill. A confrontation like the one with Radovic is sure to go bad for you, he told himself. This guy won't have to call for help; he could kick the shit out of a Toyota all by himself, take on two at a time. Dorsey sighed with relief when Damjani stepped out from a drugstore, opening a tin of Skoal and shoving a plug deep into his mouth. After sucking at it to his satisfaction, he moved down Merchant Street at a double-time step. A man with an appointment to keep, Dorsey thought.

The sidewalks of Merchant Street grew more crowded as they moved along, mostly men of Damjani's age, all dressed like him and moving in the same direction. Also in the crowd, Dorsey spotted a sprinkling of older men, mill pensioners, wearing fedoras and navy or black windbreakers. A block farther, police cruisers could be seen, along with a station wagon bearing the logo of a Pittsburgh television station. In the denser crowd and with better camouflage, Dorsey closed in on Damjani, twice brushing against his arm as they passed bars, coffee shops, and hardware stores.

When they came to the hall of the steelworkers' local, Dorsey realized that Damjani had reached his destination. The crowd came to a halt on the sidewalk before the hall, and a ring of police and sheriff's deputies barred the entrance, allowing people to go in slowly in single file. Dorsey watched as Damjani waved to another young man standing inside the police cordon. The man returned the wave and had a word with one of the deputies, pointing at Damjani. The deputy stood aside, and Damjani moved quickly ahead of the rest and was inside the union hall as the deputy retook his position.

Whatever it is, Dorsey thought, it's big and this guy looks to be part of it. He dipped a shoulder and began to glide and angle through the crowd, jockeying for a position in the entry line. Twice he was rebuffed but then found a soft spot in the line and slipped by some retirees. He took a few hard looks and curses but found himself moving single file through the police cordon and into the union hall.

Staying in step, Dorsey walked through a thin lobby and into a long, low-ceilinged auditorium filled with rows of wooden chairs. Ushers, dressed in work clothes and looking like union brothers, moved the line along toward the front of the auditorium, where a low stage rose. Standing along the side walls were camera crews from local TV stations in Pittsburgh and Wheeling, each with a reporter giving his appearance one last check before the film rolled. Dorsey was directed to a chair in the eighth row, between a frail-looking young man in his twenties and one of the blue-jacketed retirees, two chairs away from the center aisle. As he sat, he spotted Damjani with several men at the front left corner of the auditorium near a flight of portable steps leading to the stage. There was a thin blond woman with the group. Damjani gave her a thumbs-up gesture.

"Hey, you." The retiree was addressing Dorsey. "You from Midland? You look new."

"From up river," Dorsey said. "On the other side near Wireton."

"This is gonna be worth the trip for ya." The retiree gestured his head toward the stage. "You'll see. I went up the Mon Valley for the last one. These guys helped save my pension, is what they did. Some of my medical coverage too."

"Figured it was time for me to see this myself," Dorsey said.

"Won't be disappointed." The retiree turned his attention to the stage.

The stage was furnished with a lectern and six folding chairs fanning out on either side. Still with his friends, Damjani glanced at his watch and turned to check the progress being made in seating the audience. Dorsey watched him consult his watch again and signal several men in the back of the room, who closed the auditorium doors. Next, Damjani led his group onto the stage to their assigned seats, the chair closest to the lectern on the left remaining open, apparently for himself. Satisfied with the arrangements, Damjani strode to the lectern and tapped the microphone twice with his finger.

"Workin', right?" His words reverberated throughout the hall. A TV camera crew did a lighting check, and Damjani momentarily shaded his eyes. "Good, real good. Wanna thank everyone for comin' today." Damjani grinned. "But, what the hell, you sure ain't missin' a day of work for this. Anybody here still on a payroll?"

The audience reacted in outbursts and angry calls. The retiree next to Dorsey and the young man on his right shouted and raised their fists. Damjani threw up his fist too and paraded from one end of the stage to the other. They'd kill me, Dorsey thought, a line of cold sweat inching down his spine; if they knew, I'd be dead. Cold meat floating downstream in the Ohio on its way to Cincinnati.

Better show that Wireton is with them all the way. Dorsey stood, whistling and clapping. TV crews and radio reporters held microphones over the heads of the seated, gathering background.

"We're here to show the man we're behind him," Damjani shouted through the mike. "To show him Midland is behind him one hundred percent. And to show them bastard sumbitches we ain't buyin' their bullshit! Kensington Steel never lost a dime in this town. Made money on us is what they did. Now they're pullin' out. No way!" The crowd went into a frenzy, and Damjani waved his arms for several minutes before he was able to be heard. "I'm takin' up too much time. The man says it a lot better than I ever could; he says it so everybody knows, so everybody sees it like it really is. You know who I mean. Father Andrew Jancek!"

The cheering was deafening as a thin man in a clerical collar walked to the lectern from offstage left. He stroked his gray and white beard, took silver wire-rimmed glasses from his breast pocket, and waited for the crowd to shout itself out.

CHAPTER 8

Why the cheering? I don't understand." Father Jancek addressed his remarks to a spot in the air a few feet above the heads of the audience. His question hushed the crowd. "Cheering takes place when something is accomplished, when a long-sought-after goal is attained. Cheering is for the state finals, the World Series. What have we attained, what have we accomplished?

"It's true, I suppose, that some of you now have more peace of mind"—Father Jancek's soft tones flowed like intimate whispers through the room's sound system—"now that your pensions will continue and your health benefits are secure. But that's just for pensioners, retirees. Please, don't get me wrong; what we have done is important, and retirees deserve their pensions. But the day when we can sit down and pat ourselves on the back will be a long time in coming. Meanwhile, save the cheering for the basketball team. We still have a lot of work to do."

Father Jancek cleared his throat and briefly scanned the notes he had placed on the lectern.

"It is our understanding, and this is from our committee members, that the final layoffs at Kensington Steel are scheduled for late December, possibly the twenty-first, just in time for Christmas. On that day, we expect all of you to be at the front gates at the end of the daylight shift, the last shift ever at Kensington. We'll form up on either side of the gate, right and left, with former Kensington employees in the front ranks. We'll be there to shake each man's hand on his last day and to invite them to join our crusade."

The audience responded in applause and wild cheering. The twelve people seated on stage signaled for quiet.

"The final demolition of the plant," Father Jancek said, once order was restored, "will be postponed by winter weather, at least until April. But remember, demolition is the reason for the closing in December. The board of Kensington Steel has voted to close in December in order to give you a winter of personal struggle to forget the plant. So, in spring, demolition can go unobstructed. Remember this: that steel plant is the tax base for this community: taxes that pay for police, road maintenance, the water treatment plant, and the school system. The plant closure will hurt us, hurt us badly. But with the plant standing we have the means to recover. It can reopen. But if we allow that plant to be dismantled, we will be lost. There will be no Midland and no way to rebuild it.

"We have no intention of allowing this to happen." Father Jancek's voice had gained strength and its timbre hardened. "We must do whatever is necessary. In McKeesport we failed. And our failure was because of our delusion that we were dealing with reasonable men, men with sensitivity. Well, we were not.

"In McKeesport we used symbolism. We gave the authorities no resistance. When we were removed and arrested, we went peacefully. Well, no more; now we fight. Come April, that plant must remain standing. At any cost, it must remain standing!

"With whatever means possible." Father Jancek's voice transcended another octave, and Dorsey felt the power behind it. He's pulling in his fish, Dorsey thought. The speech begins with his giving them plenty of line. And then he does what he's doing now, takes up the slack, prepares for the big finish when he lands them in the boat. He must've studied the old man's technique.

"If it means forming a picket line, we'll form one. If it means putting the bulldozers and wrecking balls out of commission, we'll do it. And if it comes down to hand-to-hand struggle, we'll fight to the last man. We'll stand against the police and state troopers, we'll stand against the national guard. Because at the end of April, that plant will be standing. And it will be standing at the end of May. And at the end of June, at the end of July, at the end of August. And when we're done, when the fight is over and the buildings and the smokestacks and the furnaces are still on their feet, *then* you can cheer!"

Dorsey felt the electric charge coursing through the auditorium, taking in the full effect of the priest's magic. The crowd was euphoric, as if the calendar read next August and the battle had already been won. Dorsey was on his feet with the others, careful to remind himself that his actions were supposed to be a cover. With his wits collected, he focused on Damjani and was shaken by the realization that the blonde standing next to Damjani, shaking Father Jancek's hand, was Karen Stroesser—the bad knee from Somerset, Dr. Tang's patient. And behind her was Mel Stark, back problem from Greensburg. Seated farthest from the right, Dorsey recognized Carl Radovic. Even more ominous was Dorsey's realization that Radovic was returning his stare, the muscles of his fat face twitching.

"Oh, shit," Dorsey muttered. "Looks like I'm that Toyota you mentioned."

Dorsey watched as Radovic shuffled across the stage and took Damjani's arm, pointing out Dorsey. The two of them started forward. Dorsey moved into the center aisle and made for the door.

It was tough going. Dorsey had to work his way through huddles of men throwing their fists in the air. Watching the empty side aisles as he angled his way along, Dorsey saw Radovic moving quickly along the right wall while Stark hustled along the left. He saw them alert their union brothers at the doors and then looked backward to find Damjani shoving his way toward him. Dorsey's stomach began to churn as it went acidic and sweat soaked his collar, flowing along his spine. His heart skipped a beat and then another. Dorsey knew he had never been so alone. Deep shit, he thought; the bad guys are after you and the locals aren't friendly. An ass-beating could be this show's second act. Maybe the priest will like the idea and ask you back to warm up the crowd at the next rally.

Damjani closed in from behind, shoving away heavy-chested men who didn't argue, and reached across several others to paw at Dorsey's shoulder, inches away from taking a firm grasp. Dorsey shrugged him off and pushed forward, watching as Radovic closed in from the right while Stark and two others neared the back of the auditorium from the left. The center doors were manned by two union men. Radovic shouted to them and pointed to Dorsey. The guards stood taller and squared their shoulders. Dorsey shook and tasted bile rising from his stomach.

Over the shoulder of one of the guards, through the small pane of glass in the door's center, Dorsey saw the head of a man wearing the visor cap of a sheriff's deputy. Hoping this was not the same deputy who had allowed Damjani through the police cordon, Dorsey prayed that help was only a plywood door away. He grabbed one of the folding chairs, having a tough time holding on to it with his sweat-slippery hands. But once his grip was true, Dorsey swung the chair high and wide at the two men at the center doors who instinctively, but only momentarily, dropped back. Dorsey released the chair at the end of its arc and dove forward, head first, slipping along the polished tile floor into the doors. One door cracked open and Dorsey wiggled through on all fours and found himself in the lobby at the feet of several deputies and borough policemen.

"The hell is this?" one asked.

"A guy is chasing me," Dorsey said, scrambling to his feet, "big crazy guy. He's nuts."

Dorsey turned his left shoulder to indicate the center doors and caught Damjani's left forearm flush on the cheek. He fell against a policeman, who let him slip to the floor.

CHAPTER 9

The glass window of the holding tank, smudged with finger and palm prints, was three feet by four feet. Through it, Dorsey watched Antonio Ruggerio wrap several ice cubes in a washcloth. Ruggerio was a squarely built but very overweight man dressed in a white shirt and black slacks. He weighed the cubes in his hand and, content with their arrangement, walked around a gray steel desk, fished a set of heavy keys from his pocket, and worked the holding tank lock. He laughed as he entered.

"Sorry to see this, my friend. You've come down in the world." Ruggerio handed the wrapped ice to Dorsey, who sat on the corner joint of a benching that went three-quarters of the way around the metal room. Ruggerio sat at the far wall. "Used to be you'd come in here wearin' a suit, big shot from the city. Used to be you were askin' the questions in the tank. Now you just sit. But don't worry, you're gettin' sprung."

"No bullshit, okay, Antonio?" Dorsey concentrated on where to apply the ice first. His jaw no longer ached despite the swelling, but the knot on his head where he had made contact with the union hall's tile floor throbbed.

"The cheek, it don't look so bad," Ruggerio said. "Some swellin', but it's okay. Bump on your head needs work, though."

Watching Dorsey apply the ice to a spot above his left ear, Ruggerio spread his legs to evenly distribute his immense weight. Again he smiled and shook his head, then spit at the floor between his legs. "Goddamn, Dorsey, how ya been?"

"Good. At least I was till that big ox flattened me," Dorsey said. "Seriously, Antonio, no bullshit. They cutting me loose?"

"Hell, yeah," Antonio said. "Ain't got shit on ya, fella. There's nothing to have on ya; all you did was get hit and fall down, way I heard it. It's the deputies, they're a little pissed. Sheriff is pissed at you for not checking in with him before you started workin' in the county. So when he's pissed, his people are pissed."

"Last-minute decision to come here today," Dorsey said. He felt cold rivulets run down his wrist as the ice melted. "Didn't expect to get around to this job for another week."

"And you weren't gonna check in then, either."

"You know how it works," Dorsey said. "I check in with the sheriff, and one of his men passes it to a courthouse worker who's related to the guy I'm looking at. That takes twenty minutes on the outside. And I'm screwed."

"Whatever." Ruggerio returned Dorsey's smile. "Figure on another twenty minutes or so in here. That's the shift change for the deputies. For the guards, too. I arranged for one of them to take you back to Midland. That's where your car is, right?"

"Thanks, Antonio, thanks a lot. I owe you."

"Don't finish thanking me yet. And don't tally up your debts yet, either." A uniformed jail guard rapped a knuckle at the window and held up a thick file folder. Antonio went to the door and took the file, examining it. "Yeah, this is the one. Thanks." He sat himself down with his weight resting on his left hip and leafed further through the file.

"How much you know about Eddie Damjani?"

"Worked at Kensington Steel, maybe he hurt his back," Dorsey said. "He also has one hell of a backhand."

"Then you don't know shit." Antonio passed Dorsey three sheets from the file folder. "Got it off the NCIC last time Eddie was in our hotel here. We don't get him much anymore, just when he falls behind on his fines and violates his parole." Antonio gestured to the papers he had passed to Dorsey. "Take a look for yourself. Lotsa stuff on the list."

Dorsey read through the teletype lists of eleven separate arrests, three in California. All reflected violence: discharge of a firearm within town limits, four assaults with intent, destruction of private property (shooting out the windows of a mobile home), and various aggravated assaults. No big-time criminal, Dorsey thought, but nobody to mess with, either.

"Local hard-ass." Dorsey looked up from the pages.

"Worse than that," Antonio said. "Tip of the iceberg. You put in enough time as a detective to know that. This is only the shit he got *caught* doin'. Other crazy shit, he doesn't get caught. Or maybe people are just scared shitless and won't file a complaint. Looney bastard is what this guy is."

"You're sure?" Dorsey set aside the reports, strained out the cloth that held the ice, and again applied it to his head.

"Don't get the picture, do ya?" Antonio leaned forward and his voice fell to a whisper. "Listen, the spades back in the cell blocks, and there's a lot of them back there, *they* don't fuck with the guy. You should find out about a guy before you start a tail."

"How am I supposed to do that?" Dorsey asked. "I can't get NCIC reports like you, and Insanity Anonymous has a confidential member list."

Antonio shoved himself from the bench and made for the door. "Still, for my sake, watch your ass with this one. He's a sick guy."

"For your sake," Dorsey said.

"If only that." Antonio unlocked the door. "One more thing. Your little escapade made the radio news, and I hear the six o'clock TV version has film. I'll get your ride in a little bit."

The trip back to the Buick was made in silence. The driver was a young black man who was probably pissed off at carting him around. It's the kid's first real job, Dorsey decided. And he's a union man; isn't a jail guard in the country who hasn't been unionized. And the family's poor. Antonio rules with an iron fist.

"You a detective?" The guard didn't take his eyes from the road. "Antonio said you was."

"Used to be," Dorsey said. "DA's office."

"You fuck up?"

"Yeah," Dorsey said. "Then and now."

At Ohio Street, Dorsey mumbled a brief thanks and quickly transferred to the Buick. He kept his head low until well out of town, carefully observing the speed limit, fearing a police roust. During the drive home he played at the car radio, searching for newscasts. Two stations labeled it a riot incited by a management agitator, another called it a spontaneous explosion of violence. Dorsey was relieved that none mentioned his name.

In the Wharton Street row house, Dorsey found Gretchen studying at the office desk. Wearing horn-rimmed glasses and taking notes from *Harrison's Principles of Internal Medicine,* she silently watched Dorsey enter the room and drop into the chaise.

"Carroll, you all right?"

"No."

Dorsey turned to face the windows and Gretchen went to the chaise, sitting at its foot. She stroked and patted his hip, coaxing him onto his back. "Tell me," she said.

Dorsey gave her the details of his afternoon. "This is a bad one. My work is supposed to be done discreetly, that's the value of it, part of the value, anyway."

Gretchen kissed his cheek and gave his hand a light squeeze. "Try to relax. Close your eyes for a minute or so. Maybe take a few deep breaths."

She went to the kitchen and returned with a damp cloth, which she placed over Dorsey's eyes.

"What happened to you today," she said softly, "explains why the phone has been ringing off the hook. I was doing some research for a case staffing so I let the answering machine pick up. About twenty minutes ago I took a break and listened to the tape. Let me get the list."

She took a written list from the desk and returned to the chaise.

"First call was from Jack Stockman. He's the lawyer, the one they mentioned on TV?"

Dorsey took the compress from his eyes and rose on one elbow, wishing that P.I. Stockman would stay out of his life. "Guess he got a call from Father Jancek and wants to threaten a lawsuit of some sort. Nothing but bullshit. Forget him."

"You won't even return the call?"

"For what?" Dorsey asked. "There's been no laws broken and no damages caused. When he doesn't hear from me he'll write a nasty letter, and I'll have the pleasure of crumpling it into a ball and shooting it at the wastepaper basket."

"And miss and leave it cluttering the floor?" Gretchen grinned and pointed at the far corner.

"That too." Dorsey returned her smile.

"Next to call was another attorney." Gretchen stroked the list with her pencil. "Louis Preach. Sounded like a black man on the tape."

"That's an unfamiliar name."

"Well, he seems to have heard of you. He said the two of you need to get together very soon and it would be of mutual benefit."

Dorsey closed his eyes momentarily and shook his head. "I can't see Damjani with a black lawyer. The guy could be a token in Stockman's office."

Lifting himself by the heel of his hand, Dorsey came to a sitting position alongside Gretchen and kissed her cheek. "Thanks. For the comfort and the update."

"I'm far from done," Gretchen said, snickering. "Now, with your return to the land of the living, let's continue. Bernie is on the list, so maybe, just maybe, it isn't all bad. His message was that he had some big news for you and you better call him ASAP. Then, two seconds after that call, Ray Corso was on the line saying you needed to get your paperwork together and get to his office ASAP."

"Better talk to Bernie first." Dorsey stood and shrugged the tension from his shoulders. "Most likely, Corso knows what happened, got it on the radio or something, and is hitting the panic button, which is a lot of physical exertion for him. So, being frightened to death, he calls the company's local counsel, which is Bernie's firm. And Bernie calls me. Who's next?"

"Your father called."

Dorsey stopped cold. "You mean Ironbox called to give me an appointment?"

"No." Gretchen solemnly lowered her voice. "It was the great man himself."

"Really? No shit?"

"Not even the slightest shit."

Dorsey shook his head. "I wonder if he's calling to rub in the embarrassment or to congratulate me on my daring escapade."

"Sounded concerned." Gretchen turned to the window and watched a red and white van pull to the curb. "Oh, boy. Seems the last guy on the list couldn't wait for a call-back."

Dorsey went to the window and peeked through the side curtains. The van parked outside, in red lettering, carried the logo of local TV Channel Three. "Now what?"

"Sam Hickcock, the news guy?" Gretchen was apologetic. "His was the last call. I thought I'd be cute and leave the worst for last."

Through the window, Dorsey watched a cameraman and a sound technician haul their equipment from the rear of the van. Hickcock, a thin man dressed in brown tweed and busily combing out a perfectly barbered mustache, urged them on, warning them that the tape had to be ready for the six o'clock lead-in.

"TV supposedly makes a person look heavier," Gretchen said, pointing to Hickcock through the glass. "You'd have to be bulimic to look like that. Just think, Carroll, all that money but you'd still have to puke after every meal."

With the camera set and the lighting perfectly calibrated, Hickcock assumed an air of grave resolve and strode up the front stoop of the row house. He pressed the doorbell twice.

"Care to make your television debut?" Dorsey moved back from the window. "Chance to be discovered."

"It's not me he's here for," Gretchen said, following Dorsey to the center of the office. "Father Jancek makes the national news every night at seven. You'd know that if you watched. Brokaw and Rather make heroes of these people. You answer the door."

"No way." Dorsey waved his hands, shooing away the very idea. "I was hit once today already. My face makes the news, and Damjani and his friends will launch an around-the-clock manhunt for me."

The doorbell rang twice more, and then they heard Hickcock's fist pounding on the door. Dorsey leaned back onto the desk and shook his head. "He'll be gone in a second. Smacking your fist into a door is too much like work and gets old fast. He'll go away."

"Shit, we have to get something," Dorsey heard Hickcock call to his crew. "Let's try this."

Dorsey and Gretchen each went to one of the front windows, which were slightly open. Outside they saw Hickcock direct the cameraman and sound tech to the curb. When the tape rolled, he took position in the middle of the pavement and pointed over his shoulder at the row house, addressing the camera and speaking into a hand-held mike.

"Behind me is the home of Carroll Dorsey," he said in his perfectly modulated voice. "Earlier today, in an activity that led to his arrest by the Beaver County sheriff's office, Dorsey totally disrupted a rally sponsored by Movement Together. Held in Midland, the rally featured a speech by the movement's founder, Father Andrew Jancek. It is now believed that Dorsey is employed as a so-called corporate agent provocateur.

"We have every reason to believe that Dorsey is now at home but, despite our ringing the doorbell and knocking at his door, he refuses to acknowledge our presence, let alone answer any questions. It was our intention to give him an opportunity to tell his version of today's events. Our invitation still stands. We'll see how he responds. Sam Hickcock reporting."

Dorsey watched Hickcock check his wristwatch and hurry his crew into the van, complaining about a five-thirty deadline. "This guy, he wants to get to the networks, and he's going to try it riding on my back."

"You're news now," Gretchen told him. "Fair game to one and all."

"And I'll be stuffed and mounted over someone's fireplace if I don't watch my ass."

CHAPTER 10

Don't worry, Bernie had said over the phone, you'll get there after the shift change. The hell's that supposed to mean? Dorsey had replied. Bernie explained further that the shift change at Al's was between six-thirty and seven when the after-work drunks, the ones Dorsey had to worry about, were on their way home to dinner. Then the evening drunks arrive, Bernie said, the old single guys who sip on beer until the eleven o'clock news is over. They won't give you trouble; you'll be safe. The young ones: worry about them. They'll kick your ass, they catch up with you.

"Wrong again, Bern," Dorsey muttered as he stepped into the bar. Three young men, about age thirty, sat at the near end of the bar, dressed in flannel shirts and blue jeans splattered with dried cement. The man sitting in the middle looked over his shoulder and elbowed his friends.

"Over there, the guy from TV," Dorsey heard the middle one tell his friends. "Told ya he came in here."

The workman nearest Dorsey pushed himself from the bar

and took a firm grip on the neck of his emptied beer bottle. Knowing he had little chance of outrunning all three men and a flying beer bottle, Dorsey moved in, crowding the guy and making it impossible for him to take a full swing. Then Dorsey locked his eyes on the workman, hoping for a stare-down. It's my only chance against all three, he thought, convinced he was about to be knocked down for the second time that day.

"Hey, fella," Al said softly from behind the bar. Gently, he tapped the workman's shoulder with the business end of a thirty-two-ounce baseball bat. The workman turned slowly, and Al worked the bat under his chin.

"Friendly place this is, civilized." Al watched all three men, alternately looking each one in the eye. "We'd like to keep it that way. You guys are disturbing the peace. As owner and operator, only I am allowed to do that. Get out."

The workman saved his dignity with a few moments' icy stare, then slowly backed toward the door while his friends scooped up their change from the bar. Keeping the bat at port arms, Al came around the bar and watched as they left.

"Al, you were beautiful," Dorsey said. "Like the new marshal in town. Fresh off the last stage from Dodge City."

"Careful, fella." Al took Dorsey by the elbow and led him to the back room. "Treasure the friends you have, us loyal ones. The six o'clock news was very popular tonight; you were not. Watch your step here."

Al's back room never failed to impress Dorsey with its size. Its walls lined with red leatherette booths and its dance floor tiled in red and white check, it had a Wurlitzer on the far wall. By the jukebox's dim light he could see Bernie sitting in a booth just to the left, peeling the label from a bottle of Michelob with his thumb.

"Missed all the action, Bern." Dorsey slipped into the booth opposite Bernie. Al remained standing, leaning on the bat. "Al just saved my relatively young ass from some guys who, according to you, should've been home and drunk and passing out in the meat loaf and mashed potatoes by now. You misled me, but Al was there to fix things."

"There's been more than enough action in my life for one

day," Bernie said, sipping his beer. "I was going to ask you if you have any idea how much shit hit my personal fan this afternoon after word of your little adventure leaked out. I surmise there is no way for you to truly appreciate it, but your opportunity to do so will come up in two days."

"Hell's that supposed to mean?" Dorsey looked at Al, who merely shrugged his shoulders. "Honest, it wasn't my intention when I got up this morning to get cracked in the head and dragged into a cell. Or to get you in hot water. Sorry. Fill me in."

"Al," Bernie said. "Couple more beers?"

"Sure, sure. Got a bar to run anyways. I'll send Russie back with 'em. But the next time one of you guys has a spare moment, bring me up to date. Following your adventures makes my day." He headed back to the bar, twirling the bat in his right hand.

Bernie leaned in closer to the tabletop. "Seriously, Dorsey, today was a bad one. About ten after four, one of the clerks walks up to my desk and says that Mr. Everette, senior, wants to see me right away. You have to put this in perspective; the only time I have words with Mr. Everette, senior, of Everette, MacLeod, and Lancer, is at the Christmas party when I get to kiss his ring. And I haven't won any big cases or landed any big accounts lately, so I was sure it would not go well. Which it did not."

"Said I was sorry," Dorsey said. Russie, unshaven and wearing a black watch cap, brought their beer to the table on a small round tray. Bernie paid for the beers while Dorsey dropped two quarters onto the tray.

"You're a good guy," Russie said to Dorsey. "Always was. You was a good kid too. How's your dad?"

"Good. Last I saw him he was good. See you around, Russie."

"Before I start up again," Bernie said, "how come you're still supporting that rummy?"

"Russie?" Dorsey said. "Russie was a ward heeler over here for the old man. County worker. He used to wash the big shots' cars at the City-County Building. The old man used to tip him three bucks for a wash, five for a wax job." Dorsey set down his beer and shrugged. "Fuck's it to you what I do with my money?

He's a good guy, loyal. Now, tell me what's going on in the so-called halls of justice."

Bernie pulled at his beer and wiped his lips with the printed napkin Russie left behind. "Well, I'm in Everette's office, and he's behind this huge desk that twelve mahogany trees gave their lives for. Doesn't ask me to sit down, but he does say it is his understanding that I know you personally. I told him we're good friends. Then he asks if I know who you are presently working for. I said I thought you were on pretty steady with Fidelity Casualty."

"The guy was playing with you," Dorsey said. "Corso must've called, right after the trouble in Midland. Everette knew the answers before he asked the questions."

"Maybe he did," Bernie said, "but not from Corso. Corso doesn't call a full partner. He talks to me or some other guy on the ass end of the totem pole. You ever hear of a guy named John Munt?"

Dorsey did a quick mental run-through of his client list. "No."

"He's at Fidelity Casualty's home office. In Syracuse." Bernie sipped his beer and silently eyed a fortyish-looking woman standing at the room's entrance, peering into the dim light. When she appeared satisfied with her observations, she left. Bernie resumed his story. "This Munt has direct supervision over Corso. The way I see it, Corso heard about you on the radio, shit his pants, and called Munt. Possibly Munt has been reading your reports."

"So he called Everette." Dorsey set down his beer and held out his palms in submission.

"No." Bernie shook his head and tried unsuccessfully to suppress a grin. "No, Munt called an old college buddy, a Mr. Charles Cleardon. And I already know you don't know him, so I won't ask. You two move in different social circles. I am given to understand he is a senior officer of the Calumet Corporation, which owns Fidelity Casualty. *He* called Everette."

"And he wants something done," Dorsey said.

"Quickly," Bernie said. "He's very concerned about corporate image. He wants something done fast, and that something involves a meeting with you."

"Just me? To find out if I'm loyal, trustworthy, and brave?"

"Not by a long shot," Bernie said. "They're going to circle the wagons this Friday at two-thirty. Cleardon and Munt are flying in. Corso will be there too, sweating bullets, I'm sure. Everette may attend and bring me along as caddy. And a guy from the DA's office."

Dorsey set down his beer, so startled he nearly toppled it. "Why the DA's office? Nobody's preferring charges. There's no complaint filed."

"His attendance will be strictly informal," Bernie said. "But face it, if your reports are right, we have insurance fraud, a conspiracy. This is Mr. Everette's idea. The DA's rep will also be sitting in for the DA offices in Westmoreland, Washington, and Beaver counties. And anywhere else you've been snooping lately."

"So I appear before all the big guns."

"That's right," Bernie said. "So you better get your shit straight."

"And how do I go about that?"

As Bernie filled him in, Russie appeared at the booth and tapped Dorsey's shoulder. Bernie looked annoyed but Russie waved him off and spoke to Dorsey.

"Al says you gotta leave inna little bit. And you gotta use the back door, through the kitchen."

"How come?"

Russie leaned in closer. "Al said to remind you about the three guys who were on your ass when you came in. He expects them to be out front waitin' on you. Al says you should be expectin' that, too. So like he says, use the back door."

"Thanks, Russie, thanks a lot and tell Al thanks, too." Dorsey turned back to Bernie. "And you ask me why I take care of the guy?"

Chapter 11

At five the next morning, the alarm clock sang out and Dorsey flopped over onto his stomach, burying his face in the pillow. Gretchen rose immediately from the far side of the mattress, punching the alarm switch as she went naked down the hall and into the shower. Dorsey listened to the pipes rattle as the hot water struggled up from the basement tank.

They had made love fiercely the night before, Dorsey erasing the previous day, Gretchen alternately responding and initiating with the passion that never failed to surprise him. But even the serenity that followed their coupling could not take the edge from Dorsey's dream, a repeating flight from men chasing him and, worse, catching him. On any other morning when Gretchen had early rounds at the hospital, Dorsey would doze until just before six and then throw on whatever clothes were handy and drive her to work. This morning was different. His dreams had one foot in reality. From all sides, he thought; they're coming at me from all sides. Won't even let a man get his sleep.

By the time Gretchen returned from the shower wrapped in

her terry-cloth robe, Dorsey had on his gray cotton sweatsuit and was sitting at the edge of the bed lacing his Brooks walking shoes, the ones with paint splattered on them. "You're up," she said. Her tone mimicked wonder.

"Sleep seems suddenly to be bad for me." Dorsey stood and tested the strength of his legs with a few deep-knee bends. "I'll be back in plenty of time to run you to work."

Dorsey took Wharton to South Sixteenth Street, then made a right onto Carson, his arms and legs pumping in unison. The trees along Carson were few in number and widely spaced, but collectively they had produced enough brown and yellow leaves to overflow the gutter and litter the pavement. On the outward leg of his walk, Dorsey kicked at the leaves and thought of Gretchen and money, his father and money, and the investigation—which could also be money. Future cases and new accounts and maybe an exclusive with Fidelity Casualty. That's money! Dorsey thought.

The return trip, after the turnaround at the foot of the Smithfield Street bridge, went quickly, now that the pace was set and the joints well oiled. The body moved on its own while Dorsey cleared his mind with a daydream of Benny Goodman's clarinet. Finished with "Don't Be That Way," he moved on to a fantasy of Ellington's piano with the horn section as backup. He was so immersed in the last bars of "Mood Indigo," when he crossed the alley bisecting the block between Carson and Wharton, he almost missed the first sign of surveillance. A few doors up the alley, its left wheels on the curb, was a radio van with the Channel Three logo across its rear double doors.

Dorsey moved cautiously down the alley, nearly doubled into a crouched position, until he was certain the van was unmanned. Peering through the passenger-side window he saw the citizen band radio and police scanner and wished he could remember the name of the thief who had sold him the telephone answering machine. Cleaning out the van would help even things, Dorsey told himself, for the shit they plan to put you through. He also wished for an ice pick to do in the tires.

He left the alley and moved down to the corner of Wharton and South Sixteenth, again crouching and staying close to the red brick of the corner house. Craning his neck past the building's edge, he saw yesterday's cameraman huddled in the doorway across from his own. Dorsey figured him to be alone until he spotted a second man sitting in a car parked halfway down the block at the far-side curb. Dorsey wondered if there was a third man on the back door.

Trotting back to the alley, Dorsey shaped his plans. Keeping at a brisk pace but mindful of his knee, he crossed South Sixteenth and took the alley for three blocks, then went back to Wharton on South Thirteenth. After waiting for a truck to pause at the intersection's stop sign, he sprinted across Wharton and continued down to the next alley, running parallel to Wharton and back to South Sixteenth. Carefully, he approached his own thin back yard. Nobody's on the back door, Dorsey decided. So they're watching the car, not the house. Simple bastards.

Dorsey entered the house through the back door and found Gretchen at the kitchen table, dunking a tea bag in her cup. She wore her work uniform. "Forget the front-door key?" she asked, smiling over the rim of the cup.

"Company out front." Dorsey continued on through the kitchen and hallway to the front office.

Gretchen followed and watched as he peeked through the drawn curtains. "Seems like you do a lot of window peeking these days."

"Channel Three again," Dorsey said. "Two of them. One's the cameraman from yesterday. Probably want not only to follow me but also to get a few candid shots as I head out for another day of evil doings. Think I'll stay put."

"I suppose that means I take the bus to work."

Gretchen watched Dorsey seat himself at the desk and lift the telephone receiver.

"Take the car," Dorsey said.

"Won't you need it today?" Gretchen asked, approaching the desk. "I thought you would. I can't see getting away from the hospital before five or five-thirty. And I wanted to go to my place tonight."

"Please, take the car." Dorsey dialed a number. "Park in the garage, like always, then give the keys to Bennie. You know, the guy you pay on the way out? I'm sending Russie over on the bus to drive the car back here. I'll get you when the shift is over."

Gretchen shook her head. "You're sending Russie? He drives? He has a license?"

"Yes and no, I think." Dorsey listened to the ringing at the other end of the line. Looking at Gretchen, he said, "Guy lives on the second floor and you have to call on the bar phone. Takes forever." Dorsey rested his elbows on the desk and spoke into the receiver. "Sorry to get you up. . . . Oh, you *were* up. Do me a favor? . . . Good, here's the deal."

Ten minutes later Gretchen left as Dorsey watched from the window. The cameraman tensed at first and lifted the minicam but stopped halfway up, disappointment registering on his face. The man in the car, which was an LTD, showed no reaction at all. Cool son of a bitch, Dorsey thought.

Dorsey caught a quick shower and dressed casually in jeans and sport shirt. In the kitchen he brewed a small pot of coffee and reheated oatmeal that Gretchen had made earlier. With one long arm he retrieved the morning paper from the front doormat—the paperboy rarely missed—and with his meal he began to wander through the sports section.

Halfway through his second cup of coffee, Dorsey heard movement in the back yard. There were three knocks at the back door, a moment's pause, and then another three. "C'mon in," Dorsey called. "It's open."

Russie walked through the door with two sets of car keys in his hand. "Car's parked up in front of the bar. Al's van's just out back in the alley. He says it's okay, he won't need it today."

Dorsey rose from his seat and pressed a ten-dollar bill into Russie's hand. "Cup of coffee? Something to eat?"

Russie accepted the offer of coffee and poured himself a cup. He took off his watch cap and opened his zippered jacket, then took a seat opposite Dorsey. "The guys outside, they here 'cause of the stuff on TV?" Russie sipped at his coffee, bending to the cup instead of lifting it.

"Because of yesterday. That's right."

"People like to hold on to hard feelings," Russie said. "Get a hard-on for a guy, they don't like to let go. Gives them something to live for. Remember Tootsie Reagan, he was pissed at your old man for years? All 'cause Tootsie had a dumbbell of a son-in-law that he wanted made into a constable. Wasn't satisfied that your father fixed up the kid with a job onna public works truck. Tootsie took it as a pride thing, and when your father told him the kid was an asshole and he could take the truck job or nothin', Tootsie said forget it. The kid didn't get shit. And Tootsie got pissed."

"Tootsie was a dipshit," Dorsey said. "Tried his best to make trouble for the old man afterward, something about splitting some ballots, I think. But he never got anywhere." Dorsey folded his paper and pushed it to Russie.

"And Tootsie just got hotter." Russie took the paper and placed his cap over it. "And when he ended up out on his ear, all he had to live for was hatin' your father. How's your father doin', anyways?"

"Good, I think. Called yesterday, left a message. I'll get back to him today."

"Still the same between you guys?" Russie asked. "Me and your father go way back. I know him good. Knows how to take care of a guy."

Dorsey ran his eyes over Russie, examining the plain work pants and cotton shirt, looking into the guileless face and eyes. Maybe he's simple, but surely not stupid, Dorsey concluded. And Bernie wonders why I take care of him. As if he needed it.

When Russie had finished his coffee and was gone, Dorsey cleared the breakfast dishes and went to the front office to check the street. The cameraman was gone but the watcher in the LTD was still in place. Resigning himself to being on the opposite side of a surveillance, Dorsey put on some music and began to peck out a brief outline of the previous day's events on the Olivetti. When he finished he took from the file cabinet the investigation reports on the four men and one woman who had shared the stage with Damjani and Father Jancek. He read slowly, taking notes on a yellow legal pad.

At ten o'clock, by Bernie's arrangement, a bicycle messenger delivered a portable dictaphone and three cassette tapes. They want to get your reports, Bernie had said in the back booth at Al's, fast as you can talk them. So they can digest them. Sounds like stomach trouble, Dorsey had told him. Try Zantac.

Dorsey turned down the music to a murmur and spoke softly into the microphone, hoping his spoken reports would play as well as his written ones. Working slowly through his outline, he touched on each of the investigations that had led to Midland. Radovic, fiercely proud of the manpower he could muster to back up his threats. Karen Stroesser, who examined bumpers like a researcher for *Consumer Reports,* looking for the safest car in which to have an accident. And Damjani, the master of ceremonies. Then there's Father Jancek, he told himself, a man you know very little about.

Twice during the dictation, Dorsey was interrupted by the telephone. He let the answering machine pick up the calls but set the volume so he could listen in.

"About yesterday," Sam Hickcock said over the line. "Don't take the stuff I said on TV seriously. I couldn't come away from your place empty-handed. I'd've caught hell if I had nothing on the day's big story, especially if I came back without film. But the offer to hear your side of the story still stands. Call me." Hickcock left his number.

"Said the spider to the fly." Dorsey rolled his eyes and returned to his dictation.

The second call was from a low-range black voice identifying itself as Attorney Louis Preach. Evenly, without threats or enticements, he suggested that Dorsey call him back. Don't make that call, Dorsey cautioned himself, not until you know who he is and what he wants. Maybe not then, either.

The bicycle messenger returned at two o'clock, and Dorsey had him wait in the hall while he closed out the dictation, hoping to concoct a brief comment on where the investigation should go from here. You know what you have, Dorsey told himself, his feet on the edge of the desk. He could hear the messenger pacing in the hall. In dictations make no conclusions, just indications. Radovic crosses town on foot like a wilderness hiker, so maybe his back isn't so bad. But is he a fraud and can you make it stick? No. Stroesser and the others wreck rented cars and maybe you have a conspiracy. But how's about a little something in the way of evidence? And connections, meaningful ones, between Damjani and the priest? Show me the evidence.

After seeing the messenger out, Dorsey checked the street for the LTD, but it was gone. He returned to the office and through the window he scrutinized each doorway and between-house walk space for its driver. Gone, Dorsey thought, like the cameraman before him. Must be a big news day.

The phone rang three times and then the answering machine picked up. Martin Dorsey asked for a return call and Dorsey broke into the line.

"Hold on," Dorsey said. "Sorry I didn't get back to you yesterday, but things got hectic."

"And public." Martin Dorsey allowed several moments of silence. "This Hickcock, I've had dealings with him, when he covered election returns. Carroll, you be careful with that one. He's not particularly smart, but he is ambitious, and that kind can be a headache. He's TV, and only appearances matter."

"The power of the electronic press has been brought to my attention."

"A lesson to be learned. You'll do better next time." Martin Dorsey sounded relaxed, conversational. "I take it there was a reason you were in Midland?"

"For once in my career I may be on to something," Dorsey said. "Something more than an insurance cheat or a husband stepping out."

"The priest, he's involved? If he's not, you made yourself famous for nothing."

Dorsey laughed, lowering his instinctive shield against his father. "Maybe. It's just that I don't know much about him. Next to nothing, really."

"Then find out about him."

"Thanks, I will."

Martin Dorsey allowed another silent pause. "Have you given it much thought? My offer, I mean. You said you would."

"I'm thinking about it," Dorsey said. "Much more so today."

"Good," Martin Dorsey said. "The project is looking even brighter. Finance is not my area of expertise, but I've been assured of great things, fortunes to be made. I want you to be part of it."

"We'll see," Dorsey said and thought of Gretchen and a life together.

"That's all we ask." Martin Dorsey permitted yet another moment of empty air on the line. "About the priest, Jancek. Do you remember Thomas Gallard? He's at the Theology Department at Duquesne."

"The one who gave me a D in Judeo-Christian Heritage? The class that was supposed to be a breeze?"

"You're my son," Martin Dorsey said. "More is expected of you. Whatever your grade, Monsignor Gallard is a friend. And he knows Jancek, I've heard him mention it. I think they were in seminary together. No, their ages are all wrong for that. Whatever, he knows him. Give the monsignor a call. I'm sure he'll try to help."

"I'll do that," Dorsey said. "And I'll talk to you soon, about the other thing."

Monsignor Gallard agreed to see Dorsey in his campus office at four o'clock. At three-thirty Dorsey left the row house through the back yard, climbed into Al's white van, and slipped the key into the ignition. After grinding the gears he went over the Tenth Street bridge and then on through the tunnel, backtracking up the bluffs to the campus overlooking the Monongahela. A campus security guard waved him away from the faculty parking lot until Dorsey flashed his leftover ID from the District Attorney's office. The guard let him through but with his thumb and forefinger he signaled for Dorsey to make it a short stay.

Gallard's office was on the second floor of one of the older red brick buildings on campus, and as Dorsey climbed the wide steps, he wondered how well the monsignor might remember him. It's been seventeen years since you hid in the last row of his classroom, he reminded himself. And the man was old then. But your father, he doesn't spare time for old fools who can't remember what day it is. Except maybe to use them for all they're worth.

The department secretary led Dorsey through a reception area that had once been a classroom and knocked at a door with a top panel of frosted glass. Rather than wait for a response, she opened the door a crack and announced Dorsey. A soft, even voice acknowledged her and bid Dorsey enter.

To Dorsey, Thomas Gallard looked every hour, minute, and second of his seventy-eight years. He wore a black cassock, and the skin above the thin red piping that edged his Roman collar hung loose and dry, blue veins running along each side of his neck. A few strands of white hair, looking like aged straw, were combed across his pate. Seated behind a scarred schoolteacher's desk, he gestured Dorsey into a seat across from him.

"I apologize for not rising to greet you." Monsignor Gallard rattled a quad cane in his left hand. "I had a stroke three, maybe four, years ago. After quite a bit of rehabilitation therapy, my arm bounced back nicely. The damned leg, though, refused to respond."

"Sorry to hear it," Dorsey said. "I hadn't realized."

"No matter." Monsignor Gallard squared himself in his seat and directly faced Dorsey. "We aren't here to discuss my health, are we?"

"No, sir." Dorsey spoke slowly, thinking that since the stroke it might be necessary. "Monsignor, do you remember me? I mentioned my father on the phone."

The monsignor smiled. "Yes, Carroll, I remember you. And no, no matter how many extra assignments you turn in, it is much too late to change your D in Judeo-Christian. Let's talk about Father Jancek. What is your interest?"

That settles any doubts about his memory, Dorsey thought, squirming in his chair. "Background on an investigation I'm conducting, that's all. The father is not central, more of a sidebar."

"Calling Father Jancek a sidebar would be insulting him," the monsignor said. "Besides, I read two newspapers each day and I catch the TV news. From what I saw yesterday, I'd say you have had your allotted fifteen minutes of fame."

It was Dorsey's turn to smile. "And I'd have to agree. But I'm into something and I couldn't tell you much about it even if I understood it. Father Jancek is involved somehow. You know him; talk to me about him."

The monsignor drummed his fingers on the desktop, then sighed and folded his hands together. "Like you, he was a student of mine, but it was twelve years before your time and it was at Fordham. Reading the historians of today, one gets the distinct impression that the nineteen-fifties were totally devoid of radical thinkers. As if the so-called left wing spent the decade in a coma. Nothing could be more erroneous."

With a slow nod of his head, Dorsey encouraged the monsignor to continue.

"There were quite a few pockets of radicalism in New York City at the time, mostly in the Village and uptown around Columbia. And Andy Jancek knew and was welcome in each and every one of them. That included the haunts of wealthy liberals on the Upper West Side. Radical chic, it was called a little later. Some of the students and faculty referred to Andy as the Subway Radical because of his successful wanderings. Fordham was still a very Catholic and conservative institution, and Andy stood out like a sore thumb. Especially with his goatee. The full beard is new. An improvement."

"Was he a good student?" Dorsey asked.

"Surprisingly so." Monsignor Gallard flicked at a speck of lint on his cassock. "I say that because of all the time he devoted to his politics. Coffeehouses, study groups on socialism; as I recall he attended every ban-the-bomb rally scheduled. And a lot more of his time was occupied in defending his activities to his fellow students. The school ranks brimmed with children of the Catholic upper and middle classes, and they had little time for him. I remember at the time I was concerned that he would grow into an embittered man."

"I can see how it could happen," Dorsey said. "Did it surprise you when he entered the seminary?"

"Not at all," the monsignor said. "He spoke to me of his vocation on a number of occasions. However, I was very much surprised that he saw it through to the end. Remember, the activist church was still a few years off."

"How about more recently? Any contact with him since he became famous?"

Monsignor Gallard tried unsuccessfully to suppress a laugh. "No, I lost track of him when I came here in the mid-sixties. One hears things, though. The priesthood has its own grapevine. From the tidbits I've picked up, I can only assume that he followed the same path taken by other young priests of the time: hunger marches, freedom marches with the black community, saying mass in private homes wearing blue jeans. I distinctly remember hearing he was heavily involved in the McCarthy campaign: Eugene McCarthy."

"All pretty standard for the times," Dorsey commented. He began to rise, thinking the well had run disappointingly dry.

"Perhaps. In some ways, yes." With the palm of his hand, Monsignor Gallard motioned Dorsey back into his chair. "Keep in mind what I said. This was a boy in his late teens when I first met him, forced to withstand extreme social pressure. There was a lot of strength there, even if it was a touch single-minded. He had little opportunity to make a friend, let alone keep one. Thank God for Jack. It's good to see their friendship has endured."

"Jack?"

"The attorney, Jack Stockman." Monsignor Gallard smiled thinly and nodded. "They were close friends at Fordham—soul mates, it could be said. Even entered seminary together. Jack left after his first year. I remember fearing Andy would follow close behind. I'm so glad I was wrong."

"Jack Stockman," Dorsey said, hoping to work the monsignor for more. "I don't know much about him either."

Monsignor Gallard's eyes narrowed. "He's a rather prominent attorney, locally. I thought your father said you've been employed by a number of law firms. Surely you know him?"

"Sure, but not well."

Cutting back across the campus to the faculty parking lot, Dorsey reviewed what he did know about Jack Stockman. Simply put, he thought, the man's the best. But he's the best in personal injury cases, workers' compensation, things like that. Not labor law. That's why his being hooked up with Movement Together never made sense until now. With Stockman being so close to the priest, he has to know it all, whatever that is. Better yet, he may have cooked up the whole deal. Maybe Stockman's the chef, and the priest just chops the vegetables.

And one more thing, Dorsey told himself. Because he's the best, if you take him down a few pegs, you'll go up a few pegs, make a name for yourself. This could be the big one.

Dorsey turned into the parking lot and saw two security guards standing by the van, one of them speaking into a hand-held radio. Quickening his steps, Dorsey felt the crunch of broken safety glass under his feet and saw the shards scattered across the lot's asphalt surface. The van's windshield and passenger window were smashed, and shattered glass covered the upholstery of the forward seats.

One of the guards, the one he had encountered while parking, took Dorsey aside.

"Listen, it's like this: we can't be everywhere. The campus is a big place. My partner heard the noise, but by the time he got here—nobody. He put in a call for the city cops, and the glass replacement truck is coming. You got insurance to cover it?"

"Yeah, I'm covered." Dorsey tugged the keys from his hip pocket and undid the driver's door. Al's gonna love this, he thought, grimacing as he brushed away bits of glass held together by the safety mesh. Let's hope he's covered, otherwise we'll have to find a way to figure this into my Fidelity Casualty expense account.

It was only after he was convinced that the broken glass was the extent of the damage that Dorsey noticed the small white envelope resting on the floor near the passenger seat. He lifted the envelope and stood erect in the doorway. Inside was a typewritten message.

THE GOOD FATHER SAYS WE SHOULD PRAY FOR OUR ENE-
MIES. I DISAGREE.

"What's that?" The security guard reached for the note, but Dorsey quickly stuffed it into his jacket pocket.

"It's personal," Dorsey said. "From a guy I met yesterday."

CHAPTER 12

Dorsey slid in the apartment door key and worked the deadbolt. It opened with the sound of metal sliding over metal. Carrying Gretchen's dry cleaning with both hands, Dorsey shoved the door with his shoulder and flicked on the overhead light switch with the back of his hand.

"Thought I had it right on the money," he said over his shoulder. "I really thought I had. It only made sense for the guy in the LTD to be the cameraman's partner. But obviously he wasn't."

"Don't be so hard on yourself." Gretchen followed him into her apartment, carrying a brown paper grocery sack, and turned left into a compact kitchen. She emptied the sack's contents into a slender refrigerator and one of several cupboards. "A slipup is all it was. You keep them to the barest of minimums, but they will happen." There was a touch of irritation in her voice that Dorsey could feel. "The dry cleaning goes into the bedroom closet. The right side, behind the door with the mirror."

Dorsey hung the cleaning in the closet and picked his way across the bedroom like a broken field runner, carefully placing each foot to avoid tripping over piles of clothes and stacks of medical journals. How does she live like this? How does she avoid passing on infections during patient examinations? Thank God for rubber gloves, he thought; they were invented with her in mind. He skirted the Exercycle near the door and walked back to the kitchen.

"Never have I seen a double surveillance," he went on. "Two watchers from separate sources watching the same guy at the same time. Unheard of. Besides, who could've expected a bunch of out-of-work mill hands to be so organized? It's Stockman; he knows the game. He tells the priest what to do, and Jancek tells Damjani. And he sends a goon to scare me into pissing my pants. I'm dry, but it was a little rattling."

Gretchen put her arms around his neck and softly kissed his cheek. Sliding into her thin smile, she slowly pulled back. "Just so you're all right. Now shut up about it. Drop it. Sit and have a beer. My turn to cook."

Gretchen handed him a Rolling Rock from the refrigerator, and Dorsey settled into one of the two metal chairs that sat around the kitchen's small glass-and-chrome table. Sipping his beer and watching Gretchen take plastic containers of leftovers from the refrigerator, Dorsey cursed himself for his stupidity. Antonio warned you, he reminded himself. Said for you to watch your ass with these guys. And you didn't. You've got to keep an eye out for Damjani and his people. But my old man, he says to keep an eye out for Hickcock. Good thing you have two eyes.

There was another matter on his mind, too. Money. The old man's money offer. Sky's the limit, that's how he makes it out to be. High tech, wave of the future. Yours and Gretchen's. Even if it's only half of what he says, and he always puts in the fix to make sure that doesn't happen, the days ahead could be eighteen carat.

"Gretchen." Dorsey swirled his beer and watched the waves through green glass. "When you're through there, when you get a second, sit down for a little while. I'd like to talk."

After putting the lid on a saucepan with a toothpick wedged in to release steam, Gretchen poured herself a glass of white wine from a gallon jug in the refrigerator and sat across from Dorsey.

"Weisswurst and kraut, sound good? My mom sent it back with me the last time I was home. So what's on your mind?"

"First of all," Dorsey said, "even to a dunce like me, it's obvious that when someone goes to medical school and then wades through an internship and residency, their career is pretty important to them." He spoke deliberately, weighing each word. "The someone I'm especially interested in is you. You're preparing for emergency medicine; that's your goal."

"Some centers call it trauma medicine, but it's all the same." Gretchen sipped her wine, watching him.

"What do you figure to pull down a year in a practice like that? In general, based on the doctors you know."

Gretchen went to the stove and uncovered the saucepan, stirring the contents. Seeming to be content with dinner's progress, she returned to her seat. "Well, Jim Clarkson, he's been there a while, he makes sixty-three a year. For me, when residency is over, something in the mid-forties sounds reasonable in the local market. Why do you ask?"

Dorsey evaded the question. "Suppose there wasn't an opening in the local market. Would you move out of town?"

"I'll answer that question, but that is it." Gretchen set aside her wine. "You get nothing more without an explanation. First of all, my prospects locally are good. My field of medicine is not the most glamorous or profitable, so the competition is not too steep. But to answer your question, if you need an answer right now, I would relocate, but I don't foresee that happening. So tell me what this is all about."

"My father's offer, the money." Dorsey's eyes were downcast.

"I don't follow."

"Simply put, I don't want to lose you," Dorsey said. "I don't want you to leave me behind."

Gretchen, in a show of exasperation and exhaustion, sighed deeply and dug the heels of her hands at her eyes. "Carroll, you know how I feel; I'm in love with you. And I know you love me, though I'd like to hear you say it more often. When I look at the future you're always in it. But honestly, that's speculation, not prophecy. I plan for a future with you, but there's no guarantee. I can't provide one."

"Maybe I can." Dorsey reached across the table for her hand. "That's where the money comes in. With money, with a cushion, you could wait things out. Say there wasn't anything available at a local hospital, you could sit tight until something came around. And later, when you're set up and don't have to rely on packages from home, we could be on common ground financially. Follow what I'm saying?"

"Don't worry about that sort of thing." Gretchen rose and began to set the table. Silently, she put out flatware and paper napkins, then divided the sausages and sauerkraut between two plates.

"You piss me off," she said uncharacteristically, speaking through a mouthful of half-chewed food. Angrily, she went on pumping forkfuls into her mouth. "As if I give a damn about the condition of your bank account or how good your prospects are. I don't half-live with a guy ten or eleven years older than I am because I think he belongs to a well-heeled family. I don't want to hear any more."

Dorsey opened his mouth to speak.

"Not a word," Gretchen said, pointing with her fork. "Eat. And be quiet."

They worked their way silently through dinner, avoiding each other's eyes. Dorsey took a fresh beer into the living room while Gretchen changed into shorts and sweatshirt and worked out on the Exercycle. No guarantee, Dorsey thought, sitting on a thinly cushioned sofa as he paged blindly through the evening newspaper. You knew that, Dorsey, that's why you asked the question. And got the only answer possible: no guarantee.

So, don't get one, Dorsey thought, awkwardly folding the paper, unable to return it to its original shape. He clenched his hands behind his neck and stretched, ending with a rough shrug of his shoulders. You know the rules; never rely on anything or anyone else. How long ago was it that you learned you were strictly on your own? How many times have you been on the stand? They used to slice your balls off before you got smart—back when you would say so-and-so said this, or so-and-so assured me that would happen. Before you learned to check things out for yourself.

Dorsey pushed himself from the couch and went to the room's only window. He heard the Exercycle's timer ring. A moment later came the sounds of Gretchen struggling out of her sweatshirt and shorts as she made her way to the shower. Outside, in the alley below, garbage was piled at the gate of each yard, ready for the next morning's collection. Dorsey drummed his fingers on the windowpane.

So depend on yourself, he thought, and only yourself. Two golden opportunities are looking you in the face, close enough to nip your nose to assure your attention. The investigation has the potential to go somewhere. People are pissed off and striking back, so you must be hitting a nerve. And the stakes are big. Bring in the goods on this one and you've got an automatic reputation. Carroll Dorsey, the guy who cracked Father Jancek and saved a bundle for the insurance company. And most of all, the guy who kicked Jack Stockman's ass. Lots of business and free drinks. Set 'em up for the guy who got all over P.I. Stockman's shit.

And maybe, just maybe, the old man's money wouldn't mean a thing. Who needs it? There'll be plenty of work and opportunity: maybe hire a few assistants, maybe slip into the security guard business. But still, the old man's money could round out things.

Dorsey turned from the window at the sound of Gretchen's footsteps. Dressed in a flannel nightgown, she worked a towel through her hair as she moved across the room. She took him by the hand and led him back to the sofa. Once seated, she rubbed the curls above her left ear, then dropped the towel to the floor.

"So you're worried about us," she said, folding her hands over his. "Don't be, please. My plan is to be with you. Plans do change, but only when something unexpected happens. Nothing has happened yet; most likely it never will."

"I worry sometimes," Dorsey said. "My day was bad too. I'm disappointed in how things went."

"Don't be."

"Got a right to be disappointed." Dorsey leaned forward and placed his chin in his cupped hands. "I should've been watching for both sides to come after me. I was preoccupied with Hickcock and his cameras. I knew Damjani was crazy; now I know he's long-distance crazy."

"You said Damjani didn't do it."

"He didn't. It was the guy in the LTD, most likely." Dorsey nodded, agreeing with his own theory. "It's the note. Damjani wrote it. He's a psycho. It's a psycho note."

He got up, stretched, and went to the refrigerator for a fresh beer. On his return he flopped onto the sofa, facing Gretchen.

"So how about you?" he asked. "On the ride over here, even before I opened my mouth, you were pretty surly. Something happen at the hospital?"

"You're not the only one who screwed up today," Gretchen said. "I had one today myself."

"I didn't realize." Dorsey touched her shoulder. "Tell me."

"A couple of weeks ago, do you remember I told you about a drunk in the ER? One we had to restrain?" Gretchen asked. "He went wild, remember? Something like that happened today."

Dorsey leaned closer. "You're okay, right? This one didn't knock you around?"

"If only that. No, this was much worse." She settled farther into the sofa's corner. "The police brought in an older man this afternoon, about three-fifteen. Well dressed with an expensive haircut. One of the officers said they had gotten a call on a drunk and had found him face down on the sidewalk in front of a Market Square bar. The liquor smell wasn't all that strong, but it was there. Besides, the guy staggered around and spoke gibberish."

"So he was a drunk."

"That was my conclusion, but . . ." She pointed into the air for emphasis. "I get the orderlies to take him to detox, and while that's going on one of the cops gives the guy's wallet to the ward clerk to punch his admission into the computer. But just as she's ready to do it, the system goes down. So the orderlies take the man to detox, and I move on to my next adventure."

"Reasonable," Dorsey commented. He sipped his beer.

"Perfectly normal procedure." Gretchen straightened the hem of her nightgown. "Never gave it another thought and never expected I would have to. But about an hour and twenty minutes later, I get a page on my beeper and take the call at the clerk's desk. It was Dr. Costello's secretary. He's head of neurology. She said to stay put; the doctor was on his way to see me.

"I caught hell from him," Gretchen said. "Really bitched me out. I was in an examining room stitching a butterfly on a man's chin. There was an intern and a nurse and me when he marched in. Dr. Costello is a big, heavy-set guy, and he just threw back the curtain and began shouting. He fumbled through the pages of this textbook he was carrying, and when he found the page he was looking for he stuck the book right under my nose. And then he shouted even louder."

"What for?" Dorsey asked, his temper kindling. "A doctor, and he acts like that?"

"It turned out he had a right," Gretchen said. "The drunk was no drunk. His name was Fiedler and he's a patient of Dr. Costello's with a history of TIA's, little strokes. Costello found out he was in the hospital when the computer system came back up. If the system hadn't crashed, we would have had the man's history and all this could have been avoided."

"But the guy smells like he's in the bag, and he can't string a sentence together."

"One martini at a business lunch," Gretchen said. "And the gibberish is called aphasia. His cognitive powers went out for a while and he couldn't process anything from his brain to his mouth. From all accounts, he probably didn't realize himself that anything was wrong. In his case it was Wernicke's aphasia. I know that now because it was on the page Dr. Costello shoved under my nose. What a scene, him screaming and the nurse and the intern trying to slink out of the room."

Dorsey slid across the sofa and folded his arms around her. "Like you said, the system goes down and takes all its information with it. Had it done what it's supposed to do, then you get a chance to do your stuff. Which is to do the right thing in an emergency."

Gretchen nestled closer. "It's more than that. I had simply decided I had seen it all. This was just another drunk, and the all-knowing Dr. Keller without any medical history divined the proper course of action. I just did it and moved on to the next patient."

"How'd he make out?" Dorsey asked. "Fiedler, I mean."

"Fine, thank God. The aphasia was temporary. He'll spend tonight and maybe tomorrow in the hospital, and if all goes well he goes home."

"No harm done," Dorsey said.

"I know." Gretchen's eyes teared and she dabbed at them with her sleeve.

Dorsey set his beer on the coffee table and cradled her. He kissed her curled hair and rocked her slowly. In this easy motion he realized that in consoling Gretchen he found his own peace. Here and nowhere else, he thought. You've got to keep her. Solve the case.

CHAPTER 13

At his row house on Wharton Street, Dorsey rose early the next morning, as if Gretchen had stayed with him. Just before sunrise he dressed in gray sweats and looked out through the window: the street was empty except for the paperboy. Regardless, he left through the alley. Once his exercise was done and he had returned home, Dorsey quickly showered and dressed without shaving. For the next few hours he paced the office and sipped coffee, waiting for the shops on Carson to open. At nine o'clock he checked the streets again, found them empty, and left, wearing a wool parka against the autumn wind, this time through the front door.

Strolling up South Seventeenth, he checked each doorway and continually glanced over his shoulder. No one's there, he told himself. But no one seemed to be watching yesterday either; the coast was clear. Yet they were there, all right, right on your heels. You just didn't see them. You old pro, you. At Carson he turned right, crossed three intersections, and entered a men's clothing store.

"Ivan, you around?" The lights were on but the sales floor was empty. "Ivan, c'mon, you've got a customer waiting. You in back? I need a few things."

A very short and slight man in his early sixties pushed through a curtain separating the sales floor from storage. Carrying a Styrofoam coffee cup, he walked the length of the shop, his free hand playing across the top of a glass showcase displaying ties, belts, and handkerchiefs. Ivan's pants were worn to chest level. Dorsey tried to remember the difference between a dwarf and a midget.

"Dorsey, good morning," Ivan said, leaning back into the showcase. His voice was thick with the sound of Eastern Europe. "Coffee in back. Want some?"

"Had some," Dorsey said, "half a pot, I think. Need a shirt, a dress shirt. Nice one. And maybe a tie. I still have credit, right? My account's paid up."

"On the fourteenth of the month." Ivan closed his eyes to calculate. "Eighty-seven dollars and thirty-one cents. A sweater and two sport shirts, bought on sale. Two months ago. You were late, but there's no interest charge so why argue? This shirt: wearing it with a suit?"

"Yeah, the dark gray with the pinstripe."

Ivan pushed himself from the showcase and shuffled to a shelf loaded with broadcloth shirts still in their plastic wrappings. As he went, Dorsey could sense him picturing the suit in his mind. "You're the one with the long arms, right?" Ivan asked. "Sixteen neck and thirty-six sleeve, that's you. And button-down collar, Arrow or Hathaway?"

Ivan held out for his inspection a conventional light blue button-down. Having placed himself, sartorially, in Ivan's hands years ago, Dorsey immediately approved. Next, Ivan led him to the tie rack sitting on top of the glass showcase. He set his coffee near the cash register. "This dress-up: business or for the girlfriend?" Ivan fingered the edge of one of the neckties.

"Very serious business," Dorsey said. "I have to impress. Keep the color of the suit in mind."

"Of course. Try this." Ivan held up a muted burgundy tie,

spreading its full length between his hands. He then gently laid the tie diagonally across the shirt.

"Very nice with the suit," Ivan said. "With the way you describe it, I mean. Give me the wrong colors, mistake's not my fault."

"It'll be fine."

Ivan produced a ledger from below the cash register and flipped through the pages to the D's. In a very clear hand, and with his nose almost touching the page, he recorded the sale. "Something else, socks maybe? Handkerchief for the breast pocket? You want to impress, the outfit gotta be right."

"This is fine," Dorsey said, scooping up the bag that held his purchases. "I'm fixed pretty well for the rest."

"Don't forget," Ivan called after him. "Shave your face. Don't forget, for chrissake!"

Two doors down from Carson, Dorsey stopped at a dry cleaner and had the shirt unwrapped and steam-pressed. While it was run through the steam table, the sleeves taking on creases as sharp as blades, Dorsey paced going through the names in his head, cataloging each with cross-references. Radovic leads to Damjani, who loops back to Stroesser, who splits, going in two directions, to Stockman and the priest. Father Jancek encircles them all and doubles back neatly to himself.

Slinging the shirt across his shoulder on a hanger, Dorsey hurried back to the row house, where he sat himself down to work up a spit shine on a pair of Florsheim's. Kiwi cream polish was followed by twenty minutes of buffing with a clean chamois, and the shoes rivaled onyx.

Dorsey took another and much slower shower, scrubbing his flesh nearly raw and methodically applying a cuticle brush to his nails. And all the time he did so, the opinions and the possibilities, names and dates, all fell into their pigeonholes to be kept at the ready. A slow and precise shave followed and then Dorsey dressed gently, respecting the fabric and the dry cleaner's skill. It took him three tries before his tie had the perfect knot.

Toting his suit jacket on its hanger, Dorsey went downstairs to the office. He laid the jacket smoothly across the chaise and went to his desk, where he again reviewed the case file. The phone rang. When he answered it, Ironbox Boyle asked him to hold for his father.

"Hello Carroll, how are you?" His father sounded particularly happy.

"Good," Dorsey said. "A little on the antsy side, but good."

"Nervous?" Martin Dorsey asked. "How so?"

Quickly, Dorsey gave his father a rundown on his talk with Monsignor Gallard, its aftermath, and the impending conference. Two-thirds of the way through, Dorsey realized his father's cheery tone had him spilling his guts, but he did it anyway.

"A lot of it will be their perception and your appearance," Martin Dorsey said. "The meeting, I mean. You've testified in court; just conduct yourself like you're on the stand. No quick answers, just calm response. This reminds me of a fellow named Johnny Reardon. Maybe you remember him?"

"Don't recall."

"Johnny was a lawyer, had a small office, I think it was in Morningside. He handled local small-time offenders, mostly kids. Played the clarinet and applied his music to his law practice. His young clients were mostly anxious types, the kind who make fools of themselves when they testify. So Johnny taught them a three-note downbeat. Answer no question until you count three in your head, he always told them. They said that when Johnny had a real dolt for a client, Johnny would stand in the courtroom waving his finger like a baton. A-one-and-a-two-and-a-three."

"Nice system," Dorsey said. "If the kids could count that high."

"All systems have their flaws."

Dorsey silently concurred with that thought. "So, Mrs. Boyle gets me on the line for you. I can't help thinking this is official, but you sound like you're looking for a chat. What's up?"

"The project we discussed the last time you were here? I collected several advances today, unexpected ones. This thing is off and running."

"Congratulations," Dorsey said. "You always knew where the money was."

Martin Dorsey laughed. "I know where the money is. Are you going to let me show you the way? You said you might."

"Give me a few more days," Dorsey said, immediately thinking of Gretchen. "Things have been hectic around here, remember?"

"Find the time. Make the time," Martin Dorsey said. "I never pretended I was doing this without strings. This is for me, I told you that. So I can sit here in my office and tell myself I'm a great father, thoughtful enough to make a fortune for you. I want that as quick as I can have it and for as long as I can have it. So make up your mind."

At precisely twenty minutes before two o'clock, Dorsey left his house through the back and walked two blocks down the alley to where he had parked the car the night before. His steps were controlled and slow as he struggled with the tom-tom beat in his chest. In light afternoon traffic he cruised across the Tenth Street bridge and through the dim yellow light of the Armstrong Tunnel, emerging into the downtown area. He parked in a Ross Street lot near the courthouse and walked one block to his appointment, past the law offices that lined the sidewalk. Entering a large office building, he took the elevator to the eleventh floor. Bernie was waiting for him in the reception area.

"Good, we've got a few minutes." Bernie took him by the arm and led the way through a clerical area where three secretaries typed from dictation machines. Bernie smiled and waved as the two men passed.

"Easy, Bern," Dorsey said, freeing his arm and rubbing his elbow. Bernie closed the office door behind them. "It's been a rough couple of days."

"Keep your sense of humor, it may be all you have left." Bernie settled in behind his desk and motioned Dorsey into the visitor's chair. "No shit. I've been snooping around the halls for the last day and a half, trying to get some idea as to how this thing is going to go, and I've come up empty. Really, you better understand. A law firm is like any other business. There are few secrets anyone can keep. All the boys bullshit after work, and the young ones have a whole officeful of secretaries they're trying to impress. A little bombshell dropped in the ear of your favorite typist might go a long way, but not this time. I haven't heard one thing, except that I'll be in the room with you. Not to add anything but just to put you at ease. Show a friendly face, I was told."

"Jesus, Bern. Am I being bounced off this thing?"

"Who the hell knows?" Bernie said. "I can't find out dick about this one."

The telephone on Bernie's desk buzzed twice. He depressed a flashing button and lifted the receiver.

"Okay, right away." Bernie put the receiver in its cradle. "That was it, my friend. We're on."

CHAPTER 14

Despite these formal settings, of which I am rather proud, I think we should proceed informally. First names all around.''

George Everette depressed a blood-colored button on the arm of his chair, and a young secretary entered the room from a side door that blended into the sea-green wallpaper. She crossed the hunter-green carpet and took coffee orders from those seated at the table, which was cherrywood, matching the chair rail that circled the room. Everette, dressed in a double-breasted navy blazer with gold buttons, nodded and smiled around the table, as if approving each beverage choice. Bernie sat in muted light at the edge of the room. The secretary left.

"Mr. Dorsey," Everette said, addressing Dorsey across the width of the table, "my junior associate, Mr. Perlac, tells me your friends commonly refer to you as Dorsey. Will that be sufficient for this afternoon's purposes?"

"Dorsey's fine." Dorsey nodded anxiously to the five men already present. Surprised by his nervousness, he kept his trembling hands below the table, with no intention of lifting his coffee cup when it came. For a guy who was slapped around by a Neanderthal two days ago, he told himself, you're really taking the heat from these guys, even before they get started. You've been grilled by the best, P.I. Stockman among them. Take the old man's advice this one time. Answer slowly, be assured. Johnny Reardon is at the podium. A-one-and-a-two-and-a-three.

The secretary returned and served coffee from a silver tray in Lenox cups. Once finished, she took a seat by the far wall near Bernie, producing a pencil and steno pad as if from the air. Dorsey's coffee sat steaming, undisturbed.

"Ms. Chapman is my private secretary," Everette explained. He pushed a well-barbered tuft of gray hair into place at his temple. "If no one objects, she will keep the minutes. Copies will be furnished to each of you. No objections? Good, let's proceed."

Everette continued in his quiet tone, pointing to each of the men as he introduced them. "Let the minutes show that in attendance are myself; Raymond Corso of the Fidelity Casualty local office; John Munt, vice president of claims at the home office in Syracuse; Charles Cleardon of Calumet Corporation, the parent company; and Carroll Dorsey. Informally representing the District Attorney's office is William Meara."

Each man opened the manila folder that sat on the table in front of him, flipping through the contents. Also provided for each were pencils and a yellow legal pad.

"Before we discuss the investigation and the events of the last few days," Everette said, "I for one would like a little background from Mr. Corso—I mean Ray, sorry. You've entrusted a great many cases to Mr.—I mean Dorsey. Tell us how this came about."

Ray Corso was of average height but with a heavy stomach that strained his shirt buttons. He wore a full beard flecked with gray that offset his retreating hairline. Considering a response, he chewed at the stem of an unlit pipe. Slow-boat pipe-smoking asshole, Dorsey thought. How appropriate.

"Mr. Dorsey is highly qualified." Corso used the professional tone Dorsey had heard him adopt so often to hide his incompetence. "Well respected in his field and experienced. Just the man for the project we initiated last spring. These recent developments were never expected, but I stand on my choice of investigators."

"I'm missing something," John Munt said. "A special project?"

Dorsey summed up Munt as the long and lean athletic type, the kind who runs ten-kilometer races every other summer weekend. His receding hair gave him, unlike Corso, the look of healthy middle age. Dorsey decided he would look more natural in shorts with a number pinned to his T-shirt.

"Normally," Munt said, "special projects and the funds for them require a proposal to my office. Yesterday while preparing for this meeting I had my secretary pull all the correspondence between you and me for the last twelve months. It was routine: expense reports, claims reserving, a couple of pay increase recommendations. Nothing about a major project."

Corso ground his teeth into the pipestem. "That's true, that *is* the normal procedure. But you'll remember I instituted a rather severe austerity program over the last several years. We cut costs, paring down our staffing with no loss in efficiency. To be honest, my recent budget proposals were a little fat, to squirrel away some rainy-day money. Originally, anyway. I was able to finance this project strictly from within my office budget, so no proposal was needed. I was not requesting any additional funding."

"I'm aware of your expense savings," Munt said, smiling sheepishly. Dorsey sensed that Munt had been outmaneuvered, and his nerves began to ease. "As I recall," Munt said, "I wrote you a commendation letter."

"Yes, that's correct."

"A special project, that was the term you used?"

Charles Cleardon smiled a gentle apology for interrupting. With short straw-colored hair, he was Munt's physical match but wore a better suit. Dorsey priced it at three-fifty, rock bottom, on the back of a truck, double at retail. And throw in another two hundred for the alligator shoes. To Dorsey, his soft voice had the sound of old, comfortable money.

"You gentlemen will have to indulge me," Cleardon said. "I'm something of a fish out of water in these matters and I will require some guidance, especially with legal and insurance jargon. Ray, tell me about your project, and keep in mind that I am a novice."

"Well, Charles, we had a problem." Corso tapped the pipe bowl against his palm. "We were right where we wanted to be in terms of office expenses and staff, but in December of last year we noticed a disturbing trend in our reserving. It was going through the ceiling."

"Reserving?" Cleardon asked.

Dorsey listened as Corso explained that reserving was the art of estimating the expense that would be incurred by each ongoing claim in the upcoming year. His anxiety waned as the pace of the meeting hit a comfortable stride and he watched William Meara, the DA's man, studiously taking notes, oblivious to Ms. Chapman's shorthand. Heavily muscled through the chest, Meara sat with hunched shoulders as he worked at his yellow pad. His hair was dark, curly, and unmanaged, and his suit was bargain basement. Dorsey pegged him for a typical dark-Irish grunt lawyer.

"But what was the problem?" Cleardon asked.

Before Corso could reply, Munt interrupted. "If there was a serious problem, one that could result in a mess like this, home office should have been consulted."

"Yes, in hindsight you are correct." Corso spoke tactfully, accepting the rebuke and allowing Munt to save face. "But the problem we saw did not suggest any murky conspiracies, such as Dorsey seems to think we now have." Dorsey could feel Corso establishing distance between them. "We were faced with an extraordinary number of claims with very high expense potentials. Mostly auto and workers' compensation. Young and unskilled people, their youth the cause of the high liabilities. Extensive lost wages, that sort of thing. Investigations and settlements seemed the only way to control claim costs."

"So you hired Dorsey," Everette said. His index finger ran along the coffee cup's rim.

"On a case-by-case basis," Corso said. "Beginning in April, I believe."

"Along with reports," Munt said, "I had the bills pulled on

these assignments. They're high, much higher than average. Overnight stays and stiff hourly rates, with no half rates on travel time." Munt turned to Dorsey. "Are these your customary rates?"

"No, John," Dorsey said. "These are about fifteen dollars more per hour."

"So?" Munt now spoke to Corso.

"I offered this rate as an incentive," Corso said. We had some potentially serious trouble brewing with these claims, and I felt there was a need for more than the standard results. And it seems that Dorsey may have delivered, if what he has is correct."

Cover your ass, Dorsey said; make some space. His anxiety had passed and he was eager for the center ring. He wondered why it had not been forced on him already.

"Well," Munt said, "I'm not entirely sure what Dorsey is trying to prove. From what I can see we have a loose and circumstantial case that says a few claimants who know each other keep showing up at the same place. With this priest they worship."

Everette cleared his throat. "John's words are right on point. Circumstantial is correct. There is conjecture and opinion but little in the way of fact. Very intriguing; anything is possible. Dorsey, we need to know what you think is going on."

Johnny Reardon had his baton in hand and threw the downbeat. Dorsey moved with the baton, struggling with the urge to blurt out his thoughts. "Actually, I don't know. But I'm sure that *something* is going on. And it looks like something big. People are out of work, and the social classes are at war in the western half of the state, the haves and the have-nots. Maybe that's why I was attacked the other day, just another skirmish in the conflict. The priest and Jack Stockman would like to have the world think so, but there's more to it than that. This thing, this ripoff, is organized: the first element of a conspiracy."

"A little proof, please." Munt's eyes flashed angrily before they settled on his note pad. So he's pissed, Dorsey thought. Who can blame him? He's got you and your mess on his hands along with having to keep an eye on Corso. And now he has to sit here with Cleardon, the top dog.

"Yesterday I was followed. Not by anybody great, but good

enough to catch me after I switched cars on them. Thought I had it beat, but they were right with me. Took out my windshield to make their point."

"Anything else?" Meara asked his question without looking up from his notes.

"There's Stockman's connection to the priest." Dorsey figured Meara for a tough cross-examiner and chose not to play with him. He told the group of his conversation with Monsignor Gallard.

"Can't say I like this business about Stockman," Everette said. He turned to Munt and Cleardon. "For your edification, Jack Stockman is a top-flight plaintiff's attorney. He handles a high volume of workers' compensation cases, but personal injury and product liability are well within his area of expertise. Some judgments he has obtained for his clients have been staggering. Criminal law is not his long suit, but he would be a formidable opponent. And I don't relish the idea of raking a fellow attorney over the coals. It's always bad business."

"Perhaps the facts will eventually speak for themselves," Cleardon said.

"But right now the facts couldn't work up a good whisper on their own," Munt said.

"Well," Everette said, again clearing his throat. It made Dorsey wonder if the road to success started with a phlegm-free set of vocal cords. "I think," Everette said, "we all need to keep in mind the spirit of this meeting. We are here to determine the course we will take. Can I assume we are all in agreement that the investigation should continue? After all, we have a great deal of smoke. Surely there must be fire to be found somewhere. John? Charles? Suggestions or ideas?"

"Certainly we must continue." Cleardon held his cup to his lips, then returned it to its saucer without drinking. "My reason for attending this meeting must be made clear. My primary concern as a corporate officer is to protect the interests of our stockholders, our investors. Don't misunderstand, Calumet and Fidelity Casualty are rock solid. No financial problems exist and none are foreseen. But there is such a thing called the stockholders' comfort level, and that has to be maintained. I can't give them any reason to doubt the competency of the corporation's present administration. And I certainly don't want panic over adverse publicity, which is what we now have. Every newscast and morning paper these days carries a story of a worker let go and his family dispossessed. We can't afford to be smeared as a result of the general public's sympathies. Make no doubt about it, gentlemen, we can be made to look very, very bad. I need your assurance that this will not happen."

Dorsey was now in total control of himself. "I think I can help with that. Sam Hickcock, the local newscaster the networks are picking up, I've been avoiding him for a few days now and I can continue to do so—no problem. He'll keep on making noise, but he'll get no ammunition from me."

"See to it," Cleardon said.

"I think we all appreciate your concerns, Charles," Everette said, "and I'm sure I speak for all when I say this will be foremost in our minds as we proceed. Now, Dorsey, perhaps you can give us a brief outline of your plan of action."

"Might that not be a bit presumptuous?" Munt asked. "To me, there is still a question about Dorsey. We need to discuss whether or not he is the man for this job. Perhaps we should hire one of the larger firms; there are several good ones with local offices here in Pittsburgh. They could place several men on the job. It would be more expensive, but the results would be quicker. Also, Dorsey is known to these people. He can't help but draw attention to himself, what with this newsman on his tail."

"You have a point, John," Everette said. "That's a concern. Is Dorsey too compromised to continue as our investigator?"

All eyes turned to Dorsey, but he was too much at ease to be drawn into that bear trap. The hell with three notes, he told himself. You pass on this question. Keep your mouth shut and let the silence weigh on them. You've seen it before. Important people need fast answers; silence puts them in a sweat. If you don't give them answers, they provide their own, if only because time is so precious. Let's see who cracks. And let's hope whoever it is provides something to work with.

"I have to say I feel the bigger firm would be a mistake." It was Corso who spoke, to Dorsey the least likely source of support. "My experience with large firms has always been poor to mediocre. They can be inflexible. They have set ways and standards, which means another bureaucracy to deal with. We tell them a case has to be handled one way, and later we find out that our way doesn't jibe with their standard procedure. No doubt they'll assure us it can be done, but from experience I can tell you that nine times out of ten the word never reaches the investigator on the case. Or the billing clerk. All we'll get for our money is the standard report; uninformative and totally devoid of insight. If we had done that last spring instead of hiring Dorsey, we would never have obtained the information we must deal with today. I think Dorsey should remain on the job."

"Sensible," Everette said. In contemplation, he ran a finger across his chin. "But in fairness to John, you've provided only half a case. Using an agency does appear to be inappropriate in this instance. But you and I know there are a number of very competent independents in the city. Why not use one of them? Why must it be Dorsey?"

Cleardon broke in before Corso could answer. "Ray, please hold your thoughts. I would like to hear Dorsey plead his own case. After all, he hasn't had much of an opportunity to speak."

Dorsey let the downbeat pass and returned Cleardon's slick smile. "I'm the one to see this thing through because I'm in it up to my neck. I'm an independent, my own employer and owner of my own business. You, Charles, work on a much vaster scale, but I think you can see me as a fellow businessman. I have to look after business, and right now my business is on the line."

Cleardon's eyes roamed the table, apparently checking reactions. He nodded for Dorsey to continue.

"This thing can end three different ways for me," Dorsey said. "You could dump me now, and I'll have some lean days ahead. With some luck and hard work, I may bounce back, but for a while nobody will want to hire a guy who couldn't keep his face off of TV. There'll be a lot of jokes, but I'll get by and things will die down like they have a tendency to do. Then I'll be back to where I was a few months ago, which wasn't so good.

"Or," Dorsey went on, "you might keep me on the job and I screw up worse than I already have. More time on TV, picture in the paper, the whole deal. Maybe even a trumped-up harrassment suit. And that, Charles, would be the end of Dorsey. I'd be out. No work from any insurance company or law firm. In a very short time, I'd be a five-buck-an-hour rent-a-cop guarding a warehouse of empty beer kegs."

"And the third outcome?" Everette grinned, approving the performance.

"I stay on the case and wrap it up." Dorsey turned from Everette back to Cleardon. He was sure of the real seat of power and wanted to play to it. "I bring the whole thing down, whatever the whole thing turns out to be. Maybe even deliver enough for a few convictions. The priest would take a fall and so might Stockman. As for me, I'd be set for good. I'd come out of this looking great. If Stockman goes down, I'll be a hero. He's burned a lot of people, both adjusters and lawyers. Those guys would all throw work my way, wanting to be my friend."

"I mentioned Jack before," Everette said. "I'm not sure I like his being entangled in this."

"Me neither," Dorsey said. "He scares the living hell out of me. He's the best: clever and slippery. And his reputation goes with him into the courtroom. He's a leg up on the defense before the trial begins. But evidence on him might tie his ankle to the plaintiff's table."

Everette lowered his head to ponder, Corso fiddled with his pipe, and Munt looked defeated. Cleardon smiled, and Meara raised his pencil to take the floor.

"Let's be clear on this." Meara squared his shoulders and adjusted his suit jacket, still buttoned. "If there is a criminal fraud case coming out of this investigation, Dorsey, either I or an assistant DA from another county will be seeking indictments, using evidence you've uncovered. So I speak for myself *and* my counterparts, because the rules of evidence don't change from county to county. What you have so far isn't going to cut it. If this is all you can come up with, don't knock on my door. If these people have something going, there'll be damned little about it written down on paper. No agreements signed in blood. You say you're good. So tell me what I need."

"Testimony." Dorsey spoke softly and turned to each of them to be sure it registered. "That's what Bill has in mind. Somebody to tell the whole sad tale to a grand jury, maybe even at trial. Somebody who can say he was part of it and saw it happen. Who can say so-and-so thought it all up. And if there is some paper somewhere, bank slips or anything that shows money changing hands, this informant can lead us to it. Bill, am I right?"

"Essentially, that's the general idea." Meara stayed in his interrogator's demeanor. "This is not going to be an easy one. Again, if you bring me crap, I don't know your name."

Everette allowed a moment for Meara's words to have their full effect. "Well, let's go around the table on this. As far as Dorsey's staying on the job goes, I have only minor reservations: He is known to the—uh, opposition and the TV fellow, Hickcock." He turned to Meara. "Bill, you're here on observer status, so I'll ask you to pass on the voting. But let's hear from the rest."

It began with Corso, but Dorsey paid only faint attention. Only one man will make this decision, he thought; the rest is blue smoke and mirrors. The man who holds the purse strings and traveled all this way to see me in the flesh: let's get to him.

Munt began to speak his piece but Cleardon cut him off. "Dorsey stays," he said.

Silently, Dorsey thanked the hand on the purse strings.

Cleardon spoke firmly, leaving no room for debate. He slid his thumb and forefinger up and down his coat lapel, a gambler calling the hand. "Excuse me," Cleardon said, "all of you. George asked for an informal meeting, with our rank insignia left in the cloakroom, and up until now I've agreed wholeheartedly. But we've just entered the realm of decision-making and responsibility-taking. I'm senior corporate officer; only the CEO carries a greater burden of accountability. The reason I'm here is because of the gravity of this situation, especially in the area of public relations. Because of these concerns and the importance of this decision, I've decided to make it myself. Dorsey stays. From the proper perspective, you should all feel very liberated. In the event Dorsey lets us down, I'm the only one on the hook for it."

"It's a real possibility," Munt said. "Letting us down, I mean."

Cleardon folded his hands on the table and faced Munt. "John, you've stated your concerns and reservations, and as of now I am rejecting them. Unless some major crisis develops, it is my decision to stick with Dorsey to the end of the line. That's final."

Dorsey gripped the table's edge, steadying himself against the urge to yell in triumph. It's yours, he told himself, right to the end of the line! Everette gave him a smile and a nod. Corso fumbled with his pipe, and it fell to the tabletop with a clatter. He took Cleardon's hint, Dorsey thought; he's liberated. His own neck was stretched and might still be after Cleardon's dressing-down of Munt. Ah, fuck 'em both, you got the case. Bernie, who had been sweating throughout the meeting, waved to Dorsey and quickly excused himself.

"I'm glad this is decided." Meara rested his pencil at last. "And now that it is, I need to point a few things out to all of you. We really have to avoid any false expectations in this matter."

"You're correct, Bill," Everette said. "Please speak your mind."

"This is fraud we're talking about, and testimony must be the cornerstone of any potential case. But we have other elements of the crime to prove as well. These have to be willful, deliberate acts. The priest and his friends have to have a clear plan. Nothing written down, but a joint understanding and intent among the actors. And the money has to add up. If this is only a few bucks skimmed to feed the unemployed, my office won't touch it.

"One last thing," Meara added. "Dorsey could be wrong. I'm warning you, my office will not participate in an attempt to manu-facture evidence to fit the theory."

"Understood." Cleardon nodded his commitment to Meara but kept his eyes on Dorsey. "Dorsey, you have your case. Coordinate things with Ray. He'll give you any help you need."

Everette took up the cue. "Well, then, we have wrapped up our business for this afternoon. I thank each of you for your time."

CHAPTER 15

Cruising across the bridge back to South Side, Dorsey brooded over Meara's words. Testimony was needed, and he had to find the person who was willing, or could be made willing, to provide it.

Dorsey considered the candidates. Radovic was out. What devotion, he's ready to sprout angel's wings streaked with slag dust. And Damjani was too incomplete a person to experience guilt or remorse. Movement Together finds its strength as a holy crusade, not as a labor union. But there must be someone, just one. There always is. One whose motives are not completely golden. One who can be leaned on.

It struck Dorsey as he unlocked his front door. Without taking a moment to remove his jacket, he dropped into the desk chair, wheeled himself to the file cabinet, and thumbed his way through the middle drawer. When he found the folder he was after, he wheeled back to the desk, spread the file's contents across the blotter, and dialed the number in the top left corner of Dr. Tang's stationery. Recognizing the receptionist's voice, he asked if she remembered him. She laughed at the question.

"Who could forget your visit?" She spoke in a hushed voice. "Took the doctor three days before he was himself again. But it broke the monotony around here. You want another appointment?"

Dorsey laughed too, telling her he never tried twice to piss off a guy who was handy with a scalpel. "That friend of yours, Claudia. I stopped by her place when I was up there. You were right, she takes long vacations."

"She's home now." The receptionist gave Dorsey a disgusted grunt. "Bitch makes me sick. Rest of us tryin' to chase down some decent work, and she gets a tan."

"Unemployed?"

"Free as a bird and getting three squares from her mother."

"Give me her number," Dorsey said. "In case I need to get hold of her."

After the call was finished, Dorsey ran through the answering machine tape. There had been only one caller: Sam Hickcock. He apologized again for the doorstep coverage and then suggested that Dorsey watch Channel Three at ten-thirty. If you want, Hickcock said, you can appear on next week's show.

"Fuck you and your show," Dorsey muttered.

Bernie took a Michelob from the office refrigerator, lingered a moment to consider the photos of Dorsey in his various basketball uniforms, then crossed the room and fell backward onto the chaise. With his legs stretched across the desktop and still wearing his now-crumpled suit jacket, Dorsey watched Bernie and awaited his critique of the meeting.

"Good job, but face it, you didn't do it alone." Bernie stared out the window at Wharton Street, now dark with the early November evening. "I'm happy for you and, yes, you did handle that hard-ass Meara pretty well. But the deck was stacked. Corso never puts himself out for anyone, friend or relative. Yet the guy goes on the chopping block for you. The rich guy, Cleardon, he probably got a kick out of slumming with you and figured he might like to come back for more sometime. But Corso surprised the hell out of me."

Dorsey waved off Bernie's concerns and swung his feet to the floor. "In some ways you're right, Corso shook the shit out of me too. I liked what he said about me, but that wasn't him at the table. Could be he was running scared and figured his only chance was to tough it out."

"Hell, I don't know." Bernie massaged the bridge of his nose, his eyes shut tight. "The guy has always been slippery. For my money he's a thief, steals his salary. Shook his hand at a meeting once and a friend suggested I count my fingers afterward. Always has that slow thoughtful answer to every question, like there's really something going on inside his head."

Dorsey sipped his beer and worked through his unopened mail. "Met Corso at a meeting, huh? When was this?"

"A year, maybe eighteen months ago," Bernie said. "We were set for trial on a personal injury case. Corso was to arrange for some expert testimony from this vocational specialist, but he fucked up." Bernie paused momentarily. "Or so I thought."

Dorsey ripped the seam of an envelope with his thumbnail. "How could he fuck up a voc expert?"

"Plaintiff was a pharmacist who ripped up his right hand when he fell in a bar and put the hand through a glass tabletop. It was one of those fern bars downtown; the tables were those wrought-iron and plate-glass deals. The pharmacist was fresh from work, so he was still sober. And four witnesses were willing to testify that a waitress had just spilled a tray of drinks near the table not ten minutes before. So the liability was undeniable."

"Go on." Dorsey knew the defense, which was no defense. Just try to settle as low as possible. With a pen, he underlined the total on his electric bill. "How bad was the hand?"

Bernie shook his head. "Total functional loss. Two fingers they couldn't sew back on and severed tendons in the thumb. Total washout. So, liability and damages are established. And the plaintiff's attorney, guy named Kendall, he plans on hitting us extra hard on the issue of lost future wages. He makes it clear up front that he considers his client disabled for life. No more working, period. The guy was a drugstore pharmacist for eleven years, and supposedly that was all he could do. Bunch of bullshit is what it was."

"Had a point." Dorsey grinned. "No more diet pills, no more Ortho-Novum products to hand out. But he could fall back on his other skills, like selling Styrofoam coolers and hair dryers. From what I see, that's half the job."

"The man was educated and could've used his skills elsewhere," Bernie half shouted. "Knows the sciences, chemistry and all. And he knew enough medicine not to poison anyone for eleven years on the job. Think he couldn't do anything else? Tell you what, he could've been a great claims examiner. The man could save an insurance company a bundle doing hospital audits. We had to pay; shit, that was obvious. But this Kendall, he wanted to soak us."

"So the vocational expert was to show that the lost future wage figure was unreasonable. He was to prove the guy could get another job."

"You got it." Bernie, in a movement made awkward by his anger, pulled himself to a sitting position and faced Dorsey. "And it was Corso's job to hire the expert. Kendall let the voc expert evaluate his man, no problem. Which should have tipped me off. The court would have made him comply, but he should have put up a fuss for appearances, show his client how tough he is."

"So, how'd it turn out?" Dorsey moved on to a notice from the county tax assessor.

"Prick crossed us," Bernie said. "Corso finds this hack with a master's degree and all those little letters behind his name that lets him charge a fee. This master's degree interviews the pharmacist for a couple of hours, runs him through some aptitude tests, and files a ten-page report and a six-hundred-dollar fee. And the report says the pharmacist will never work again unless he is completely retrained. Any chance of a fair settlement was gone. We paid through the nose."

"Got stiffed. It happens." Dorsey shrugged his shoulders and looked back at his sports photos. Involuntarily, he flexed his arthritic fingers. "By and large, Corso is an asshole, you'll get no argument from this corner. And in your case he picked the wrong guy. Unless you think there's more to it."

Bernie rose and paced across the front of the desk, reminding Dorsey of a schoolboy being forced to admit a prank. "I figured the same: we got burned by our own expert. And, yes, it does happen. But early this year, February, I was having lunch with this other guy in the firm, name of Millender. He handles divorces. So we're bullshittin' and he tells me he's got this case where the husband is being hit for child support payments so high he needs a second job. And the payments are based on an earnings-potential study done by a vocational expert hired by the wife's lawyer. And the lawyer is Kendall. And the voc man is the same one who burned me on the pharmacist."

"Keep going," Dorsey said. "You've captured my interest."

"Millender tells me Kendall has been using this vocational hack for years. You know, the hack estimates the husband's wage potential, and he and Kendall cook up a high child-support demand. But the point here is that Kendall and the hack have been in cahoots. And the hack is the guy Corso hires."

Dorsey watched Bernie move about the room; he felt Bernie's eyes cutting through him. So Corso maybe sold a case, Bernie's case. He just fucks up, or so it looks. And Kendall provides a kickback. "Ever tell anybody about this?"

"Tell somebody what?" Bernie gazed out the window at the street, aglow with the light of mercury lamps. "No proof, just the association between the hack and Kendall."

Dorsey leaned forward and planted his elbows on the corners of the blotter. His chin rested in his cupped hands as his fingertips worked at his fatigued eyes. "I know, Bern, I know. But in the meantime, I'm stuck with Corso, who you tell me I can't trust. Maybe on this one he'll be too frightened of Munt and Cleardon to put out a palm to be greased. Hopefully."

Bernie took his suit jacket from the back of the chair, slipped it on, and straightened his tie, concentrating on the empty far wall as if it held a mirror. Dorsey tore open the last piece of mail and read the two-line message.

"Hold it a sec," Dorsey said, rising from his seat and holding out the letter for Bernie's inspection. "Before you're out the door, look this over. You know a lawyer named Preach, Louis Preach? He's called a couple or three times leaving messages on the tape. Sounds black on the phone."

"Naw, he's new to me," Bernie said, taking the letter. "Says you two ought to get together. It could be of mutual benefit."

"Figured him to be representing one of the Movement people," Dorsey said. "That's why I haven't bothered returning his calls."

Bernie folded the letter and dropped it on the desk. "Lemme ask a friend, a guy I know at the county Bar Association office. See what Preach is all about. I'll call you when I have something."

"Don't forget the TV program tonight," Dorsey said. "Gonna catch it? Might want to pick your brain about it."

"Can't say." Bernie was in the hall, fishing in his pocket for his car keys. "If I'm still awake at ten-thirty."

In the kitchen, Dorsey put a cassette into the portable player, spent a few calm moments resting against the counter admiring George Shearing's touch at the keyboard, and then dug into the refrigerator for half a used onion and some bologna wrapped in white butcher paper.

So maybe Corso sold a case, he thought, slicing down the onion. Just maybe, now; there's no proof. You always figured him for lazy, maybe he's a thief too. Dorsey took an iron skillet from the cupboard. Maybe he's ambitious, like most everybody else. You always figured he moved from company to company to cover his incompetence. Maybe it was his crimes he's trying to avoid. Naw, that's impossible. Nobody could keep that up for long.

Dorsey broke the sliced onion into thin rings and tossed them into the skillet, allowing them to pop in their own juice. He stripped the skins from the bologna slices and cut four tiny slits in each slice, then added the slices to the onion. Watching the meat brown and curl evenly at the slits, he gently turned the onion with a fork. George Shearing glided through "Lullaby of Birdland."

Concentrate on Cleardon now, Dorsey told himself. You're

his choice, not Corso's anymore. He's the man to please. And if you do, you're his man, right to the end of the line.

Dorsey made two sandwiches of bologna, onions, bread, and ketchup and ate at the table. From his hip pocket he took the torn page of notebook paper and again read Claudia's telephone number. It was a start, he decided. The only way to go, as a matter of fact. Claudia Maynard was the obvious choice. She's in no danger of losing the house or having to feed the kids from the food bank. And she gets a couple of months at the seashore for faithful service to the Movement. Tipping Radovic to a layoff doesn't rate that kind of payment. There must be others she helped out. And Fidelity Casualty is the carrier at the mill.

Dorsey went to the office and wrote himself a note to call Corso in the morning and ask him to pull all the comp files on Carlisle Steel employees. Let's see how many friends Claudia Maynard has made, he thought. He also played with the idea of asking Corso if he'd had lunch with Attorney Kendall lately, but decided to stick to business. While writing the note, the telephone rang and Dorsey allowed three rings to pass, listening to the metallic click of the answering machine. It was Gretchen's voice.

"Hold on," Dorsey said, grabbing the receiver. "It's me, I'm here."

"Thank God. I love you, but I hate your voice on tape."

"You're running awfully late."

"Four-car pileup on the Fort Pitt bridge," Gretchen said. Ambulance drivers brought them all here; worked on six people myself. Lucky we were so close. Otherwise, two of them wouldn't have made it."

"You ready to get out of there? Should I come for you?"

"One of the nurses is giving me a lift to my place. I'm beat, done in. Tomorrow's an off day and I may spend it in bed." Gretchen paused. "So tell me, how'd it go?"

"Still on the job," Dorsey said. "The head man, he gave me his seal of approval, and the rest reluctantly fell in line." Now Dorsey paused. "You and the nurse keep an eye out, okay?"

"Seriously?"

"For safety's sake," Dorsey said.

"Really, just try to relax." Gretchen's voice was laced with fatigue. "What about tomorrow, you'll be over?"

"Sure," Dorsey said. "One o'clock. How would you feel about taking a ride with me? Up into the mountains?"

Gretchen laughed. "What do you have in mind, a day trip to Wyoming?"

Dorsey returned the laugh. "Something more local, like Johnstown. Those are mountains, technically. You could be of help."

"Business, huh?" Gretchen asked. "I'll sleep on it. Love you. Sleep well."

Dorsey put down the receiver and checked his watch: ten-twenty. He stripped his necktie from beneath his collar and let it fall to the floor. She could help, he told himself. If you can't get through to Maynard, maybe Gretchen can, just by being there. Make you look like less of a monster. It's a shitty position to put Gretchen in, but this is for her too. She may not see it that way, but she's got a stake in this. Swing Maynard over, and the rest could fall into line. She gives up her part in the scheme, comes up with some names, and we can squeeze them. Or maybe at that point Meara can do the squeezing. Whichever, we win.

At ten-thirty, Dorsey turned on Channel Three, adjusting the volume. The screen showed a series of Pittsburgh neighborhood scenes followed by some quick frames of farms and pasture. A voice-over announced the beginning of "The Western Pennsylvania Report." The footage ended and Sam Hickcock appeared on camera.

Hickcock greeted his electronic audience, advising them that this was the local area's only magazine of the air and that tonight's report would cover the state milk pricing board's impact on local dairy farmers and a Clarion County man who sculpted heads from apples. Jesus, Dorsey thought, apple heads covered by Sam Hickcock, that no-nonsense reporter?

"Before we get to these stories," Hickcock said, "we have another report concerning the area's vast numbers of unemployed. In this installment we'll speak briefly with Father Andrew Jancek, director of Movement Together."

There was an awkward jump in the television screen, telling Dorsey it was a videotaped interview. Hickcock, in the same suit, sat in a swivel chair. After a few opening remarks, he introduced Father Jancek, who sat opposite him dressed in a black clerical suit and Roman collar, his silver beard well trimmed.

"Father Jancek, you are certainly no stranger to those of us in the media or, for that matter, to our viewers," Hickcock said, gesturing to the notes held by the clipboard on his lap. "Just the same, give us a brief statement on the goals of Movement Together."

"I'd be more than happy to do so." Father Jancek spoke softly, conversationally. "Primarily, we are attempting to restore dignity to a large section of society. I don't want to bore you with figures concerning the local unemployed and homeless; I'm sure every member of the viewing audience knows at least one worker who has lost his job. We intend to reverse this trend and restore these jobs, which were needlessly lost because of the refusal of local corporations and banking institutions to invest in the local economy—to reinvest in the workers, the original source of their riches."

Hickcock posed with a finger to his lips, as if taking a moment to absorb the priest's comments. Illusion, Dorsey knew; the man is a master of illusion. And the priest runs a close second, gaining on him from the left.

"The jobs have been lost needlessly?" Hickcock asked. "Could you elaborate on that?"

"It's a matter of investment." Father Jancek held out his palms, indicating the issue's simplicity. "Steel companies, other large manufacturers, and our banks are not reinvesting their enormous profits locally, profits that since the beginning of the Industrial Revolution have been generated by factory and mill workers. Mills are not repaired and modernized, and I would challenge anyone to name one large manufacturer who has recently opened a plant in western Pennsylvania. Granted, we had Volkswagen come here, but expectations were greater than reality. Rather than returning their profits to the local economy, businessmen have invested them in industry overseas. Movement Together wants to see the money come back here."

"There has been some criticism of your methods." Hickcock ran his finger through a number of items in his notes. "Rotten fish left in bank deposit boxes, pickets outside the homes and churches of executives, closed factories blockaded to prevent demolition."

"Sam, I must state right now that I do not believe there is a man alive who is evil." Father Jancek's eyes cut to slits and he pointed at Hickcock as if instructing a student. "Blind, yes; we have those men among us. I think our corporate leaders number among the blind. We are trying to give them vision, to enable them to see the misery that surrounds them. We have invited them to Braddock and Homestead to see the houses of the dispossessed, but they decline. So we have to bring the poverty and despair to them.

"The demonstrations at the mills were originally conceived as symbolic acts of our purpose and resolve. But we realized that if we wish to rebuild the area, we had to save the physical plants. Otherwise, there would be nothing to build on. The mills must remain standing. Without them, we might as well throw in the towel."

"Lately, we've heard some distinctly political sounds coming from your camp." Hickcock shifted in his seat and smiled at the priest. "As we understand it, you're a resident of Westmoreland County, in Congressman Dayton's district. He's been a supporter of yours."

"In word only," Father Jancek said. A little too eagerly, Dorsey thought. "His actions have been disappointing. His office has not generated any new legislation to protect the jobs and homes of his constituents. I don't think he can count on the workingman's vote any longer. The seat is up for election next year. Perhaps a more responsive candidate will emerge, I don't know."

Hickcock thanked the priest and turned to the camera. The screen jumped as the videotape ended, and the live Hickcock reappeared and was followed by a dog food commercial.

So the priest goes to Washington, Dorsey thought, on Fidelity Casualty's money. Maybe it wasn't the original plan, but Father Jancek's going to run. He and Stockman have a war chest, and they'll kill Dayton in the May primary. All that dough, and it goes for TV time, billboards, buttons, and straw hats. Jesus Christ.

The telephone rang. Thinking it might be Gretchen having changed her mind, Dorsey picked it up on the second ring.

"The priest is very convincing." It was Cleardon. "Better get going. Don't let me down."

CHAPTER 16

Pacing the office carpet, Dorsey checked his wristwatch for the third time in five minutes. C'mon, Corso, he thought, jiggling his car keys in his pocket. You're late. You're slow and you're late. It suddenly struck Dorsey that it was silly to worry about being late to a job he was sure to detest.

Sixteen minutes later, at half past noon, Dorsey watched from the window as a bicycle messenger pedaled his way down Wharton, braking to a stop at the front steps. Dorsey met the boy at the door and recognized him as the messenger who had delivered the dictaphone.

"Do I gotta wait again?" the boy asked. "Last time you held me up a long while. Beat hell outa my schedule. Work on volume, ya know? Only make money when the wheels are rolling."

The boy was thin with a deeply pocked face. Dorsey watched him adjust some greasy blond hair under a railroad bandanna and was reminded of a junkie he had run across while with the sheriff's office. He had met the guy twice, the first time in a Braddock housing project when the junkie denied any part in a string of East

End burglaries. The second encounter was in the morgue, all blue lips and frozen limbs. He had died in a sitting position, and the coroner's crew had had to break his legs to straighten him onto the stretcher.

"Hey, kid. You got any relatives in Braddock who were—" Dorsey held his tongue. "Skip it and hand over the package."

The delivery consisted of a fourteen-by-eleven-inch padded envelope. Dorsey slit the edge and allowed the contents to spill out on his desk. Stapled to the front of a manila folder was a two-line memo from Corso reminding Dorsey that clipping services were expensive. Flipping through the pages, Dorsey found articles on Father Jancek from the two Pittsburgh dailies, a local Catholic weekly, newspapers in Beaver and Westmoreland counties, and a feature article from *The New York Times*. He was tempted to sit down and review the material at length, a temptation born from both his curiosity and his wish to avoid the work he had cut out for the afternoon. He overcame the urge. After checking Wharton Street by peeking through the curtains, Dorsey left the house. On the way to the Buick to pick up Gretchen, he formulated an excuse for being forty minutes late.

As he had promised Gretchen, Dorsey took the scenic route to Johnstown, along U.S. 30 and through the Laurel Mountains and the Ligonier Valley. He drove in an anxious silence, oblivious to the panoramic views. At the far end of the front seat, huddled under a quilted comforter, Gretchen paged her way through the fourth edition of Cawle on *Fractures, Strains, and Sprains*.

Intimidation—frightening people—had never been Dorsey's bag, and he knew it. During his days as a county detective he had left the role of heavy to his partner, choosing to be the understanding cop, willing to listen to the suspect's story. Now he had no partner to play the villain, making threats that were based only loosely on truth. You've got to scare the shit out of this girl, he reminded himself. She's got what you want, and you have to get it.

"There may be a new procedure in here," Gretchen said,

mercifully invading his thoughts. "For your hand, I mean. You know, to give you more flexibility. A second coming for the running hook shot."

"Thought you wanted to see the foliage. That's why we came this way."

"Sorry." Gretchen pulled the comforter tight at her chin against the mountain cold. "Can you get a little more out of the heater? I'm freezing." She reached from beneath the comforter and poked Dorsey in the ribs. "And another thing. You owe me some explanation as to where we're going and how I'm to help."

Dorsey slowed the Buick to thirty-five as he passed through Jennerstown, then gunned it to sixty once past the village limits. At the junction of U.S. 219 he headed north. "Here it is," Dorsey said. "Remember me mentioning a girl named Claudia Maynard? Well, I want to talk to her. I want her to confess to a few things. Not to everything she may have done in her life, but certainly to a few things. And she won't do that just by me asking her to. I've got to make her think she's in hip-deep shit, maybe even looking at some jail time. Which isn't likely, but what the hell? It's the only way I know to do it."

"How am I supposed to help with that?" Gretchen asked. "Forget it, don't answer. I won't be part of it."

"You could help the girl through it, provide a little comfort at the right time. Soften the blow. It could be rough on her."

"That's crap."

No shit, Dorsey thought, passing the exit to Scalp Level and watching for the one to Mundys Corners. It's crap, but it's going to happen. Give the girl your compassion, Gretchen; be the good guy to my bad one. She may tell you what she won't tell me. Protect her from me. Jesus Christ, help me.

In the high country around Johnstown it had begun to snow, and by the time Dorsey parked in front of the Maynard house a quarter inch had accumulated. The walkway was snow-covered, and Gretchen and Dorsey held on to each other for balance as they made their way to the front door.

"Go 'way," Mrs. Maynard said. Only her right eye and cheek were visible through the space allowed by the door's safety chain.

"We see you on the TV. The news. Go 'way or I call the police."

Dorsey moved away from the door and introduced Gretchen, hoping the sight of her would calm the old woman. "We're just following up," Dorsey said, "on the job I was on before. I'd like to speak to Claudia about this Radovic fellow."

"Bullshit, Radovic." The eye at the door turned mean. "Trouble for Claudia because of that damned priest. She should stay away from that priest. I said that before, the last time you showed up. I tell her that too. But she don't listen."

"Maybe we could talk to her about that," Gretchen said. "For her own good."

"Hell you would. She's not home anyway."

"She go somewhere special?" Dorsey asked.

"That damned priest." Mrs. Maynard shut the door.

Back in the car, after turning over the engine and adjusting the heater, Dorsey suggested to Gretchen that he just might know where Claudia could be found. "Like the old lady said." Dorsey chuckled. "That damned priest."

He drove south to the lip of the crater that held Johnstown at its basin and began the descent, playing at the brakes for both his and Gretchen's peace of mind. At the bottom, by a now-quiet foundry, they crossed a WPA-vintage bridge of gray steel that spanned an offshoot of the Conemaugh River and went left, pulling onto Otterman Avenue. Once he found Radovic's house, Dorsey retraced the route he followed on the day of the surveillance until he found himself in front of the Movement Together office. He pulled to the opposite curb, halfway down the block.

"Now you can earn your first private-eye solo hours," Dorsey said, turning to Gretchen. "You're going inside because I can't; Radovic may be in there minding the store. And the girl may just be there too, based on what her mother said. If she is, we wait for her to leave and then we follow."

"How am I supposed to pull this off?" Gretchen shook off the thought and laughed. "I don't even know what she looks like."

"Neither do I," Dorsey said. "So you have to snoop around a little. Play up to them and find out who's who. These guys love attention, so give it to them. Ask some questions. Play a role, like a small-town reporter; better yet, be a social worker. I like that. Somebody who could refer others to the Movement. Yeah, try that."

Reluctantly, Gretchen left the car and crossed the street, using the comforter like a shawl to cover her head against the falling snow. Dorsey watched her in the rearview mirror as she entered the storefront, praying she would relax, coaching her. Take your time, check out the wall posters, look at the pamphlets. Cool and casual.

If this craps out, Dorsey reminded himself, you're in trouble. You may hate what you're about to do, but screw it up and you're in for a long haul. It will mean backtracking over old ground, looking for an opening in any of the claims you've handled since spring. The investigation goes flat and you'll be out on your ass. The only people willing to hire you will be lawyers and claims managers who have spent the last few weeks out of the country.

Again in the rearview, Dorsey saw Gretchen emerge from the storefront and make her way across the street. A part of him hoped she had failed, hoped she had come up empty. No, she learned something in there; she's too bright to have missed anything. She'll get us to the girl. And then you'll do your part. No choice.

"Had the pleasure of meeting Carl." Gretchen slipped into the passenger seat and adjusted the comforter around her. "He's a tough one. I asked a few questions, but all he did was point at a stack of leaflets." She held a handbill out to Dorsey. "But I think I found something. They're calling it an Outreach Meeting. It's this afternoon in Ebensburg. Where's that?"

"Just a little north, not far." He looked at the handbill. "The address is familiar, too. It's the mineworkers' local. Used to go there a lot. There's three attorneys with an office on the second floor. It's a large old house that's been renovated. The attorneys have a corner on the comp cases."

"So what do you think?" Gretchen asked. "Are we going?"

"We're going."

The snow was falling heavier now, and Dorsey slipped the Buick into second gear to climb out of the crater. Gretchen went back to her textbook, and Dorsey's stomach churned acid as the confrontation grew closer. To distract himself, he told Gretchen about his first visit to Ebensburg.

Dorsey was with the Allegheny County detectives at the time and had received a call from the Cambria County sheriff's office about a prisoner in the Ebensburg jail. The prisoner was named Sturgis and was serving a sentence of two years minus a day, the longest sentence allowed in a Pennsylvania county jail, for murder by vehicle. The Cambria sheriff had told Dorsey over the phone that Sturgis wanted to sell information on an auto theft ring in Pittsburgh. In return, Sturgis wanted someone to whisper in the sentencing judge's ear that he should get work-release privileges. "So he can work half a day," the deputy said, "and screw his girlfriend the other half. You're welcome to him, but you'll have to come up here. Too expensive to deliver."

Dorsey and his partner had made the trip to Ebensburg and interviewed Sturgis at the jail. The plan had been to grill Sturgis with Dorsey's partner as the heavy, but one look at the man told them he was forty pounds overweight and fifty points below the average intelligence quotient. Sturgis told them not about an auto theft ring but, instead, how a single car had been stolen by his brother-in-law three years earlier: a '71 Impala taken from the Civic Arena parking lot during a hockey game.

In Ebensburg, which unlike Johnstown was set on a hilltop, Dorsey turned onto a side street lined with once-elegant homes, large wooden structures with wraparound porches. Halfway along the block, he pulled to the curb and directed Gretchen's attention to the house at the end. At the edge of the porch, just out of the snow, two men dressed in heavy coats and woolen caps held handbills and searched the street for any interested party.

"Snow's put a damper on things," Dorsey said.

"Well," Gretchen said, "tell me what you have in mind."

"We find the girl." Dorsey shifted in his seat to face Gretchen. "You're at bat again. Go inside and snoop. Like I said, I've been there before. Through the door you'll be in a big central hall with a receptionist's desk and a waiting room off to the left. Looks like it might have been the living room once. Play your role and see what you come up with. Ask around for the girl if you have to."

"Can't say I like this a lot, but it *is* interesting." Gretchen smiled and slipped smoothly from the car, again covering her head with the comforter. The men on the porch, stomping their feet to keep warm, forced handbills on Gretchen and ushered her to the front door.

Moments after Gretchen had stepped inside, a late-model Omni came down the street from behind Dorsey, moving much too fast for the snow, fishtailing as it passed the Buick. Dorsey watched the driver, an attractive dark-haired young woman who looked to be in her mid-twenties, emerge from the car after accomplishing an awkward parking maneuver in front of the corner house. Dressed in close-fitting jeans and a belted suede jacket, she waved off the greeters and trotted across the porch into the building. Moments later, Gretchen stepped out onto the porch and hurried back to the Buick.

"Got her," Gretchen said. To Dorsey she sounded as if she liked the hunt, now that she had a whiff of the prey.

"She's in there?"

"Just arrived." Gretchen wiped snow from her lashes and eyebrows. "The dark-haired one who just walked in." She grinned slyly. "The good-looking one."

"You're sure?"

"Positive," Gretchen said. "There were three guys at a card table looking pretty bored, complaining how the weather had kept people away. But when the girl walked in they all snapped to, all smiles and optimism. Hi, Claudia, good to see you. How was the shore? She just smiles and drinks it all in and then mentions she can only stay a second, so many things to do. That's why I left. We follow her, right?"

Jesus, Dorsey thought, she *is* enjoying this! Early success, clean and easy, with the dirty work still to come. How will she like it then? Much less than you will, Dorsey.

"That's her." Gretchen tapped at his forearm and gestured toward the union building. "Here she comes."

Dorsey turned over the engine and watched Claudia Maynard

give the man on the porch a quick good-bye and climb into the Omni. Recklessly, she fishtailed again as she pulled from the curb. Dorsey moved out behind her, slowly. The Omni made two left turns, then was forced to halt at a red light. With no cars between them, Dorsey had no choice but to pull up directly behind. It's okay, he assured himself. You can drop the precautions because the girl takes none. She's a fool, or chooses to act as one. Drives like a fool, and like a fool doesn't hide her association with the priest. Lording it over the men at the union local and spending the Movement's money on trips and clothes. She's ready to be taken with one sharp blow. Which you will deliver.

The light turned green. The Omni and the Buick both turned onto a street lined with shops and offices. Following the girl, Dorsey watched Gretchen from the edge of his vision. She leaned forward into the dashboard and studied Claudia through the Omni's rearview mirror.

"Something you want to share?" Dorsey asked.

"Look at her," Gretchen said. "She's a live wire, primping in the mirror. I'll bet she's blasting the radio, from the way she's jumping around. Looks shallow, like she's in over her head and doesn't realize it. You won't have trouble talking to her."

Really into it, Dorsey thought, aren't you? More than one young woman might be in over her head.

Dorsey followed the girl out of the business district, heading for an on-ramp leading to U.S. 219 southbound. Lagging behind but keeping the Omni's taillights just visible through the falling snow, Dorsey saw the turn signal flicker and the Omni climbed the on-ramp, accelerating. Dorsey did the opposite.

"Why are you slowing down?" Gretchen asked. "You'll lose her."

"It's okay." Dorsey moved up the ramp in low gear, letting the right tires dig into the berm for traction. You smell blood, Gretchen, and you're getting overanxious. Wait until you taste it. You may have other thoughts. "Once we're on the four-lane we'll catch her. Even in the snow, we can keep her in sight. We can sit in the lane right next to her and she'll never guess."

The two southbound lanes were snow-covered but empty of

traffic, so Dorsey moved to their center, where the dotted line would be. Now he hit the accelerator, taking comfort in the extra space on either side of him in case of a spin-out. At her end of the front seat, Gretchen slapped at the dashboard and urged him on. A mile farther the Buick fishtailed, but Dorsey went with the slide and corrected his course. "It's okay, we're all right," he said and realized only he needed reassurance.

Just north of the Sidman exit, one exit before Johnstown, Dorsey spotted the Omni's taillights, bright red against a white backdrop. It was a downhill grade, and Dorsey slipped the Buick's transmission down a notch, wanting control instead of speed. Both cars ground out the last two miles to Johnstown.

"I was afraid that with the weather she might be heading home," Dorsey said. He drove down the exit ramp and watched as Claudia Maynard took a local road into the outskirts of Johnstown. "But this could work out. Better stay close."

"So, close up the gap." Gretchen had a so-why-are-you-telling-me tone to her voice.

Dorsey got the Buick close, slowing only at curves the Omni slid through. There were two rights and then a left-hand turn before the Omni slowed and slipped over to the curb. Dorsey took the first parking spot on the street, half a block behind. "Jesus Christ," he said. "We're back where we started from."

Coming from the opposite direction and knowing only the route he had taken while shadowing Radovic, Dorsey was startled to find himself a block up from Movement Together's Johnstown office. Radovic's place, he reminded himself. Dorsey let the motor run and the wipers cleared the windshield. They watched Claudia Maynard leave the Omni and carefully make her way to the storefront door and work the key into the lock.

"Now," Gretchen said, "I suppose we wait some more, right?"

"Really into it, aren't you?"

"Can't help it," Gretchen said. "And you knew I wouldn't be able to."

"Well, pay attention, because the waiting is over." Dorsey shut down the engine. "You're an apprentice in the field, so allowances can be made. But did you see what the girl just did? She unlocked the door, which means the door was locked. And that door is never locked when someone is inside because the office is full of posters and handbills and a glass jar for donations. They want the public coming in. Catch the foot trade."

"The point, please," Gretchen said irritably.

"Unless the toilet's broken and Radovic locked up shop to go take a leak, Claudia Maynard is in there all alone. Now is our chance to have a talk."

Gretchen entered the office first, followed by Dorsey, who backed his way in, hunched over and brushing snow from his hair. "Excuse me," Gretchen said, removing the comforter and folding it over her forearm. "Are you Claudia Maynard?" Dorsey kept his back to the woman, waiting on the reply.

"Yes, I am, and I'm very busy. I have to leave."

Turning, Dorsey realized that Dr. Tang's receptionist must have envied Claudia Maynard for more than her easy life. The girl was striking, and much younger than Dorsey had thought. No longer bundled against the cold, she was exquisitely thin, almost fragile. And her hair, Dorsey thought: it's so dark, nearly coal black. He found it hard to believe he had come this far to take her apart. She's too young, he thought again. Yeah, just like the bicycle messenger's look-alike who was a housebreaker at fifteen, in Camp Hill State Correctional Institution at seventeen, and in the morgue at nineteen.

"I'm ready to close up, just stopped to drop off a few things." Claudia Maynard stepped around the church basement folding table and attempted to shoo them out. "Tomorrow we're open early. Come back then, and there'll be somebody here to answer all your questions."

"We asked for you by name, Claudia." Dorsey leaned back into the closed door. "Movement Together? We know all we need to know about that. And we know about you."

Dorsey ignored his cramping stomach and concentrated on the flash of recognition in Claudia Maynard's eyes. That's right, the guy from the TV and newspaper, Dorsey thought. The same guy Eddie Damjani probably warned you about.

"Jesus, have you got balls." The girl turned about and went for the telephone. Gretchen pleaded with her not to be angry, they only wanted to ask a few questions.

"She should be pissed," Dorsey said, disregarding the flush of excitement that drained from Gretchen's face. "And she should be scared." He faced Claudia Maynard. "Didn't you think we'd figure you out? You're up to your ass in this one, and your friends have you stuck way out in front, all alone."

"Bullshit." Claudia lifted the receiver.

"Don't think so?" Dorsey moved to the table and leaned in, bracing himself with his arms, taking the pressure off his aching stomach muscles. "There's Carl Radovic and all the others you've helped. Insurance fraud, plain and simple. You tip off a guy to a layoff and he does a fall-down, fakes an injury."

The girl began to dial.

"You'll be indicted with the rest. And they'll all say they did it for a good cause, and so will you. They did it for the working-man. And they'll get off. But not you."

The girl stopped dialing but held on to the receiver, as if for comfort.

"Naw, for you it won't work," Dorsey said, his voice gathering heat. "Because some of the money stuck to your fingers. A nice trip to the seashore and who knows what else? That was your end of the deal. No high-minded motivation, so no judge will let you walk. I know, trust me. Ever been to the Women's Correctional at Muncy? A little cleaner than where they keep the men, but stocked with bull dykes. You'll be most welcome. Keep up the hard-ass shit with me, and you've got a future of broomsticks and Coke bottles."

"Fuck you."

But it was a weak fuck-you, Dorsey thought. So show her the ace, the hole card. The last lie.

"You're right, what's prison to a hard rock like you? But don't forget about all the rest. Father Jancek is a media personality, and this mess will get a lot of coverage. And so will you, as his girlfriend."

"What?"

"That's how it will look." Dorsey worked a fiendish grin across his face. "That's how it can be made to look. Your friends and family, they're going to love it the first time a TV reporter sticks a microphone in your face and asks when it was you first slept with the priest."

Claudia Maynard dropped the receiver into its cradle and fell back into the folding chair near the table. Dorsey shoved his trembling hands into his hip pockets and turned to check on Gretchen's reaction to his performance. He found her backed to the far wall, a look of shock across her face. No time for consolation, Dorsey knew; he had to keep hitting at the girl's crumbled defenses. He found a chair, one of several beneath the front window, and pulled it to the table.

"This is it," Dorsey said. He sat and took a pen and a pad from his coat "If you want to avoid total fucking humiliation, give me a list of names, all the guys you helped out at Carlisle. Radovic wasn't the only one. Saving him doesn't rate a month on the beach. Take the pen and write out the names."

The girl was crying now and spoke with difficulty. "I'll try, but please, I don't think I can remember them all."

"How many are we talking about?"

"Seventeen," the girl said. "I remember maybe thirteen or fourteen names."

"Do what you can. Don't bullshit me."

Claudia Maynard took the pen, shaky at first, and began to write. Gretchen came to her side and gave her a tissue to wipe her face and then gently squeezed the girl's shoulder for strength. Dorsey rose and paced the room, studying the posters of immigrant workers that covered the walls, as he had done on his first visit to the office. He concluded that the photos had all been taken at the shift change. Men with metal lunch buckets, their faces smeared with coal dust, walking away from the pit mouth. Other workers, again with lunch buckets, exiting the steel mill gate. And still other men, turn-of-the-century men, carrying lunch buckets across railroad ties. And that plaster crack that ran from one poster to the next. My God, he thought, you're Carroll Dorsey, son of Martin Dorsey, champion of the workingman in so many elections, here to sink the workingman's boat. Look at the side you're on. As if anything as simple as taking a side made sense. As if either side had a clean case to make for itself.

When he returned to his chair, the girl had completed her list. "Let's see what we've got." Dorsey took the steno pad and studied a list of unfamiliar names. By some she had written the hometowns. Holy Christ, he thought, fighting a headache. Seventeen men at maybe three hundred and fifty dollars per week. Just at Carlisle. Add that to workers at other plants and the bogus auto accidents. It had to be big to be worthwhile? Well, it's enormous.

"All these guys," Dorsey asked, "some old and some young, but all single, right? No married men on the list?"

"Because of the money." Claudia Maynard wiped at the corners of her eyes and Gretchen stood behind, gently stroking the girl's hair. "Family men need their whole check to make ends meet. The single fellas, they can get along on much less. They kick in half their checks, sometimes more. To make up for it, they draw free groceries from the food banks."

From behind the girl, Gretchen signaled to Dorsey. "She's had enough shock for the day. You've got the list, let's leave."

Dorsey shook his head. "Just a few more things to cover." He turned his attention to the girl. "When did it all start?"

"Not this summer, the one before. The first man was a guy who worked in the furnace, second helper."

"Who asked you to do it," Dorsey asked, "the priest? Your father says you're in tight with him."

"No, no!" Claudia Maynard shook her head violently, causing Gretchen to back away. "Not Father Jancek. We can talk about anything else, but not him. I never even met him till later on. It was two guys; one was a lawyer, I think. The other guy was named Gretz."

Dorsey chose to allow the exclusion of the priest and concentrated on the lawyer. "The lawyer, you get his name?" he asked. "Stockman, was that it? Older guy, mid-fifties?"

"The age is right," the girl said, "but I only met him one time, and it was a real short meeting. Never gave his name. He just assured me there was nothing illegal in what I was doin'."

A technicality, Dorsey thought. Splitting hairs. Leave it to P.I. to discuss the act but leave out the intent, the intent to defraud. Oh, Jack boy, if I could only connect you to this! One meeting and no names given. A short meeting to impress upon the small-town girl how very important she was. Long ago and so quick she could never identify you. So slick you are, Jack.

"This Gretz, the other guy at the meeting?"

"Darrell Gretz." Claudia Maynard held her face in her hands, staring down at the tabletop. "Used to date him. He's a couple of years older than me. Lives here in Johnstown."

"He worked at Carlisle Steel?" Dorsey asked. He looked past the girl at Gretchen and estimated her anxiety level. Nothing to be done about it now, he told himself. Concentrate on the girl.

"He did, but he was low on the seniority list. He was on layoff long before I met him. He eventually introduced me to Father Jancek."

Dorsey again placed the pen and pad before the girl. "So far you're doing fine. Now you're going to supply me with a full statement, written and signed, covering all your activities with Movement Together. It's your story, but I can help you find the words. When we're done you'll have a chance to read it over a few times, to be sure it's complete and true. No rush, take all the time you need. And when you're satisfied with its accuracy, sign and date it. And Miss Keller will sign as witness."

Her eyes dull and red-rimmed, the girl slowly twisted in her seat, facing Gretchen. "No. I can't do any more."

"What I said before will come true." Dorsey forced the girl's attention back to him. "Prison and those hungry inmates. But that's only after you get famous for sleeping with Father Jancek."

The girl cried out and again turned to Gretchen, burying her face in Gretchen's midsection. "Is this necessary?" Gretchen asked, stroking the girl's hair. "She's all done in. We have to let her rest."

Dorsey rose from his seat, shaking his head. "No. This is what we came for." He wished it wasn't so. He wished it were over and done with.

"You have the list." Gretchen's eyes held his. Dorsey was sure it was the cold and clinical look she had when warning an asthmatic to give up smoking. Or a juicer to lay off the booze. All business, blocking out anything that might obscure her meaning. "Fourteen names. That's fourteen leads for you to chase down. One of them is sure to tell you all you need. Besides, you can always come back to her."

Dorsey moved around the table and gestured for the girl to stay in her seat. He took Gretchen by the elbow, gently, and led her to the far end of the room. She followed him stiffly, hesitantly.

"Listen, just for a second; listen to me." Dorsey spoke quietly, taking care the girl did not overhear. "The list could be useless. It could be a list of men dedicated to the priest, like Radovic. Imagine it, fourteen Radovics. You're right, I could get their claim files and maybe cause them some trouble, but that's not good enough. Claudia, she knows the priest. And even though she can't connect him to a conspiracy, she proves a conspiracy exists."

"Not now. No." Gretchen's voice was clear and loud, disregarding the girl. "Look at her, for God's sake; she's a wreck. She might collapse on us. The statement can be gotten another time."

"She'll run," Dorsey said. "She'll run for a long time, and she'll get help. And when she gets back, P.I. Stockman will erect an eight-foot legal wall around her. He won't let anyone talk to her alone, and she'll be in a position to deny everything she's said so far. It's now or never."

With a shake of her head, Gretchen dismissed his words and turned away. Her hand came to her mouth and she gently rested a knuckle against her lips, pensively staring out at the snow.

"This has to end. I'm sorry, Carroll." She faced Dorsey, her expression telling him that for her the matter was closed. "So far today I've seen you tell lies and half-truths and tear away this girl's dignity. What comes next? She's likely to hold out. And you'll know if she does; you're too good to be fooled by her. What do you have left up your sleeve? I don't want to find out. I don't know you when you're like this. And I don't want to know you."

Dorsey had no answer. The stakes were too high to blurt out some tough talk of the trade. You play it right, he warned himself, do the job right and get what you need from Claudia Maynard, and you'll lose what you're playing the game for: a chance to put some bread in the bank and to keep yourself in Gretchen's income bracket. To keep Gretchen.

Dorsey stepped past Gretchen, his head hanging in frustration, and moved around the table to face the girl. He took the pen and pad and settled into the chair.

"We're through for now," he told the girl. "You're not doing so well, so there's no sense to push it. But believe me, you'll have to make a statement sometime. You're going to have to tell all you know. I'll try to call and set a time, but don't be surprised if you hear from some other people instead. There's a guy named Meara I'll be checking in with. He's a prosecutor in Pittsburgh. Most likely, he'll talk to the Cambria County DA, who will send out his detectives to see you. And trust me, you will write out a few things for them, bet on it. So if you hear from me first, you can consider yourself lucky. It'll be easier to talk to me."

Sick of himself, Dorsey pushed away from the table and went out into the street, walking the half block to the Buick. Looking back through the storefront window, he saw Gretchen comforting the girl, guessing that she was suggesting that Claudia calm herself before trying to drive home through the snow. Once at the Buick, he started the engine, turned up the heater, then stepped back out to scrape ice from the bottom of the windshield.

Say good-bye to the Maynard girl, he told himself, tearing the wiper blades from the frozen glass. She'll call Gretz and Gretz will call the priest. The damage will be assessed and the girl goes back on vacation. Fourteen men will be warned and told to watch their step. And Ed Damjani, the priest's personal lunatic: he'll know you were up here. Watch your back, Dorsey, Damjani is on his way.

CHAPTER 17

Al set a seven-ounce Rolling Rock and a short beer glass in front of Dorsey, then moved off to the stainless steel sink at the center of the bar. Meticulously, he scrubbed out draft beer glasses and dunked them in a clean rinse, then followed this with thirty seconds of polishing for each. Outside, the streets were silent with snow, and the only sound to penetrate the barroom walls was the churning and clanging of the occasional salt truck passing by.

"Painted into a corner is the way I see it." Al finished the last of the glasses and dried his hands on his white cotton apron. "Hurts like hell, I bet. Halfway to cleaning up the whole mess, and then you gotta walk away from it."

"Big mistake is what it was," Dorsey said, pouring his beer.

"Of course it was." Al stepped from behind the bar and began turning off the neon beer signs that decorated the bar's windows. After he finished, he took the stool next to Dorsey. "There are businesses where a couple can work together, and there are some where they can't. Like with me and Rose. She heads up the kitchen, does all the cooking except when I make the bean soup, and I stay out here. She does all the buyin' for the kitchen, and I keep the accounts for beer and liquor up to date. Works out good. Your line of work is something different altogether. There's no room to navigate around each other. One-man job. In this place, I can bitch out the beer distributor or harp about the deadhead civil servants at the state store, and Rose is not out here to be embarrassed by it. Same thing with her; the food purveyors live in fear of Rose, but me, I'm too occupied with the bar to feel bad about it. Your job won't let you do that." Al left his seat and walked back behind the bar. "So how did you leave things with her?"

"The ride home was pure hell," Dorsey said, sipping at his beer. "Like driving a hearse, it was so quiet. And with the weather it was a three-hour ride. I'd try to talk, start a conversation and get it off the ground, but she'd just stare out the window or stick her nose in this textbook she brought with her. Not reading, just flipping through the pages."

Al turned off the small lights that illuminated the rows of liquor bottles behind the bar. "That's what really threw the wet towel on it for you two. Most people, couples, when they get their noses out of joint at each other, one of them can get up and go in the next room or leave the house, maybe. Just get a chance to come up for air."

"Not this time." Dorsey poured the remainder of his beer into the glass and shot it down. "Dropped her off at her place. No 'call me tomorrow'; nothing like that." Dorsey slapped the bar with the flat of his hand and rose to his feet. "Ah, Jesus. I better go."

"Right, you get some sleep." Al followed Dorsey to the door and held it for him. "Early snow," Al said, looking out on Seventeenth Street. "Early snow always takes me by surprise. Tomorrow it all melts. Things'll work out. They blow over and straighten themselves out."

"With Gretchen or with this mess of a case?"

"Say one prayer at a time."

Dorsey stepped out into the snow and heard Al slide the door's deadbolt into place. Five inches had fallen, and although the showers had stopped, the sidewalks were yet to be cleared. Across

Seventeenth, in a basketball court surrounded by hurricane fence, Dorsey saw the tall figure of a man standing beneath the near backboard. Above his head, the hoop's nylon cord net had frozen and was filled by wet snow, looking like a snow cone from a street vendor before the syrup is poured. The figure was motionless and appeared unaware of Dorsey. Trying to discipline himself to think only of the case and certainly not of Gretchen, Dorsey dismissed the man as a drunk or a street bum without a doorway to sleep in. Keep your perspective, he told himself. Hope for the best. Maybe the girl won't run. Then, Monday morning, check out the files on the fourteen names on her list and search the Carlisle Steel workers' comp claim files for other workers who fit the mold. Dorsey decided to call Corso at home to arrange it for Monday.

Twenty feet from Carson Street, an alley bisected the block. As Dorsey hopped across the slush pond that had gathered at the gutter, two men stepped out from the alley's shadows. Both wore ski masks and fatigue jackets. The shorter of the two, a man of average height and weight, carried a tire iron. The second man was much taller and twice the width of the first and held an eight-inch wrench in his right hand. Startled at first, Dorsey gathered himself and slowly backed away, stepping through the slush.

"Ed Damjani." Sure of the identity, Dorsey addressed the larger man, wondering how such a big man could hope to hide his identity with a ski mask. Like a train robber's bandanna on King Kong.

Neither man responded, and the smaller one moved into the street, flanking Dorsey's right, cutting off escape in that direction. Slowly moving backward, Dorsey glanced over his shoulder and saw what he expected; the man from the basketball court was closing in behind him. As the man passed beneath a street lamp, Dorsey saw that he was black and carried more metal in his hand. Three hours from Johnstown, Dorsey thought. They could set up anything with three hours of lead time. Dorsey dropped into a defensive crouch, arms out and up, intending to protect his head at any cost.

"Back the fuck off, both you sumbitches." It was the black man speaking, and the metal he held was a blue steel automatic. He pointed the gun past Dorsey and trained it at Damjani's sternum. "Big mafucka, you specially. Back off."

Damjani's partner waved the tire iron in the air, coming toward the gunman. "This got nothin' to do with you. Take off, spade, and we'll forget about it."

Dorsey searched the gunman's face but was unable to place it. As tall as Damjani but sleekly built, he kept his knees bent in the shooter position, both hands gripping the gun. With his thumb he cocked the hammer.

"Don't even know what this man's name be," the gunman said, indicating Dorsey. "But I ain't gonna let you mafuckas kick his sorry ass, not tonight anyways. And watch that spade shit. Might just put a hole in your fuckin' head for the fuckin' principle of the thing."

For several moments that seemed like an eternity to Dorsey, the scene was frozen and silent, none of the players able to fight through the tension, none willing to end the standoff. Dorsey faded back across the pavement until his back was against the brick wall of an auto repair garage. The palms of his hands went to the wall and his fingertips dug into the mortar seams between the brick, as if gripping for safety at a dangerous height. At what he thought was surely the moment of no return, with both sides about to engage the other, the night was shattered by a wild scream and Dorsey heard his name shouted from far up the street. The gunman eased the hammer back into place and made a quarter turn, keeping Damjani, his partner, and Dorsey in sight, while he checked out the shouting.

Down the center of the street, through a lane that had been cleared and salted by the city trucks, Russie charged toward them waving an aluminum softball bat. Dressed only in T-shirt, slacks, and bedroom slippers, he sidestepped patches of lingering snow and slush, shouting Dorsey's name all along. The few wisps of hair remaining on his head seemed to stand on end as he ran.

"I'll help ya! I'll help ya!"

Russie wiggled between two parked cars and onto the sidewalk, blowing by the gunman to take up a position in front of Dorsey. With the bat held at arm's length, Russie turned to each of the men, his eyes small and fierce. "Gotta go through me, bastards. Gotta go through me."

The gunman snickered. "The fuck is this shit? Easy, now. These two guys, they's the ones to be pissed at. Me, I'm here to help your friend."

"Easy, Russ, loosen up," Dorsey whispered over Russie's shoulder; he took hold of a belt loop in Russie's slacks, slowly guiding him away from the men in ski masks. "Lighten up, Russ, it's gonna be all right. Take it slow, we're gonna get out of this one. You saved my life. You did, Russie, you saved my life."

Later, Dorsey would repeatedly tell a city detective that he could remember Damjani laughing but did not see him coming at Russie. Instead, Dorsey told them he felt Russie pull away from him and saw Russie take a strong rip with the bat, landing it solidly against Damjani's shoulder. No, Dorsey told the police, the big prick didn't fall, barely moved.

"So what happened next?" the detective taking notes asked.

"Damjani's buddy, he slipped in behind Russie and took a cut with the tire iron. A full cut, brought it up from the sidewalk right over his shoulder. Russie, being just a little guy, he caught the iron on its way back down. Jesus Christ, you could hear the bone crack, like when you snap wood. Russie just crumpled to the ground."

"Hold on just a sec." It was another detective speaking. "The guy with the gun, he was on your side, right? What did he do during all this?"

"Held back," Dorsey said matter-of-factly. "Stood his ground, kept the pistol pointed up in the air."

"Bullshit."

"Listen," Dorsey said. "I know what you're thinking. But when it was done and those two guys took off, I asked him, 'Where the fuck were you?' Seriously, I asked him."

"So what did he say?"

"He said, 'They said to look after you. Didn't say shit about him.'"

"Father Melcic says there can't be a mass." Al sat on the edge of the office chaise, sipping at a coffee mug. "Can't prove Russie was Catholic. There's a birth certificate but nothing about a baptism. I guess his bein' around here, I just figured him for some kind of Catholic, Greek or some other Orthodox. Anyways, I can't prove he's Catholic. So no mass and no burial in consecrated ground. I did get the priest to agree to say a few prayers in church. It'll be Tuesday morning. We can't get the body before that because the postmortem is Monday. Burial will be in the county cemetery out in Lawrenceville. Gonna be there, right?"

Still wearing the clothes he had worn to Johnstown, Dorsey sat in his swivel chair, where he had gotten five fitful hours of sleep. The police had released him shortly before dawn and he had taken a cab home from the Public Safety Building. Later, awakened by Al pounding at the door, he had gone through the motions of making coffee, double strong, as if fighting his way out of a trance.

"Sure, I'll be there," Dorsey said, rubbing sleep from his eyes. On the desktop were his coffee mug and two empty beer cans, drunk when he had returned that morning. "Feel kind of responsible, I guess. I'll be there, sure." Dorsey sipped at his coffee and again tried to figure out the identity of the gunman.

"Of course you're responsible," Al said. "So am I. Not for him gettin' killed, but we were his only family, if you think about it. The guy would've gone through a brick wall for either of us. Even for Bernie, for some reason." Al drank coffee and shook his head. "Way I figure it, he must've been watchin' out of the apartment window. He did that a lot. Saw you leave and then saw the spade follow after you. So Russie grabs the bat and off he went. Showed me that bat lotsa times. Said he'd protect his place and the bar. Loyal guy. Kinda dimwitted, I suppose, but loyal."

"I'll be there," Dorsey said. "And I'll call my father. He'll want to be there too."

Al rose to his feet, stretched his arms, and moved off to peer out the window. "So tell me," he said, not looking at Dorsey, "you hear from your bosses yet? The guys at the insurance company?"

"Not yet, but I certainly expect to." Dorsey pushed back into his chair and studied the ceiling. "Somebody's going to call, Sunday or not. I suppose they're drawing lots right now to see who gets the pleasure of firing my ass. Munt, I'm sure he's chomping at the bit, dying for a chance."

"So you get fired," Al said. "So you get a new boss."

Dorsey watched Al settle into the chair at the side of the desk. "Who in the hell is that going to be? No new bosses, no new cases. Not for some time."

"C'mon, Dorsey." Al spoke in a fatherly tone. "You're gonna finish this business, this case. You do the legwork, I'll cover expenses. And your fee. Russie's dead. The guy who mopped my floors and hustled your beer to you. The guy who thought he was saving your life."

Dorsey straightened himself and stared at the desktop blotter. The idea of finishing the case, with or without pay, had been forcing its way through his fatigued mind throughout the police interrogation. But later, in the cab ride home, he had dismissed the thought as an emotional and temporary remedy for his shock and guilt. Now it was presented in a new light, by someone who had spent the night in a bed and hadn't watched a man's skull being split open. The poor dumb bastard, Dorsey thought, dead because you befriended him. Dead because you pissed off Ed Damjani and maybe the goddamned priest. And Stockman, the son of a bitch. Good ol' Personal Injury Stockman. And because, Dorsey, you've underestimated these people at every turn, every step of the way.

Oblivious to Al, Dorsey's thoughts surged forward. Some very smart and not so smart people get together to steal some money, and it's okay because a lawyer shows them the way. White-collar crime, so it's white-collar killing, as sure as if Russie's head were crushed by a business ledger. Can you do it? Dorsey asked himself. Can you try?

"Me, I got the money," Al said. "You got no idea how much I put away. Own the bar and the building. The only employee is my wife, and Russie was around to clean up or serve beer in the back room. I drive a ten-year-old car, and my idea of a vacation is three days at Lake Erie. Whatever you gotta do and for as long as it takes, I'll cover it. But you're the one with the know-how. You gotta do the work. All the money you need."

So you're the one, Dorsey told himself. Out of this tight little circle of people that gives a shit about this guy being dead, you're the man. To the end of the line.

"Let's get clear on a few things." Dorsey moved a quarter turn in the swivel chair to face Al. "Damjani and the prick who killed Russie, it's up to the police to catch them. They can do that job much better than I can. And Damjani, he wasn't the one who slugged Russie, so he might not get anything at all. Believe me, I'd love to see him do twenty years, but there's not much I can do about it. You're clear on that, right?"

Slowly, silently, Al nodded.

"So what we want to do is get the people who caused it, the ones who set things in motion. The things that got Russie killed."

"Absolutely."

"Well, then," Dorsey said, "I'm going to wreck the priest. And Stockman. Pin all this shit on their chests and parade them downtown at high noon. Get them indicted, maybe convicted."

Al placed his mug on the desktop corner. "You can do that?"

"I can try," Dorsey told him. "Because I have to look into the mirror for the rest of my days, too."

CHAPTER 18

Corso's voice later that day was heavily laden with anger and sarcasm, and the telephone line did nothing to conceal it. "You are aware of what it is I'm telling you, right? Went to the wall for you with Munt, that hardhead. Munt wanted you fired, and from the way he talked it sounded like he didn't give a shit what Cleardon has to say about it. Think about it. It's the second time I came through for you."

The call had come just as Dorsey was stepping out of the shower. Wrapped in a towel, he wondered what was keeping Corso on the job. Where was Corso's payday? There had to be one.

"Hey, Ray, it's appreciated. I mean the effort you've made for me. Must've been tough."

He sat on the edge of the bed and allowed Corso a few more moments of rambling before cutting it off.

"Okay, Ray, here's what I need." Dorsey wanted the files on all Carlisle Steel workers' compensation claims to be ready for his review on Monday morning. "You can do that for me, right?"

"Sure," Corso said. "But you gotta realize—"

"Thanks, Ray, have a good weekend, what's left of it."

He saved you again, Dorsey thought, or so he says. And if he did, you still don't know why and that's one hell of a question. Your ally is the man who sells cases, the one you better not trust. Is he busy selling your case too? He could be out taking bids from Stockman right now. Corso would know how to get in touch with him. Steady, Dorsey, steady. One crime at a time. This is your case now, the property of Carroll Dorsey of Wharton Street, with financial assistance by Albert Rosek, restaurateur.

Feeling a bit fresher in clean clothes, Dorsey went downstairs to the office and answered the telephone on the fourth ring. It was Western Union, verbally delivering a priority mailgram. The message was from Dennis Tesso, a Johnstown attorney, informing Dorsey that he now represented Claudia Maynard concerning any matters arising from her former employment at Carlisle Steel. All communications with Miss Maynard were to be directed through his office and, as Miss Maynard was not presently residing in the Johnstown area, a lengthy period of time should be allowed for a response. The operator assured Dorsey that written confirmation of the message would be forthcoming.

Fortified by a mug of coffee, Dorsey checked his messages.

The first three were from Bernie. First he said he had information on Louis Preach and told Dorsey to call. Next, he told the tape he had to go to his kid's soccer match so don't call until later. The third message said, "The hell with it, here's what I found out.

"You were right, Preach is a lawyer, black, office up on Webster Avenue, the Hill District. He's in his late forties, maybe fifty. The guys I talked with said he was a real sixties activist, sort of a civil rights rabble-rouser. If there's a black pressure group, he's a paid-up member. No one hears much from him anymore, but I think he does a mix of things: small claims, title searches, and some JP hearings. Hope it helps. By the way, Al told me about Russie. You okay?"

"I'm okay," Dorsey mumbled to himself.

The tape whirled on. Two newspaper reporters and Sam

Hickcock requested interviews. Ironbox Boyle told him his father was in Harrisburg but would be in touch on Monday. The last voice was Gretchen's.

She was taking a few days off, had arranged it with the ER chief. Just a little time to take stock of things. "I'll be in Lancaster, at Mother's. We'll talk when I get back."

Dorsey had hoped to reach her quickly, before any bruise became too deep-seated. Now, he thought, she'll run through it all with her family and maybe old girlfriends. With a mother who is bound to question her daughter's relationship with a man ten years her senior, when she could be out trapping a fellow doctor. Friends will shudder when she tells them what he does for a living. Where, oh, where, is your father's money? Dorsey asked himself simplistically, as if it resolved all issues.

Not now, Dorsey, he reminded himself, not with a job to do. And a dead friend. Screw your courage, he thought, remembering an English class from long ago. Think only of the job, like you did two nights ago. When they killed Russie.

Finishing the coffee, Dorsey switched to beer and took a can from the office refrigerator. He turned on the TV and returned to the swivel chair. The late-afternoon football game, the four o'clock game, was on with a score of twenty-four to six. It isn't baseball, Dorsey thought, and it sure as hell isn't basketball, which is an art form. Sweaty, but an art form just the same.

Squaring himself in his seat, Dorsey opened the manila folder Corso had sent him. The first few pages of the media report contained articles taken from the Pittsburgh dailies, factual accounts of specific events. Father Jancek speaks to the workers at the Neville Island barge works. Father Jancek arrested as he and his followers attempt to force a debate at a church attended by corporate executives. The priest appears at a hearing for a proposed injunction against picket lines established at several factories. At the hearing, he tells the judge he does not accept the judge's authority or jurisdiction in this matter and spends two days in jail for contempt.

The information gathered from the *Beaver County Times* and the Greensburg-Westmoreland newspaper was similar, with the exception of several editorials, which were strongly in support of

Movement Together. But when Dorsey reached articles taken from the *Sunday Home Visitor,* a local Catholic paper, and *The New York Times,* he began to take copious notes.

The *Sunday Home Visitor* provided a brief sketch of Father Jancek's activities after arriving in Pittsburgh in 1966. Assigned to one of the diocese's black congregations in south Oakland, he immediately involved himself in civil rights demonstrations. The first publicity for Father Jancek came with attempts to open the construction trade unions to black membership. In the spring of 1967, Father Jancek stood in the front ranks of a protest march in which thousands of unemployed blacks and their families demonstrated at major construction jobs in the downtown business district. At the site of a partially completed office building, while giving a brief but thunderous speech, Father Jancek was struck in the cheek by a rivet dropped from several stories up. The writer suggested that the ensuing disfigurement led to Father Jancek's allowing his goatee to spread into a full beard.

The remainder of the article wrestled with the issue of Father Jancek's status as a priest. In a brief interview, the bishop of the Pittsburgh diocese clearly indicated that in his opinion Father Jancek's activities with Movement Together were inviting official censure.

> The papal edict concerning the political activities of the clergy is not, as some Catholics seem to believe, directed only to the priests of Latin America," the bishop said. "Without a doubt, it has universal application, and Father Jancek is running afoul of the Holy See. I am compelled to take action in this matter.

A week later, Father Jancek was relieved of his pastoral duties and provided with quarters at a monastery for retired priests in the city's Lawrenceville section. This occurred despite the published opinion of a prominent intellectual monsignor who challenged the bishop's decision.

Rather than being purely political, with the objective of achieving a fundamental reformation in the country's ruling regime, Father Jancek's actions fall into a socioeconomic classification. He is involved only with a specific sector of society, attempting to promote and improve that sector's economic standing in relation to the rest of society. I doubt that the Holy Father intended religious orders to curtail this type of activity.

The feature article taken from a Sunday edition of *The New York Times* provided a much more detailed history of the priest, indicating that his ordination in 1964 had been placed in jeopardy by his political activism. In particular, there had been three warm-weather absences from the seminary when he filled a seat on a Freedom Riders bus bound for Mississippi. Several elderly priests, seminary instructors, petitioned for seminarian Jancek's dismissal, citing a likely inability to commit to a vow of obedience. Seminarian Jancek was saved by a younger, more sympathetic priest who arranged for him to face his detractors in closed session. At this meeting, employing his already well-respected powers of oratory, Jancek presented an argument that explained away his absences and assured the priests of his acceptance of their authority. Several priests who had been present at that meeting were contacted in preparation for the *Times* article, and although none could remember the content of Father Jancek's argument, all agreed they had been moved and reassured of Father Jancek's faith by it.

The last of Father Jancek's accomplishments recorded by the *Times*, before the creation of Movement Together, was referred to as the "Shifting of the Ashes" speech. In April of 1968, following the assassination of Dr. King, the blacks of Pittsburgh, as in other northern cities, put sections of the city to the torch. For the most part, the damage was confined to black neighborhoods, but one incident, the burning of a lumberyard on Twenty-fifth Street, occurred in the Strip, which at the time was still populated by working-class whites who lived near their factory jobs. The burning of the lumberyard and the fiery death of its owner, who had been standing guard against looters with a deer rifle, became a rallying point for white backlash and a demand for the capture of the arsonists. When it became apparent that the identity of the arsonists would never be known, the demand was changed to a call for stiff sentences and fines for all arrested looters.

In July of that year, the City Council held open hearings to determine the root causes of the riots. Early on, spokesmen for a number of white working-class neighborhoods made appearances, again calling for swift and sure punishment for the rioters. Dramatically waiting for the final day of the hearings, Father Jancek led a contingent of blacks and liberal whites to council chambers to present a response. In a stirring speech before radio microphones and TV cameras, he beseeched city residents to search their souls for the seeds of revenge, "just as workers now sift through the ashes of that lumberyard. And cast out those seeds just as those workmen clear away that structure's charred remains." In the spring of 1969, a playground was constructed on the lumberyard site.

Dorsey remembered little of that day, other than his father's jubilant response to the priest's speech. Sipping at his beer, Dorsey recalled the dinner table that night and his father saying that the Democratic Party was off the hook. "The Democratic Party runs the city and county," Martin Dorsey explained to his son. "So the police and the DA are the Democrats. If the police don't arrest the rioters and if the DA doesn't convict them, the whites will think the Democrats let them down. And if the rioters get long sentences, the black pressure groups will be angry with the Democrats. But the priest has the whole city ashamed of itself. He fixed it for us. Reconciliation is on the way."

So when did he change? Dorsey asked himself as he crossed the room to turn off the lopsided football game. When did the priest switch from community advocate to political messiah? Or instead of changing, did he just come of age? Either way, he put into motion the wheels that ground up Russie.

Dorsey passed the desk, grabbed his beer, and moved on to the front windows. Peering out onto Wharton Street, bathed in the weak glow of mercury lights, he thought of the others in Movement Together, the rank and file. The people who ate at the soup kitchens and dressed in secondhand clothes provided by Movement Together. Old men and women who donated money at Father Jancek's call in the hope that he could preserve their way of life, that families and communities could stay intact. Fuck 'em, Dorsey thought, Russie's dead.

You'll find a way, Dorsey told himself. There's a way to derail the priest and old Personal Injury himself. Just find it.

Back at the desk, Dorsey pushed on to the last pages of the media search report. These were photos, with captions, taken of Father Jancek over the last nineteen years. None were of Father Jancek alone, and Dorsey became intrigued in trying to identify the people sharing the photos with the priest. My God, Dorsey thought, it's a Who's Who of liberal politicians. A 1967 photo of Father Jancek bestowing Holy Eucharist on the tongue of Bobby Kennedy at the communion rail. A 1968 shot of him shaking hands with Eugene McCarthy. The last photo on the first page was a 1972 group shot including Father Jancek and, of all people, County Commissioner Martin Dorsey.

"Both ends to the middle," Dorsey mumbled. "Both ends to the middle."

The second page held five photos. Dorsey breezed through them until he reached the fourth. It was a picture of Father Jancek, Jack Stockman, and a black man in what Dorsey guessed to be his forties, considering the gray at the temples. Smiling, the three men were grouped closely together, their right arms extended and their hands one on top of the other, as if in a prayer huddle before the big game.

"Jesus Christ," Dorsey said, reading the caption. "I'm fucking surrounded."

FATHER ANDREW JANCEK, JACK STOCKMAN, AND LOUIS PREACH AT THE NATIONAL URBAN LEAGUE DINNER. PITTS-BURGH HILTON, 1978.

CHAPTER 19

The front page of the morning paper ran a picture of Dorsey taken several years earlier when he was with the DA's office. Next to that was a photo of Russell Anthony Bartok. The closed eyes and squared jaw and grainy quality identified the photo as a release from the coroner. So that was his full name, Dorsey thought.

The Fidelity Casualty claims office was like the hundreds of police squad rooms Dorsey had visited, only longer. Located on the fourth floor of a downtown office building, illuminated by fluorescent lighting, it consisted of a large open area with rows of desks manned by adjustors instead of police detectives. At the far end, away from the elevators, were glass partitions housing the claim manager's office and an enclosed conference room. Dorsey set up shop in the conference room.

Equipped with a large black coffee and two Danish, he had arrived at ten o'clock. He had a brief, perfunctory conversation with Ray Corso, who reminded Dorsey that it was he, Corso, who had saved him from the sharp edge of John Munt's ax. Dorsey had mumbled his thanks and settled himself at the head of the conference table. Piled before him were the files of twenty-seven active workers' compensation claims on Carlisle Steel employees.

Dorsey began by reviewing the files of the fourteen men on Claudia Maynard's list. The diagnosed conditions varied: back injuries being treated by Dr. Tang or one of several chiropractors; leg injuries; and several occupationally induced psychiatric conditions. But the profiles met the Movement Together mold: young, single, no dependents. More important, attached to each of the file folders was a Western Union Mailgram, its message similar to the one Dorsey had received concerning Claudia Maynard. Delivered earlier that morning, it indicated that the injured worker was now legally represented by one of several attorneys in the Johnstown area. Again, as in the case of Claudia Maynard, all communication was to be conducted through the attorney's office.

How far would you have to dig, Dorsey asked himself, to find the connection between these lawyers and P.I. Stockman? Maybe just through the topsoil. Stockman could have his name on each of these notices and it would mean nothing. What would it prove? A high-powered lawyer like Personal Injury can pick up fourteen new clients on a slow day. The man could use a turnstile for an office door. Stockman's connection, without testimony, means nothing. Dorsey was reminded of how valuable Claudia Maynard could have been, and how, short of a subpoena, he would never speak to her again.

Of the thirteen remaining files, Dorsey was easily able to eliminate nine: workers in their mid-fifties, some with children and grandchildren. And all nine had undergone a series of back surgeries: disc removals and fusions. None met the Movement Together stereotype.

Unable to disregard any of the remaining four, Dorsey wondered if Claudia Maynard had helped eighteen workers to file fraudulent claims, not seventeen. The remaining claims were those of young single men with less than two years on the job. Two back strains, one cervical injury, and a worker claiming an acquired seizure disorder.

"Just a little off," Dorsey said, watching the door open. "You look a little off for most people. But considering your usual appearance, you look like hell. You sleep in the park last night?"

Sam Hickcock slipped into the first chair to Dorsey's left. His tie was slightly loose at the throat and his moustache was wet with hangover sweats. His hair, which normally showed the results of careful blow-drying, was slick and combed straight back, obscuring the usual neat part line. Slumped in his chair, Hickcock tried to rub away the redness from his eyes.

"You came alone?" Dorsey searched the main floor for a cameraman. "How'd you know I was here? There was no tail on me this morning, I'm sure of it."

Hickcock pulled closer to the table. "I was told you were here. Don't ask by whom. Privileged information."

"Really?" Dorsey knew he would get nowhere by pressing. "Then *why* are you here? Let's try that one. Expecting a release for the media?"

"No, nothing like that. Just want to talk."

It's not just his appearance that lacks its usual flair, Dorsey decided as he studied Hickcock. There's no command in his voice, none of his famous sense of urgency. And he has yet to try to startle me; he's not trying to put me on the defensive. "So talk to me. And take some of this." Dorsey pushed the Styrofoam coffee cup across the table to Hickcock.

"I turned forty-five over the weekend." Hickcock sipped at the coffee. "And I have reached the conclusion that life does not start at forty or forty-five. In fact, for me, it's the kiss of death."

For a few moments, Dorsey allowed Hickcock's words to hang in the air. "You know I have nothing to say. My work is confidential."

"I've been on your ass. I apologize." Hickcock wiped his palms on a handkerchief. "Let me make it up to you."

"How and why?" Dorsey asked. "Begin with why. If it's not good enough, you can ditch the how."

Hickcock played at his tie knot before speaking. "Turned forty-five on Sunday. That's a milestone in my business. If you're not with the networks by forty, forty-five on the outside, you don't get in ever. So I'll never get in, right?"

"If you say so."

"And I've been trying," Hickcock said. "About two months ago I got my last rejection. You send demo tapes to New York, that's how it works. Most of the stuff I sent recently was coverage of Movement Together. I figured with the national interest, it was the way to play it. Figured I was in. But it was no good."

"I feel bad for you." Dorsey skimmed through the file folder in front of him. "What's this have to do with me? You'll stay in Pittsburgh and be a big frog in a little pond."

"That's not all of it." Hickcock nervously went through his pants pockets, as if searching for something. "A demotion of sorts came my way last Friday. Father Jancek, even with competition from the other stations and the papers, has been my story. The public thinks of the two of us together.

"Friday changed all that. I was pulled into the news director's office, and in there with him was the station manager. They started telling me what a great job I was doing, which is always a bad sign. So, as a reward for hard work, they were giving me an assistant, someone to split the duties with. Then we watch a demo tape of this girl they're bringing in from Cincinnati. Early twenties, blond and good-looking, with one of those tougher-than-a-guy stares they all have these days."

So he's on his way out, Dorsey thought. Eased out of his job and soon out the door. No chance of getting anything better, and what he has is being pulled out from under him. You have the why, now see what he has to sell.

"So you're on thin ice. Tell me, how do you plan on saving your sweet ass, and how do I come out ahead?"

"From what I see, Movement Together has crossed the line." Hickcock's words were pressured, showing signs of being rehearsed. "When your friend was killed, I mean. The other stuff they pulled, dead fish in bank vaults and stink bombs in department stores, those were attention-getting pranks. With the priest's popular support, and the harmless nature of the pranks, I had to slant the news their way. Now something serious has happened, I can take a wider view of events, give both sides a little credit. And I can make you look good."

"You, criticize Movement Together?" Dorsey asked. "Jesus, Hickcock, you invented these people. You're the one who first brought me to tears with all those poor folks out of work. You're in the middle of the race. How in hell can you change horses now?"

"Bit by bit. Until the new girl gets settled in, the priest is all mine. I'll shift my outlook a little, each night, at six and eleven. Put a little distance between us. By the time the girl gets here she'll have to fall in line."

Dorsey rose from his seat and walked to the partition. Drumming his fingers against the glass, he watched a young secretary as she walked from desk to desk distributing memos. She wore a tight black skirt. Did she make Corso chomp down that much harder on his pipestem?

"Cut the shit," Dorsey said, returning to his seat. "You're about to get canned. Some hot blonde is moving you out. It's only natural in your line of work, you being forty-five and not nearly as pretty. The best you can do is catch on as the noon weatherman. And you want to help me for all the trouble you've caused." Dorsey's eyes zeroed in on Hickcock. "I have no fucking idea where this conversation is headed. What is it you want from me? Now or never."

"We could be partners," Hickcock said. "On a book. We could write one together."

"A book? C'mon, please."

"Really, I was in newspapers. Before I started with a station in Buffalo."

"Good," Dorsey said. "Good for you."

Hickcock put his hands to his chest, imploring. "I can do this, believe me. I can do nonfiction." Hickcock grinned.

"You're something," Dorsey said. "No shit, you really are."

"The project is already under way," Hickcock said. "For some time now I've been planning a book on Father Jancek and the movement. Nothing very ambitious, but a book on him would sell. Up to now the plan was to make him look like a saint. That's what the research indicated. But you've changed that."

"Me?" Dorsey asked. "How how did I manage that?"

Hickcock wagged a finger at Dorsey. "Now it's my turn to tell you to cut the shit. You're on to them, and you've got a dead friend to prove it. There's something there, all right. I don't know what, but it's there. Look at it this way. I put together a nice little book about the priest and the poor folks he helps, it'll be published with no problem. But I won't get any recognition from it. It's like writing the biography of the quarterback who won the Super Bowl. In a week it's old news. But if we work together, if you give me what you have, I can put together an exposé that will make the best-seller list. The two of us could split fifty-fifty and sit around autographing copies. And for me the station could go fuck itself."

Dorsey tipped back in his chair and studied the ceiling. Of course you can't trust him, he told himself, but you can use him. For what he may know about the priest and maybe Stockman too. To get the justice Al may end up paying for, the justice you want.

"Worth thinking about," Dorsey said, dropping the chair back on all fours. "But that's about the best I can do for now. From you I need something, an act of good faith. Show me your intentions, an example of what I can expect."

"In the bag." Hickcock rose to leave. "Catch me on the six o'clock show. You'll be impressed."

"Maybe." Dorsey watched Hickcock open the door. "I'm still interested in knowing how you knew I was here."

Hickcock shook his head and left.

At twenty minutes past six that evening, the news anchor turned to his left and introduced Sam Hickcock, Channel Three's investigative reporter. The camera panned along the news desk to Hickcock, who looked like his old self, and he and the anchor traded a few seconds of small talk.

Sitting at his office desk, Dorsey pushed away his dinner plate and settled back into the swivel chair, sipping at a mug of coffee. Let's hear it, he thought. Show me the change.

Hickcock quickly recapped Russie's murder and indicated that the police were unable to locate Edward Damjani, who was wanted for questioning. Next, Hickcock introduced a film clip of an interview of Father Jancek held earlier that afternoon. The location was a food bank in Ambridge. As they conversed, the camera swept the room, focusing on blue-collar men and women accepting sacks of groceries from two union reps standing behind the closed lower half of a Dutch door.

To Hickcock's question as to whether or not Movement Together officials would cooperate with the police in finding Damjani, Father Jancek, in an even voice, replied that he and the other steering committee members had already been contacted by the Pittsburgh and Pennsylvania State Police organizations and had shown complete cooperation. "However," the priest added, "we can only tell what we know. And that, I'm afraid, is very little. Ed is a Movement Together member, but his alleged involvement in any crime is not a matter for my comment. Also, let the term 'alleged' be stressed. My personal knowledge of Ed leads me to believe there is some mistake."

Ed, Dorsey thought, his personal knowledge of Ed. Yeah, priest, there's a mistake, all right, and you've made it. Just a matter of my finding it.

Hickcock reminded Father Jancek of reports that Mr. Carroll Dorsey, who had witnessed the killing, was investigating Movement Together. He asked the priest if he knew of any connection between the attack and the investigation. Hickcock also asked Father Jancek to comment on the basis of the investigation.

"Your first question doesn't deserve the dignity of a response; what it suggests is simply ludicrous. For the second question, I propose you ask that question of Mr. Dorsey. Or to his unnamed employers. As I understand it, that is a matter which Mr. Dorsey is unwilling to discuss."

Dorsey watched the interview scene dissolve and Hickcock reappear at the news desk. Crap, Dorsey told himself. Hickcock didn't press the guy. Two simple-ass questions and he gets two stock answers, and the priest is allowed to remain serene, his feathers unruffled. This is a change in direction?

Hickcock faced the camera and continued. "Despite Father Jancek's minimizing of Edward Damjani's involvement with Movement Together, Mr. Damjani participated in, or perhaps instigated, an earlier altercation with Carroll Dorsey at a Movement Together rally in Midland. The tape you are about to see was provided by our sister station WPGT. In it you will see Mr. Damjani's actions of a week ago."

The tape was of the Midland Union Hall rally, and Dorsey watched an image of himself angling through the crowd. Jeez, TV does make you look heavier, he thought, squeezing an inch of fat at his hip. The camera angle was from the rear of the room, and Damjani could be seen closing in on Dorsey in slow motion, Damjani's head and shoulders above the throng. Watching the tape, Dorsey felt a tingle run up his spine and rooted for the taped Dorsey to get away. Shoving his way down the center aisle, Damjani pushed people aside, adding to the sense of menace. Damjani reached across several heads and took hold of Dorsey's collar. As Dorsey began to struggle, the tape froze and the camera closed in on Damjani's face, twisted in rage.

"This," Hickcock said as the picture dissolved, "is Edward Damjani."

Choreography, Dorsey thought, paced well for dramatic effect. The camera as image maker. You should hire this guy for a publicity agent, he told himself.

Hickcock returned to the screen to make some more small talk with the anchor, who now captured the camera's attention.

"Well," Dorsey said to the television, "you were impressive, just like you promised. But I still don't trust you."

CHAPTER 20

All of ten minutes. That's as long as he took.

Dorsey watched Father Melcic standing over the coffin, mumbling his way through a small black prayerbook. The coffin sat on a wheeled gurney standing at the communion rail's center gates; the priest held the prayer book to his chest and blessed the air above it with the sign of the cross. Finished, he motioned for the undertaker to wheel the coffin away, up the center aisle of the church.

All of ten minutes, Dorsey thought again, and you sleep-walked all the way.

The six mourners had taken the first two pews to the right of the center aisle, three in each. Dorsey stood in the second aisle behind Al and watched Father Melcic retreat across the altar to the sanctuary. "Give anything to the priest yet?" Dorsey asked, tapping Al on the shoulder.

"Cash." Al tilted back on his heels to whisper his reply. "Twenty-five. Should've used a check. Could've stopped payment."

Martin Dorsey, dressed in dark blue and wearing a black mourner's band on his left upper arm, stepped from the first pew to follow the coffin. In the aisle he waited to take the arm of Mrs. Rosek, and Al followed solemnly behind. Waiting in the second pew for Bernie and Ironbox Boyle to step out ahead of him, Dorsey considered the difference between Father Melcic and Father Jancek. This guy here, Melcic, he's only got ten or twelve years on Jancek, but they've been hard ones and they show. Years spent putting the fear of God in guys who got drunk and beat their families and slapped their wives around, and years spent knocking the stuffing out of kids who were two steps away from the juvenile detention center. So Melcic is all business and hard at the edges, a little bitter and disillusioned, while Jancek stays young drinking the elixir of public acclaim. Young enough to have an older man die.

Dorsey started up the center aisle, keeping a few paces behind Mrs. Boyle. As they moved outside to the church steps, facing the cramped row houses of Twenty-second Street, Dorsey spotted a white van with a Channel Three logo parked ten feet behind the hearse. A two-man film crew kept the light and the camera trained on the coffin as it was wheeled down a handicapped ramp and across the sidewalk to the hearse. Without success, Dorsey searched the street for Sam Hickcock.

"The voice-over, they do that later." Martin Dorsey stood at his son's side. "In the studio. The reporter adds the narration as they play the tape for editing. You learn that when you try to get elected in the so-called Electronic Age. They'll want shots of us, too." Martin Dorsey gestured to Mrs. Boyle, and she followed as he descended the steps and crossed the sidewalk to his rented car and driver. As he had predicted, the camera followed him each step of the way.

Bernie told Dorsey he had to get back to the office and left, saying he would call later. Out on the sidewalk, satisfied that the coffin had been loaded into the hearse without mishap, Al told the undertaker he could start for the cemetery. "We'll visit the grave later," Al said, after rejoining his wife and Dorsey at the top of the steps. "The priest won't be there for the last farewell, so there's no sense in goin' now."

Rose agreed and invited Dorsey back to the bar for lunch. "We hoped Bernie and your father would've come. Hoped to make something of a wake out of it." She was all South Side in Dorsey's eyes. Short and squat, with years of hard and devoted work showing on her face but not in her eyes. They stayed clear and bright with love. That face could work you over but good, and the eyes said you were better off for it.

"I'll be along this evening," Dorsey said.

Rose dug into her square black purse. "Better give this to you now, then. Good thing I brought it along." She handed a small note-sized white envelope to Dorsey.

Slipping a thumbnail under the flap, Dorsey tore open the envelope and took out a color snapshot of Russie and his father sitting at dinner. The setting, decorated for Christmas, was his father's dining room. On the back, in what must have been Russie's scrawl, the photo was dated *Christmas Day, 1973*. When you were in the service, Dorsey reminded himself. Most likely, Ironbox took the shot.

"It was in the drawer where he kept what he figured to be his important papers," Al said. "Russie, I mean. Him havin' no family anybody knows of, we had to sort out the stuff. The clothes, they all went to St. Vincent de Paul's. There was some more stuff like this: souvenirs. There was a stack of old ball-game tickets, thick as your hand is long. Mostly from Forbes Field and basketball at the Arena. Some of your old games, I bet. We might frame a bunch of 'em, hang it behind the bar."

Dorsey slipped the photo into the envelope and put it in his coat pocket. "Thanks, Al. You too, Rose. Thanks a lot."

"Take care," Rose said, patting his arm. "You look after yourself. The big one, the guy they showed grabbing at you on the TV. That son of a bum, he's still around. You take good care."

As Al and Rose walked away, descending the church steps, Dorsey dug into his pocket to retrieve the snapshot. Dressed in coat and tie, Martin Dorsey sat at the head of the table, his glass raised in a holiday toast. Russie sat to his left, wearing a plaid flannel shirt and a dark green tie. Neither one—neither the old man nor Russie—ever mentioned it, or any other get-together that might have taken place, except for when the old man slipped Russie a five for a new wax job on his car. The old man must have it in him, he thought. Look at him: one hell of a picture, and it never made its way into a newspaper or election brochure.

The heavy oak church door behind Dorsey opened and Father Melcic stepped out, pulling at the hem of his black cassock to keep it from catching as the door closed. Against the cold, he wore a heavy sweater of matching black. Taking Dorsey's hand, he offered his condolences. "Nice thing you and the others did, arranging for the memorial service. Wish I could have done more for you, but with no proof of the deceased being Catholic, there was only so far I could go. But it was a very good thing you did. Most indigents go from the morgue to the grave without a blessing."

"He was no indigent," Dorsey said, his voice carrying a sting. "He had a roof over his head that he paid the rent on each month. The guy worked all his life and had a pension coming from the county. He was just alone."

"My misunderstanding," Father Melcic said in an even voice. "Still, it was a nice thing. I suppose you're waiting for your friend?"

"My friend just left. In the back of a hearse."

The priest looked at Dorsey and shook his head. "You feel bad, I know. But I was referring to the fellow who is still inside." Father Melcic again shook his head and walked off.

Dorsey stepped into the vestibule, ticking off a list of possible mourners, wondering who he and Al had forgotten. None of the names caused a stir as he worked his way through the bar patrons and Carson Street people who might have known Russie. County workers were out too, he thought. Russie had been retired for years.

Dorsey slipped through the swinging doors into the church proper and spotted a man who had not been there before, kneeling in one of the front rows near the altar, far to the left and near the side door. He wore a trenchcoat with the collar turned up, leaving only his bald pate exposed. Dorsey started down the center aisle, walking softly, respecting the man's prayers. When Dorsey was halfway down the aisle, the man blessed himself, rose to his feet, and began moving to the far end of the pew. Dorsey was somewhat surprised; he had not expected the man to be so short. Stepping out into the side aisle, the man made a half turn toward the altar and genuflected. Only then did Dorsey see the gray and white of the beard and the silver wire-frame eyeglasses.

"Jancek!"

Dorsey watched the priest jump at the sound of his voice and quickly turn to face him. As recognition worked its way across Father Jancek's face, Dorsey started forward, sliding sideways through a pew, careful not to trip over the kneeler. Backpedaling, Father Jancek made for the side door, reaching backward for the door handle. He went through the door as Dorsey reached the aisle.

Sprinting to the door, Dorsey seethed, outraged at the desecration. No cameras, no press release, he thought, pushing open the exit. There's no mileage to get out of this, no chance to show his piety and his ability to pray for the enemy's casualties. Dorsey chugged down the steps to the sidewalk and spotted Father Jancek climbing into the rear seat of a worn and rusted Chrysler. He watched as the Chrysler screeched away from the curb toward an intersection, where it blew through a stop sign and turned right, disappearing onto Carson.

Standing at the curb, Dorsey wiped the sweat from his face with the back of his hand and pulled at his tie. "Fuckin' bastard round-collar. The fuck is he doin'?" He spat into the gutter. Helps the deceased become the deceased, and he wants the honor of saying the requiem. Dorsey shook his shoulders to work out the hatred, rolling his head to loosen the neck muscles. Satisfied, he gathered his coat around him and smoothed the lapels. It was then he felt a gentle yet firm nudge at the base of his spine.

"Slowly, very slowly."

The gunman, Jesus Christ, the gunman. Dorsey recognized the smooth southern voice, free of the hard edge of a northern city. He made a cautious half-turn and faced the black man who had sent Damjani and his partner packing. Sent 'em packing, he thought, after Russie was face down in the slush. The gunman worked a wide smile across his face, exposing a gold-capped tooth, just left of center. He was as tall as Dorsey but slender. Dorsey likened his skin tone to well-polished black marble.

"Hell of a gun you got there," Dorsey said, looking down at the automatic, its barrel pointed just to the right of his coat's center seam. Stay with it, he told himself, stay calm and play it out. As if there was a choice. "No Saturday-night special, right?"

"That's true," the gunman said. "Forty-five. It'll get you through the whole week."

A dark late-model Riviera pulled up to the curb and its black driver slipped across the front seat and pushed open the passenger door. "Hop in," the gunman said, pushing Dorsey inside with the gun barrel.

"Thought you were sent to look after me." The gunman had climbed into the backseat and Dorsey addressed him through the rearview mirror.

"The other night," the gunman said, "I was lookin' after you. Today I'm fetchin' you."

The Riviera cruised across the Birmingham bridge, away from South Side. In the rearview Dorsey watched the gunman, pistol hanging loosely in his hand, and wondered if the Chrysler carrying Father Jancek had just taken the same route. Well, Dorsey, at least you get to ride in a nicer car. Jancek or Stockman, either one, sent two guys to crack your skull and the strong-arm man in the backseat pulls you out of the fire. Now the same strong-arm man is the snare in the trap baited with the priest. You're the detective in this car, so where's the logic? Tell us how it all comes together.

"I'm meeting the priest, huh?" Dorsey asked.

"Sure, if that's what you want." The gunman peered out the window and down at the river. "Headed for the Hill. You ever hear this one, Dorsey? This is supposed to be the longest bridge in the world. Goes from Poland to Africa. Polacks in South Side, niggers on the Hill. A white guy told it to me. But I like it."

At the foot of the bridge, the driver, silent and concentrating on the road, pushed the accelerator, and the Riviera roared through the intersection and up a steep grade. Dorsey watched the streets go from mean to worse, block after block of gutted buildings and collapsing wooden homes, some with Insulbrick hanging in sheets from the walls. Between the buildings were weed-covered lots with paths beaten through them. City weeds, Dorsey thought, the kind that look eternally gray and stand seven feet tall. Excellent spots for dumping stolen cars, moving junk, or just taking a wine-drunk piss. And Father Jancek's old parish, the black one, is nearby. Dorsey's palms went wet and clammy, and he tried to convince himself that he was safe. That whatever this was he'd come out in one piece. The media coverage, it makes you invulnerable. Your picture's been all over the papers and the tube. You turn up dead, and the only suspects are the priest, Personal Injury, and the Movement. But who says you're going to turn up? Think about it. Might be different if you just disappeared. No body, no crime, and no charges. And it blows over when the cops get tired of looking. My God. Jesus fuckin' Christ.

The Riviera went left onto Centre Avenue, the driver handling the steering wheel with just the tip of a finger. Thick through the shoulders and thicker yet at the waist, he wore a slouch cap with the visor pulled low. Dorsey wondered if he was armed but realized it made no difference. He knows you won't make a move when the car slows for a turn, which it hasn't. Or if we have to stop for a red light. Must be one bad son of a bitch in the back seat.

They went another two blocks along Centre, and Dorsey's pulse quickened with each black face and boarded window they passed. The driver made a fast right and then an even quicker left into an alley running parallel to Centre. The Riviera pulled over by the rear door of a building facing Centre, the driver's-side tires resting on the curb. The driver killed the engine and struggled out from behind the steering wheel.

"This is it." The gunman tapped Dorsey's shoulder with the gun barrel. "Gotta go inside."

Dorsey stepped out onto the asphalt, and although the gunman was a few steps behind, he could feel the gun on him as surely as he felt the cold wind cutting across his face. There'll be no running, he assured himself. This has to be played out; make a move only if it looks like the worst is going to happen. Like begging on your knees.

The driver opened a steel security door and ushered Dorsey inside and up a flight of steps, the gunman trailing behind. Dorsey jumped at the sound of the steel door slamming shut and the smell of rotting wood and corroding plaster assaulted his nose. Dorsey remembered the smell from a thousand suspect roundups in mill-town slums where the heat source was a cheap open-flame gas burner.

At the top of the steps was a second steel door, and the gunman reached past Dorsey to unlock it. The lock snapped crisply and the gunman forced Dorsey forward. "Watch your feet," the gunman said. "Gotta step up."

Dorsey found himself in a small windowless office with a third steel door at the far wall. Paneled in imitation wood, the room held a well-polished desk of dark wood, matching swivel chair, and two cushioned visitor's chairs facing the desk. Diplomas hung on the wall behind the desk, but before Dorsey could read the name of the diplomate, the gunman pushed him into the first of the visitor's chairs. The gunman rested on the edge of the desk, squarely in front of Dorsey, blocking his view of the diplomas. Dorsey wondered if it was intentional and came to the conclusion that everything this man did was intentional.

"What's it gonna be?" Dorsey asked, hoping to discern his fate. "The priest, he comes in and gives me the Last Rites, then you take it from there? That's how it's starting to look. From my seat, anyway."

The gunman shook his head and partially suppressed a smile, sending tremors up Dorsey's spine. My God, he thought, maybe you're right. This guy can pull it off. Complete detachment when he needs it, like with Russie. For Russie to get it was okay, this guy could stand for that. Two feet away and he could let it pass, because he was paid to keep an eye only on you.

Dorsey heard the door behind him open, and the gunman rose from the desk and trained the automatic on Dorsey's chest. Gripping the chair arms, white-knuckled, Dorsey watched as a tall, stocky black man, immaculately dressed in a suit the color of charcoal ash, rounded the desk. The ends of his jacket sleeves showed French cuffs with gold cuff links. He tugged at the tops of his pant legs when he prepared to sit. Dorsey figured him to have gained fifteen pounds since the photo was taken, and the gray had spread beyond his temples. The diplomas, now plainly in sight, confirmed it: he was sitting in the office of Louis Preach.

"Please, you should relax." Preach smiled. "It's been a tough day for you so far. Said good-bye to a friend and now this. I regret it, I really do, but it was necessary. I gave you plenty of invitations, over the phone and in the mail." Preach smiled again. "But you never called. I felt rejected."

"You've got my attention now," Dorsey said. "Using the priest like that, how could you fail?"

Preach's face took on a puzzled look, the lines of his forehead deepening, and he turned to the gunman, now positioned at the side wall. Pushing himself away from the paneling, the gunman came to the desk and crouched down to speak in Preach's ear. Dorsey watched Preach as he listened, wondering if the gunman was passing along last-minute instructions. And if he is, Dorsey was sure, the instructions were the joint product of Jancek and Personal Injury.

"Sure about this, Dexter?" Preach said as the gunman retreated to the wall. "The priest was there? And Dorsey, he thinks he's here to see him?" Preach turned to Dorsey, a grin working its way across his face. And then, studying Dorsey, he threw back his head and laughed so loudly it bounced off the office walls.

"Oh, Jesus, you think Father Jancek brought you here?" Preach asked.

"Yeah, I think the priest brought me here. Cut the bullshit." Dorsey found some of his fear turning to anger at being the obvious butt of a joke between Preach and Dexter, who was shaking with laughter too. "You enjoy your work, that's nice. But don't jack me around, okay?"

"Dorsey," Preach managed to say between laughs, "I didn't bring you here to see Father Jancek. You're here so I can show you how to nail him."

Preach wiped his face with a monogrammed handkerchief and started to send the gunman into the adjacent office for a bottle he said was in the secretary's desk. "Dex, hold on a minute," Preach said. "Mr. Dorsey's a beer drinker. Hustle across to the Circle for a six-pack."

Dorsey watched Dexter slip out of the room, quietly closing the door behind him. "Beer, huh? You know a little bit about me."

"Secondhand knowledge is all it is. Like I said, you wouldn't return my calls." Preach rose for a moment to shove the handkerchief into his rear pocket, then settled back into his chair. "After Dexter gets back, I'm going to send him out again. You don't carry any armor, and if you take off—well, these streets are top-heavy with what journalists used to call angry young black men, the dispossessed. You're much better off here. We'll talk; then you'll be taken home. By the way, if you want, there's a bathroom just out the door and to the left."

Cautious and weary, Dorsey rose and crossed the room, watching Preach over his shoulder. The next room was a reception area furnished with a secretary's desk and two worn sofas. Like the inner office, it was without windows, and the door facing Centre Avenue was the same steel make as the other. Dorsey found the bathroom and concluded it was a closet with plumbing as he wedged himself between toilet and sink. Leaning over the bowl, he took a long and furious fear piss, his anxiety lessening. Next he filled the sink with cold water and dunked his face, killing the heat in his facial nerves. He wiped his face with a paper towel and returned to the inner office.

"Security doors and no windows." Dorsey settled into his chair. "You'll scare away business, along with keeping the burglars out."

"Too often," Preach said, "they're one and the same."

The outer steel door slammed and Dexter entered the office dangling a six-pack of Budweiser from its plastic ring. Preach motioned for him to give two cans to Dorsey. "He'll drink fast. He's had a shock."

Dorsey took a can in each hand and popped the snap-tops with his thumbs. "That's right, a trying day it has been." He took a long pull from the can in his left hand. The beer hit his stomach fast and cold, soothing the tremors in his knees.

Dorsey placed the remaining cans on the corner of the desk and left. Preach moved them onto the blotter and used his elbow to wipe at the wet ring left on the wood. "Now that you're more composed, let's talk about Father Jancek. You're getting closer, I know you are. But I also know, as sure as my face is black, you haven't got him yet."

"And what is it I'm supposed to be getting him for?"

"Of course," Preach said. "You don't trust me. And why should you? You think I've thrown in with the priest."

"The two of you, you look really good together." Dorsey took another long pull on his beer and wiped his face on his sleeve. "Together, you two are downright photogenic."

Preach leaned back into his chair and spread his arms. "A photo opportunity is what it's called. "Pictures were taken, that's right. But there's a few years on them now, and times change. Father Jancek and myself—our little fallout was, I think, two years ago."

Calmed by the beer, Dorsey began pulling his thoughts together, hoping to initiate instead of reacting. Talk to me, he thought. He'll say the words, Dorsey told himself, and you'll shove them through the strainer to glean the truth from the bullshit, if any. "What's the matter?" Dorsey said. "Won't Father Jancek let you join him in praying at the steel-mill gates? You may have missed another photo opportunity. While they load you into the sheriff's wire-window bus."

"Oh, my delegation and myself, we were there at the beginning." Preach flashed the grin again, but this time it was much shrewder, and Dorsey watched for a knuckle ball. "But a year or two ago Father Jancek began seeing things in a different light. A different shade, perhaps." Preach pointed at Dorsey. "Think about it, just take a minute. You've been to one of the rallies, and you can't tell me you haven't seen the television. How many black faces have you seen? One, maybe two, if the good father is in an expansive mood on that particular day. Movements are coalitions. And, as is customary, to attract one specific group you may have to drop another. In the case of Movement Together, the dropped group is black. Disenfranchised, that's what we are."

Dorsey finished the beer and reached to place the empty on the blotter. There had been a few blacks in the union hall in Midland, he remembered, but they were fly shit in the sugarbowl. And the media-search photos in the manila folder. The earlier ones were pretty dark, but the tone lightened as the years rolled by. The demagogue develops.

"If you're on the outs with the priest, like you say, why was he willing to play out his role in church today?"

"Right now," Preach said, "you'll find this hard to swallow, but he wasn't there by my design. Pure coincidence. Dexter was told to get you here today, that's all. As I say, you may not believe that. But let me set my cards out on the table by telling a story."

Dorsey finished the second beer and took another from the desk, jerking the can away from the plastic ring. He nodded for Preach to begin.

"I've known Father Jancek for some time now," Preach said. "Since he came to Saint Agnes. Me, I'm not Catholic, guess you could say I'm a part-time Baptist, but we met through the community action groups. When he was at the head of the hunger and housing marches, I was one rank behind. I saw him wrap himself around politicians, and believe me, I loved the things he could accomplish. He never changed the city's social structure, but here and there, and maybe just temporarily, things got a little better. Job programs, help for the elderly and shut-ins, assistance to single mothers. Reagan's doing his best to undo it all, but it was better."

Dorsey nodded. "So you knew him way back when."

"And maybe not so way back," Preach said. "Like I said, it's only been the last two years that he and I have been on the outs. Me and my people were in on the ground floor when the Movement was formed, when the economy nose-dived. We were pretty well organized around here, and to be honest, a lot of it was Father

Jancek's doing. We were his first power base. But the Movement, it had to grow. New groups had to be attracted, enticed—union locals up and down the river valleys. And those guys like white faces best."

To Dorsey, it had the ring of truth. More than possible, he thought; damned likely. It's skin against skin in those towns, not class economics. And nobody there wants to do well if doing well leaves you with a nigger next door.

"It was a union local up in Brackenridge that finally did us in," Preach said. "Oh, sure, we were being nudged out before that. Little by little, white faces replaced the black ones in the committees. But this local up in Brackenridge, Christ, they were fat. Big and rich, with bank accounts that would make you drool. They wanted to be part of Movement Together, and Movement Together wanted them. But this local, the head men didn't want coffee mixing with the cream. And that's when the last black member of the executive committee, me, lost out in a special election."

"When you lost out?" Dorsey returned Preach's sly smile. "I thought your efforts were all in the service of your people."

"Me, my people: one and the same," Preach said. "My people, they need success stories, role models. So I should be one. But get this straight. We've been disenfranchised and I want that changed."

And the priest takes a tumble, Dorsey told himself, and Movement Together goes flat. And a new leader emerges. Louis Preach and his well-organized black faction at the center of a new coalition.

"So things get a little crazy for a while," Preach said, as if reading Dorsey's thoughts. "There'll be a lot of splinter groups looking for a vocal, high-profile leader. I can be very vocal when necessary."

"And you'll be very powerful," Dorsey said. "And there's more than one congressional seat up for grabs next year. I hear your local man plans on stepping down."

"I've never been one to be locked into one goal," Preach said, "and it's an interesting possibility. But regardless, you have my reasons for wanting to help you; we now understand each other. That's good."

"So how do I get Jancek?"

"You're going to pay a visit to a man I know," Preach said. "A man who was in on the planning, a man who sat at the table when it was all put together. It's arranged for you to talk to him tomorrow, late afternoon."

"And where's this going to take place?"

"Huntingdon State Penitentiary," Preach said. "He's doing three to five."

Chapter 21

Through the windshield, frost creeping in from the edges, Dorsey watched her emerge from the wooden side porch of the brick farmhouse. Leisurely, she crossed the yard and did leg stretches against a rough wood fence, her navy sweatshirt riding up as she bent forward. Finished, she adjusted her woolen cap and began moving down the driveway at a jog, her long arms and legs synchronized. Although the car sat on a knoll above the house, at a hundred-yard distance, he could see the morning air catch her breath and hold it in small white puffs. She made a right where the driveway met the county blacktop, then climbed a steep grade and disappeared down the far side.

Dorsey checked his watch and figured on forty minutes, twenty out and twenty back, her routine whenever she was away from her Exercycle. And the twenty minutes, they'd tick off in her head, never second-guessed by a wristwatch, Dorsey was sure. He turned over the engine to allow himself three minutes of heat and dug into the file folder on his lap, reviewing the criminal career of Arthur Demory.

The morning before, after Dexter had delivered him to his row house, Dorsey had put in a rush call to Meara, asking him to turn on the juice and get all he had on Demory, Preach's jailbird. Impressing Dorsey with his influence, Meara had the material compiled and delivered to Dorsey by early evening. The messenger was the same blond kid with the junkie look-alike. Was he the only messenger the agency had who could find South Side, or was South Side the only place this messenger could be trusted to go?

Dorsey had hoped to spend the evening writing his report on Louis Preach and plowing through Demory's file, but his discipline crumbled and thoughts of Gretchen overwhelmed him. Instead of pecking away at the portable Olivetti, he wandered from office to kitchen, peered into the refrigerator, and then paced back to the office to watch Wharton Street from his front windows. At eleven o'clock he caved in completely, hastily packed an overnight bag, and began the five-hour drive eastward across the state to Lancaster County.

Now, as he pushed through Demory's file, he sipped at the last of three coffees he had stopped for in Strasburg. The first two had coated his tongue, and the acrid taste of the third led Dorsey to dump most of it out the window. He wiped his mouth with a paper napkin, vowing to begin a love affair with tea.

At the top of the folder was a parole officer's presentencing report for Demory's first felony conviction, twenty-one years ago. Twenty years of age at the time, he had been charged with three burglaries and agreed to plead guilty to two. The report stated that Arthur Demory was the son of Agnes Demory, father's identity unknown. He had been raised in the Plan Eleven section of Aliquippa, a place Dorsey thought of as a smaller and meaner version of Pittsburgh's Hill District. Twice Dorsey had worked Plan Eleven, searching for auto accident witnesses, and both times he had gone in with local police escort. It was a white man's no-man's-land.

Arthur Demory had left high school at sixteen, and by age twenty he had failed to establish any employment history. Although he had by this time fathered a son, the court had shown only mild compassion, disregarding the parole officer's plea for leniency based on an impoverished childhood and the need to support a child. Demory had drawn thirteen months of county time.

Dorsey slipped the presentencing report to the bottom of the pile. With no employment record prior to his arrest, Dorsey figured Demory for a busy little burglar. A pro, a child prodigy in his profession. And Preach says to trust him?

Next in the file was a National Crime Index Computer report, a brief summary of arrests and convictions. Six months after his release from the Beaver County jail, Demory had been arrested for another burglary, but it didn't stick; no conviction. A year later, he'd been acquitted on a charge of receiving stolen property. Dorsey chuckled at Demory's advancement from burglar to fence. From labor to management.

At twenty-six he was given six months' probation for terroristic threats against the mother of his child. Two months later the Aliquippa police had collared him on a drunk-and-disorderly in an after-hours club. His probation officer issued a violation order on the arrest, and Demory did another four months for Beaver County.

Demory's sheet was clean for a little over three years, and then a drug bust put him in Pittsburgh SCI. Western Pen, Dorsey thought, the Wall. And he comes away from there a master of deception, the primary survival art inside a state correctional institution. Trust him, Preach said.

For the next nine years, according to the NCIC report, Arthur Demory's record was clear, confirming Dorsey's belief that the Wall had been Demory's finishing school. Then at age forty, Dorsey concluded, the man forgets all he's learned and is cracked for armed robbery, taking off a Seven-Eleven. And he ends up with his present address, maximum security at Huntingdon. Perhaps to relearn what he had obviously forgotten.

Dorsey skimmed the remainder of the file, thumbing through inmate records, hearing transcripts, and work-release reports. After packing it all away, he climbed out from behind the steering wheel. Shaking the cramps from his legs, he circled the Buick and checked his watch. Gretchen had ten more minutes of roadwork, by his figuring. Resting against the car hood, he studied the farmhouse: two stories of red brick, front and side porches, and stone chimney.

Gretchen had told him the fields and pasture beyond the fence no longer belonged to the Kellers: sold off, parcel by parcel, by Gretchen's late father to finance her medical training. And, Dorsey remembered, Mother lived on a schoolteacher's pension, Father's life insurance and social security. You need to settle things with her, he told himself. Don't leave without a promise. Even if it's only a promise to think it over.

Back behind the steering wheel, Dorsey allotted himself another three minutes of heat, watching the crest in the county blacktop. First came the puffs of steam put out by churning lungs. A speck of woolen cap was next, then head and shoulders cleared the crest. Gretchen came over the top and quick-stepped down the steep grade, struggling with gravity. But elegantly, Dorsey thought. The movements, finely timed legs and arms: always so goddamned elegant. He watched her puff her way up the driveway, kick off her shoes, and enter the house. Dorsey slipped the car into drive and made for the farmhouse.

He parked at the top of the driveway, climbed the two front steps, and knocked. Her mom would answer the door, he was sure; Gretchen was a fast shower artist. As predicted, an elderly version of Gretchen came to the door. The face was weathered, but the lean strong build was the same, and the hair was a tight curly crown. Introducing himself, Dorsey's heart was stung by how handsome Gretchen would remain through the years to come.

"You look awful," Mrs. Keller said, smiling to soften her words, a habit Gretchen had picked up. She was dressed in pressed khaki shirt and pants as if, despite its being November, she planned to spend the day gardening. "Better come inside. Some coffee?"

The mere thought cramped Dorsey's stomach. "No, no, thanks," he said. "Lately I've been trying to stay away from it."

"Then some juice and oatmeal." She took his jacket and led him through a hallway papered in a cornflower print and into a small kitchen. Even the mannerisms and the movements, Dorsey thought; they're the same. She'll be beautiful forever.

Dorsey sat at a rectangular oak table while Mrs. Keller poured orange juice. "She'll be a surprise," she said. "I've heard a lot about you the last couple of days. You know you're not really perfect, are you? Please don't get me wrong, now; I like it that she hasn't hung a halo on you. A lot of people do that, but I'm glad Gretchen hasn't. This way, if the two of you stick it out, she won't have too many disappointments. You either."

"Thanks," Dorsey said. "For the juice and the backhanded compliment. And for letting me barge into your home so early in the morning."

"No thanks necessary." Mrs. Keller placed a bowl of oatmeal in front of Dorsey and took the seat across from him. "It's romantic, you coming all this way at night. I'm impressed."

Dorsey poured milk from a pitcher into the oatmeal, mixing it with a spoon. "She still angry with me?"

Mrs. Keller sipped at her coffee. "That's where you're wrong. She never was angry; she was disappointed. As I said, disappointments are what we have to keep an eye out for in life. Keep them to a minimum and get them out of the way early on, the worst ones, anyway. Then you'll know if you're good for the long haul. Like the two of you are doing now, although I don't think either of you realizes it. I must admit, it's nice to be here and watch. It's touching."

Dorsey wolfed down the oatmeal, surprised at his appetite, now that the threat of coffee had passed. He washed it down with the last of the orange juice. Overhead he heard a dull thud, followed by the rattling of the house's plumbing. The shower was over; he knew the routine. She wipes down with a bath towel and then works it over her wiry hair. Then a few seconds to brush her teeth and apply deodorant, and then she wraps herself in a terry-cloth robe. Five minutes puts her down the steps for breakfast. Five minutes.

In sync with Dorsey's thoughts, Mrs. Keller began arranging a place setting to his right: juice glass, spoon, cloth napkin. A few silent minutes passed; then at the sound of footfalls down the stairs, they nodded to each other.

"Ah, Mum?" Gretchen called out from the hall, her voice

coming closer. "I might pass on the oatmeal today. Just some coffee and maybe a little—"

As she stopped, framed in the doorway, Dorsey looked her over from head to toe—from brain stem to bunghole he remembered Bernie saying once. The once-over confirmed that five hours of turnpike driving had been worth it. And looking at both her and her mother, he knew the long haul would be worth it, too, whatever it took.

"Good morning," Dorsey said cautiously. Gretchen remained in the doorway, knuckle to her lips, as if pondering his appearance.

"Coffee and juice is on the table." Mrs. Keller motioned her into the room and toward a chair. "Something needs tending to, I'm sure. Enjoy your breakfast, both of you."

As her mother left the room, Gretchen spent a few moments silently staring into her coffee. "I said I would call when I got back to town," she said, looking now at Dorsey. "On your machine. I said I needed time and I'd call."

"You needed time," Dorsey said. "Me, I'm afraid of time, scared shitless of what it might do. Like one day you're away and that day gives birth to two more, which split into a week or a month. And the longer you're away the easier it is for you to get used to the idea of my not being around. It scares the hell out of me."

"And your work scares me." Gretchen sipped at her juice, then moved the glass away from her. "That day with Claudia shook me up. You put her through the wringer. From the stories you tell, I thought all you did was keep watch on dishonest people, people who want something for nothing. The stories were always funny, with plenty of irony. There was always a nice little twist about the lengths people will go to for a buck. Now I'm faced with the lengths you'll go to for a job."

Dorsey smoothed his napkin. "I've never had a big case like this before, not since the DA's office. And what's worse, I've got my neck stretched out pretty far. It's a make-or-break deal for me. I go big-time or hire myself out as a rent-a-cop. So I fell back on what I knew, which is that every informant is dishonest. I needed to know what Claudia knew, and she didn't want to share it."

"So what's next?" Gretchen asked. "When does round two with her take place?"

"It doesn't." Dorsey explained that nothing short of a subpoena could get him within earshot of her, and he was following up another lead that could wrap up the whole affair very quickly.

"And then you get another tough case as a reward, right?" Gretchen gently rotated her cup, swirling the brown liquid. "And each time you get a tough case, you fall back on what you know."

"Succeed or fail," Dorsey said, "there won't be another tough case. Success will guarantee me plenty of work, enough to hire help and pick and choose my cases. So all I'll do is watch a guy's house to see if he's reshingling the roof. And if I fail, there'll be no cases at all, period."

Dorsey searched her face, finding nowhere to advance, no sign of how to proceed. He gave his mouth an abrupt swipe with his napkin and dropped it on the table. "Your mother and I, we had a good talk before you came down. Bright woman."

"Don't tell me." Gretchen chuckled. "The disappointment routine, right? Anything bad happens, it's a disappointment. We don't see things for what they are, so we expect more than is reasonable. And she applies it to us."

"Worked for me." Dorsey hoped for a laugh that didn't follow. "Could you give it some thought? You've got—what, another two days off? You get back to town, I'll stay away for a while if you need more time. But just one thing: keep some of your stuff at my place, okay? At least till you figure out what you want. It's only a bone, but I love you, so I'll settle for it."

Gretchen began to cry softly, the tears welling up from the bottom of her eyes, then brimming over, in a way Dorsey had seen before and had committed to memory. "I've been here since Sunday," she said, her chin resting on her hands, propped on the table. "And I've done nothing but think about us. On the ride out here, I missed the turnpike exit, almost ran off the road. Even with the snow, I wasn't paying attention."

Dorsey took her empty cup to the sink, rinsed it, and stacked it in the rack. There was a half window above the sink, and Dorsey looked out on the fields that had once been the Kellers', down payments on Gretchen's future. So it all goes back to a storefront in Johnstown, he thought, where you had to put the heat on the chain's weakest link. Then three silent hours through the snow. She gets a night's rest and an early start for Lancaster. And you miss her call because you're at the police station.

The realization struck him as he moved away from the sink. Frozen on the kitchen tile, Dorsey pulled it all into one piece. Jesus Christ. Sunday morning, early on. Before the papers or even the radio had the story. And after a few miles east on the turnpike, the car radio gets only the farm report and prayer meetings. Good God, she doesn't know.

"Look, something happened Saturday night." He slipped back into his chair and toyed with a spoon. "It might not help you see things my way, but—whatever. You think nothing could be worse than what you saw, but believe me, everything is relative. And there's always another notch to take things up to." Dorsey told her about the assault, Russie's death, and the funeral.

"That's where it stands." Dorsey took her hand, softly squeezing it. "The job I did on Claudia Maynard was pretty low, but it's not the worst. Death is the worst—unless Father Jancek has enough pull in the hereafter to fix me up for eternal damnation. Don't put me in his league."

Dorsey watched her go to the sink and wipe her face. "I didn't know," she said, her back to Dorsey as she gazed out the window. "He was your friend. I'm sorry. He got the car that morning, the day they were watching the house. Kind of an odd guy, but even still."

"Odd?" Dorsey said. "He was damned strange. But he was my friend. And I was the target, the one they came for."

Gretchen turned to him. "So you'll see this thing through; I suppose you have to now. We'll talk when it's over. I can't promise anything, except that we'll talk."

CHAPTER 22

Dorsey left the Buick in a parking lot near the perimeter of the prison compound, located in a windy hollow between two mountains. Looking for the visitor's check-in, he crossed through an area that might be taken for a mobile-home court, filled with Airstreams and Avions. But Dorsey knew it for what it was: housing for the trusties who worked the prison farm. He recalled a time several years earlier when he had interviewed an inmate who had begun pulling in compensation checks just before sentencing. The inmate claimed to be in constant excruciating back pain. After the interview, using binoculars from a perch atop one of the guard towers, Dorsey watched for two hours as the inmate bounced along on a tractor, jumping on and off during breaks, plowing a field.

At the visitor's check-in, still outside the high red-brick walls, Dorsey found that Preach was as good as his word: Dorsey's name had recently been placed on inmate Demory's list of approved visitors. Dorsey was given a brief lecture on prison regulations and the penalties for smuggling things inside. After he browsed for a few minutes in a gift shop that carried inmate art work, mostly depressingly dark sketches of prison scenes, Dorsey's name was called and he was escorted to the main gate. Next to the barred gate was a walk-through entrance, the final security checkpoint. A gray-uniformed corrections officer handed Dorsey a plastic tray, instructing him to empty his pockets into the tray, along with his belt. The officer then motioned to a second officer seated in a glass observation booth overlooking the gate. Holding his pants up by the belt loops, Dorsey passed through the metal detectors and entered the maximum security area of Huntingdon SCI.

Dorsey retrieved his belongings and walked through a small garden, brown with winter, following a sign for the visiting center. In a long one-story wing, he found a lounge equipped with easy chairs and vending machines where inmates, dressed in uniforms of varying colors depending on their housing and work assignments, mixed with visitors. At the far end were three doors; Dorsey made his way through groups of families and girlfriends to the door marked ATTORNEY'S CONFERENCE and slipped inside, locking the door behind him. The room was ten by twelve, divided by a waist-high counter across its middle. From the countertop to the ceiling was wire-reinforced glass, with a metal speaking portal at the height of a sitting man. A chair sat at the portal; a companion chair was beyond the glass.

Dorsey sat at the divider, took a pen and steno pad from his coat pocket, and placed them on the counter. As he watched the door at the opposite end of the room, his thoughts trailed back to Gretchen and that farmhouse, now three hours away. She'd be back, he was sure . . . almost sure. She'll be back and you'll make it work, he promised himself, or nothing's ever going to go right again.

With a metallic clang, the steel security door's deadbolt was released. Dorsey nervously ran his hands down his sides, checking his appearance, as if he were the subject of the interview. A short, heavily gutted guard swung open the door and motioned an even shorter black man into the room. Unlike the officer, the black man was very thin and looked to Dorsey as though he was only beginning his recovery from a serious illness. The skin of his face was tight to the bone, and his eyes were more brown than white. The sleeves of his orange coveralls were rolled to the elbows and ballooned out from there. His hair was trimmed close to the scalp with a razor part on the left, and when he came opposite Dorsey at the glass he fished two packs of cigarettes from his pockets. Dorsey checked the two vertical scars on his chin and figured them for a cell game that got out of hand.

"Word is you've got the room for as long as you want." The guard turned to Demory as he began to close the door. "Art, bang on the door when you're through. Or if you need more smokes. Just keep at it, I'll hear ya eventually. Okay?"

Demory watched the door shut then dropped into the chair. "You Dorsey? The guy Lou Preach sent?"

"That's me," Dorsey said. "You believe me, don't you? How many visitors you get up here in the mountains? I could show you some ID, perhaps a major credit card?"

Demory snorted out a laugh. "Fuck, no. This is good. Preach said you'd be good for a talk. But you're who you're supposed to be?"

"Yes, I am. I is me." Dorsey flipped open the steno pad.

"This is gonna be okay," Demory said. "You gotta realize. My day is full of hangin' out with cons or bullshittin' to guards, assholes like the one that brought me here. On a good day I get to pull the psychiatrist's leg." Demory lit a cigarette. "I shouldn't call the guy who brought me here an asshole. He ain't bad. But here you are, my fuckin' diversion for today."

The ground rules were set, as far as Dorsey could tell. No hard-ass bullshit, no threats, valid or otherwise. You've seen him before. He wants to talk, to impress on you that he is no ordinary jailbird. Lead him a little and sit back for the ride. And, of course, make sure he's not a fraud, a put-up job by Lou Preach.

"I read up on you on the way here," Dorsey said, tapping at the glass. "Your home turf, I'm familiar with it."

"Fuck you know about Aliquippa?" Demory laughed and took a deep pull on his smoke. He flicked the ash to the floor.

"What you know, maybe, is the Serbian Club, some Italians, and the mill. You don't know shit."

"Somebody say something about Aliquippa?" Dorsey registered confusion. "Plan Eleven, that's the place I had in mind."

Demory grinned and wagged a finger at Dorsey. "You know the Plan? Damn straight. The Plan, that's where I spent what I like to think of as my formative years."

"And learned your profession?"

"That's right." Demory shook a cigarette free from one of the packs on the counter. He lit the fresh smoke from the butt of the one he was finishing. "Doors, locks, windows, iron bars. Ain't nothin' could keep me outa your house. If you had something I wanted, you could bet your sweet ass I'd take it away from you."

"Don't know about that," Dorsey said. "No matter how good you are, even the best get caught. They caught you and put your skinny black ass in Beaver jail. With our mutual friend Tony Ruggerio."

"Antonio motherfuckin' Ruggerio." Demory drew it out through his teeth. "That fat-ass. Me and Tony was tight. He's a hard fuckin' guy, gets on your shit, but we was tight. I was in Beaver County twice. Second time, I made trusty. We was tight."

"Good man," Dorsey said. "Not many like him."

"Shit, ain't nobody like him." Demory hit off his smoke. "Up at the Wall there ain't nobody like him. Hard place, know what I mean? Fuckin' hard."

It was starting to move for Dorsey. Give it a little push, he thought. The inmate is ready to talk. Dorsey watched him take yet another cigarette and light it off the butt. Good Christ, Dorsey thought, his lungs must resemble the walls of a coal mine.

Dorsey didn't have to push. The jailbird was moving under his own power.

"The Wall," he said. "Can't help but pick up a few things in a place like that. I learned plenty."

"Heard a guy call it a finishing school once." Dorsey chuckled. "What courses did you take? Must've done pretty well. You stayed clean a long time."

The compliment drew a nod from Demory. "Picked up general stuff, first year or so. Stuff everybody learns. Like how to lie so well you believe it yourself. So you could fool anybody."

"What you might call the core courses?" So this is what it boils down to, Dorsey thought. You're sitting in this room with a guy who likes to think of himself as the master of deception, and you've got to hang on his every word. The crapshoot of a lifetime. "Then what?" he asked.

Demory pulled at his cigarette and coughed back the smoke. He spit on the floor and shrugged his shoulders, collecting himself. "Preach was right. He said you'd be worth talkin' to." Demory stared back at his cigarette. "It was this white guy I knew at the Wall. It pissed off the brothers, me hangin' with him, but it was worth it. The guy really knew some shit. Called him the Professor; me and three other guys called him that. The Professor stayed in his cell most all day except for chow. He was older, fifty or sixty; he was afraid some guys would fuck with him. But it was okay because me and these other guys would spend our time in there with him, on the floor by his bunk, squattin', kind of. Just hung with him till whenever."

"Sounds like story time at the children's library," Dorsey said.

"Weren't no fuckin' kids in that cell," Demory said. "And the Professor, he knew a game that beat shit outa creepin' around somebody's house in the dark. This guy pulled in more on one job than I ever did in a month of doin' houses. The Professor was a fall-down artist. He was behind the Wall for likin' little girls too much, but he made his livin' on beatin' insurance companies. And he taught it all to me."

Verification, Dorsey realized, was in his own backyard. This is your turf; he can't bullshit you. It's why Preach put us together. He knows you and he knows this jailbird, and he knows one can't fool the other. "Tell me about it," Dorsey said.

"For a while," Demory said, flicking ashes to the floor, "I did most of my work in department stores. On escalators. Had this shoe with a ragged toe. I'd head down the escalator when it was crowded. At the bottom, I'd fall down and start screamin'. I mean really bawlin'. And then I fell flat on my face. Nobody could see what was happening, but even still, with all the screamin' and the nasty end of my shoe, they thought they was witnesses. After the first-aid room I went to the risk manager's office, a guy who knew a nuisance claim when he saw one and wanted out. So I'd sign a release for a check and head down the street to the next target."

"Slick, very slick." Dorsey stretched and linked his hands at the back of his neck. "What else?"

"Icy sidewalks in winter, maybe a fall down a flight of steps. Some of that, anyway. And auto accidents: whiplash. Used rental cars, always used rentals. The rental agency pushes through the settlement. That way, nobody gets the idea their cars are a piece of shit. You better believe that takes a certain touch, hitting a bus or a car just so, especially if you want it to look like the other guy's fault. Make the other guy look like an asshole. Which he fuckin' is."

Carmen Avolio and his Brownsville rent-a-cars flashed through Dorsey's mind, along with Kenny Borek and all the other happy motorists. They had taken it one step further. They got the liability settlements and cashed in on disability policies.

"This drivin' business," Demory said, his cigarette at the corner of his mouth. "The Professor, he could only tell us about that. No cars behind the Wall to practice on. Had to develop the touch on the job."

Demory continued, explaining how it had been necessary to stay on the move, going from city to city in an east-west direction. He kept to the larger urban areas, where one injury claim looked much like the next and overloaded claims adjustors paid out settlements quickly to keep the paperwork flowing. And where a fall-down man could, at least for a time, remain invisible. Dorsey liked the feel of it. It was all genuine; the ring of truth was there from the first. Only one stumbling block remained. Why, Dorsey asked himself, if the money is good and easy, why branch out to armed robbery?

"And through this—ah, private practice of yours, you came to meet up with Jack Stockman, right?" Dorsey caught the grin on the inmate's face, his reaction to "private practice." "You two being colleagues and all, in the same line of work. And through P.I. you met the priest. Tell me I'm wrong."

Demory fired a cigarette off of the security glass, laughing when Dorsey instinctively ducked the red embers. "That's about how it went," Demory said. "but I only met the priest once, and that was later on." Demory lit another smoke. "I did a job in Pittsburgh. Figured it would go easy like all the rest. During regular visiting hours, I go to this hospital and look for the housekeeping department. You know, the janitors and shit? What I was lookin' for was a janitor with a mop and bucket, to lead me to that nice wet floor where he just mopped up somebody's puke. But I can't find any. So, like a million fuckin' other visitors, I go to the snack bar for a milkshake, the only thing my poor sick relative can keep down. From there I find a nice quiet wing of the hospital and step up to the counter at the nurses' station. The shake goes on the edge of the counter and while I ask for directions to my loved one's room the cup goes over the side, and there's milkshake all over the floor. I fumble around sayin' how sorry I am while they call housekeeping. Fifteen minutes later, just after the janitor finishes the floor and leaves, I come on back to apologize again. And my feet fly out from under me on the wet tile and I hit the deck. All because of one slick spot the janitor left behind. Instant fall-down."

Dorsey laughed. "Sounds easy, the way you tell it. But I guess it takes a true artist. Tell me about Stockman."

"The fuckin' hospital risk manager turned out to be a hard motherfucker. Must've read the report on how it happened and decided not to pay."

"And you being a smart-ass, you pushed him."

"Should've let it pass." Demory shrugged. "Pissed me off, him not payin' up, so I figured on calling his bluff. Asked some people I knew and heard Jack Stockman was the man. Looked like an easy case, so Jack took it. Without checking me out first."

"P.I. never knew it was fake?" Dorsey asked.

"Never got around to that part. Jack said he knew the risk manager, and the two of them would work it out. Jack said the guy knew how the game was played and there'd be some money coming my way. Anyways, Jack and the hospital guy had a meeting, and Jack read the accident report. Next thing Jack did was boot my ass out of his office. But he must've liked me, 'cause he called when he needed me."

"Just a second," Dorsey said, working up an inquisitive expression. "Needed you for what? To consult on a case maybe?"

"In a way." Demory coughed, gagging, and nearly doubled over before overcoming it. "Who you think taught all them union boys? Personal injury, auto, workers' comp. Gold mine of knowledge, that's what I am. Them union boys didn't know their ass from first base. I'm the one changed all that."

So we've finally arrived, Dorsey thought. But should we go further? He's a talker, but is he a bullshitter? Let's not waste any more time entertaining this jailbird, not in this green metal cage. C'mon, man, call for the check.

"I could listen all day." Dorsey gave one last smile before going serious. "But war stories I can get anytime. You want to tell me about P.I. Stockman and the priest. And believe me, I appreciate it. But I gotta be straight with you. Something doesn't feel right."

"Fuck you talkin' about?" Demory ground out his cigarette on the countertop, then pushed back his chair, screeching across the tile floor. One hell of a reaction, Dorsey thought, impressed. Wasted half a cigarette.

Dorsey rose to his feet and braced himself against the counter, his face inches from the glass. "I'll tell you what the fuck I'm talkin' about. So you think you're hot shit, no insurance scam you can't pull off. The money pours in and you live the good life, nice stable income. It's all going great, no reason to stray. But just the same, you grab a gun and hit a convenience store. What the fuck is that about? Why didn't you stay with what works? Tell me; I'm anxious to hear all about it."

"Can't do that shit forever," Demory said.

"Why the fuck not?" Dorsey watched the anger drain from the black man's face; his lips and tongue worked silently in a search for words. "That's right, Arthur, you've got a job here to do. And you're supposed to convince me to believe you. So get going, Arthur, make a believer out of me."

"They know, man." Demory spoke to the floor. "I've been indexed."

"Yeah, sure, I've seen the Criminal Index report on you. Inspiring, but who gives a shit?"

"No, no, not that." Demory held his hands with palms out as if surrendering. "Ain't talkin' about the Criminal motherfuckin' Index. This is the Claims Index. They got my identity. So I'm fucked."

"And that's how the hospital risk manager caught on to you. And that's why P.I. Stockman sent you packing. He's handled shaky cases before. But you being on the index, that must've really pissed him off. Tell me I'm wrong."

"You got it right," Demory said. "Congratu-fucking-la-tions."

Dorsey pulled back from the glass and paced the room. There's no doubt this man is the genuine article, he thought. Only an insider would know the indexes. Somewhere along the line some adjuster knew Demory for a fraud and gave his ID to an index service, those noble listings of repeat claimants. Guys who have a habit of falling down on every other sidewalk they cross. Dorsey laughed as he thought of the hospital risk manager running Demory's name and statistics through the service. He pictured the computer lighting up like a Christmas tree. Son of a bitch, this guy is the real thing.

"Which index service has your name?" Dorsey stood behind the chair, leaning into the back supports. "Or didn't the Professor tell you the names?"

"He told me everything." Demory pulled his chair close to the glass and sat and fired a cigarette. The grin was back on his face. "Cleveland Index for sure; that's what fucked me locally. Probably one or two more, I figure out west. That's where I did most of my work. Satisfied?"

Dorsey stepped around the chair, took his pen and steno pad from the countertop, and sat. "I'll be satisfied if you don't kack out from the smokes before we get through." Dorsey clicked out the tip of his ballpoint. "Now tell me all about it."

With Dorsey interrupting with questions, it took four hours to get the whole story. Twice they called the guard to bring more cigarettes for Demory, who never missed a link in the chain; one cigarette ignited the next. Dorsey didn't dispute the facts; his questions served only to fill in the gaps in the story. Relaxed, the inmate explained that his second contact with Stockman was after the robbery.

"It was maybe three weeks after the cops cracked me. I was in county jail, Pittsburgh, all that time. My record, and the gun, sent my bail through the fuckin' ceilin'. Judge decided I was a danger to the community and a sure bet to take off. Which I was planning to do. Bail was set at seventy-five thousand. Like I was some kinda motherfuckin' baby raper or some shit. Anyways, there was no way to get up bail, so I sat."

"And in steps P.I., right?"

"That's it. Fuckin' P.I." Demory shook his head, laughing at the nickname. "Guard just took me off the range and walked me to this office. And get this, the office was outside the security area. And right behind this desk is Stockman. The guard sits me in the chair and leaves, shuttin' the door. Now, check it out. I got no cuffs on my wrists and no manacles on my legs, and I'm outside of the range in a room where a guy could hand me a howitzer. In an office, not no glass and telephone like on visiting day. So I knew Stockman had clout, pull like I never seen. And I know if this guy says he can do something, he can."

"And what was that? What did he say he could do?" Dorsey took notes and got the date of the meeting. Feed me P.I., he thought. C'mon, serve him up.

"Said he could get me out," Demory said. "Said he could get the bail lowered and that he would come up with the bond money. Then he tried to flatter the shit outa me. Said a man of my experience was wasted in jail, that my talents were needed elsewhere."

"But still, what was it the judge had said?" Dorsey concentrated on the inmate. "You're a potential jumper, considering your record, which you're proud of. P.I. is one savvy son of a bitch. How'd he figure to keep you from running?"

Demory smiled and tapped the ash from his cigarette. "You got it right. P.I. is one savvy son of a bitch. He promised some money I could hold onto if I went inside, which is where I am. And he never doubted I would go inside. Must admit, he got me a good lawyer, free, and that lawyer cut a pretty fair deal. Sentence could have been a lot worse. And one other thing. P.I. said if I jumped he'd send private detectives to bring me back to Pennsylvania, and that my legs might break on the difficult journey back."

"C'mon, hell," Dorsey said. "A hard-ass like you, afraid of P.I.?"

"Get fuckin' real, man," Demory said. "I'm a fuckin' inmate in a county jail, a dangerous motherfucker as far as the world is concerned. Surefire maximum security material. And I'm in a closed room with a guy from the outside. I knew if a guy could arrange this, he could do the job. Besides, I could've jumped bail once I was out, but I done time before. And bein' a fugitive, it's a real fuckin' drag."

As Dorsey continued to take notes, Demory explained that bail had been lowered the next day and bond posted. On release he was met on Ross Street, at the jail's public entrance, by two burly and capable-looking men. He was taken to a second-floor apartment on Penn Avenue in Greensburg. The place was clean and the refrigerator was stocked with food and beer. One of the two men told him to rest up, take a few days off.

"Should've seen the ride they drove, piece of shit. This rusted-out Chrysler."

Dorsey chuckled and remembered the car that had rescued Father Jancek at the funeral. Must be Movement Together's company car. He had Demory repeat the address and the date he arrived.

"And two days was what I got," Demory continued. "Laid around and worked on the refrigerator. Didn't see a soul. And then, seven o'clock on the third morning, Stockman showed up. From then on I didn't get a rest till I was sentenced here. I *needed* a vacation."

"Let's hear about this meeting," Dorsey said. "All you can remember."

Demory wheezed from deep in his chest and spat phlegm at the floor. "Maybe he didn't think I was all the way on his side, because he started in with the flattery shit again. How I was this great resource. I guess I'm *your* resource now."

"Just keep going."

"So he tells me how my talents could be used in the interests of the people." Demory coughed and spat.

Interests of the people. Dorsey rolled it around on his tongue. P.I. the closet radical, Father Jancek's college chum. The radical gospel according to Father Jancek. "And so you served the people."

"Damned straight. Now I was the Professor."

Dorsey grinned as he thought of how even the most corrupt learning is passed by word of mouth, generation to generation. Taking notes, he listened as Demory laid out the scope of the conspiracy. The auto accidents were Stockman's idea, but Demory insisted on using rental cars. "P.I., he knew some stuff, but this would've never flown without me. Why wreck your own ride?"

"Can we get into the workers' comp and disability side of the deal?" Dorsey peered at the inmate over the top of the steno pad.

"Again," Demory said, "P.I. had some good ideas, and he came up with the people who were willing to play the part. But no fuckin' organization. Bunch of guys don't fall down all on the same day without somebody catchin' on. Has to be spread out. They wanted the money fast. Takin' our time was hard to sell to these people."

"Carlisle Steel, that was the biggest operation," Dorsey said. "Am I right?"

"Biggest I ever saw." Demory stuck a cigarette in his mouth and applauded the idea. "Moved on greased wheels. It was an inside job; a girl in the personnel office was in our pocket. She let us know if our people were going in the next layoff. The boys found it easier to play along when they were about to lose their jobs anyway. The fall-down is easy when you know you'll be taken care of."

Dorsey switched gears and moved from the big picture to the details, the individual brush strokes. He pressed for meeting dates and who attended and who said what. In the time it took to do in five cigarettes, Demory provided a detailed chronology that hung the Carlisle employees, Claudia Maynard, and P.I. Stockman. Impressed with the inmate's powers of recall, Dorsey told Russie's memory that one of the big ones was in the bag. Now for the other.

"So far, you've maybe left someone out?" Dorsey asked. Demory expelled a packet of gray smoke and gently nodded his head, looking at Dorsey as a teacher looks at a star pupil.

"The priest," Demory said. "Like I mentioned before, he showed himself only once. But that's enough if it's done right."

Demory told Dorsey it was three months into the fraud before he met Father Jancek. "It was up and going, fan-fucking-tastic. My people learned quick and stayed smart. So, and you're thinkin' we were fuckin' crazy, we threw a party. Stupid, right? Fuck it, that's what we did. Had it in the back room of this bar in Latrobe. P.I. covered the whole thing: beer and liquor, food, and some of the guys blew a couple joints. And after things start to cook, when they are really goin', Father Jancek kind of slips in. No round collar, just a sweater, and hardly any of these guys even catch on to who he is at first. P.I. took me by the arm and just about drags me across the room to meet the fuckin' guy. So then the priest starts in on how he was aware of my contribution. That's what he kept calling it, my contribution. That must sit better with him than theft by deception. And he kept on telling me, more for his own benefit than mine, that my contribution was necessary for the economic recovery. And how nobody would really understand it, so it was best to keep it under our hats."

"Keep going." Dorsey flipped a page on the steno book. "What else about the priest? There's more, I hope."

Demory took a long pull on his cigarette and held it, thinking. "Not much. The man shook a few hands, patted a few backs, and left."

Dorsey took down the date of the party and the bar's address and asked Demory about any other meetings he had with Father Jancek.

"Never saw the man again," Demory said. "Except on TV."

Only P.I., Dorsey told himself, you might just have to settle for his ass. Demory's testimony and some further corroboration from a few more reputable Movement Together members once they crack under pressure should nail him. But in court, the priest walks. But not on TV and not in the papers. And not in the book Hickcock puts together, if that slippery bastard is to be trusted. Sorry, Al, sorry, Russie, it's the best I can do.

Dorsey flipped through his eighteen pages of notes, checking for any inconsistencies. Satisfied, he closed the steno book and clicked his pen, retracting the point. "Look, from what I can see you've got more pull around here than the warden's wife."

Demory grinned.

"What I need," Dorsey said, "is for you to call that guard in here and arrange for me to use a typewriter in one of the offices around here. It'll take me a little while, but I'm going to type up your statement. And then you'll sign, right?"

"Yeah, I'll sign," Demory said. "But you be quiet about this shit, especially while you're here. Lotta shit can happen to a guy, and Lou Preach ain't got that much pull. I'll sign and I'll testify in court, but that's later, after indictments are handed down and I become too important to fuck with. Be cool, and I'll sign."

"Guaranteed," Dorsey said. "I'll type. You sign,"

CHAPTER 23

Dorsey awoke to find himself at his desk, the early light of a winter sun cutting through the window, catching flying dust in shafts. Lifting his head from the blotter, he wiped grains of sleep from the edges of his eyes and took a fast inventory of the desktop: two beer cans, both crunched in the middle; the Olivetti portable with an empty ribbon box beside it; his steno pad, thinner now that the pages of notes had been torn away and crumbled. Neatly stacked to the left was the final draft of his report.

He took the report in hand and began to proofread, impressed by his ability to compose in a state of near-exhaustion. The first fifteen pages were all he remembered typing, yet the narrative flowed easily through the remaining twenty-three. It weighed about a pound, Dorsey estimated. But like a hundred-pound millstone, it would take P.I. Stockman straight to the muddy bottom.

Dorsey checked his wristwatch, confirming four hours until his lunch date. Upstairs he stripped and took a thirty-minute shower, scrubbing away the ink under his nails left by the typewriter ribbon, the dirt of six counties, and the animal-sweat stench of the penitentiary. He dressed casually in corduroy slacks and rag sweater topped off by a camel-hair sport jacket. After retrieving the morning paper from the front door, he went into the kitchen and brewed a four-cup pot of coffee. He downed all four cups while scanning the paper and listening to a tape of the Ellington band, Johnny Hodges taking off on alto sax.

The day's first stop was at a copier service on Carson. Dorsey ordered three copies of the report, one each for Corso at FC, Meara at the DA's office, and Cleardon at corporate headquarters. Waiting on the copier, he stared out at Carson, the sidewalk peopled with deliverymen and shoppers, and thought back to Bernie's warning about Corso. The man sells cases, Dorsey thought. This one could bring a high price. Stockman has a lot riding on this and he could raise enough cash to convince Corso that the risk was worth taking. The set procedure is for Corso to receive a copy of the report; that's what you agreed to. But he sells cases. Sighing, Dorsey turned from the window and considered his options. Fuck it, he decided, Corso gets shit. The report can go to Munt, tucked safely away at the home office in Syracuse.

With the copies in a legal portfolio next to him on the front seat, Dorsey drove through light traffic on the Tenth Street bridge and into the Armstrong Tunnels, moving slowly to allow his eyes to adjust to the abrupt fall of night. Just off of Ross Street he pulled to the curb, stuck a quarter in the meter, and trotted up the steps of the Allegheny County Courthouse. A short elevator ride to the third floor let him off opposite the District Attorney's office.

"Mr. Meara can't see you now, he's in deposition."

The receptionist was in her fifties. A thick paperback was open and face down at the center of her low steel desk. Dorsey figured it to be the type that promises the reader young American women in Paris and bedroom scenes every seventy pages.

"Like I said, he's in deposition," the receptionist repeated. As she spoke her left eye closed against the smoke of a cigarette stuck in the corner of her mouth. "After that he's got meetings. He's tied up all day. Gotta call ahead. I keep telling you people—"

Dorsey raised his right hand, pointing his index finger to

center the woman's attention. "Okay, honey, let's get this straight. I don't want to see Bill Meara. What I want is to leave this little package for him. And it's something important, so it better get to him. I'll be back this afternoon, and at that time Bill Meara will want to see me, no matter what needs to be canceled." Dorsey dropped a copy of the report onto the desk. "Another thing: what's this 'you people' stuff? And one last thing: quit reading that crap. It'll ruin your eyes."

Out on the sidewalk, Dorsey pumped four quarters into the parking meter. There was still time to kill before lunch. It was dangerous to arrive early. Don't look anxious and come off as the needy one, because you are not. Demory's statement is a trump card, ace high. Nobody can take the trick away.

At a stationery store he purchased two large envelopes, addressed one to Charles Cleardon and the other to John Munt. He took them to the postal window at the Federal Courthouse, mailed the reports by overnight express, and started back along Grant Street for his appointment. Passing the county courthouse again, he took a detour and walked through the center courtyard, where the judges and politicians had once parked their cars and Russie had washed and waxed them. Dorsey stopped by the fountain at the yard's center, picturing how Russie must have looked, his sleeves rolled to the elbow and his hands plunging into buckets of sudsy water. And always in a hurry, Dorsey remembered, keeping so busy the joke was that there was no way he could be a county employee. Should've had the memorial service here. Could've saved the priest's fee and Russie would have been home. But it's okay, Dorsey told him, it's okay. The checks are in the mail. For the payback.

It was Dorsey who had insisted on the Wheel Café. Hickcock had suggested a lunch date at a small Greek restaurant near the TV station, but Dorsey had no intention of going onstage, allowing Hickcock to show him off to his fellow reporters, impressing them with his insider connections. Use him, Dorsey warned himself; don't let him use you. He'll get his chance at the book-signing party, if it gets that far—and maybe it will. Things are turning in your direction. Now, if Gretchen . . .

Dorsey stopped just inside the café doors and took in the restaurant, appreciating the continuity; it never changed. Long and wide, the room had a thirty-foot ceiling covered with old worked tinplate. The bar was dark wood and ran from the front entrance to the swinging kitchen doors, deep into the gloom of the poorly lit far corner. To the right was a line of booths, and a bartender signaled Dorsey to the last of them.

"Jesus Christ," Hickcock said as Dorsey slipped into the booth. "This is your idea of a place to eat? The room needs paint. Maybe five or six coats. What's the attraction?"

"It's old," Dorsey said. "Not restored, not refurbished. Just old."

A bartender dressed in white shirt and dark pants topped with a white linen apron, double-wrapped, passed the booth and slapped down two menus. Dorsey pushed them away and hailed the bartender. "Hey, Cas, we made up our minds already." The bartender backed up to the booth and yanked a bill pad from under the apron. "Give us the hot sausage," Dorsey said. "Two each, and two drafts." Hickcock began to protest but Dorsey cut him off. "They're small, the sandwiches. And they're different."

The beer came before the food and Dorsey thanked the bartender as he headed into the kitchen. He sipped his beer and turned to Hickcock. "So, what's on your mind?"

"I'm here to find out what's on *your* mind."

Hickcock looked much more composed than at their first meeting. His hair was freshly cut and there was no way his suit was off the rack. Healthy and in control; no longer a beggar.

"You've been watching the news regularly, I assume. My reports, I mean. And the new girl, the one I told you about, there's another couple of weeks before she gets here. By then the news direction will be solid and she'll have to toe the line I establish."

"You came through." Dorsey drank his beer, tipping the glass to Hickcock. "What you said would happen—well, it happened. Good as your word. So what's next? You called me last night, not the other way around."

Hickcock drank off a little beer, pensively swishing it about on his tongue. "What's next is for you to trust me. And for you to tell me what you know."

"Some of it, maybe." The bartender returned with the sandwiches and Dorsey quieted. The sandwiches were on smallish buns, the sausage split and grilled with onion. Dorsey dug in, taking half of a sandwich in one bite.

"C'mon, Dorsey. No fuckin' around, okay?" Hickcock took a neat bite of his lunch. "We have to be together on this. And besides, I need more. I need it now. I can't keep repeating the same things I already know, and people in general already know. Viewers get bored; they'll switch the channel to catch a "Benny Hill" rerun. You want to string it out, give it to me in small portions, that's okay with me for now, as long as the information comes in a steady stream. Do it in steps, but someday soon you'll have to give it all up."

Dorsey drank the last of his beer and tapped the tabletop for a refill. "It'll keeping coming, as long as you stay straight with me. And yeah, I do have something for you today. Two things, actually." Dorsey told him about Father Jancek's appearance at Russie's memorial service, omitting his own kidnapping and conversation with Louis Preach. The bartender set a fresh beer in front of Dorsey and left.

"So who else saw?" Hickcock asked. "Give me the names."

"No witnesses." For a moment Dorsey toyed with the idea of giving up Dexter, but the memory of Dexter's forty-five urged caution. "Just me."

"Is this bullshit? I have no use for bullshit, things that can't be confirmed."

"Since when has confirmation of a story ever been a hot issue with you?" Dorsey finished off the second sandwich, chewing as he spoke. "You just tell the good people out there in TV land that the information came from a trusted and knowledgeable source. I've heard you use that phrase in the past. And maybe the priest won't deny it, hoping to prove his compassion for all men. He'll get some mileage out of it, but you, you'll prove to your audience that you're the man with the inside information. I can hear those tuner dials clicking away, leaving "Benny Hill" far behind."

Dorsey watched the concentration on Hickcock's face, revealing the struggle within. Buy it, Dorsey thought, and hoped for ESP. C'mon, you can use it. It'll work. And you like film. The station already has the footage taken outside the church. It'll work.

"Okay," Hickcock said, the tension draining from his face. "You said two items."

"There's a balding fat man in Johnstown," Dorsey said. "He mans the Movement's local office, a few blocks from Otterman Avenue; you know, where the hospitals are? He knows maybe just a little more than nothing, but he thinks he's important and he's got a temper. You waltz into that office with your crew and shove a microphone into his face and let him take it from there. He'll threaten you and hang himself in the process. Maybe he'll even attack the fearless reporter right on tape. That's you, buddy."

Bill Meara wore half-moon glasses at the end of his nose as he skimmed the last few pages of Dorsey's report. His sleeves were rolled up to mid-bicep and the knot of his tie hung loosely, several inches below his collar. Irish grunt, Dorsey thought again, sitting across the desk from the attorney. And the office, a grunt office: a picture of the county commissioners mounted on a gray wall, one metal desk, and four filing cabinets. And one window overlooking Ross Street.

"Looks good," Meara said. He flicked on his desk lamp against the fading light of the November afternoon. "But we have some problems too. The first one is your stoolie." He closed the file folder and slipped it across the desktop to Dorsey. "We'll have to offer some immunity, at least to the extent that no further time can be added to his present sentence. That'll take the okay of my higher-ups. The other problem is there's no grand jury in session right now—not that I would put this before a grand jury here in the city. Not in this county."

"Why not?" Dorsey asked. "You seem capable."

Meara scratched at his dark wiry hair and laughed. "For the son of Martin Dorsey, you're a little light on political sense. You expect me to try a case against a priest *here?* This is a large industrial city, or a former one anyway. And that means people like you and me. Catholics, Catholics by the bushelful. Forming a jury with a chance of convicting would be next to impossible. And another thing. I have a career in this office as long as I can keep the present DA in office, which he wants very badly. Which he won't be if I get into the habit of prosecuting priests. Most of the crime took place in Cambria and Westmoreland. Cambria expects to enpanel a grand jury in January. We'll give it to them, out in the hills where they can latch on to all the Protestants they need."

Dorsey was dumbfounded by Meara's words. The priest; he thinks he can pull in Father Jancek, at least for an indictment. "You'll have to back up some," Dorsey said. "I can't touch the priest with what I've got. Only P.I. can finger him."

"You don't know that." Meara shook his head, frowning. "You left the Sheriff's office too soon, before you learned to be an investigator. How did you get so far on this job? P.I. won't rat on him, you're right. But the guy's only a priest, and even with good advice from P.I., he fucked up somewhere along the line. Pros fuck up, so he must've. Like going to your buddy's funeral. It'll come to light. Don't worry; save your worrying for other problems."

"Like corroboration," Dorsey said, ecstatic over the renewed hope of bagging the priest but wanting Meara to move off the subject. Don't dwell on shortsighted conclusions. "We need more than Demory. Testimony from someone a little less tainted than him. I'll see what I can do."

Meara gazed thoughtfully out his window and Dorsey wondered what was next. "There's another thing," Meara said, turning back to Dorsey. "About your Mr. Demory, something you neglected to mention in your report. I checked with the prison medical staff: Demory's a lunger. And along with his lungs, the majority of his coronary arteries are clogged. The man is inoperable. There's no guarantee he'll even live to testify. Maybe there's just enough bullshit in his story for him to have a laugh on his way out."

"I know what you're saying," Dorsey said. "That's why I got the written statement. In case he's not around when we need him."

"No, no." Meara waved his arms as if flagging down a truck. "Forget it. I know, a signed dying declaration. Don't bullshit me. I'm the one in this room that finished law school, remember? They exist, but not in a vacuum. All we have is a signed statement, with only you as a witness. My friend, you are no officer of the court, and the man who signed it is a known felon. For all I know the guy's a pathological liar."

"You're a hard-ass; no one had to tell me." Dorsey left his chair and walked to the window, peering down at Ross Street. "But you're right. We need more."

"And that's up to you." Meara neatly arranged some papers on his desk. "No county people yet. And maybe never from this office, depending on the sales job I do on the Cambria DA."

So maybe it goes to trial in Ebensburg, Dorsey thought, because of the priest. And who knows how competent that DA will be? But more important, Father Jancek might just be sitting at the defense table. The priest and P.I. and everyone on Demory's list will be sitting there. Better get a big table.

"In the meantime," Meara said, "this report of yours, along with anything else you come up with, stays confidential. I can vouch for myself, and I'm assuming you can vouch for yourself. Keep your mouth shut. Something gets out before we are ready to try for an indictment, we may never get to court. They'll cover their tracks."

"I know the drill." Dorsey was tempted to tell Meara about Corso, but that would take an explanation he wasn't ready to defend. "I'll manage."

"Good." Meara turned his attention to a thick file he had taken from a desk drawer. "Now we get back to work."

By five-thirty night had fallen, and a misty rain began that helped further to entangle rush-hour traffic. Dorsey drove away from downtown along Liberty Avenue, and the twenty-minute drive to Gretchen's apartment took forty-five. Once past the curve near the

Bloomfield foot of the bridge, Dorsey began searching for an open parking spot along the curb, which was lined with small shops, Italian restaurants, and the Chinese restaurants that were beginning to infiltrate the area. It took several swings to do it, but Dorsey got the Buick into a spot meant for a Yugo, two doors down from the florist.

Inside, an elderly florist suggested a flower arrangement, promising to make it up fresh. His English was good but the Sicilian roots slipped through. "I showa you," he said. "You see, justa minute."

"Carnations," Dorsey said as the proprietor stepped behind the shop counter. "A dozen."

The florist leaned forward, resting his forearms on the counter. "Wife? Girlfriend maybe? Something special is whata you want. I show you."

Dorsey waved off the idea and insisted on carnations. "A dozen. You have them, right?"

"Okay, carnations." The florist headed for the workroom in back. "Carnations, they worka for you, good. You get carnations."

The carnations were wrapped in extra plastic against the rain. Traffic was still heavy, but it was only another three blocks before the turnoff for Gretchen's apartment. Dorsey turned left onto a street made up of row houses with aluminum awnings, except for Gretchen's building, an older apartment house of yellow brick with gargoyles stretching out from the roof. He pulled to the curb about fifteen feet past the building.

The apartment showed signs of a fast getaway. Dorsey maneuvered through the four rooms, encountering a sinkful of dishes, towels on the bathroom floor, and half-open drawers with clothing spilling out. Worse than usual, Dorsey thought, much worse. But you want to have a surprise waiting for her tomorrow, so hop to it.

Policing the apartment took a little over two hours, with Dorsey scrubbing away, sweaty and bare-chested. The shower and tub were the worst, and Dorsey used a wire brush against the mildew, scratching the porcelain. The bathroom sink took more of the same.

Finished, Dorsey washed his arms and torso at the sink and slipped back into his shirt. He checked the carnations in the fluted glass vase he had found in a kitchen cabinet, ensuring that each flower stood independently. After placing the vase at the center of the kitchen table, he took his jacket and left.

The rain had gotten heavier, and Dorsey paused in the building's lobby to fish in his pocket for his car keys. Isolating them between thumb and index finger, he hunched his shoulders against the rain and started for the Buick at a trot. Ten feet from the car he heard a pistol shot and felt a sliver of yellow brick slice his forehead, an inch above his right eye.

Instinctively, Dorsey dropped to the sidewalk on all fours and began scurrying along toward the Buick, using parked cars as cover. He could hear the sound of running from the far sidewalk and from behind the trunk of the Buick raised his head for a look, and the footfalls went silent. The muzzle flash illuminated the big man behind the gun, and a bullet cut a gash in the Buick's bumper. Another bullet went a little high, and the flash allowed Dorsey to confirm that it was Damjani. Dorsey took off in a low crouch and heard the ringing of the spent shell dancing along the cement. Jesus Christ, Dorsey thought, looking for a walkway between row houses and finding none. He has an automatic. Pray for a jam.

Blood streamed down Dorsey's cheek. He stayed on the move, keeping an eye on the far pavement. Damjani kept pace, holding the automatic at the end of an outstretched arm. He fired again, the bullet smashing into the cement at Dorsey's feet as he dashed between parked cars. Dorsey made a fast turnaround and doubled back in the opposite direction, hoping to juke out Damjani. Over his left shoulder he saw Damjani execute a neat turn with surprising agility for such a big man. There's nothing this way, Dorsey reminded himself, and turned again. Damjani followed easily.

"Motherfucker!" Damjani shouted across the street. "Next shot and you're dead, motherfucker!"

The muzzle flashed again and the bullet passed through the backseat windows of a car Dorsey was using for cover. Searching for a way out, Dorsey saw lights being flashed on at the row house porches and hoped they might frighten off Damjani. Bullshit, this guy is psychotic. He doesn't frighten, he kills. And forget about counting the shots. The spent shells make it an automatic. The clip might hold as many as twelve, and a blind man can hit one out of twelve. Keeping going, keep moving; movement means you're alive.

Dorsey started down the line of cars again; Damjani stayed right with him, step for step. Dorsey counted six cars to the intersection and open ground. The intersection, he thought, where Damjani shoots you. The intersection, it's a no-man's-land.

Hunkered down behind a car hood, he saw Damjani crab-walking between two cars, crossing the street. He's not waiting for the intersection; he's coming for you. Dorsey searched for an escape; the prospect of a mad sprint across the intersection was looking better and better. He slipped into a sprinter's stance, his legs tensed and ready to kick off, when, in the light of a mercury streetlamp, he spotted a walkway between two row houses, four doors down and two short of the intersection. Hoping to fake Damjani into setting up a shot at the intersection, Dorsey burst out of his stance, pumping arms and legs for the corner. He heard the automatic fire and prayed for a miss and for his knee to hold up as he cut hard and fast into the walkway. The knee stayed steady as he bounced off a wrought-iron porch railing and into the wire gate blocking the walkway. It wasn't locked and Dorsey worked the latch until his eyes fell on the sign at the gate's center—GUARD DOG, BEWARE—complete with the face of a police dog. Fuck it, he decided, and pulled open the gate. He ran the length of the walk-way, his ears sharp for the sound of a menacing growl. As he ran he tore off his jacket and wrapped it around his left forearm, intending to jab it at the dog's snout. He reached the end of the walkway unmolested, jumped into the center of a small brick-paved yard at a wrestler's stance, and heard the rustle of a chain leash to his left. He turned toward it, ready to fight.

It was a beagle. A puppy. On a leash.

"Everybody's a fuckin' comedian." Dorsey took two strides and vaulted over a low cyclone fence to the next yard and then into the next. He heard Damjani's running feet echoing in the walkway and, much more distantly, the wail of police sirens. The fourth yard had a three-foot cinder-block wall and Dorsey hopped over it, steadying himself on one arm, and dropped to his knees as two shots threw mortar dust from the top of the wall. Dorsey found hope as the sirens grew louder, closer. He can't be that crazy, Dorsey thought; nobody sticks around to get caught. C'mon, Ed, run for it. Prison is prison, and you won't like it. Ask Demory.

Another shot was fired, a loud, forceful cough. Not the automatic, Dorsey was sure. He peeked carefully over the wall and saw, two back yards down from Damjani and the beagle, a short round man dressed in T-shirt and bathrobe. In the man's hands was a deer rifle, complete with telescopic sight. Dorsey turned to see Damjani dropping back into the walkway, a billow of brick smoke coming from the wall where the bullet had struck.

"Later, motherfucker!" Damjani's voice rang inside the walkway. "Can't hide for fuckin' ever. I'm on you forever!"

Dorsey listened to Damjani's footsteps running toward the street. So it takes a rifle shot to break through his madness. Thank God for the rifle-toting neighbor. Wonder how many friends and relatives he bags each season?

He turned and slid down the wall and sat on his ass, his back resting against the cinder blocks. At rest he could feel the shaking in his legs and hands, and the wise-ass comments weren't coming through. The shaking moved inward; Dorsey felt as if the organs in his chest were vibrating. The copper taste of blood rolled down his cheek and across his lips.

He hadn't been followed to Gretchen's, Dorsey was certain. Not in this weather and traffic, he told himself, not with the precautions you've learned to take. No way; Damjani was watching the building. Watching for you or for Gretchen? Would it make a difference to that flipped-out bastard? The psycho knows where she lives and she comes home tomorrow. And Damjani's on you forever.

That was the moment Dorsey decided he would have to kill Ed Damjani.

CHAPTER 24

Two uniformed officers took a shoulder each and firmly lifted Dorsey, wet and limp, from the yard's brick floor. Grabbing him by the belt, one officer turned him to face the cinder blocks while his partner forced Dorsey's hands to the wall and kicked his feet out wide. Each took a turn at frisking him, apparently disappointed when they came up with only a wallet and key ring. Even in his state of near collapse, emotional and physical, Dorsey was sufficiently coherent to critique the officers' performance. Lazy and in a hurry, he decided; they never checked the small of the back, right along the spine, where a bright guy could dangle a razor blade or even a small flat knife along a thin thread looped around the shirt label. Probably disappointed with the night's catch. Hoped for more than a scared and bloody and sopping mess.

Again taking Dorsey by the arms, the officers led him across the backyard fences and through the walkway. The street was alive with porch and stoop lights where old men and women watched the flickering red and blue lights of four prowl cars. Stepping out

of one of the cars was a burly officer in his mid-fifties, as far as Dorsey could figure, wearing a white cap with a plastic cover and a white uniform blouse. Another officer draped a black slicker over his shoulders. Dorsey recognized the uniform and manner of a precinct inspector. In command at the scene, Dorsey was certain, and politically attuned.

The inspector gave Dorsey a quick look, then examined the wallet handed to him by the officer on Dorsey's left. He flipped through some cards and passed the wallet back to the officer. "He's your old man, am I right?" the inspector asked.

"Yeah," Dorsey said, seizing one of the few moments in which he was glad of Martin Dorsey's pull.

"Give it to me slow," the inspector said. "I warn you, no bullshit, or maybe the old man don't mean shit to me."

Dorsey gave it to him quick and dirty, a simple chase story. After hearing him out, the inspector stepped away, buttonholed one of the officers, and towed him along. Dorsey trained an ear at the hushed conversation, only able to overhear one phrase, the inspector saying, "No dead bodies this time around, right?" The inspector motioned for two other officers on the scene to join him, listened for a few minutes, and dismissed them to their cars. He then returned and spent a few moments examining Dorsey's cut.

"That'll need stitches." The inspector took a nightstick from one of the officers. "Which is yours?" he asked, indicating the line of parked cars. Dorsey motioned toward the Buick.

The two officers moved Dorsey along, trailing the inspector to the Buick. Approaching the driver's side of the windshield, the inspector took a firm grip on the baton, his knuckles four inches from the business end. With the index finger of his free hand he sighted a spot directly over the steering wheel, reared back, and jammed the end of the baton into the glass, sending spider webs from the point of contact. He regarded his work, looked satisfied, and walked back to Dorsey, returning the officer's baton.

"And that," the inspector said, "is how you came to cut your head. Accidentally." He instructed the two officers holding Dorsey to get him and his car to the emergency room at Allegheny General, far across town.

"Inspector," Dorsey called, as one of the officers moved him into the Buick's front passenger seat. "The guy with the rifle did us both a favor when you think about it. I'm alive, and you're saved the bother of cleaning up a messy dead body. Go easy on him, okay?"

"Never saw him, never heard anything," the inspector said. "Not a noise or a word."

One officer drove the Buick while the other followed in the prowl car. At the hospital they took him directly to an examination room over the protests of the triage nurse. Dorsey's key ring was slipped into his hip pocket as he was placed on the examination table, and after one of the officers checked him in they both left.

The cut took three butterfly stitches. Flat on his back and looking up at a ceiling light fixture, Dorsey listened to the resident assure him that he was the ER's best stitchman. "The fingers," the resident said. "These fingers are very limber. From piano. I play, or used to play, at a couple of local clubs."

Dorsey considered asking the resident which clubs these were, but his mind was already too deep into the plan he was hatching. It was pulling together, each segment of equal importance. The gun, the knife, the phone call, and the meeting. And the acting job, he reminded himself. Sell it to Damjani. The naked fear, the absolute fear of God. Sell that, sell it hard, or the rest is of no consequence. And it won't all be acting, this fear, will it?

At a few minutes past ten the next morning, in a light snow that had just begun to fall, Dorsey crossed the intersection of Carson and Twelfth streets, and entered the Iron and Glass Bank. His head ached with tension and the butterfly stitches nipped at his skin, but he managed to keep his composure when the assistant manager, a young man in a gray suit, asked for two forms of identification and a signature sample to check against the one on file. The assistant manager asked Dorsey to remain seated as he went to a file cabinet to check the signature. While he sat, Dorsey cut through the pain and anxiety to admire the bank building itself, classifying it with the Wheel Café. The floors and counters were white marble and the

tellers' windows were framed in copper that gleamed in the light coming through long high windows. And the vault, Dorsey thought: good as any, even without an electronic timer. The way you like it, he told himself, old and maybe just a little older yet.

The assistant manager returned to the desk with a white index card and, while Dorsey watched, compared the signatures. "Will you be taking the contents with you?" The assistant manager asked. "If you're only interested in viewing the contents, we do have a private office you can use. You won't be disturbed."

"There's no need." Dorsey absentmindedly ran a finger across his cut, following the contours of the stitching. "I'll be taking it with me."

Both men rose and took key rings from their pockets. Dorsey followed the assistant manager into the vault, which was lined from floor to ceiling with numbered boxes; Box 487 was near the ceiling in the far left corner. The assistant manager inserted his and Dorsey's keys, turned them, and handed the box and his key to Dorsey.

Dorsey set the long thin metal box on a nearby stepstool and flipped open its hinged lid. Inside were three blue flannel bags that had once clothed fifths of Crown Royal. They were gifts from Al when Dorsey had mentioned that he wanted something soft, nonabrasive, in which to store his goods. While the assistant manager stood by, Dorsey took a plastic grocery bag from his pants pocket, shook out its folds, and put the three flannel sacks inside. The manager slipped the safety deposit box back into its perch and inserted the keys, closing both locks. Taking his key back, Dorsey put the bag under his arm and left the bank.

The snowfall began to pick up in intensity, and a stiff wind funneled along the row of cramped storefronts on Carson causing a near white-out. Dorsey hurried along with his chin tucked to his chest against the weather, assuring himself that no one following him could keep him in view. Winter's early, he thought. Autumn is all done in and so nearly are you. But if you pull this off, you'll at least last long enough to finish your Christmas shopping.

At Seventeenth Street, Dorsey turned right, walked half a block, and crossed the mouth of the alley where Russie had been killed. It came full circle, he realized: one dead last week and another, Damjani, very soon. And if it doesn't happen soon, there will be more deaths.

Dorsey covered the rest of the block and knocked firmly at the barroom door, knowing Al never opened before eleven o'clock. He waited a moment, knocked again, and heard Al hustling down from the second floor. Seconds later he heard the deadbolt slide free.

"Sorry, sorry." Al motioned Dorsey inside and started for the back room. "The apartment, Russie's place, I was up there. Gettin' it ready, in case anybody wants to look at it. Not that Russie was anything but army barracks clean, but things need freshenin' up."

Heading for the back room with Dorsey in tow, Al stopped for a moment and took a white canvas bank deposit bag from behind the bar. He directed Dorsey to the last of the booths and slipped in across from him, placing the deposit bag on the table.

"How much did it come to after all?" Dorsey asked.

"Three thousand."

Dorsey worked open the bag and pulled out a wrapped stack of twenties.

"That's good, real good. You only figured on two."

"Checked the accounts after we talked," Al said, sounding distracted. "Kind of surprising to see how well Rose and me been doing. I figured I could pull out three and get it back in tomorrow without much notice."

Dorsey shoved the wad of bills back into the bag and yanked the cord, cinching it closed. "Thanks, Al. I figure it'll find its way back to you tomorrow; next day, tops."

Al ran a hand across his bald head and rubbed at his eyes. "Slept bad last night. Kept Rose up too. First time in years I didn't drop off soon as my head hit the pillow. This thing, I guess I had to run through it a few more times. Well, maybe more than a few."

"Don't like it any more than you." Dorsey met Al's eyes and spoke softly. "If it could go otherwise, I'd try it."

"It's a bad thing," Al said, "but it's not the first time. You ever hear about a guy named Joey Nikita? His real name was Nikowicz, something like that, but everybody called him Nikita. Like the Russian guy."

"Maybe once," Dorsey said. "Must've been one of the older guys mentioned it. One of the guys you get in here."

"That sounds about right," Al said. "Had to be one of the older guys. After all, it happened in 'sixty-one, maybe 'sixty-two. The mill was going good again, just after Kennedy fixed the strike. Anyways, this Nikita, he was a lot like this guy you're tellin' me about. He worked at the mill, at J and L, and he thought he was a big mountain man, wore these bib overalls all the time. Maybe he was from West Virginia originally, who knows?"

"What about him?"

"Looked for trouble. All the time."

"Did he find some?" Dorsey asked.

"More than expected," Al said, nodding his head. Dorsey picked up the signal. This was solemn truth. "Like most guys," Al said, "guys like Nikita, he got a hard-on for one particular guy, a little guy named Danny Kelso. One of those real quiet guys, you know the type?"

"I'm followin' so far."

"Kelso was at the mill too, and Nikita rode him all shift and then picked it up again afterward at the bar—not here, they drank at one of the places on Carson. Nikita got physical when he was drunk, and one night he started slappin' Danny around. And Danny was on the light side so he couldn't put up much of a defense, not right away. So he left, or so Nikita thought. An hour later Nikita is climbing into his car and Danny catches him over the head with a piece of pipe, or maybe a rod of rolled steel. Nobody knows for sure and nobody knows how many times he hit Nikita, but it was a closed casket funeral."

"How many years did Kelso do?"

"Not a day," Al said. "Never questioned. Nikita was not popular, so no one who had been in the bar that night could remember anything about him, except he drank quietly and left when he was finished. And the cops, they had little interest in finding the killer. They knew what Nikita was like too."

"So you're saying nobody'll care if all goes well?"

"Well, yeah," Al said, "but there's more to it. More than how people felt about Nikita, you have to take a look at Nikita himself.

See, and this may sound stupid, but there are guys out there lookin' for people to kill them. Nikita was one, without a doubt. It had to happen. If not Kelso, somebody else would have done it, sooner or later. Fate, whatever they call it these days. And this sounds like the same thing."

Dorsey looked away for a moment, staring at the far wall. "Thanks, Al," he said, turning back to him. "But it's hard."

"Like I said, this is a bad thing." Al reached across the table and put his hand on Dorsey's. "But I agree, Damjani won't stop. I'm gonna feel bad for a long while. You're gonna feel a lot worse. But remember three people. Gretchen, you, and Russie. You and her have to be safe. And Russie, he has to be put to rest."

Dorsey placed both the deposit bag and the grocery sack on the desktop and slipped a tape into the tape player. As he took the three flannel bags from the sack, Dinah Washington began to sing "September in the Rain."

Sitting at the desk, his fingers loosened the gold cord of the first bag. The cord came free and, tilting the bag, Dorsey allowed a black-handled switchblade to tumble out onto the blotter. He picked it up, resting it loosely across his palm. With his thumb he moved the release slide near the top, and the spring loader shot five inches of steel blade out of the handle. Dorsey was pleased to see it working despite years of disuse, but couldn't help but smile and think back to his boyhood. They had all held it to be solemn law that any knife with a blade longer than your palm was illegal. Even then, Dorsey recalled, he had wondered whose palm they had in mind.

Dorsey released the slide and, pointing the blade at the blotter, gently allowed the blade to retract. He worked the slide again, and the blade sprang true. After again retracting the blade, he set the knife aside and took a cartridge box from the second flannel bag. With the box open he counted twelve .32-caliber shells, examining each to be sure it was clean and intact. Satisfied, he placed the box next to the knife and turned his attention to the third bag.

He didn't lift this one but instead allowed it to sit flat on the blotter as he worked the cord open. Inserting three fingers, he took hold and pulled the bag away, revealing the barrel, cylinder, and trigger loop and finally the hand grip. Dorsey took the gun in his right hand and hefted it, estimating the weight, and recalled the specifications. Meridian Arms break-top revolver, .32 caliber and nickel-plated. The contents of all three bags had been lifted from the sheriff's evidence property room four years earlier.

"A couple of throwaways" is what Mindes, his last partner, had called them. Dorsey had been saddled with fat sixty-three-year-old Carl Mindes. Because Carl was coasting toward retirement, he and Dorsey were assigned to easy duty, mostly following up on leads developed by other detectives, allowing plenty of down time for Mindes to lecture Dorsey on inside politics and to tell war stories of his thirty years of duty. Around noon one day, as Dorsey was stepping out to grab some lunch and a stretch of peace of mind, Mindes buttonholed him and suggested that they meet at the property room in the courthouse basement.

Dorsey arrived first, never sure of his read on Mindes. The property room attendant, an elderly sheriff's deputy, peered out through the wire mesh, a quick nod his only acknowledgment of Dorsey's presence. When Mindes arrived, the attendant opened the security door and ushered them both inside, exchanging greetings with Mindes.

"The box," Mindes said. "It's in the back, am I right?" He led Dorsey past shelves of evidence: guns, knives, TV sets, stereo equipment, and a complete set of Norton anthologies.

"Kid in college," Mindes said, noticing Dorsey's interest in the paperbacks. "Couldn't pay for his own books, used his mom's money for dope maybe, so he followed the kid sitting next to him in class to the bookstore. Once the kid buys his books, our boy kills him to get them. He was ready to compete for good grades, I'd say."

Near the back wall Mindes stopped and lifted a hatbox from the middle shelf. Looking at the box, Dorsey thought he was about to be presented with Jack Webb's fedora. Mindes pushed the box into Dorsey's hands and lifted the lid.

"This is an old practice," Mindes said, "and a damned good

one. You need throwaways, you understand? Every cop, city or county, should have them, but the young ones, the smart shits, they don't go for this. Some day they may end up wishing they had."

"These some kind of backup?" Dorsey whispered conspiratorily. "Second gun and a knife, that's a lot to carry. Really, when you think about it, if I don't stop a guy by emptying my service revolver into him, the guy deserves to win."

"Looking at it all wrong is what you're doing." Mindes replaced the lid, tapping it firmly in place. "Throwaways, not backup. Say you're chasing a guy and it's dark and all of a sudden the guy stops cold and turns on you. His hand goes up, so you figure he's got a gun and you shoot him first. Dead. But when you search him there's no gun, maybe a flashlight instead. The way it stands, you surrender your gun, face an internal hearing, a coroner's inquest, and maybe even a manslaughter charge."

"A plant," Dorsey said. "Make the sides look a little more even."

Mindes smiled, as if proud of a star pupil. "Exactly. These weapons, they're cold, can't be traced. Just lost in the shuffle. You put either one in the corpse's hand, who's gonna think it wasn't his? And the worst that can happen to you is a coroner's inquest that says it was self-defense."

Dorsey tried to decline the gift, telling Mindes that he had no intention of chasing anyone, day or night, down an alley, let alone pulling his gun. But Mindes was adamant, as if he were giving a gift from father to son. "Some things I can teach you, explain to you," Mindes said, "and some stuff you gotta take on faith. Listen to an old man for once. Do as I say, please?"

Dorsey accepted the hatbox, and later that same day he leased the safety deposit box to house the weapons, ensuring that he would never be tempted to pull his service revolver. There'll be no way to hide a mistake, he had told himself, no way to rake the dirt and cover your tracks. Bad judgment and a pulled trigger will mean your ass.

Now, at the desk while the tape cycled through twice, Dorsey painstakingly cleaned and oiled the revolver until the break-top snapped smartly, the chamber, cylinder, and barrel slipping firmly into the firing position. Dinah Washington sang "Manhattan," inviting someone to "go to Coney and eat baloney on a roll," as Dorsey pointed the revolver at the television and pulled the trigger, the hammer making a metallic snap and the chambers rolling along for six phantom shots. Satisfied, he opened the break-top and loaded the chambers. From the left-side drawer he took a pair of ear guards stolen from the county firing range years ago and went down the hall to the basement door.

Dorsey flicked on the light, closed the door firmly behind him, and headed down the steps, keeping the revolver muzzle pointed upward. The basement walls were unfinished rock and at the far wall at the front of the house Dorsey had hung an old mattress, bound over double. Nine feet from the wall was an old wooden table left behind by the house's former owner. Dorsey stood behind the table and placed the ear guards over his ears and worked loose the muscles of his neck and shoulders. Keeping his arm straight and his elbow loose, Dorsey lifted the revolver and sighted. He emptied the chamber into the mattress, and even with the ear guards he felt the six shots echo along four stone walls and become twenty-four blasts. He had hoped for the stone to contain the blasts, and his ears rang with the success of his plan. Massaging his ears, he hurried upstairs and returned to the office, putting the revolver and the ear guards on the desktop and dropping into the swivel.

So, Dorsey dryly concluded, the gun works. And your aim was good enough to hit a queen-sized mattress, which is a significant improvement. But it's okay because the idea is to be inches from the guy when the gun goes pop. So a gun in working order is all that's called for. And three thousand dollars strewn across the top of a roll bag loaded with paper wads will look like ten thousand. So you're all set; only the phone call and the act itself remain. And the call has to sound like the real thing. Like you're on the ragged edge with the fear of God Almighty in you. Nothing artificial will do; you've got to find the fear in you. That seam of ore may be easily mined.

He called directory assistance, area code eight-one-four, for the number. A computer-generated voice repeated the number and

Dorsey hung up halfway through the second go round. He dialed again.

"Carl Radovic, please," Dorsey said, after the call was answered on the fourth ring. He had a moment's fear that the office was closed and his one sure contact to Damjani was out for the day—the day Gretchen returns.

Over the line, Dorsey heard approaching footsteps bring the curtain up on his act. "This is Carl. Who's this?"

"Carl," Dorsey said, "please don't hang up, this is Dorsey. We need to talk." Dorsey's words were pressured, overlapping and running together. "Carl, this is really important."

"Fuck you want, bastard? Heard you slipped by a couple of times. Felt real bad, wished you woulda died. You're too lucky."

Dorsey left his chair and paced in front of the desk holding the phone in his hand. His voice became even more pressured, and he realized it was no act. "Listen to me," he said, "at least do that. This shit is too much for me. I never bargained for this kind of stuff. Man, I'm just a follower; trailing people and peeking into windows is my line. Believe me, I never meant to mess with you guys. It's too fuckin' much."

"Tough shit," Radovic said.

"No, no," Dorsey said. "I have to get to your man, Damjani. I want him off my back and I know he ain't gonna do it for nothing. I could make it worth your while. Know what I mean?"

There was a tense moment of silence for Dorsey before Radovic replied. "Scared shitless, aren't you. I like you that way. Maybe things should just stay as they are, with you lookin' over your shoulder all the time. Make you go fuckin' nuts."

"Listen," Dorsey said. "Don't tell me the priest looks at things that way. He's in it to help people, even when it gets a little rough. And I said before, I could make it worth your while. Yours, Damjani's, even the priest's."

"With what?"

"Money," Dorsey said. "Heard you people could use some. Ten thousand. Damjani has an accomplice-to-murder rap hanging over his head from last week. So make it going-away money. Or give it to the priest and show him what a contribution you've made. Do what you want, just get Damjani off my back."

Radovic laughed. "Want to make a contribution, send in a check. Then we'll see."

"I need some assurance from Damjani," Dorsey said. "And payment is in cash. The guy could keep this shit up even after I sent the money. Look, there's a bag here on my desk with the whole load inside. In twenties. All I got and all I can raise. Best I can do, now or ever."

There was another silence on the line. Dorsey could picture the concentration on Radovic's face as he weighed his options. C'mon, Carl, Dorsey thought. Ten thousand, for Christ's sake. It'll make you a hero, make you important. You'll have the recognition that can get you away from sitting all day in that drafty office. Yeah, you sat on stage with Father Jancek, but that was a crumb you were thrown; the next day it was back in that meat locker of a storefront. C'mon, man, go for it.

"Get the money up here to me," Radovic said. "Do it right away and I'll see what I can do for you. I think I can fix it."

"Carl, c'mon, man," Dorsey said. "You know Damjani. You know him a hell of a lot better than I do. So you know I got good reason to be worried. The deal is the money for him laying off. The deal is between him and me. I'll hand over the money to Damjani, and he can say it's all off. That he'll get off me."

"Fuck is this shit?" Radovic screamed and Dorsey feared he had moved too quickly. "Got it in mind to set him up, right?" Radovic said. "He shows and the cops are waiting, right?"

"It's not that way," Dorsey said. "You can look at it that way, but that ain't how it is. I'll go anywhere to meet the guy; you name the place. Just so it's him and me, and it's got to be outdoors so I'll feel safe. You don't trust me? Jesus, I'm the one who almost died twice. Why I should trust you? To get this guy off me I'll go anywhere."

"What a bullshitter," Radovic said, laughing. "And you never give up. What a bullshitter."

The whole deal, Dorsey reminded himself, was to play on the

egos of two men, Radovic and Damjani. Radovic, so his stock will go up in Movement Together. And Damjani, so he can get a real charge out of it at your expense. For destroying you. So he can take the money and laugh and call you a pussy. So he can get his psycho rocks off. You've got to get to Damjani.

"Carl, I'm under fucking siege here!" Dorsey shouted with a nervous crack to his voice. "You want to pass on this, okay, fine. I guess you got a right. But fuck, man, at least tell Damjani about it. See what he says. I'll meet the guy anywhere. C'mon, Carl, you have to do that much. You have to."

Dorsey dropped into the swivel chair and wiped the perspiration from his face with his sleeve. The line was silent. While he listened for Radovic's response he extended his left arm out straight and checked for tremors; his hand fluttered in midair. Help me get him, Carl. It'll put you in solid with the priest.

"Let me see what I can do," Radovic said, sighing. "Stay by the phone while I put something together."

"I'll be here."

CHAPTER 25

Dorsey stood at the kitchen sink, thoroughly soaking a dish towel under the faucet. He had toyed with the idea of a shower, wanting to rinse away a clammy sheen of fear, but thought better of it. The telephone could not go unmanned. Even Radovic was not stupid enough to tell a recording machine that he knew how to get in touch with a wanted man. Miss the call and miss the chance, the only one you can figure on. And until the cops find Damjani or until Damjani finds you, you'll spend your time looking over your shoulder and suggesting to Gretchen that she change her address.

On his way back to the phone he stopped at a hall closet and pulled out an olive-drab field jacket complete with MP patches. He went to the office, draped the field jacket across the chaise, and sat down wearily in the swivel chair. Gently, with his head back, he laid the dish towel across his eyes, the pull of the towel causing his stitches to sting. For the next hour he did not move. The phone remained silent.

Refreshed, calmer, Dorsey lifted the telephone receiver and

dialed Gretchen's number. After eight unanswered rings he returned the receiver to its cradle and took an address book from the desk's center drawer. This time he dialed the emergency room at Mercy Hospital. A triage nurse answered, then went to find Gretchen.

"Dr. Keller is unavailable at the moment," the nurse said, coming back on the line. "She said to let you know she will call you, but probably not today. She's got double shifts, today and I think tomorrow."

So that's how she found the time to take off for home, Dorsey thought as he hung up. Sarcastically, he told himself it was a good thing he had Damjani to keep him occupied.

Dorsey took the revolver from the desktop; holding it upside down, he broke open the cylinder and shook out the spent shells. After fitting the barrel and stock back together, he picked up the field jacket and shook it out before putting it on. It hung loose and baggy from the shoulders despite Dorsey's having gained fifteen pounds since the day he was mustered out, and he recalled it had been three sizes too large on the day it was issued.

Taking the revolver in his left hand, he worked it up his right sleeve, bringing it to rest at the midpoint of the forearm with the barrel pointed downward. Next, he let his right arm fall straight from a cocked position and the revolver slipped freely down his arm onto his palm. He tried it several more times, and with every repetition the revolver dropped into his hand. Perhaps too freely, Dorsey thought, but what is the alternative? In the jacket's flap pocket it would show. And when Damjani sees you go for it you'll never get there. The right sleeve is the only place.

He practiced for another ten minutes, tensing his forearm muscles to hold the pistol more firmly. Satisfied that it would work, Dorsey stripped off the field jacket and reloaded the revolver. As he did so, the phone rang.

"Hello," Dorsey said, hoping it was Gretchen. He let the field jacket fall to the floor.

"Mr. Dorsey?" The voice was that of a young man.

"Yes?"

"Mr. Dorsey, this is Jay McGregor. I'm one of Mr. Hickcock's assistants here at Channel Three. We're running a story live tonight on "The Western Pennsylvania Journal," and we need you to confirm or deny on several issues."

"You have Sam Hickcock call me," Dorsey said, dismissing the caller. "And when you see him, tell him for me he should know better than to have a go-fer do his work for him."

There was a silence as McGregor paused before speaking. "Ah, actually, Mr. Dorsey, it was at Mr. Hickcock's insistence that I called you. We need to run a few things past you. Just a few points on your investigation of Father Jancek and Movement Together, especially the statement you obtained from this Arthur Demory person."

Now it was Dorsey's turn to pause, giving himself time to come to grips with what he had just heard. Jesus Christ, Hickcock has my report!

"Tell Hickcock to call me. That's all." Dorsey hung up.

He sat in the swivel chair, but it wouldn't recline far enough for him. It wouldn't go all the way back, to where everything went dark. And the walls and ceiling, he wanted them to close in around him, isolating him from the outside where everyone could read his report. Jesus, he thought again, Hickcock has the report! How and from whom? And who do you talk to to get the answers to those two questions?

Corso, he thought, had to be him. But he didn't get a copy. Not from you, anyway, but from someone else, sure as hell. Maybe like this. The report is express-mailed to Munt. He calls Corso after reading it, wants to talk it over with him. But Corso says he doesn't have a copy, so Munt faxes it to him. Corso reads it, calculates a price, and sells it to Hickcock. But why not sell it to the priest? And then again, he could have sold it to both. Fucking Corso. Fucking Hickcock. They've got my report.

The telephone rang again and Dorsey, certain of who it would be, was tempted to let the tape machine pick it up. He lifted the receiver on the third ring. He had guessed right; it was Meara.

"Listen," Dorsey said. "I just got a call from—"

"Oh, no, you listen." Meara's voice bit at Dorsey's ear. "I just had a call too. Actually it was a couple of calls. Some kid named

McGregor called to allow me the opportunity to confirm or deny most everything I read in what I thought was your confidential report. What the hell did you do, sell it to the news guys? You bastard! Don't tell me; you get to play yourself in the movie version."

"Wait, now, hold on." Dorsey was out of the chair, pacing circles around the desk. "I issued three copies of the report. You, Munt, and Cleardon. That was it. Didn't even send one to Corso, who was supposed to get a copy. Even still, it had to be him that released it. He's pulled this shit before."

"Give it a rest," Meara said. "If it wasn't you, it must have been one of your many fuck-ups that let this news guy have it. Maybe you left a copy in the photocopying machine. Something idiotic like that."

"So don't believe me," Dorsey said. "It doesn't matter now. What matters is what we do from here on in."

"Drop the 'we' shit."

"Huh?" Dorsey grunted, fearful.

"What I'm saying," Meara said, "is the same thing I just told McGregor. Neither myself nor anyone in my office have had any dealings with you. We are not presently conducting an investigation of Movement Together, nor do we intend to do so in the future. I told you from the start; fuck up and I don't know you."

"Hey, slow down," Dorsey said. "You're forgetting our ace, Demory. We still have him and he can tell it all to the grand jury. We get them to indict and maybe some others can be convinced to come forward."

"Like I said before," Meara said, "there were a couple of calls this morning. You remember yesterday, what I said? I told you I checked on Demory, spoke to the medical staff at the prison. Well, one of the nurses called me this morning. It seems a TV film crew is camped at the main gate. They were there to interview Demory, asked the warden for permission. News like that goes through a prison like beer through a bladder. Demory got word before the warden did. And when he figured out what was up, he keeled over."

"Dead?" Dorsey pictured the jailbird. How sickly and wasted he looked and how he pumped in the nicotine despite it all.

"Close, very close," Meara said. "In fact his heart did stop for a couple of minutes, but the paddles brought him back. They took him to the ICU at Logan Valley."

"Good, he's alive," Dorsey said. "Then we still have him; he can make a case." Dorsey's voice was strained; he was struggling for a toehold.

"Will you please listen to what the fuck I'm saying?" Meara was shouting now. "There is no fucking case in this office. And that's because there is no investigation being conducted by this office. The only investigation is yours, and it gets local prime-time coverage at ten tonight."

Dorsey heard the connection break as Meara hung up. He tried to put the receiver in its cradle, missed, and tried again. Stepping away from the desk, he crossed the room and peered out the window at the late-morning emptiness of Wharton Street. It's down to this, he thought, picturing Demory near death, flat on his back in the ICU, plastic tubing in every available orifice. And then he shifted to a second image, of Russie dead, face down in a slush puddle, the indentation in his skull seeping blood. The bad press that goes over the airwaves, Dorsey thought, directing his thoughts to Russie, I hope the bad press is enough. The priest gets off: no trial, no exposure. But the bad press will put a shadow over him. Yours. Best I could do, along with ridding the world of Damjani. Corso, you bastard. You made me come up short.

Back at the desk, Dorsey found Corso's number in his address book and dialed. A secretary told him that Mr. Corso had called in sick. Dorsey hung up, called the home number, and got no answer. The next call was to Hickcock on his direct office line. McGregor answered.

"Get your boss," Dorsey told him. "I only talk to him."

"Ah, Mr. Dorsey?" McGregor said. "Mr. Hickcock specifically said that he did not wish to take any calls from you. I'm sorry. Perhaps I can help?"

"Help me by putting your boss on the line." Dorsey pushed McGregor. "Get him on the fucking phone. Now."

McGregor told Dorsey that he would be hanging up now.

"One more thing," Dorsey said.

"What's that?"

"Fuck you." Dorsey slammed down the phone, wishing he had maintained his composure. Childish, he told himself. But it was all he had left.

The long-term consequences began to nip at Dorsey. From the desk's center drawer he took two bankbooks, one savings and one checking. On a sheet of blank typing paper he copied the two balance amounts and did a rough estimate of the fee he had coming from Fidelity Casualty. That'll be good pay, he told himself, but it's likely to be the last for some time. The stakes were high; you knew that going in, if that's any comfort. Because, my friend, who wants to hire an investigator who can't keep his report off the ten o'clock news? No more referrals. Not from Fidelity Casualty and not from Bernie's firm. So you're down to the old man's money, the investment money. The only other option is to have yourself fitted for a security guard's uniform. And don't forget to buy yourself a new lunch bucket.

The tape cycled through for the fifth time and Dinah Washington did another encore of "September in the Rain." Dorsey returned to pacing the floor, stopping now and again to stare out the window, collecting his thoughts: Gretchen, Damjani, the old man's money. First you kill Damjani to keep yourself and Gretchen alive. Then you take the old man's money so the two of you can stay together. For Christ's sake, is it worth it? Hell, yes. Again, it comes down to this.

He dropped back into the swivel, lifted the phone receiver, and dialed his father's number. The line rang three times and then Mrs. Boyle's electronically reproduced voice requested that he leave his message at the beep. Dorsey hung up, deciding that even a recorded Ironbox was too much for him. He thought of calling Bernie to see if he could plead his case to the senior partners. Bernie could tell them he was born an asshole but that he'd try to do better in the future. Besides, Dorsey realized, it's better if Bernie keeps some distance, for his own protection. If they link him to you, the senior partners will find him stupid by association. What's left is to finish off Damjani and live with Gretchen.

The telephone rang and Dorsey speculated over what he might lose this time if he answered. It was Radovic.

"This is it," Radovic said. "Listen up."

"Whatever," Dorsey said. "What-fucking-ever."

Chapter 26

With the snow, it took Dorsey an hour and forty minutes to travel north to Beaver. He had planned—hoped—to be in place at least thirty minutes before the 10 P.M. meet. Now he had only ten minutes to check the side streets leading to the meeting place, check the doorways and alley ways where a second man could be waiting. Waiting to take him out after he gave the money to Damjani.

The streets of Beaver were straight and wide, and the new snow reflected the purplish glow of mercury streetlamps. Dorsey made for the center of town, past elegant well-kept homes, thinking of the struggle it must have been to keep the working classes out of this county seat, a county dependent on heavy industry for its survival. And a dry town, he reminded himself, smiling. No place for a thirsty mill hand fresh off the swing shift.

He turned left at Third and Market with the Beaver County Courthouse, its vast sandstone mass illuminated by spotlight, to the right of the intersection. Moving along Market, the courthouse now to his back, Dorsey could see the high stone wall of the county jail, where Tony Ruggerio had given him the story on Damjani. To Dorsey's right, between the courthouse and the jail, was a city block's worth of flat park lawn, with tall trees and park benches at the edges. Dorsey pulled to the curb. Through the falling snow and the faint light he could see the dark outline of the gazebo at the center. The meeting place.

The snow was a blessing, Dorsey decided. No one moves silently across crisp new snow, except maybe an Indian in moccasins, and the priest doesn't have much of a following on the reservations. And no one can stalk you against a white backdrop. But the coin has two sides. You'll be out there on your own. And maybe, just maybe, Damjani learned something from the old man in Bloomfield and got a scoped rifle of his own.

Dorsey pulled back onto the street and moved slowly along, reminding himself that the possibility of a long-distance rifle shot was the only problem he could not resolve. He hoped Damjani's hatred still had an edge to it, one that wouldn't be satisfied unless he did his dirty work close up. You said it had to be outside, he told himself. So you'd feel safe. And you are, relatively, considering the situation. Which you created. So the hell with it.

Past the park, Dorsey drove along the side wall of the jail, then turned right and circled the park and the jail twice. All clear, he decided; the park was empty and the jail and courthouse parking lots held only official vehicles. He drove past the jail once more and stayed straight on Market, parking the Buick one block beyond the jail by an empty grammar school building.

Dorsey stepped out of the car and worked his way out of the field jacket, laying it across the front seat. Stretching toward the far door he took the switchblade from the glove compartment and slipped it into one of the jacket's flap pockets. He dug back into the glove compartment, this time retrieving the revolver. Holding it in his right hand, he slipped his arm into the jacket sleeve, extending his hand but allowing the revolver to come to rest inside the sleeve, several inches above the cuff. He put on the jacket and maneuvered the pistol until he was sure he could get to it when needed. From the top of the dashboard he took a black watch cap, working it over his head and folding it back just above the ears. Locking the doors, he took the roll bag from the back seat, two layers of twenties over wads of cut paper, and headed for the park.

At the edge of the park, from behind a tree, he checked the lawn and the gazebo for the last time. Again there was no movement and Dorsey started across, estimating seventy feet of open ground ahead of him. The snow was lighter now. Dorsey wiped flakes from his mouth and eyebrows as he considered Damjani's choice for a meeting place, concluding that it fit his plans as well as any. It looks good, he thought. The jail is at one end, high stone walls for the shots to echo against, and all personnel are inside where the walls let no sound penetrate. Same with the courthouse. Most likely, the night staff consisted of a retiree watchman asleep in the basement. And open space on the left and right where the noise can travel, diffuse, and die.

Nearing the gazebo steps, Dorsey wiggled his right arm and hand, assuring himself once again that the revolver would be there on cue. In his pocket he felt the weight of the knife, recalling that it was there for an emergency: a witness. Someone sees you do it, sees you plainly and is sure to make an identification. While the witness runs for the cops you plant the knife in Damjani's dead hand and come up with a story about how Damjani tried to stick you. Cooperate with the police and get yourself a bright attorney and charges are knocked down to voluntary manslaughter, maybe less. Sentence is suspended because of your past being clean, and you never see the inside of a cell.

Dorsey climbed the gazebo steps and, once under its shelter, dusted snow from his shoulders and neck. The gazebo had a low wooden railing with support poles leading to the roof, and Dorsey stood near the pole farthest from the street, where the shadows were darkest. He checked his watch. It was time.

Two cars passed along Third Street, silhouetted in the courthouse light. Both drove through the intersection without turning onto Market. A few moments passed and then another car slowed at the intersection and turned onto Market and slowed even more, cruising by the park. Dorsey recognized it as the rusted Chrysler that had picked up Father Jancek at the church. Good Lord, he thought, it really *is* the Movement Together company car.

The Chrysler picked up speed and continued down Market, going out of sight as it passed the jail. Dorsey figured it for a safety check and waited for the car to circle around, guessing on two men being inside: Damjani and a driver who would leave after delivering him. Two men, he thought. If only one steps out, stick to the plan. If two come for you, let them come within your mattress-shooting range and open up on them, Damjani first.

The Chrysler came by again, turned onto Market, and stopped. One man emerged from the passenger seat and closed the door, and the car moved on past the jail and out of sight. Shoulders hunched and bent forward against the snow, the man started toward the gazebo. Dorsey watched as he was highlighted by the snow, then obscured by tree shadows, then highlighted again. At the hem of his jacket Dorsey wiped his hands clean of the sweat that collected there despite the cold, then moved forward with the roll bag, crossing the gazebo's hardwood floor. He rested the bag on the railing.

With two thirds of the distance covered, the moving figure emerged from the last of the shadows. Dorsey felt the sweat rolling down his neck and he worked his wrist, moving the revolver down his sleeve so the barrel tip was at his cuff. This is it, he thought. Jesus Christ, this is it!

The man crossed the last of the open ground and stopped at the steps of the gazebo to kick the snow from his shoes. His face was darkened, visored by the cloth cap he wore, and Dorsey could not see his features, but when he straightened to his full height, Dorsey knew things had gone sour.

"Oh, shit," Dorsey murmured. Too short. This guy is too fucking short; it isn't Damjani. The second man, the driver: shit, where the hell is he?

Dorsey dropped to the wooden floor and pushed with the heel of his left hand until the revolver was firmly in his right. He rolled to the center of the gazebo and came up on one knee pointing the gun toward the jail wall, searching the snow for the driver. For Damjani. He spotted no one.

There were footfalls on the gazebo steps and Dorsey turned to meet them, the gun held high. "Close enough!" he shouted, moving forward. "This is a gun, make no mistake, it's on you. Where's the driver, the second man? Where's that big son of a bitch Damjani?"

"Ed won't be coming tonight." The man's words were slow and even. "He won't be bothering you any longer."

Dorsey recognized the voice and moved forward, the revolver aimed at a spot at the base of the man's throat. "My God," he said. "It *is* you. Son of a bitch, it's you. You're here by yourself, no Damjani?"

"All alone." Father Jancek climbed the steps, took a handkerchief from his pocket, and wiped his glasses free of snow. The flakes in his beard had turned it from salt and pepper to white. "You're safe. Could we have a talk? There's a lot to be said."

Dorsey kept the gun on the priest. "Where's Damjani?"

"In the custody of federal marshals," Father Jancek said, leaning back onto the gazebo railing. "He'll be put away. Either prison or a mental institution; one is as good as another, and I truly don't know which is more appropriate. The important thing is that you are safe from him. You and perhaps so many others. But, please, let's have a talk, indoors and away from this weather. There's a place nearby. A bar."

"Not in this town." Dorsey moved to his left and picked up the roll bag. The gun never left the priest.

"Just across the line, in Bridgewater," the priest said. "Only a few blocks over. We'll have a sip and go over a few things. I assure you it's safe. Put your gun away. And keep the money."

As smooth as his rally speeches, Dorsey thought, and as endearing. And as reassuring. He's got a touch, St. Francis calming the deer and petting a robin. Ah, well, follow where he goes. Dorsey slipped the gun into the right-hand jacket pocket. Roll bag in hand, he followed the priest down the gazebo steps and into the snow.

The snow began to taper off, and snowplows and salt trucks passed them by as they walked along Third Street. Father Jancek did most of the talking. "The killing of your friend," he said, "it sickened me. I was heartbroken, and believe me, I prayed and meditated for some time. I almost reached the conclusion that I should leave Movement Together, turn the whole thing over to men with a more temporal point of view. This violence, so personal and directed toward one person, this was never anticipated."

Dorsey plodded along in the snow, cautiously planting each footstep, and thought of Louis Preach. "A mutual friend put it best," he said. "He suggested that you wanted to fight a war and not get bloody."

"Who said this?"

"Doesn't matter." Dorsey braced himself against a cold gust. "Go on with what you were saying."

"It was a terrible thing," Father Jancek said. "I felt compelled to attend the church service. I remember the anger in your eyes when you saw me. When I ran, I ran for my life. Please believe me, I was not there to offend anyone. It was not my intention to desecrate the service."

"But you left Damjani to continue roaming around on his own. Most likely you and yours helped him stay at least one step up on the police. Gave him a second crack at me. That's tough to forgive in a priest."

"No, never," the priest said, shaking his head and sending wet snow from his beard in every direction. "We never helped him, not after the death of your friend. Admittedly, we did not turn him in to the police at that time. But we gave him no aid in avoiding arrest."

"So," Dorsey said, "tell me about the federal marshals. You said he was in their hands. Who arranged it? You?"

The priest scratched at his beard, then wiped his wet gloved fingers on his jacket. "By answering that question as put, I admit it was arranged and I had a hand in it. Ah, so be it. You'll hear more than that tonight. I think I owe you this for your friend. Anyway, we did arrange it. Not a happy task despite the necessity for it. Ed was totally beyond control, and it was apparent that he recognized no limits."

"And you delivered him to federal cops?" Dorsey said. "Murder is local stuff, a local crime. He was part of the killing."

"And he would have spent precious little time in jail for it as only an accomplice with a bargained plea." The priest raised a finger as if reaching the linchpin of a thesis. "A federal warrant was issued this morning. There was a bank robbery, armed robbery, three years ago in West Virginia. Two of the three men were captured and sent away for long stretches in Lewisburg. These two men never identified the third member of the gang until this morning. The inmates cut a deal with an FBI agent who was summoned to the prison. They were able not only to identify Ed as the third man but also to tell the agent where Ed was to be found. A federal judge signed the warrant by noon and Ed was picked up in an apartment in New Castle."

"Well done."

"We have friends all over."

"The robbery," Dorsey said. "Damjani did it? Or is this a put-up job?"

"He did it, all right. That is true. Ed was heading for prison all his life, if not for the robbery or your friend's death, then for something else, something even worse. Justice is served, and you are safe."

Dorsey laughed and shook the snow from his hat. "My safety, you make it sound like Movement Together's top priority."

"My work is not to take life." Father Jancek spoke sharply. "My work is to save a way of life."

Dorsey explored the priest's face and concluded that his words were sincere. Nothing so clean, so sharp, could be a deception. C'mon, Father, Dorsey thought, what's it going to be? Good guy or bad guy?

At the foot of the bridge where Third Street ended was a flight of cement steps that led down the hillside to Bridgewater. Silently, concentrating on each snow-covered step, the two men descended. At the bottom, Father Jancek turned to Dorsey.

"You will have to try to understand our association with Ed Damjani," the priest said. "You have to understand how it began. We knew he was something of a local character and that he was a radical union man. Being so colorful, he had a following among the other workers, the young ones. Leader-of-the-pack sort of thing.

They were drawn to him, so we knew he could recruit younger workers for our program."

"Recruits for the program," Dorsey said. "You mean for the scam. I learned that much. The young single ones, with the exception of Radovic, were your fall-downs. The ones in car accidents with whiplash and the ones who fell off the loading dock a week before the plant closed."

"That's right, you do know that much. As I understand it, you know a lot more." Father Jancek started across the street. "We're almost there. Just another block or so."

Dorsey fell in step with the priest, who was making his way in the direction of the Beaver River, a quarter mile up from where it meets the Ohio. The bar, a one-story wood-frame building, stood across the road from the river. Dorsey and the priest stopped underneath the bar's aluminum awning to shake the snow from their shoulders.

Father Jancek pulled open the door and Dorsey followed, finding himself in a cramped room with just enough space for the bar counter and a walking space on both sides. The bartender, whom Dorsey figured to be in his late fifties, was the room's sole occupant. He signaled for them to advance. Father Jancek led the way along the bar to a door at the far wall, which he unlocked, and Dorsey followed him in as the priest flicked on the light switch.

The room was a small square addition attached to the bar; Dorsey could see where one set of timbers ended and the next began. There was a swag light hanging over a round felt-topped card table, and an old refrigerator stood in the far corner. While Dorsey dropped the roll bag and sat at the table, Father Jancek dug into the refrigerator.

"This should suit you." The priest placed an icy glass and a twelve-ounce Rolling Rock on the table. Dorsey watched as he got the same for himself.

"We may have a third joining us," Father Jancek said, taking the seat across from Dorsey. "It depends on how bad the roads are. It's Jack, Jack Stockman, I'm referring to."

"Your dear school chum. And, for a little while, fellow

seminarian." How's that for a return? Dorsey thought. You know my beer, I know your life. "Before we get to whatever this is supposed to be about," Dorsey said, "I guess I should thank you for Damjani. It's a relief, having him out of the picture."

"You're welcome," Father Jancek said. "As I said, he was a serious error on my part."

"Okay." Dorsey ignored the glass and drank from the bottle. "Let's talk."

"Jack Stockman tells me you have integrity, a quality, he also tells me, that is rare in your line of work." The priest filled his glass and lifted it to his lips, nibbling at the foam. "I have integrity too. I keep my own counsel, and normally the motives for my actions stay between God and myself. But your friend—Russie, you called him?—your friend changed things around. Then, this afternoon, I found out just how much you've learned about our activities. I feel a couple of things. I feel compelled to explain myself because I owe you that. Also, being something of a religious maverick, I have no confessor. Actually, it's been years since I've been on the receiving end of a confessional. So indulge me, please?"

"This is no confessional," Dorsey said. "I can't take a vow of silence. You tell me something useful, I'll have to pass it along."

Father Jancek shrugged his shoulders in resignation. "To what end will you use this information? Bill Meara is burning his file on the matter. There is to be no prosecution, so what does it matter in the long run? I just want you to know."

"So you know about Meara?" Dorsey ran through the Irish and Polish and black faces working in Meara's office. And each has an out-of-work relative if you look hard enough. It could've been any of them.

"It's true," Father Jancek said, as if reading his mind. "We have friends most everywhere."

"You said something before about how I know so much," Dorsey said. "You said you found out this afternoon. From whom?"

"Ray Corso."

"Ah, Corso. Your spy." Dorsey drank again from his beer. "Be careful, spies are a fickle bunch. Poor sense of loyalty."

"So I have learned." Father Jancek began to explain further, but a knock at the door interrupted him. The priest went to the door and Dorsey's right hand went into his pocket, gripping the revolver. Father Jancek admitted the tall gray-haired Stockman, who dropped his hat on the table and removed his topcoat before taking the chair to Dorsey's right.

"P.I., how are you?" Dorsey said, sizing up the cold blue eyes that cloaked the maneuvering inside. But this is his turn to talk, Dorsey thought. The scalpel he's used on you in the past, in court, is put away. You hope.

"We were just about to discuss Ray Corso," Father Jancek said. "Mr. Dorsey is sure he was our spy."

Stockman, his eyes still cold, rapped his knuckles softly on the table and looked at the priest. "Andy, I'm going to say this just once more. This meeting is a bad idea. It has no purpose; we gain nothing by it. Let me handle things. Hickcock, the rest of the press: I can take care of it."

"No." Father Jancek held Stockman's gaze. "For what I allowed to happen, I owe Dorsey this. He's been through quite a bit, and there is more to come."

Dorsey's hold on the revolver in his pocket went tighter. "More of what? You said Damjani was put away."

There was a silent moment until Father Jancek gave Stockman a go-ahead nod. "The lawsuit, of course," Stockman said. "We have to sue you and Hickcock after tonight. We'll get nothing from it, but otherwise we are admitting that what you have to say is true. It's the only way."

"It *is* true," Dorsey said.

"But not verifiable." Stockman leaned back in his chair, a wry smile cutting across his face. "You have so little. A few insurance cases that may or may not appear strange, depending on the listener's point of view. The Maynard girl in Johnstown, a hysterical girl whom you threatened with lies. Most important, you have Art Demory. But all that remains of him is in an oxygen tent. I can make him look like a half-dead career criminal telling lies so he can have one last laugh on society. Also, Father Jancek and I will forever deny this meeting took place."

Dorsey released his grip on the revolver and took out his hand, running it across his chin. Goddamn son of a bitch. First there's no payday on this case, he told himself, at least not the big score you hoped for. Now they want to take what little you already have. "The suit," Dorsey asked. "No way I can talk you out of it?"

"Sorry," Stockman said. Dorsey rose to leave.

"Please, don't leave just yet." Father Jancek met him at the door. "I'm sorry about the suit, but there is a lot to consider." The priest spoke softly, endearing despite the message. Preach is right, Dorsey thought, there's more than a little St. Francis in this guy. Dorsey returned to the chair, almost before realizing it.

"Well," he said, "you two are going to sue me and there's jackshit I can do about it. All right, tell me about Corso."

Father Jancek returned to his seat and sipped his beer. "I assume you knew Mr. Corso was corrupt."

"Not until recently," Dorsey said. "Before that, I only knew he was dumb and lazy."

"Which led to his corruption," the priest said. "Jack had known about Mr. Corso for some time, about how he sabotaged lawsuits for the plaintiff. Back when we first hatched our plan, Jack and I had conversed about Mr. Corso and it was decided that Jack should approach him. Mr. Corso was very receptive to our offer."

"Which was the reason for so many of these fakes being with Fidelity Casualty. How much did you pay?"

"There's no need for particulars," Stockman said. "Listen to the story and save the questions until later, and we'll see if we choose to answer."

"Fuck you, thief." Dorsey met Stockman's chill look with one of his own, then turned back to the priest. "Go on. Tell me the rest."

"As part of our working agreement, Mr. Corso was to quash or divert any investigations into our people's claims. We knew there would be initial evaluations, but our concern was to avoid a more in-depth review. Like the one you performed. This Mr. Corso was to block. And we thought he had, until you showed up in Johnstown checking on Carl Radovic. Even then we thought little of it. Mr. Corso explained it away as random chance, a routine check. But then your name cropped up again as you interviewed several others who were working with us. We went to Corso for an explanation, but before he got back to us you appeared at the Midland rally."

"So you stopped asking for an explanation," Dorsey said, "and demanded one. What did Corso have to say for himself?"

"He said he had new orders from his higher-ups," Stockman said. "That was his story, anyway. There was a new VP at the home office who wanted investigations on all active claims. He gave us the man's name—Munt, John Munt—along with a promise that he could sanitize the reports before they were forwarded to Munt."

Dorsey's thoughts wandered back to the conference room with Corso and Munt fencing across the table. Corso telling Munt that the investigations were his own idea, defending his decision to carry them out. And Munt, seeming genuinely angry with Corso, going on about Corso having stepped beyond his authority. Who was the fraud in that exchange, both?

"At our end of things," Father Jancek said, "we slowed things up a bit. We had several more claims waiting in the wings, ready to file. But we held off and relied on the established ones. Which we are continuing to do to this day. And in doing so we thought we were safe. Please understand that before today we had no knowledge of your contact with Arthur Demory."

"That's one I'll have to live with," Stockman said. "Never did I figure he could turn on us."

Dorsey laughed. "Why shouldn't you be forgiving? The guy is half dead in an ICU ward. What'd you have in mind, cutting a hole in his bedpan?"

Father Jancek loudly cleared his throat, gathering the attention of both men. "So we need to come to today. I received a call from Mr. McGregor, as did Jack. We discussed the matter, and it was decided that we needed to speak to Corso. We found him at his home, heading out to his doctor's office—to have his blood pressure checked, he said. The two men we had sent persuaded him to remain at home for a talk. Perhaps his blood pressure was abnormal. Our men told me that he fell apart and volunteered everything. His confession was complete."

Father Jancek paused for a moment and wiped his finger along the wet rim of his beer glass. "I suppose it should not have come as such a surprise to me. We enter into deceptions, and we should not be shocked when we become the victims of yet further deceptions. For lack of a less dramatic term, Mr. Corso has been operating as a sort of double agent."

"Double agent?" Dorsey asked, scoffing. "Keep looking for a less dramatic term. Corso's too lazy to lead one life, let alone two."

"Well," Father Jancek said, "that's how he explained it. It seems that word of his basic dishonesty had filtered back to the home office, and approximately one year ago most all his work was the subject of a confidential audit. Like a secret investigation. As you can imagine, there was plenty to cover. Corso was confronted and, just like today, confessed to everything, including his involvement with us."

"Slow down," Dorsey said, wondering what Munt's role was and waving off Stockman's objection to his interruption. "Who was this confessing done to?"

"A man named Stiers, head of the audit group."

Where was Munt? Dorsey wondered. His anger at the conference was definitely the real thing. But who knows? If you suspect a major crime by an employee, you have to also suspect his immediate supervisor, the guy who is letting it happen. Sure, the auditors looked into Munt's work too. So Munt was kept in the dark. Poor Munt, sincerely angry, and never knew the reasons why.

"So they knew about you," Dorsey said. "Why didn't they move against you?"

"We put that to Corso, but he had only guesses." Stockman went to the refrigerator. He returned with one for Dorsey too. "But we do know that Stiers came back to him with instructions to hire you."

Dorsey grinned. "You mean he had orders to hire a detective."

"No, no," Father Jancek said, waving off the idea. "He was told to hire you. Told by name to hire you. And to offer you a free hand to run the cases as you saw fit."

And unlimited expense money, Dorsey recalled. Remember what Bernie said about the arrangement, he asked himself. It's bullshit, he said; it can't happen. Corso's authority doesn't extend that far. "Corso did as he was told," Dorsey said.

"And took our money all the while." Stockman drank off half his beer. Dorsey was taken by the man's anger, hot and true. It's a rare occasion, he told himself: the iceman is pissed. P.I.'s hidden side.

"So who's behind Corso?" Dorsey asked. "And who does Stiers report to? And most important, why does an insurance company hire me above all others to find out what they already know? They could have terminated the files and waited to see if you had the balls to sue. And Corso could've been quietly discharged to save customer confidence in the company. But no, you say they turned Corso and sent him to give me money. Where's the reasoning?"

"We fucked up," Stockman said. Dorsey caught the look of distaste on the priest's face before turning to Stockman. "Took on the wrong people," Stockman said. "Fidelity Casualty is owned by Calumet Corporation."

"That I knew," Dorsey said. "I've met one of the officers, a fellow named Cleardon."

The name fell like a stone upon the table.

"Charles Cleardon," Dorsey said. "What's wrong?"

"My being a priest," Father Jancek said, "gives our movement a shade of righteousness. We become saints and walk with God. In keeping with this, our opponents become demonized. Cleardon might be said to be Satan. We've tried to picket corporate meetings that he attends, but he's hard to pin down. You see, Calumet is the major financial backer in what is called the revitalization of our local economy. What they have done is steal industrial property at rock-bottom prices, tear down the existing plant, and install some type of light industry. As a result, they acquire prime land very cheaply and a ready labor force hungry for work at reduced wages, because they're the only game in town. That's why we've blocked the demolition of the older plants and mills, as proposed in Midland. Face it, we are Calumet's only opposition."

"So," Stockman said, "it looks like this. Calumet has strung us along for what I can only figure to be some big kill, some kind of master stroke to finish us off by murdering us in the public eye, arresting our leaders, along those lines. But I think Demory's ill health may have saved us and finished you. All that's left is to sue you. And for you to share a little information with us."

Dorsey absorbed it all en masse, then tried to line it up in order. Calumet and Cleardon ran Corso through a middleman, Stiers, cutting Munt out of the chain. So it was Cleardon who gave the report to Corso with instructions to get it to Hickcock. But why? Where does Cleardon come out ahead? And then there's you, he told himself, the man Cleardon wanted for the job. He wanted you, no substitutions, no duplications. And your work, in the past, has not put you in a class by yourself. Where does a corporate big shot get your name? Busy man, Cleardon. He has an insurance company to keep tabs on while he tried to buy up the western half of the state. And still he takes the time to look you up. Where's the connection to you?

Sipping at his beer, the images flashed and collided before his mind's eye. There were black-and-white photos, stark and bleak, of rundown industrial plants with disused railroad tracks. And other pictures, artist's renderings of what was to come. Sketches of large barnlike structures of prefabricated steel surrounded by gray cement fields of parking lots. And all the photos and prints were bound in a brown leather album resting on the corner of a familiar desktop.

"Jesus Christ," Dorsey said, his voice flat. "I have to leave." He rose, slipped into his jacket, and took the roll bag from the floor.

"One damned minute!" Stockman shouted. "It was misguided, but this man just poured out his heart to you. Why did they pick you?"

"That's where I'm going," Dorsey said, realizing that this question was why he was here. "I'm going to find out why."

"I think I deserve better than that," Father Jancek said. "I do think an answer is in order. I did think we could have a dialogue."

Dorsey went to the table, leaning in at the priest. "I owe you shit. You showed up tonight to be forgiven for killing a man you never knew and to see where I fit into this whole mess."

Stockman began to rise but Dorsey turned to him and forced him back into the chair with a white-hot glare.

"And what you deserve is this," Dorsey said, turning back to the priest. "You deserve to be interrogated, to be questioned again and again, to find out how it all comes to pass. To find out where the devoted liberal, the man of peace, crosses the line from demonstration and civil disobedience to crime. Pure fucking crime. Where did you cross the line?"

"I never did," Father Jancek said. "I found the line to be irrelevant. So I erased it."

CHAPTER 27

Already cleared of snow, the brick wall and driveway shone a glistening red under the glow of the lamppost. Dorsey wondered who had been given the job. A city snow-removal crew, as a courtesy, or did Ironbox volunteer? She's the devoted type, he decided. Devoted to the old man for the last twenty-four years. All those years to that old bastard.

Dorsey left the Buick at the curbstone and kicked open the black wrought-iron gate. Inside the walls, the walkways were cleared too, and Dorsey's footsteps rang off the brick as he marched to the door. He hit the doorbell, leaning his weight into it, for three long blasts. There was no immediate response, so he kicked at the door until it opened.

"It's late, and you weren't invited." Mrs. Boyle, dressed in a flannel nightgown, spoke through the space allowed by the door chain.

Dorsey reared back, collected his strength, and hit the door, leading with his shoulder. The chain tore away from the doorjamb, showering wooden splinters at Mrs. Boyle as she retreated to the far wall of the foyer.

"In there," Mrs. Boyle said, her shoulders flush to the wall. "In his office, goddamn you!"

Dorsey brushed past her and walked through the parlor to the office door, his wet shoes staining the carpet. He opened the office door and stood there looking in. Powerless to stop it, he felt his hand go into his pocket and grip the gun.

"Answers," Dorsey said. "I want answers to this whole thing. Every fucking one of them."

Martin Dorsey, in white pajamas and maroon robe, sat at his desk. He calmly removed his reading glasses. "Come in, sit down. This may take quite some time. Should I ask Mrs. Boyle to put on a pot of coffee?"

"No," Dorsey said. "Just talk. Tell me how you put it all together. And why I was dropped into the middle of it."

"So, for once, you would have some money in your pocket." Martin Dorsey rose, went to the liquor cabinet, and poured two fingers of whisky into a cut-glass tumbler. "But that would be getting ahead of ourselves, and you want to know everything. In chronological order."

"If that's easiest," Dorsey said, finding a touch more control, taking his hand from the gun. As his father sat at the desk, Dorsey dropped himself into one of the room's wing chairs.

Martin Dorsey held his drink in two hands, running his fingers across the raised edges of the glass. "Big Steel is dead, as you should know. Oh, there will be some production from a small mill here and there, but the heyday is over. Yes, Big Steel is dead, and if you don't agree, there's little to discuss."

"The mills are dead. Looks like it to me, anyway," Dorsey said. Maybe, maybe not, he thought. But I'll agree to the moon being made of green cheese to hear the whole story.

"That's good," Martin Dorsey said. "Very astute of you. Most people just won't let go. All those mill towns have mayors and other politicians who want to cling to the past. In some ways, I can't fault them. After all, it was the past that made them, pandering to the workers. An uncertain future makes for an uncertain political career. You understand?"

Dorsey worked a sad smile across his face. "The first twenty-odd years of my life were spent in this house, eating meals and listening to the dinnertime lecture. I know some about politics. So these backward types out in the mill towns, they couldn't see the percentage in Calumet buying up the mill property, right?"

Martin Dorsey saluted his son, drink in hand. "There is much you already know. I would hate to bore you. Please let me know if I get dull."

"Most of my evening," Dorsey said, "was spent with Father Jancek and P.I. Stockman. The priest, he felt bad about Russie, so he used his sorrow to try for some information from me. He told me a lot about how this thing got started. Most of it sounded like the truth. And he answered some questions for me. But I had one last one to pass on."

"You'll get your answer," his father said. "Where was I? Ah, yes, you were right, Calumet was being shut out of some of the more promising locations. They had a few things going up, some light manufacturing sites, but too few to justify the effort and commitment to the development plans.

"And by justification, I mean justification to the stockholders who like to see their dividend jump by leaps and bounds each year. So, Cleardon himself and his CEO were personally on the hot seat. And there is nothing more precious in business than saving your own sweet ass. So they came to me for help. For a very large down payment and an overall percentage, I've made most of their problems go away. Some politicians loosened up when they found a deal could be cut. Others tried to hang in there, but I spoke to them personally."

"Threatened personally," Dorsey said.

"In some cases, yes." Martin Dorsey sipped his whisky, pursing his lips as it passed them. "Some had it in mind, just because times change and new powers replace the old, that the political game has somehow changed. As if the rules were now more strict and the players less ambitious. None of these types could handle anything along the lines of a scandal. And they had been bad boys: women, money, even dope. With that, Calumet Corporation began breaking ground all over the western part of the state."

"So you were able to scare the guilty." Dorsey leaned out

from the chair, watching his father swish whisky in his glass. "But what about the innocents, the babes in the woods? The ones who had fallen in line with the priest? You had nothing on them, so they couldn't be frightened off."

"Right," Martin Dorsey said. "They were, in a sense, untouchable. Most were turning their homes over to the bank; they had nothing further to lose. You're right, you can't scare a person who has nothing for you to take. Still, normally there should be traitors in every organization. But the priest seems to have the ability to leach out the larceny from every soul. His leadership moves his organization into the realm of heaven. It becomes an ideological force instead of a temporal labor union looking for a pay hike. When there's a new messiah, it's tough work trying to buy off an apostle. We tried. Not a Judas in the crowd."

Dorsey made his way to the liquor cabinet, where he took a beer from the lower-level refrigeration unit. "You're right," he said, opening the can as he returned to his seat. "This may take some time and I should be as comfortable as you. But no bullshit, please. Let's have the whole story, for once." He took a long pull on his beer. "So who cooked this up? How was the plan first suggested?"

"Good fortune presented an opportunity." Dorsey's father leaned into the desk, grinning. "Somebody in Syracuse, at the FC home office, met a colleague from Etna at a conference. They struck up a conversation over the lunch table. The fellow from FC told his new friend that he had just hired a former Etna employee, Ray Corso. Our man found out that Corso left Etna under a cloud, so to speak. About selling cases; that was the term used."

"This fellow from FC," Dorsey said. "Any chance that was Munt?"

"No, no," Martin Dorsey said. "Munt was kept in the dark, both then and now. In fact, he was suspected because of his association with Corso, for a time. I hear he was convincing as the outraged VP in your meeting. Reality *is* convincing."

"Let's hear about Stiers," Dorsey said, sipping his beer. "The guy they sent after Corso."

Martin Dorsey again raised his glass to his son. "Very good, you have learned a great deal; good work." He finished his toast with a pull on his whisky. "Walter Stiers is an investigator and auditor who does all FC's internal investigations. That's because he is Cleardon's fraternity brother. They both went to the same expensive school in New England, somewhere up in the woods. Cleardon was there on family money, but Stiers was that poor scholarship boy the rich kids like to cozy up to, to show how humane they are. You know, take him home on weekends, show him some well-to-do hospitality? Anyway, Cleardon takes care of him. So Stiers does his job on Corso, realizes how big, how intricate the setup is, and calls Cleardon."

Dorsey shifted in his chair and kept his attention on his father. C'mon, he thought, get it all out. Let's get to the big question: What did you expect from me? "Okay," Dorsey said. "So Cleardon comes to you, knowing what a clever guy you are, and the two of you cook this thing up. Am I right?"

"I can't take much of the credit," his father said. "Cleardon is a bright fellow, a good thinker. What I always thought you could've been. He came up with most of it. He was a man with two problems, and he came up with a way to solve both of them."

"Corso and the priest?"

"Exactly," Martin Dorsey said. "Corso was an embarrassment and Father Jancek was a barricade. It's one thing to be the victim of an insurance scam by your own employee. It's quite another to be the victim of an outside group of conspirators. FC could have been rocked if word of Corso's dealings got out. Policyholders would cancel, potential new customers would look elsewhere. But if you have clean hands, the attention goes to the wrongdoer and not the victim. A way had to be found to put the white hats on the correct heads."

"Corso could have just been gotten rid of," Dorsey said.

"But what of the priest and his people? That was the greater of the two problems. So Stiers went back to Corso with instructions from an anonymous source—Cleardon. He was to begin assigning the fraudulent cases dealing with Movement Together, and in time you were innocently to uncover the conspiracy and bring Father Jancek and his friends to justice. *Pari delecti*. With clean hands. The good name of Fidelity Casualty saved, and Movement Together wrecked."

"One loose end," Dorsey said. "Corso. Somebody in Movement Together, at least one somebody, would make a deal with the prosecution and inform. And Corso's role would be reversed."

Martin Dorsey waved off the problem. "Corso denies it from day one to the end of his miserable life. We own him. As of now, the thief bastard gets to keep his job and feed his family. If he flip-flops on us, he'll lose the job he's got and never find another one anywhere. We can do it; make no mistake, we can do it. He stays loyal and he'll work. Change his mind and he starves."

"So it was all set," Dorsey said. "All that was left was to plop me down in the middle of it."

"And lead you along by the nose." Martin Dorsey laughed and shook his head. "Corso was to give you the Movement Together cases one by one, and we expected that you would naturally catch on to the conspiracy. But you were a horse that was tough even to lead to water. At one point, it was suggested by Corso that you had put it all together but were dragging your feet to hike up your fees. I convinced Cleardon otherwise and threw Monsignor Gallard your way. Later, I had a talk with Louis Preach, and he put you on a faster track."

"For what?" Dorsey asked. "In the next campaign, will there be billboards announcing your endorsement of Preach for whatever office he may have his sights on?"

"That's really not much," his father said. "I have no interest in any of his potential rivals. The endorsement costs me nothing."

Dorsey finished his beer and went for another. "All right," he said, crossing back to his chair, "so I learn everything there is to know. Demory gives it all up to me, and I write my report and send it to Munt and Cleardon. You and Cleardon get together and decide to forward it to that hungry son of a bitch Hickcock. Why's that?" He sat and opened his beer.

"To smear the priest, of course."

"That could've been done in a criminal trial for fraud."

"He would have been acquitted," Martin Dorsey said. "Meara, from my understanding, thought the priest could have been convicted in another county, but I don't see it. A priest loved by the masses? If it came down to his going to prison, anything he was found to have done would have been excusable. There's no way to convict him, even if Demory was in the pink of health."

"So you do it through the press," Dorsey said, "and in my civil trial."

Martin Dorsey held still for a moment, studying the desktop. "That's definite, is it? The possibility of a suit was always there. But I think you will find that after a few weeks or months of publicity, the case will be settled for a fraction of the original demand. You won't be hurt too badly, considering the fees that FC will be paying you for your continued services."

"Not hurt badly?" Dorsey left his chair and glowered at his father. "I'm a detective who can't keep his reports confidential, and because of that I've no future in the business. And I have a dead friend. You remember him? You should. After sharing Christmas dinner way back when."

"Knew about that, did you?" Martin Dorsey drew on his whisky. "Poor Russie, so loyal. Violence was never expected to be an issue. And for him to die—that was regrettable."

"Yeah," Dorsey said. "Tough break, wasn't it?"

"It's my one true sorrow in this business."

"But not me," Dorsey said. "How this is ending for me. You have no problem with that?"

"No, not the slightest," his father said. "You'll come out okay."

Dorsey left the beer on the desktop and turned away, stepping behind the chair. He rested his arms atop its back. "Enough. Let's get to the bottom of this. Why in the hell did you do this to me?"

"Because," his father said, setting his glass on the desktop. "Because you embarrass me."

"What the fuck is this?"

"Yes, what is this?" Martin Dorsey answered mildly, as much the patrician politician as ever. "Every time I look at you I ask the same question. How could you be mine? Doing the kind of work you do and living in that shack. I move mountains for people. Everything I touch turns to money. But then I see you—and, more important, other people see you and wonder what the hell is going on. They see my failure in you. I'm tired of it and I'm old. I want this problem settled."

"Are you serious?" Dorsey started around the chair and nearly stumbled as his foot caught on one of the legs. He shoved the chair onto its side. "Fuckin' ridiculous. You linked me into your game to punish me for the life I've led? Ridiculous!" Dorsey addressed the ceiling as if searching for divine guidance. "I'm ruined so you can feel better for setting me straight."

"You're not ruined," Martin Dorsey said. "You're saved, despite yourself. You'll still have your fees paid by FC, and you're still in line for the cut I promised you from my piece of the action when Calumet's project matures. Meanwhile, I have plans. Cleaning you up politically will not be nearly as difficult as most people will think. Remember the magistrate's job we once talked about? I can still deliver it for you. And, in time, the Pittsburgh City Council would not be out of the question. Besides, it's all you have."

"Kiss my ass, you have plans." Dorsey dropped his hand into his jacket pocket and clutched the revolver. "You have plans. Well, I've sidestepped your plans in the past. I've come out okay, all by myself."

Martin Dorsey smiled. "Is that right? Sidestepping is all I ever allowed out of you. Let's see, your greatest rebellion was what, when you left law school and enlisted in the army? Hard, tough Ranger, that's what you had planned for yourself. Back then, all the Rangers were dropped into the bush in Vietnam. All but you. In your last week of training you were reassigned as an MP. Normally that doesn't happen. To waste all that training on a fellow who will never pull the trigger on some little yellow guy in black pajamas? Think about it, for your entire enlistment, you're never sent any farther away then New Jersey. As if your assignment was to protect Ocean City from invasion. Would you like to know how I did it?"

Dorsey remained silent. His finger wormed itself inside the trigger loop.

"Congressman Dogal," Martin Dorsey said. "He sits on the

Armed Forces Committee. Politics are the same at every level. We raised the campaign money and he owes the local folks. So he took care of this for me."

Dorsey felt light-headed. His fingers tingled.

"You'll do as I say from here on in." Martin Dorsey sat and finished his whisky. "You'll do well as a city councilman. At least appear competent, and maybe there will be a run at the mayor's office or maybe we'll dump Dogal out of Congress. But that's all down the road. Sit back and relax, just leave me at the controls."

"Low-life son of a bitch," Dorsey mumbled as he shook his head to keep his balance. His instincts raged against each other, one voice demanding he take a clear, independent stand, while a sad and hollow voice of doubt crept through his thoughts. You thought you had a life without him at the controls, but it doesn't look that way now, looking back. The old man stood behind a curtain, like the Wizard in the Emerald City, pulling levers of his choice, making the magic happen. All he wants now is to remove the curtain. Would it be so different?

"Yes, it would," Dorsey said, watching the puzzled look on his father's face. He took the revolver from his pocket, aiming for the chest. Martin Dorsey grinned and shook his head. Don't dismiss me so quickly, Dorsey thought. No bluff is without some possibility of a follow-through. He matched his father's smile with the ones he wore in the photos that hung above his head on the back wall. The same toothy, soft-cheeked smile. While he bent forward to shake a black child's hand at a Martin Luther King memorial service. As he slapped the back of the governor from three terms ago. With his arms locked with those of the state's two senators. And ten more like them.

Dorsey returned the smile and elevated the revolver's muzzle. All five shots rocked the room and Martin Dorsey threw his arms up, protecting his head from the shower of glass and wood. Five of the mounted photos danced against the wall before slipping away, and a bluish cloud of cordite smoke gathered at the end of Dorsey's reach and wandered over his father's still ducked head. Mrs. Boyle whipped open the door from the parlor but only stuck in her head, tentatively.

"Well," Dorsey said, turning to Mrs. Boyle with a grin. "Nice piece of work. And I thought the mattress was a tough shot."

Chapter 28

Early the next afternoon, in a warm sun that cloaked the chill of a stiff wind, Dorsey parked the Buick two doors from his house, the closest available spot. His eyes watered and his skin had the slight crawl of a hung-over man who had already showered and slipped into clean clothes. Which, he admitted to himself, he was.

Dorsey moved along the sidewalk at a slow gait, holding his head still to protect himself against the dull ache in his temples. He climbed the front stoop to his door, inserted the key, and found it unlocked. Pushing softly, he let the door turn back on its hinges, exposing the empty hallway.

"Should have kept the gun with you," he told himself, regretting his earlier decision to leave the gun on the desktop when he stopped for a shave and shower. Even if it wasn't loaded, you could maybe bluff your way through. Keep in mind, Damjani's partner is still on the streets, his face unknown.

Listening but finding only silence, Dorsey slipped off his shoes and started down the hallway, past the office door, and on to the kitchen. The kitchen, he thought, where the weapons are. Iron skillets, bread knives, and Gretchen's rolling pin. The knife is out, Dorsey decided, reminding himself that the military police and the sheriff's department had taught him how to defend against a knife but never how to use one. He took a frying pan from a cabinet above the sink and stood motionlessly at the kitchen, again listening down the hall.

Halfway to the front door, Dorsey picked up on a noise coming from his left: short, repetitive, and rhythmic. He moved a few steps farther and the noise was better defined, reminding Dorsey of a dog's panting, only slower. At the office door he put an ear to the wood, listening, and the sound seemed more like a grunting. Dorsey choked up on the frying pan handle, took hold of one of the sliding door grips, and threw the door open along its track.

Her legs were draped across the desk and her stocking feet rested on the typewriter's carriage. She wore her customary working clothes: corduroy slacks, oxford-cloth shirt. Her running shoes were at the foot of the swivel chair, the chair reclined to its limit, and her curly hair was smashed into the chair's cushioned back.

"How about that," Dorsey said. "She never snores in bed." He allowed Gretchen three more long pulls through her nose and mouth, then dropped the frying pan to the wooden floor with a clang.

"Holy Christ!" Gretchen yelped, pulling up straight in the chair and turning to Dorsey. "Good Lord, you just took twenty years off my life."

"Twenty years?" Dorsey picked up the pan and crossed the room, kissing her cheek and patting her curls away from her face. He placed the frying pan next to the typewriter. "You're acting as if those twenty years had already been assigned to you. Now, it's you who keeps saying that life has no assurances. And today I agree."

"You sound like a life insurance salesman," Gretchen said, laughing. "And you sound nothing like your old insecure self."

Dorsey grabbed a beer from the refrigerator while Gretchen left the swivel chair and stretched out on the chaise. Dorsey dropped into the chair and rested his heels at the edge of the desk.

"It's been a very busy couple of days. You may hear about it from some of your neighbors. Let me tell you about it while I have a hair of the dog."

"My neighbors?"

Dorsey told her about the chase, right down to the rifle-toting neighbor. "Big rifle," Dorsey said. "Looked like Frank Buck's, you know, from the old movies?"

Shaken by the story, Gretchen went to the refrigerator for a beer of her own and sat on the corner of the desk. She asked what had gone on afterward and Dorsey brought her up to speed, concluding with the fireworks at his father's. "And you're all right?" Gretchen asked, gesturing toward his forehead. "Those stitches, they look irritated."

Dorsey told her he was okay. "They pull on the skin a little. But all in all, I've held up fine."

Gretchen left the desk and returned to the chaise. She took a long swallow of beer, then held the cold can to her cheek. "About ten-thirty last night," she said, "I went on break and wandered into the staff lounge. Three interns were huddled in front of the TV. One of them turned when he heard me come in and said he thought I knew you. I said yes and he filled me in on the first ten minutes of Sam Hickcock's show. The rest I saw for myself. I tried to call you most of last night. Where in the world were you?"

"First," Dorsey said, "I got drunk and made some plans. Then I puked over the railing of the Tenth Street bridge."

"Thought you looked a little pale." Gretchen smiled.

"I'm starting to come around." Dorsey sipped at his beer, grimaced as it hit his still tender stomach, then sipped again. "Anyways, after that relief, I slept a few hours in the car. Didn't trust my driving at that point."

Gretchen set the beer on the floor between her feet and her eyes bore into Dorsey. "Carroll, are you nuts? That's stupid, dangerous! Anybody could have come along and robbed you, killed you. Where were you parked?"

Dorsey waved off her concern. "On Bingham, where the Salvation Army drunk tank is. I was one of the boys, so far as they were concerned." He sipped at his beer again. "But let me get back to what I was saying. When I woke up, the sun was coming up. I drove back here and made for the kitchen, where I downed a quart of tomato juice, the universal cure-all. Straightens you up fast. After that I put in an hour under the shower. Kept changing the temperature, hot-cold, cold-hot. And the cure was complete."

"I'm the doctor," Gretchen said, shaking her head. "And I'll be the judge of who's fit for duty and cured of what. You're pale and my prescription is rest and abstinence. But c'mon, I don't want to hear about your folk cures for self-inflicted diseases; where else were you?"

Dorsey reminded her of the threatened lawsuit. "There's going to be a real need for ready cash around here. So I did a few things. Went to the real estate office on Carson, about three blocks over from where you turn to get to Al's? Anyways, I put this place up on the block. They tell me they can move it pretty fast and for a good price. Rich folk want back into the city. Take this row house and put four months of work into it, and it becomes a town house. Gentrification, that's what the agent called it." Dorsey took a drink of beer. "And I talked to Al. I'm taking over Russie's place, the apartment over the bar."

"You don't have to do that," Gretchen said. "It's not necessary. I can help with money. And if you don't want money, move in with me. We could live together, full-time basis. Might as well."

Dorsey slowly shook his head. "No. It won't work and it's not what I want. Oh, let's get it straight. I love you, and yes, I do need and want you. But the pushy days are over. If you find yourself in a corner, believe me, I don't want to be the guy who painted you into it. So have your life and give me all the time you can. But don't steal any from yourself to give to me. And plans? I won't make any plans further ahead than next week."

"My God, you really have been through hell these last few days." Gretchen left the chaise and came to Dorsey's side, running a knuckle along the edge of his jawbone. "This doesn't sound like you."

"Things change," Dorsey said, turning to Gretchen. "More or less, that's how things are. You've always said that, and it's finally sinking in."

Gretchen laughed. "It's funny, and a little frightening, to hear you say such things." She laughed again. "Maybe I liked it better when you were crowding me. It was good for my ego, you being insecure."

Dorsey grinned and held out his hands, palms up, as if summing up a sales pitch. "This will be good for you too. You know how I feel, and you know what I hope to see happen. Let's see if it happens."

"Fine with me," Gretchen said. "But now that this business with the priest is over for the present, what will you be doing for work? You're not likely to be a popular detective, not with anybody who's willing to pay you to be one."

Dorsey stretched out and flipped his legs across the desktop, gulping beer. "Only yesterday, a very bright fellow led me to believe that everything, but everything, blows over. Let's just sit back and see if he's right."